FOR ALL THE RIGHT REASONS

A Novel of Suspense and Redemption

Peter Riddle

CCB Publishing
British Columbia, Canada

For All the Right Reasons: A Novel of Suspense and Redemption

Library and Archives Canada Cataloguing in Publication
Title: For all the right reasons : a novel of suspense and redemption /
by Peter Riddle.
Names: Riddle, Peter, 1939-
Issued in print and electronic formats.
Identifiers: ISBN 9781771435048 (hbk).--ISBN 9781771435055 (pbk).--
ISBN 9781771435062 (pdf)
Additional cataloguing data available from Library and Archives Canada

Cover artwork: Musical score © Peter Riddle,
Lonely young frightened woman © AlexVH | Shutterstock.com,
Old expensive vintage two-masted sailboat © Alex Stemmers | Shutterstock.com,
Flag of Nova Scotia by Kooma is in the Public Domain.

Publisher: CCB Publishing
              British Columbia, Canada
              www.ccbpublishing.com

Dedication

As always, for Gay, who has done it all: career woman, devoted mother to our children, first reader and editor of my books, committed foster parent in two countries, proud grandmother, and my loving companion and support for over six decades.

Other Books by Peter Riddle, writing as Peter H. Riddle...

Fiction

Keeping Rebecca

Whistle Up a Wind

Coming Home Again

Running Away

Fourteenth Concerto

Thirteenth Summer

Twelfth Birthday

The Painted Ponies of Partequineus and The Summer of the Kittens

Children's Poetry
with illustrator Shelley Patterson

No Room

Non-Fiction

Trackwork For Toy Trains

The American Musical

Wiring Your Toy Train Layout

Track Planning Ideas For Toy Trains

America's Standard Gauge Electric Trains

Easy Lionel Layouts You Can Build

Tips & Tricks For Toy Train Operators II

Tips & Tricks For Toy Train Operators

Greenberg's Guide To Lionel Trains 1901-1942: Vol. III

Wiring Your Lionel Layout, Vol. III

Wiring Your Lionel Layout, Vol. II

Wiring Your Lionel Layout

Trains From Grandfather's Attic

And those who were seen dancing were thought to be insane by those who could not hear the music.

—*Friedrich Nietzsche*

Surely I have the right to remove millions of an inferior race that breeds like vermin.

—*Adolph Hitler*

Acknowledgements

My gratitude toward those who helped move this novel along its way over the past several years is boundless. Among them:

Barbara and Robert Rushton, music and education colleagues and steadfast friends to both my wife Gay and me for decades. I owe much of my appreciation for the art of sailing to Bob's generosity and expertise.

Dr. Christoph Both, colleague and cellist extraordinaire.

Michael Caines, a man of many talents, especially his computer wizardry and expertise in the game of golf.

Bill Molnar, for perspectives from rural Ontario.

Dr. Sonia Thon, Acadia University colleague and Professor of Languages.

And those unnamed, whose characters, talents and personalities served as models for some of the people in the story. I hope they may recognize themselves.

Author's Preface

In an era dominated by the concept of "fake news" and holders of high office with no regard for the truth, you may be reasonably confident that the following information is true.

The Commonwealth Nation of Canada has been governed mostly by just two political philosophies since its founding on July 1, 1867: *Liberal* and *Conservative*. The latter party has functioned under a variety of names, including *Liberal-Conservative*, a temporary offshoot labelled *Unionist*, the cumbersome *National Liberal and Conservative Party*, *Progressive Conservative*, and most recently, *Conservative Party of Canada*.

Ostensibly this dichotomy (Liberal vs. Conservative) should represent opposing objectives. In the current Canadian context, however, both of these philosophies would be considered left of center, especially when compared with the diverse political climate in the United States. Canadian Conservatives have much in common with that country's Democrats, and our Liberal platforms tend to embrace moderate social democratic policies. Canada entertains no nationwide party equivalent to the present-day American Republicans.

As in most democratic countries, a number of lesser parties have existed in Canada from time to time, although with varying influence upon the future of the country. Only one, the New Democratic Party (NDP, founded in 1961) has ever risen to true national prominence, with an aggressive socialist orientation that places it to the left of the Liberals. But except for a brief period under a charismatic leader named Jack Layton, the Party has never come close to forming the federal government.

Under the parliamentary system, the leader of a party that is elected to the largest number of seats in the House of Commons is called Prime Minister and is responsible for heading up the government. The names of the twenty-two men and one woman who have held that office predominantly represent British Isles ancestry and, reflecting the dual linguistic nature of the country, French origin.

A person of colour has never served as Canada's Prime Minister.

Canada is divided into ten provinces and three territories, roughly equivalent to but mostly larger in area than the average American state. The provinces are governed in a manner similar to the country as a whole, with Legislatures akin to the national House of Commons. Provincial governments are managed by a person identified as Premier (First Minister), normally the leader of the party with the most seats in the legislature. Liberals and Conservatives have headed most provincial governments over the years, although the New Democrats have achieved that goal in six provinces and one territory.

For the most part Canadian political parties are considered progressive in their policies and socially aware. Unlike the United States, Canada has not seen the development of nationally influential extreme right-wing parties to date.

What follows is fiction, set in the near future, but it could happen. Stranger things have occurred.

Wolfville, Nova Scotia
July, 2021

FOR ALL THE RIGHT REASONS

Prologue:
Rolf Niemand

I first encountered Caitlin Sheridan aboard the Chilean America liner *Santiago Vagabundo* in the eastern Caribbean. At the time I could not have foreseen how our crossed paths would derail the carefully orchestrated pattern of my guarded, secretive life.

I was a last-minute addition to the cruise ship's entertainment staff, playing keyboard for the Jay Neilson Trio in the Dios Del Mar lounge. Neilson spotted me during a solo gig in a backwater tavern in Fort Lauderdale the night before the sailing and buttonholed me between sets with a tale of woe. His piano man was in lockup, caught *in flagrante* with an underage prostitute and facing multiple charges. He was sure to miss the boarding call the next day. Would I fill in? Four days at union scale plus meals, a private cabin, and lots of free time.

Why not? As if I had anything better to do.

But back to Caitlin, about whom I was to learn so much over the next year. If you passed her on the street, you wouldn't give her a second glance; well, maybe one, should she happen to favour you with one of her appealing smiles. She was a conventionally pretty young teen, cute rather than beautiful and otherwise unremarkable—until you tried to keep pace with her extraordinary intellect. Her outstanding characteristics were unlimited energy and sparkling pale blue eyes that spoke of places to go, things to see.

Judging by her slight frame, a carnival barker in a guess-your-weight booth might estimate her age at thirteen, her height at five-foot-one (both correct), and her weight at eighty pounds (seven pounds too light). Several regional championships in competitive swimming and a love for gymnastics had given her the muscle density of a mature athlete.

I learned of her athletic prowess much later, of course, and also her precocious scholastic facility, as revealed by the eclectic nature of her personal library. She had exhausted the possibilities of Nancy Drew mysteries by age six, and the fantasy of *Harry Potter*'s wizardry quickly gave way to the poetry and philosophy of Samuel Taylor Coleridge and dour old Immanuel Kant, whose writings on the autonomy of the human spirit fed her flair for independence. She aggressively dog-eared the pages of William Shakespeare's insights into the human condition. She devoured Richard Dawkins' scholarly critiques of religion and delighted in the logic to be found in his passionate defence of Charles Darwin's ground-breaking treatise, *On the Origin of Species*.

Her sleepovers rang with the latest in top forty, rap and hip-hop, but place her before a piano keyboard and you would be hard-pressed to accept her tender age, such was her mastery of classical technique and expression. In short, Caitlin Sheridan was a study in contrasts— prodigiously talented, athletic, intensely curious, marginally hyperactive, and yet strangely insecure when forced by circumstance to be the center of attention.

She was not a novelty in her seaside Nova Scotia community of Bournemouth. Her talents had much in common with those of a similarly gifted youth named J. J. MacIsaac, whose birth in that small town preceded hers by fifteen years and whose mysterious disappearance at age twenty-two had never been solved. Caitlin treasured the few recordings he had made before vanishing from Canada's artistic scene, and sought to imitate his style and the freshness of his interpretations of the great masterpieces of piano literature.

Caitlin and J. J. had never met prior to the voyage of the *Santiago Vagabundo*, but all of our lives were to become inextricably bound together. To quote Caitlin's beloved Elizabethan Bard, "thereby hangs a tale."

One:
Banished

—April, thirteen years ago.

Fifteen-year-old Sabrina Dickenson sat silently and alert in her bedroom as the first hint of overcast December daylight filtered into her room. She listened to the sounds of her father's Sunday morning routine, knowing he would leave the house that morning without telling her goodbye. He had made it clear the night before that she was to be gone by the time the early morning services were over. She was fully dressed, her pathetically small suitcase already packed and awaiting her departure.

She knew she would not see her mother again before she left. That had been the pastor's orders, that his wife should avoid all contact with their daughter and remain behind closed doors until Sabrina was out of the house. There would be no fond farewells, no promises to keep in touch, no gestures of affection. Her father's word was law.

When at last Sabrina heard him exit by the back door on his way to the Church of Immanent Revelation, she stole silently down the stairs to the kitchen. She debated making herself one last meal, but inner turmoil predicted inability to keep any food down. She placed her handbag on the table and removed the contents for one last inventory: a small amount of cash (her mother's contribution, a brave act of secret defiance against her husband), a few personal items, and her birth certificate. She saw possession of the latter as a symbol of permanent estrangement from the strict and unyielding autocrat whose rules she had dared to violate, resulting in her expulsion.

I should have expected this, she thought, *after what happened with the others. But I dared to hope that he might have loved his own daughter enough to forgive my transgression.*

There was no point in lingering. She moved to the closet in the front hall where her winter coat hung in forlorn isolation. Except for the contents of her suitcase, all of her other belongings had been given away, recycled, or discarded. She glanced around the room and for the last time surveyed the mantel. Her gaze passed over the photos of her parents and lingered on that of her older brother, gone for nearly two years, taken from them by the cruelty of incurable malignancy before his eighteenth birthday. Empty space now yawned where once her own portrait had stood among them.

She made one more stop for a last loving communion with the beloved Steinway grand piano that filled one corner of the room. Stacks of music rested on top of the case, and she chose a Schumann sonata, the slow second movement, and placed it on the rack. She sat down and opened the keyboard, and with her foot planted firmly on the soft pedal, she caressed the keys in a flawless rendition of a melody so beautiful, so melancholy, that tears blinded her to the notes on the printed page.

She abandoned the effort at the end of the second theme. She shrugged into her coat, lifted her suitcase, and left by the front door without a backward glance. The road ahead would take her to an uncertain future, an unknown destination. She tried to cast out all thoughts of the beloved one who would not learn of her departure until she was far away. She was sure he would soon forget her, even though she was taking a part of him within her to whatever fate had in store. They would forever be separated by her father's rigid code of conduct and iron-fisted control of their insular and sectarian community.

As the front door closed with a soft click, a distraught Arabella Dickenson gripped the banister at the top of the stairs tightly. "Go with God," she whispered softly.

Two:
Politics

Early in January, well over two hundred men of similar backgrounds attended a private gathering in the convention centre of the Castleton Resort Hotel, overlooking the snow-covered Annapolis Valley from the foothills of the North Mountain. The gathering was exclusively male, exclusively Caucasian, and by all appearances, relatively prosperous and well fed, having paid $2500 each for the privilege of dining with the movers and shakers of the Freedom Party, Nova Scotia's latest and arguably fastest-growing political entity.

Should there have been any doubt as to the philosophical predisposition shared by those in attendance, it was quickly dispelled by the likeness of ousted US President Donald J. Trump that adorned the front of the lectern. Had this been a public assembly, however, that portrait would have been nowhere in sight. Although the term "alt-right" did not appear in any record of the Party's proceedings, Freedom's ultra conservative stance was far outside the mainstream Canadian norm. But given the influence of the populist movement that had swept through both the United States and parts of Europe in recent years, the time was ripe for a credible challenge to the status quo.

In Canada's mildly socialist society, both of the old-line Conservative and Liberal parties stood somewhat left of the American Republicans and Democrats, while the more progressive New Democratic Party had much in common with their socialistic European counterparts. The tiny but vocal Green Party had also forced the government to pay attention to ecological issues.

On the federal level, the Liberals and Conservatives traditionally prevailed under the Parliamentary System, but provincial elections sometimes produced more adventurous results. Since their founding in 1961, the New Democrats had formed majority governments in the Yukon Territory and six provinces, including Nova Scotia, although they were strongest in the west. But right-wing and especially ultra-right-wing politics had attracted little following until recently.

Central to the evening's agenda was an address by the Party's charismatic leader, a successful Halifax lawyer named Carter Williams. He projected an attractive image of competence and success, a man-of-the-people whose penchant for casual attire, even when working, was attractive to the working man. Less well known was the fact that his wardrobe was custom tailored in order to disguise his tendency toward weight gain and lack of physical conditioning, the result of a lifestyle attuned to backroom manoeuvrings and overindulgence. In public he was a chameleon, folksy and down-home among rural constituents and cultured and urbane when the situation required.

His public persona was that of a political moderate, although it was common knowledge that he opposed third-world immigration. Less well known was his belief in white supremacy, and the close ties he maintained with like-minded affiliates in the United States. He strove to conceal his biases and ignorance behind a talent for telling constituents what they wanted to hear.

While attending Dalhousie University in Halifax, his interest in theatrics and participation in dramatic productions both on campus and with the independent Neptune Theatre had come to the attention of a major Hollywood studio that specialized in pop culture potboilers. While never achieving starring roles, his presence in these films kept him in the public eye, contributing to his popularity when the opportunity to seek public office called. Admirers and critics alike often compared him to former US President Ronald Reagan, with his folksy manner of speech, his quick repartee, and a well-tuned gift for turning aside criticism and political attacks with a disarming witticism that tended to distract from the issues at hand.

His speech to constituents that evening was generally non-controversial, stressing the Party's successful fund-raising efforts and especially their sharp upswing in the polls, fuelled by widespread dissatisfaction with both the Liberals and Conservatives. A pattern of corruption and scandal over mishandling of the Provincial budget had ballooned the deficit almost to the breaking point, and opponents scented blood. He carefully and effectively outlined the platform of the Freedom Party and predicted that it would lead them to victory when the ruling Liberals were forced to call an election within the next year.

After concluding his remarks, Williams opened the floor to questions, and for the next forty minutes he rallied the troops, focusing on formulating strategies for achieving a majority of seats in the Legislature. At the very least, they hoped to form a minority Freedom Party government that could offer an attractive alternative to the old-line parties.

Only the recent resurgence of the New Democratic Party posed a real threat to their plans. The Provincial NDP had avoided any taint of scandal in recent years. Whether they could achieve more broadly based support among the voters was seen to depend upon the person who would take them into the election, following a party leadership convention planned for early summer.

The topic shifted toward the relative strength of the opposition, spearheaded by a young radical named Archibald MacInnes. "The Conservatives are no threat," MacInnes insisted, "with that fool Maurice Baxter at the helm. Everyone knows he's had his hand in the till, what with the new golf course he shoehorned into his home riding. It's just a matter of time before the auditors find the smoking gun. And the Liberals are no better."

Heads nodded in agreement. Despite maintaining his personal integrity while in office, Liberal leader Shawn DeWolfe's lax discipline within the ranks had led to charges of sexual indiscretions and embezzlement among his colleagues that badly tarnished his image in recent years.

"Even the Greens are turning their backs on DeWolfe," Grant Keillor offered. "But we all know where those left-wing whiners will throw their support now."

"Which brings us to our biggest problem," Arch MacInnes said.

"The New Democrats are the elephant in the room," Keillor said. "And most specifically, that brown Paki, Vachan Sharma."

"His family came from India, not Pakistan," MacInnes said.

"Same difference. Not a real Canadian in any case, but given the ethnic vote and the way both the Liberals and Conservatives espouse inclusion, he's the biggest threat to us. If the NDP chooses him as leader… Well, enough said."

Williams scanned the faces before him, collectively white and most bearing testament to the northern European ancestry they shared. "Let's not go there," he said quietly. "Any public hint of racism could play well in certain quarters but alienate us in others. It's a trade-off that I would rather not test at this juncture."

"I agree," MacInnes offered. "This topic is best considered behind closed doors. I urge you all to seek your own counsel on the matter of Mr. Sharma's fitness to hold office in our beloved New Scotland, and to ensure that his racial origins will not become the focus of public debate. Is there a motion to adjourn?"

As the majority of attendees filed out of the room, led by Carter Williams, a few remained behind to gather in a quiet anteroom, intent on pursuing their own agenda.

* * *

Most members of the Freedom Party considered the increasing diversity within Canadian society to be a threat to the mainly Anglo-Saxon majority in Nova Scotia. More than one hundred and fifty years after Confederation, Canada had been governed by a succession of Liberal and Conservative Parliaments led by Prime Ministers with Scottish, English and less frequently French surnames that reflected the country's founding fathers.

It became apparent in 2017 that winds of change were just over the horizon, when an Ontario-born lawyer and politician named Jagmeet Singh ascended to the leadership of the national New Democratic Party and was subsequently elected to a seat in the House of Commons. As Singh worked toward making the NDP a viable alternative to the Liberals and Conservatives, his presence raised the potential for the election of a Prime Minister whose Asian background was prominently on display. His ever-present turban advertised an ethnicity that had its roots in India, rather than Great Britain or France. The potential for a person of colour to become Prime Minister was anathema to some citizens, just as the election of Barack Obama to the Presidency of the United States had raised the ire of a substantial segment of that population.

When the New Democrats of Nova Scotia seemed poised to choose a respected physician and political activist named Vachan Sharma to lead the Provincial party, the threat to the upstart Freedom Party became apparent. Sharma cut an imposing figure, tall and youthful, and despite eye, hair and skin colouring that revealed his Punjabi background, he was mainstream Canadian in manner and speech, having been born and raised in Halifax.

Sharma's ancestors had converted to Christianity during British rule in India. He professed adherence to the Anglican faith, although that was mainly for the benefit of his more devout constituents. By nature, he was an agnostic to whom religion held no appeal, but he recognized and approved of the power of religious conviction to bring comfort to believers and to spur them to work for the common good. For that reason, he attended church regularly and endorsed such declarations of belief as expressed in the national anthem ("God keep our land glorious and free"), while remaining ever alert to perversions of faith that might threaten society; perversions such as those represented by religious elements in the white supremacy movement.

With a Provincial election mandated before the end of the year, the public's anticipation of an NDP led by Vachan Sharma rapidly gained popular support as an alternative to the moribund Conservatives and Liberals. Whereas just a few short months earlier Freedom's appeal to the public seemed to predict victory at the ballot box, Sharma's progressive platform was poised to overtake the splintered opposition and take control of the Provincial Legislature.

Certain advocates of the Freedom Party were not about to let that happen.

Three:
Caitlin Meets Chloe

—February, Fort Lauderdale, Florida

Caitlin Sheridan folded her pyjamas and slipped into her Nike racing suit. Without turning on a light, she gathered a towel around her shoulders and padded barefoot out of the motel room, carefully easing the door shut behind her. She made her way to the back stairway and hurried down to the fenced-in outdoor pool at the back of the property, using her key card to gain entrance through the locked gate. She dropped the towel on the nearest table and plunged into the deep end, ignoring the posted admonition against swimming before nine in the morning.

Caitlin's father, cardiac surgeon Russell Sheridan, blinked in the weak early morning sunlight that filtered into the motel room, wondering what had awakened him. He checked his watch and adjusted his thinking to account for the time zone change—Atlantic Standard to Eastern—that had prompted the family to turn in early the night before. Careful not to awaken his wife Jessica, who lay deeply asleep beside him, he eased out of bed and discovered the second queen-size bed empty, the covers disarrayed.

Russell sighed. *Might as well try to cap a volcano*, he thought. Thirteen-year-old Caitlin's excitement had made his daughter restless and enervated the evening before. When she finally crashed, Russell thought she would probably sleep late, although he was not surprised to find otherwise. As quietly as possible he pulled on shorts and a tee shirt, collected his room key, and scribbled an ironic note for Jessica: *Sleeping Beauty is probably in the water already. Back soon.* He propped it up in front of the clock radio.

In the motel corridor he located the elevator and descended to the first floor, where a sign directed him to the pool. He pushed his way into the enclosure to find Caitlin churning back and forth, head down, slender muscular arms and legs driving her forward in a smooth Australian crawl. She flipped over at the wall and charged back in a powerful breaststroke, reversed again, and flailed the water in an awkward-looking but efficient butterfly.

Russell sprawled in a deck chair, grateful for the coming of warm Florida sun after having boarded an Air Canada 737 a day earlier on a bitterly cold Nova Scotia February morning. Caitlin completed another half dozen laps, then boosted herself up onto the apron. She squealed at the sight of her father and jumped to her feet. Heedless of the slippery tiles, she ran to his side and threw herself into his lap.

"Hey! You're all wet!" he protested.

"You don't care, you love me," she laughed, planting a fat kiss on his cheek.

"What have we told you about going swimming alone?" he said, trying to sound stern. "It's not safe."

"Couldn't wait, been awake for *hours!* I didn't think you two would ever get up."

"What's your hurry? We can't board the ship until after one o'clock."

"When do we catch the shuttle?"

"At noon. We'll need an early lunch. The cruise port's only twenty minutes away."

She squirmed off his lap and gathered her towel from a nearby table. She knotted it around her waist. "Let's get some breakfast and go exploring. I want to see what Fort Lauderdale looks like."

As Russell climbed to his feet they heard the building's door open, and three figures emerged and approached the fence. A slim girl about Caitlin's age swiped her room card and entered the enclosure. She was striking in appearance, with a heart-shaped face and a placid, stoic smile that one might believe concealed secret thoughts, mysteries. Her café au lait skin and huge, almost black eyes suggested Asian ancestry. Under a sheer cover-up she wore a modest two-piece swimsuit, trimmed with ruffles and more for show than for serious aquatics.

Close behind her came a slight woman with Oriental features, ahead of a muscular young man of medium height wearing a dress shirt and necktie. He moved down the pool apron and sat at a table beneath a sun umbrella.

"Is the pool open yet?" the woman asked.

"Not this early," Caitlin answered her, "but my room card worked, so I came in anyway. I guess you can, too." She looked toward the other young teen. "I'm Caitlin."

"I'm Chloe," the girl said shyly. "This is my mom."

The woman stepped forward and, while smiling at Caitlin, offered her hand to Russell. "Elizabeth Wu," she said by way of introduction.

"A pleasure," he said. "Russell Sheridan, Caitlin's dad. I'm glad to know we aren't the only early birds."

"We're still on Atlantic time," the woman said. "We flew in from Halifax late last night."

"Really? So did we, but on the noon flight. Do you live in the city?"

"In Bedford, actually. My husband is a physician."

"No kidding!" Caitlin said. "My dad, too. We live down near Lunenburg, little nowhere town called Bournemouth."

"Are you taking a winter vacation?" Russell asked.

"A short cruise," Elizabeth said. "Something to do with my husband's latest project. He's flirting with politics."

"Not the *Santiago Vagabundo*!" Caitlin exclaimed.

"That's the one," the woman said.

"Us too!" Caitlin grinned at her father. "You always said it's a small world, but I didn't believe it until now." Then to Chloe, "Let's get together when we're on board. Do you know your cabin number yet?"

13

The two girls moved to sit at a table and put their heads together, comparing notes on their anticipated trip. Russell said to Elizabeth, "Looks like a friendship in the making. Caitlin was afraid she wouldn't know anyone on the cruise."

"Chloe felt the same way. She can be almost painfully shy, not nearly as outgoing as your daughter."

"Funny you should say that. Caitlin is actually insecure in new situations, and has been fretting about this adventure, even though it was all her idea." Russell glanced toward the man seated at the shaded table and tilted his head in that direction. "Is that your…?"

The woman laughed gently. "He's part of my husband's team."

"Team?"

She sighed. "He's making a run for the leadership of the provincial New Democrats. There have been a couple of veiled threats, so in addition to a secretary and an aide, the party insisted he travel with some security. That's Jacob Shaffer, second in command, and he keeps track of Chloe and me most of the time, even though it isn't really necessary."

"You've been threatened?"

"Nothing serious. It's just routine, Vachan says."

"That name sounds familiar. Is your husband Vachan Sharma?"

"Guilty as charged. I admit to being a bit ambivalent about this newest venture of his. Don't get me wrong, he's a wonderful man, a great husband and father, but he heads the cardiac department at Victoria General Hospital, and if he leads the party, I don't know what that will do to his work there. Politics can be very demanding."

"I've followed his bid for the leadership," Russell said. "He's been very forthright with his ideas, and if the party adopts them, it could mean good things for Nova Scotia."

"That's kind of you to say."

"What's more, from what I've read he could be our next Premier come November, if he can put together a strong campaign."

"Yes…" Elizabeth looked toward the girls.

"You're not in favour?"

"If it's what he really wants, and I'm sure it is, then I'm completely behind him. He's always been something of a, how do you say, a shit disturber." She shrugged nervously. "And our Province could use a little shaking up."

Russell laughed softly.

"I mean that in a positive sense," the woman said. "He likes to stir the pot, knock people off their comfortable perches and get them moving."

"We could certainly stand a little of that."

"I suppose. But it means a big change in our lives."

"Your name rings a bell with me, too. You're a teacher, right? Or a professor?"

"Part time, in the St. Mary's English Department."

"And you're a novelist! My wife has mentioned your work. Favourably, I might add."

"Thank you."

Caitlin hurried back to them, Chloe trailing along a bit slower. "I have their cabin number," she told her dad. "Same deck as ours, so it's probably a suite." She turned toward Elizabeth. "Are you guys somebody important?"

"Caitlin!" Russell said. "Manners, please."

Elizabeth smiled. "It's not a big deal," she said to Caitlin. "My husband is in politics, and his Party treated us to the cruise."

"Cool!" Caitlin turned to Russell. "Chloe wants to get wet, and I'm hungry. We're gonna meet up later and ride the shuttle together." She looked toward Elizabeth, "If that's okay, I mean."

"I think we can work it out."

"Give me a call when you get back from the pool," she told Chloe. She grabbed Russell's hand and tugged him toward the security door. Russell shrugged and smiled. "It was very nice meeting you, Elizabeth.

And you too, Chloe. I hope we'll see a lot of you on the ship."

"Come *on*, Dad!" Caitlin fished her room key card from the top of her swimsuit and swiped it through the reader. The door clicked open, and they pushed their way inside.

"You think Mom is up yet?" she asked as they headed for the elevators.

"Still asleep when I left," he told her.

"Let's roust her out."

Russell grinned and followed along, marvelling at the girl's incredible vitality. Her limitless enthusiasm sometimes tired him out, but invariably made him proud. "Hurry up, Dad!" Caitlin called out over her shoulder, repeatedly pushing the elevator "up" button.

Hurry up, Dad, Russell thought. *How often I have heard those words over the past thirteen years.*

His mind wandered back to the first time he saw her, impossibly tiny and deceptively fragile at barely six pounds, dwarfed by her bassinet. Her forehead bore a deep red blush, a temporary birthmark that still occasionally blossomed in times of stress. Her translucent skin was paper thin, her hands like tiny starfish; helpless and dependent. But her intense blue eyes were telling him, *Come on, Dad! Take me home! Let's get things started!*

Twice he and Jessica had tried to start a family, each pregnancy ending in sudden miscarriage in the second trimester, and they decided to abandon the effort. But then came the surprise of an unplanned conception. *Third time will be the charm,* they told each other, and by the eighth month it seemed as if they might be right—until that terrible night in a Toronto hotel room when Jessica awoke doubled over in pain, blood staining her nightdress, Russell dropping the phone in his panic, the shrill cry of the siren as the EMT van careened into the parking lot, Russell throwing the door open, heavy boots charging into the room, heedless of dirt and snow staining the carpet, a hurried IV line in Jessica's arm, electronic probes slapped on here and there, a gentle but hurried transfer to a wheeled stretcher, van doors slamming shut, siren again, clearing the way to the medical centre, Russell's rented Lexus glued to the back bumper.

Controlled terror.

Russell shook his head, banishing the terrible memories that too often woke him, sweating and disoriented, in the middle of the night, heralding the end of sleep.

"Mom, you awake yet?" Caitlin called out as the motel room door swung open.

I'll think about all that later, Russell thought to himself.

Four:
Back Room Boys

The eight-man Executive Committee of the Freedom Party gathered in a private dining room located in an annex to the Harbourside Restaurant and Lounge in Dartmouth. Acting as Chair was Archibald MacInnes, considered a sure bet for a major cabinet position should the Party succeed in the next election. Randall Cruikshank was the senior member of the Party, well into his seventies with a record as a stalwart Progressive Conservative in the Diefenbaker years. He sat in quiet conversation with Maurice Saulnier, who had served as a Liberal Member of the Provincial Legislature when Pierre Trudeau was Prime Minister. Both men were committed converts to the ultra-conservative cause.

Grant Keillor was a moving force behind the Party's anti-immigration campaign whose virulent bias against minorities was only thinly veiled. He and Alexander Mackenzie, named for his distant ancestor, the famed and knighted Canadian explorer, huddled in one corner in deep conversation, awaiting the start of the meeting. The youngest and least experienced of the attendees was Alistair Barclay, whose main claim to fame was his friendship with Keillor. Claude Freemont and Harris Paulson rounded out the committee membership.

The agenda called for discussion of the current state of the campaign to seize control of the Provincial Legislature. Arch MacInnes brought with him advance copies of a recent Canadian Broadcasting Company poll. He passed them around the table.

"Good news and bad," he announced, "so let's start with the good. Page one, standings for the Liberals and Conservatives. Twenty-one and seventeen percent respectively, it's their lowest showing in years, and expected to fall even farther."

"I suppose we can't count them out entirely," Grant Keillor said, "but it was to be expected. What's their demographic?"

"Urban support has bottomed out. Both parties still show well in their traditional rural areas, but neither one can command enough seats to form a government."

Keillor was a data specialist, like the others barely into his thirties and full of passionate belief in neo-conservative ideals. He placed great faith in social media to manipulate public opinion. "What are our figures?" he asked.

"Top of page two," MacInnes said, flipping over the first sheet. "Thirty percent, a gain of almost eight points in just three weeks and expected to grow."

"Who's taking the hit?" Paulson asked.

"Mostly the Conservatives."

"And the rest of the field?" Maurice Saulnier asked. He was the latest recruit to the management team for Freedom, a former Liberal who viewed his old party as ill-equipped to deal with what he considered to be a mounting threat from the far-left New Democrats.

"The poll has the NDP pegged at twenty-nine," Keillor said, "and the Green Party at three, both down from last month. It's hard to say who they've lost ground to, but the raw data doesn't tell the whole story. Take a look at the predictions on the next page. The table at the bottom is the important one, the relative strength of the Party leaders."

The men shuffled the papers and began reading. When they had digested the information, they sat back, frowning. "We could be in trouble," Al Barclay offered.

"We *are* in trouble," Keillor said. "It all depends on what the New Democrats do at their convention. Despite the gains we've made with union support, especially in Cape Breton and Colchester-Cumberland, the so-called working man still likes what those goddamn socialists are promising; minimum wage increases, more favourable contract negotiations, all that."

"But still, we've got a slight edge on them."

"Flip over to the last page," MacInnes said. "That's the bad news I was talking about."

In the final table of the report, the CBC pundits compared the expected election results as vulnerable to a number of variables. Most important was the matter of party leadership. The incumbent Doug Kauffman of the New Democrats was facing a vigorous challenge to his leadership. Should he maintain control, the poll was predicting a minority win for the Freedom Party in the fall, with the NDP in opposition.

But Vachan Sharma was a rising star for the NDP and the new darling of the media. If he replaced Kauffman as leader, the results were expected to be different. All things being equal, the New Democrats would sweep the urban areas of Halifax-Dartmouth, Sydney and its suburbs, the northern counties, and even much of the South Shore to form a majority government. Freedom would come in second, but with too few seats to have any real influence.

"That's it, then," Keillor said. "We go to Plan B. We have to take that damn Muslim or Hindu or whatever he is out of the picture."

"According to his bio, he's Christian. Anglican," Barclay said.

"That's just for show. People like him never change. He isn't one of us, and we have to stop him in his tracks."

"We should wait. A lot can change before November."

"That will be too late," Keillor said, turning to MacInnes. "If we act now, we can just sit back and watch our popularity grow. We'll be the only real alternative. The other leaders, including Kauffman, are old news, and the voters will turn to us. If…"

"Yes. If."

The men fell silent for a few moments, lost in thought.

"I repeat," Keillor said at last. "Plan B is our only alternative."

"Are we all agreed?" MacInnes asked. Everyone nodded, the elderly Randall Cruikshank a bit reluctantly. "Then we remove Sharma from the equation permanently, no matter what it takes. There's no other choice."

Five:
Gustav

Concert pianist Gustav Schreiber was born to Wilhelm and Marielle (nee Archambault) Schreiber in Vienna during the ominous year of 1935. It was apparent to his parents that the growing National Socialist movement in neighbouring Germany would soon threaten the independence of their native Austria. Although a confirmed atheist who professed no religious affiliation, Wilhelm knew that his Jewish origins endangered the family's security.

Wilhelm and Marielle relocated to Paris via Switzerland in late 1937, less than five months before Hitler's storm troopers annexed Austria. They planned to settle there permanently, hoping that young Gustav would flourish in the rich musical environment of that capital city, but long-term safety anywhere in Europe was far from guaranteed. When Nazi forces massed to cross the Belgian border in May of 1940, Wilhelm quickly booked passage to Canada and settled his family in Quebec.

However, less than three months of living under the militant Catholicism of the Maurice Duplessis government drove them to seek a more tolerant atmosphere, and they relocated to the seaside town of Bournemouth, on Nova Scotia's South Shore. Wilhelm secured a teaching position at Irvine University, and fearing that their Germanic accent would suggest allegiance to the Third Reich and its atrocities, he and his wife immersed themselves in the English language with uncommon zeal. Both German and French were spoken in the household, however, and little Gustav grew up fluently trilingual, overlaid with a cultured French accent and vocabulary absorbed from his mother. Nonetheless, the child was cautioned by his parents to conceal his linguistic ability, and at school he developed patterns of speech indistinguishable from his east coast schoolmates.

Gustav inherited his father Wilhelm's aptitude for the piano and was proficient by the time he enrolled in the Irvine School of Music. Soon after graduation he commenced a successful career as Artist in Residence at his alma mater, an uncommon honour for one so young. He concertized extensively throughout the provinces of Nova Scotia and New Brunswick.

Gustav married another Austrian expatriate, Shoshanna Weiss, early in 1958, and their daughter and only child, Rachel Rebecca (always called Becky) was born four days after Christmas in 1959. Becky devoted three intensive years to the Humanities program at Irvine after graduating from high school in 1977, and followed that with an Education degree. Three months after completing her studies she joined the faculty of Bournemouth Elementary School. In 1985 she married Angus MacIsaac, a high school science teacher, and Gustav and Shoshanna converted four spare rooms on the second floor of their three-story Victorian home into an apartment to welcome the young couple.

In September of 1990, their first and only child, Jonathan James, was born.

Six:
J. J.

Jonathan James MacIsaac stunned the music world at the tender age of nine, appearing as soloist with a chamber orchestra at Carnegie Hall in New York City. His reading of Beethoven's Fifth Piano Concerto, the *Emperor*, may not have been technically flawless. Given the diminutive size of his hands, that was not unexpected. The emotional depth and fiery execution of the piece, however, resulted in a standing ovation lasting several minutes.

J. J. (as he was always called) was the product of a curious pattern of genetic development that sometimes causes precocious talent to skip generations. While his father and mother appreciated good music, they exhibited no particular aptitude, but reviews of their child's performances frequently drew comparisons between the boy's technique and that of his grandfather Gustav.

When just a few months old, the child passed into the daytime care of his grandmother Shoshanna, his Oma, because of the demands of Becky's teaching position. The boy walked at ten months, began to talk in complete sentences before age one, and showed intense interest in the huge Bechstein piano that stood in the parlour. He would resist any effort to remove him from his preferred place, standing on the overstuffed sofa from which he could observe Gustav's hands as he played.

Once J. J. grew tall enough to reach the keyboard, he began to experiment with and delight in the sounds the magnificent instrument could make. Gustav was astonished to discover that the child could pick out the melodies he had heard. Formal lessons began shortly before the child turned three. Within a few months, and seated upon two thick books, tiny J. J. had mastered more than a dozen compositions, two-part inventions by Johann Sebastian Bach and juvenile sonatinas of the similarly gifted young Mozart.

Gustav established a regular pattern of physical training to develop his grandson's talent, plus instruction in reading music and the written word. The child absorbed knowledge like a sponge. By the time J. J. entered public school, he could read and write both English and French at an elementary level and could perform basic mathematical computation. He began the study of such diverse compositions as Debussy's impressionistic keyboard pieces, Beethoven's andante movements, and the demanding sonatas of Alexander Scriabin.

J. J. raced through abbreviated years of public education, severely challenging the best efforts of his teachers to keep him interested in what they had to offer. By age twelve he had mastered basic Spanish and, despite his family's abandonment of their mother tongue, was becoming fluent in German with clandestine help from his Oma Shoshanna. Although technically enrolled in the local school, his attendance was sporadic, and most of his learning was entrusted to a succession of private tutors. He spent little time with children his own age. His reclusive demeanour made him the target of incessant bullying.

It seemed as if there could be no limit to what the boy might accomplish. He began taking lessons at the Irvine School of Music at age fourteen, but quickly outpaced his instructor's pedagogical expertise. Gustav began making inquiries among his colleagues, searching for an artist teacher whose affinity for contemporary music might introduce the boy to the next logical step in his development.

Then suddenly, one blustery day in April, fifteen-year-old J. J. MacIsaac simply disappeared.

Seven:
A Gift

In the Fort Lauderdale motel, Caitlin and her mother discussed plans for the upcoming cruise as Russell reflected on events that had brought them south on an unexpected adventure. On the morning of Valentine's Day, the child presented her parents with an elaborate handmade card shaped like an ocean liner and festooned with stickers, sparkly red and white hearts, and tiny black and white piano keyboards. Inside was a letter from the head office of Chilean America Cruise Lines, inviting Drs. Russell and Jessica Sheridan and their daughter Caitlin to join the maiden voyage of their newest and largest ship as honoured guests of Captain Eugénio Ramos.

Although relatively small by international standards, where ships capable of hosting four thousand or more vacationers were common, the South American company had bravely entered the competitive Caribbean holiday market less than a decade earlier. The line's first two modest but well-equipped vessels could handle just eleven hundred passengers each, but their third ship, the *Santiago Vagabundo*, was nearly twice that size, boasting enough staterooms and suites to accommodate slightly more than two thousand.

The previous year Caitlin had come upon an advertisement offering employment opportunities aboard the new ship, including a call for performers to provide entertainment during the initial voyage in February. With the help of her beloved grandfather Orrin, Russell's father and a recently retired surgeon with an international reputation, Caitlin emailed an application to work aboard ship, in which she outlined in great detail what her contribution could be while avoiding any mention of her age. A representative of the cruise line responded with a request for a recorded audition, and Caitlin downloaded her

Canadian Broadcasting Company performance of Mozart's *C Minor Sonata* and a Beethoven piano trio in which she was joined by the world-renowned duo of violinist Josiah Melanson and cellist Radojka Kowalski.

Within an hour an email arrived inviting Caitlin to participate in a video interview. The following morning Orrin drove her to the local radio station where audio and visual equipment and a grand piano were available. When a call came from Enrico Sanchez, the Human Resources Administrator at Chilean America, the video feed opened on the piano bench where Caitlin was seated, diminutive in a simple skirt and cap-sleeved blouse. She introduced herself nervously to the camera.

The urbane Sanchez reacted with predictable surprise, but to his credit he almost succeeded in hiding a tolerant smile that seemed to say, *Is someone putting me on?*

"Miss Sheridan," he said, "I think there may have been a misunderstanding."

"My granddad told me you would probably say something like that," she said, "and I understand. But since you've already gone to the trouble to set up this video conference, may I play for you anyway?"

Sanchez hesitated, then shrugged and waved a hand toward his computer screen, and Caitlin launched into the lush *Eighteenth Variation* from Serge Rachmaninoff's *Rhapsody on a Theme of Paganini*, then segued to the love theme from the movie *Titanic*. Without pause and improvising a few chords to change the key, she ripped into a barrelhouse version of *Maple Leaf Rag*, her left hand a blur as it flew back and forth between the bass line and the backbeat harmonies. As the last notes died away, she swung around on the bench, grinning widely, her eyebrows raised as if to say, *See what you could be missing?*

"Miss Sheridan..." Sanchez began.

"I'm Caitlin," she said, "and I bet you're going to say I'm too young, you can't pay me, child labour laws and all that, and that kids my age can't go on your cruises alone. Right?"

"Caitlin, your playing is very impressive. You would be a real asset to our maiden voyage, but…"

"We've got it all figured out. You won't have to worry about paying me, and I won't be on board alone. Here's how my granddad says it could work."

Before the interview was over, Caitlin had been invited to appear in the ship's chamber music venue, times and repertoire to be determined. "The respected Canadian doctors, Russell and Jessica Sheridan and their daughter" were to be installed in a spacious suite as special guests of the Captain, "in honour of Caitlin Sheridan's contribution to the launching of the cruise ship *Santiago Vagabundo*." This nonspecific language avoided the legal complications that would result if the company tried to employ an underage entertainer, no matter how talented.

With the Valentine card in hand, Russell explained to his daughter that he could not take leave from his duties at the hospital to accompany her. Nor could her mother abandon her clients in the county mental health clinic on such short notice. As the second ranking psychologist on staff, and the only holder of a Ph.D. in Counselling Psychology, she would be hard to replace on short notice.

"Granddad already took care of all that," Caitlin announced smugly. "Everyone at the clinic offered to do overtime to fill in for Mom, and all your surgeries for that week are elective, so the hospital reassigned them. Anyway," she said, stretching the truth a bit, "I have to go on the cruise because I've already agreed, even if you insist on staying home."

Faced with his daughter's impressive organizational skills, Russell acquiesced, and the day for departure was now at hand.

Eight:
Rolf

Ever since relocating to the Caribbean, I've guarded my privacy carefully. I have no fixed address, no provision for receiving personal mail, and no conventional bank accounts or record of employment. I've ghosted through life for years, rarely needing the services that taxation is designed to pay for. My lifestyle comes as close to living off the grid as anyone could desire.

My sole companion is a silky, long-haired tortoiseshell cat named Jenny, a skilled acrobat to whom no nook or cranny of my yacht is inaccessible. She adopted me on a decrepit pier in a backwater cove on Grand Cayman by presenting me with the corpse of an imposing wharf rat that attempted to stow away by climbing my bow line. She sat looking smug as I deposited her gift overboard, then curled up under the dodger atop the cabin as if to say, "You need me."

I agreed; she stayed.

As far as officialdom is concerned, I don't exist. I pay no income taxes and feel no guilt over it. In my opinion, massive institutional corruption and complex tax codes that favour the rich and famous mean that the average citizen pays far more than his or her share of the burden of government. Too many million- and billionaires manipulate the system to avoid federal taxes entirely.

Fraud and dishonesty permeate all levels of society, extending even—perhaps especially—to those who occupy the highest levels of office. I'm content to stick it to these elitist crooks, elected and otherwise, who manipulate the system to their own advantage. It seems as if the human race has made little progress since the medieval period, when the privileged few luxuriated in their castles at the expense of serfs whose labour supported their greedy lifestyle.

If all of this makes me a criminal in the eyes of the law, so be it.

I try to keep my dealings with people to a minimum, but when necessary I can communicate in Spanish, German and Dutch, making me completely at home in the polyglot islands. My appearance is unremarkable. I keep my naturally light brown hair dyed medium dark brown and let it grow somewhat over my collar, albeit neatly trimmed. I'm clean-shaven except for a pencil-thin moustache. My vision is perfect, but I wear glasses with plain lenses when I'm ashore, clear or tinted to protect my eyes from the sun. The frames are simply camouflage.

My clothing choices, shorts or deck pants and pullover shirts, befit a solo sailor. Most would find it difficult to estimate my age, and having encountered me, people almost certainly retain little impression afterward. In any case, the chances of meeting someone down south who knows me from years past are fairly slim.

"Home" is a forty-foot Taiwanese Canadian yacht of indeterminate vintage. Its cryptic name *Versteck*—"Hideaway" in German—is displayed in elaborate script across the stern. One of very few similar boats ever constructed, this beamy craft allows me the freedom to roam from place to place alone, according to no itinerary or agenda. Purposely built for single-handed sailing, she requires no crew if her skipper possesses reasonable strength, agility, and mechanical aptitude. Which, forgive my immodesty, I do.

I came upon her abandoned in a backwater cove on St. Croix, U.S. Virgin Islands. Despite a fire that had gutted much of her topside superstructure, the hull was reasonably intact, and I liked her lines. A few inquiries among the locals revealed the name of the owner, a Brazilian TV personality who was willing to let her go for a song.

Further inquiries led me to Felix van der Westhuizen, a Dutch national with a reputation for fussy and obsessive craftsmanship. His English was appalling, and I became his instant best friend when he discovered I could converse with him in his own language. We struck a deal whereby he would restore the boat in his well-equipped yard while allowing me to perform whatever chores fell within my areas of expertise.

As work got under way, putting a deep dent in my cash reserves, I decided to cut all ties with everyone back home. It was not an easy decision to leave friends and family behind, but I needed to escape from troubling events in my youth that had left me traumatized and vulnerable. Nor would I return to the demands of my former profession, which I found restrictive and demanding. I no longer wished to dance to the tune of agents and various other hangers-on who fed off my talent, parasites whose appetites increased in direct proportion to my success. I was tired of all that.

Following six months of intensive work, *Versteck* emerged from the Westhuizen yard pristine and competent, her mechanicals and electronics state of the art and her ambiance that of a luxury hotel. Despite his aw-shucks air of modesty, Felix was justifiably proud that every piece of joinery below decks displayed true craftsmanship. When we took her to sea for a shakedown cruise, expecting to have to make all sorts of corrections and adjustments, I was pleasantly surprised to find her close to perfect for my purposes.

Versteck is cat rigged with just two sails, main and mizzen, and no jib to keep track of. I can pilot her from the cockpit without assistance. A powerful diesel engine underfoot gives me good speed when there is no wind. *Versteck* is remarkably stable even in the roughest conditions. She is exceptionally large below decks and offers more interior living space than many larger yachts, roomier than a typical studio apartment.

It's important to me that no one be able to predict my movements, and I never stay in one location long enough to attract attention. My range extends from the Florida-Alabama border to Barbados, and I can always find an isolated cove or uninhabited islet when the need to escape the open sea comes upon me. I give larger destinations such as Cuba, Jamaica, and the Dominican Republic a wide berth.

Versteck boasts a substantial array of electronic equipment in support of safety and comfort, including redundant navigation devices and an elaborate bank of radio receivers to alert me well in advance of any threat to my security. This warning system allows me to skirt the destructive hurricanes that threaten the Caribbean each summer and autumn, and to circumvent commercial craft plying the sea lanes. I can also monitor governmental and police bands for information about political or criminal activities in such a volatile part of the world.

Having an almost blank slate to work with, my skilled Dutch friend invested the yacht's living quarters with a host of unconventional features. Dual diesel generators guarantee ample power for air conditioning, a microwave oven, and the musical apparatus essential to maintaining my skills. The main head is twice the size of sanitary facilities aboard most yachts. In addition to an efficient marine toilet and basin, it contains a shower stall spacious enough to accommodate my six-foot-three frame. Whereas I rarely invite others aboard overnight, I specified that just two berths be installed, which freed up extra space for my extensive library and a small spinet piano.

My main concession to civilization's rules involves economic security. Deep within the bilge a waterproof safe holds emergency funds, but it isn't prudent to keep the bulk of my resources aboard. Even given my reasonably competent skills as a sailor, the sea can be dangerously unpredictable. There's no such thing as an unsinkable boat, and so I maintain safety deposit boxes under assumed names at discrete banks in several easily accessible ports, although not in major centers such as Nassau or San Juan.

Otherwise, most of my assets are invested anonymously in tax shelters managed by a friend from university days, a partner in a Bridgetown, Barbados law firm. He is entrusted with the dispersal of my estate in the event of my death, or if I fail to make contact at least once in every twelve-month period.

In short, I am a seagoing hermit. By choice.

Nine:
J. J.

After leaving home one unseasonably warm Saturday morning, young J. J. MacIssac failed to return for lunch as expected. The family was not unduly concerned, but with still no sign of him by early evening, they contacted the Royal Canadian Mounted Police. An extensive investigation failed to find any trace of the boy over the next few days. Fearing a kidnapping, the Mounties assembled a task force to deal with the expected ransom demands, but more than nine months passed with no contact of any sort.

Grandfather Gustav was devastated, but the family never abandoned hope that one day they would discover the boy's fate. As the Hanukkah and Christmas holidays approached, there was debate over whether to decorate the house. J. J.'s continued absence overshadowed any feelings of seasonal joy, but ultimately it was decided that a token spot of color might help to lighten their spirits. Unfortunately, the forlorn little artificial tree that they brought home from Canadian Tire had the opposite effect, as if underlining the emptiness of a home that had once rung with so much wonderful music.

Shortly before midnight on December 29th, Gustav's daughter Rebecca's birthday, the recently retired pianist sat reading in his recliner near a front window. A half-empty cup of warm milk sat on an end table by his side. The house was quiet, and he realized that he could not recall the content of the last few paragraphs he had read. He laid the book aside, took a few sips from his cup, then was distracted by a shadow that flickered across the window shade. Next came a gentle tapping as hesitant footsteps crossed the porch, and the hinges on the screen door squeaked softly. The doorknob rattled. The old man levered himself upright and approached the door. He hesitated with his hand on the deadbolt, then twisted it and turned the knob to find the screen door slightly ajar.

Gustav pushed through and stepped outside, peering into the shadowy snow-covered yard which was only dimly lighted by a lamp post on the opposite side of the street. Seeing nothing, he turned to go back inside and nearly tripped over Jonathan James, who was huddled to one side of the threshold, knees drawn up to his chest. The boy wore a threadbare oversized sweater that did little to augment the lightweight clothing in which he had disappeared six months before.

Other than shivering from exposure to the December cold, J. J. appeared unharmed and in good health, although seeming to have lost the power of speech. His joy at being home among those who loved him was apparent, but when questioned about his disappearance, he couldn't, or wouldn't, utter a word. Over the next few weeks his parents sought the help and advice of medical doctors and mental health professionals, who diagnosed emotional trauma. It was not until the first leaf buds began to forecast a typically late Nova Scotia spring that J. J. began to communicate haltingly, as if learning to speak for the first time. Still, he said nothing about where he had been living, or with whom.

The family was astonished, however, to discover that he had lost none of his expertise at the keyboard. To the contrary, he had mastered a number of new and challenging compositions during his absence, as if having spent the intervening six months in an intensive period of study and practice. In the face of his inability to explain how this could have happened, his parents accepted the situation and tried to help their son return to a normal existence. Even when his powers of speech fully returned, he could not be persuaded to say anything about the time he had been away.

The Jonathan James who returned home was moody and introspective, given to long periods of silent contemplation as if reflecting upon topics or emotions that would forever be hidden from others. His parents suspected some form of abuse, although the doctors who examined him reported no physical signs to suggest it.

If anything, J. J. was stronger and healthier after nine months of continued growth and development, somehow more mature both physically and in his demeanour. He seemed self-possessed well beyond his years. He had gained weight, and his appetite continued to be strong. His face filled out, and there were signs of a beard developing. There were no major indications of impairment, other than prolonged periods of meditation during which he could barely tolerate the presence of his family. They soon learned that to deny him privacy at such times was unproductive.

Becky and Angus were surprised when their son asked for membership in a commercial gym. J. J. had never expressed interest in physical fitness or any type of sports, and now he concealed the true reason for his request. For in addition to providing the usual array of body-building equipment, the gym conducted classes in self defence, including boxing and martial arts. The boy threw himself into this new pastime, and soon became surprisingly proficient. Bullies would never trouble him again.

Nor anyone else.

It quickly became clear that J. J. was only marking time in the small Irvine University music department. With his parents' reluctant approval, his grandfather Gustav arranged for admission to a summer session at New York's Juilliard School, where he fell under the professional tutelage of composer and pianist Arthur Ivchenko. He was invited to join the Ivchenko household in Lower Manhattan, where he remained for the next four years.

Before reaching his nineteenth birthday, J. J. soloed with six major North American orchestras and both the London Symphony and the Vienna Philharmonic. He divided his time between performance and extensive research into musicology, which he published in both English and German. His keyboard repertoire was as diverse as his academic interests, including sonatas and concertos by every important Classic, Romantic and late nineteenth century composer. Upon turning twenty, he threw himself into exploring the seminal twentieth century compositions of Schoenberg, Ravel, Shostakovich, Aaron Copland, and Leonard Bernstein. For the next two years he was seldom out of the public eye.

He kept himself physically fit and was generally considered handsome, his appearance enhanced by neatly trimmed facial hair. He rarely smiled but never scowled, his expression neutral and rigidly controlled. In contrast to the intense emotional content of his performances, he was quiet and aloof when away from the keyboard. He pursued no social life and had few if any close friends.

In addition to accepting multiple invitations to perform, he wrote carefully crafted essays, analyses, and theoretical treatises for a variety of periodicals and university publications in North America and abroad. His research into the piano literature of the first half of the eighteenth century, before the advent of Mozart, produced new insights into the period when that instrument was in its infancy.

His recordings and publications brought him accolades, awards, and substantial income, although he lived frugally—some would say monastically—with a bare minimum of possessions. His personal fortune accumulated quickly. He qualified for a driver's license but did not own a vehicle. He maintained no permanent residence. Instead, he leased cramped quarters on a month-to-month basis in whatever city and country he was professionally active.

And then, as suddenly as the flaming comet of his extraordinary talent had illuminated the musical universe, he vanished from the scene, his whereabouts unknown.

Ten:
Orrin

The day before the flight to Fort Lauderdale, where his son's family would board the *Santiago Vagabundo*, Orrin Sheridan sat quietly next to the bedside of his wife Marjorie and gently stroked her unresponsive hand. On the wall across from the foot of the bed, a game show flickered from a large television screen, the sound muted. Although he knew she could not understand what the images represented, the colors and movement seemed to sooth her and forestall the agitation that sometimes caused her to cry out in wordless confusion.

A massive stroke two years earlier had destroyed her cognitive abilities to the extent that she no longer recognized her husband or other family members. Language had deserted her. As the weeks passed, Orrin reluctantly accepted the fact that no significant recovery was likely, and that his beloved wife of fifty-four years no longer lived within the sad shell whose unblinking eyes followed the shifting shapes on the screen in uncomprehending silence. His only solace was her freedom from pain. She remained mostly relaxed and at peace, at least as long as her basic needs were met.

When available long-term care facilities failed to meet Orrin's demanding expectations, he outfitted a large ground floor room at the back of their house with a motorized adjustable bed, state-of-the-art monitoring equipment, and such furniture as was necessary to make bathing and caring for Marjorie's dietary and sanitary needs as easy and comfortable for her as possible. It soon became apparent that at his age, Orrin's good intentions were insufficient to cope with the demands of round-the-clock care of a bedridden patient. Although his ability to handle her medical needs was unquestioned, as were his patience and willingness to spend untold hours in her company, his domestic skills were not up to the task. Nor was his ability to go without sleep unlimited.

He hired household help five days a week to handle routine cleaning, laundry, and cooking, but Marjorie's personal care rested entirely on his shoulders, and he was afraid to be absent from the house for more than a few minutes at a time in case she needed him. Finally recognizing his declining stamina and resigned to the inevitable, he engaged the services of a highly recommended registered nurse named Evelyn Mae Hulse to relieve him of at least some of Marjorie's care.

Contractors arrived to install French doors overlooking the garden at the back of the house, and a concrete patio where he could sit with his wife when the weather was warm and pleasant. Even in February, when snow buried the carefully tended landscaping, he could place her in a wheelchair in front of the doors to watch the activity around three bird feeders flanking the patio, a busy substitute for television. He chose to believe that she enjoyed seeing the redpolls, chickadees and finches that filled the air with constant activity, promising continuity of life.

Like most long-married couples, Orrin and Marjorie had given little thought to the end of life until it became imminent, and by then it was too late for him to discuss it with her. He felt immensely grateful, however, that his personal health was such that he would probably survive her, and not leave her to the care of others. Ironically, it was he, Orrin, who was now alone, in all the ways that mattered. He had his family, of course, Russell and Jessica and his lovely and talented little granddaughter Caitlin, but with the loss of Marjorie's companionship, his life now felt empty and without purpose.

The next day he would leave his beloved wife to the care of Nurse Evelyn just long enough to drive the others to Stanfield International Airport, north of Halifax. He would hide his pain as he did every day, as he knew he must. His old enemy, time—intransigent and

37

unstoppable—demanded no less of him.

Marjorie's hand stirred in his, and his gaze wandered to her placid face. "Hello, my dear," he seemed to hear her say, "it's so good to have you sitting beside me." Silent tears leaked from the corners of his eyes.

Eleven:
Caitlin

Caitlin Sheridan loved her grandfather, deeply and without reservation. He supported her in all the ways that mattered. Not that her parents were indifferent to her needs; she knew how fortunate she was to enjoy their unconditional love, although she sometimes wondered if her father would be less attentive, had she been what she considered to be a "normal," less talented daughter. But Granddad Orrin *understood* her. She relied on his wisdom and advice whenever plagued by the trials of navigating the back roads of adolescent insecurities.

From an early age, Caitlin knew she was different. As she grew aware of the gulf between her and less gifted peers, she went to extraordinary lengths to hide that difference. She affected interest in the fads her friends pursued, whatever television or pop music personalities they favoured. She tried to separate the demands of her talent from her day-to-day activities, and to compartmentalize everything to do with the piano as if she led two lives. When seated at the keyboard she was transformed by sounds and emotions that filled her mind and heart with unimaginable beauty, as necessary to her wellbeing as food, drink, and sleep.

Even before reaching the proper age to enter public school, Caitlin ran afoul of social conventions that set her apart. She found it hard to hide her boredom when invited to participate in ordinary childhood games and didn't at first have sense enough to conceal her disdain. But soon she grasped how candid comments would alienate other children. She began to pay close attention to the ways in which her friends behaved toward each other and learned fast. She moderated her own behaviour, told herself that she *ought* to like what other kids liked, and acted accordingly. With unexpectedly mature perception, she discovered what many adults never learn—that to show sincere interest in other people was the quickest route to acceptance.

Although Caitlin tried hard, some things could not be hidden. When she was five and enrolled in school, a perceptive kindergarten teacher quickly discovered that she was already reading well above a fifth-grade level. The woman probed the child's abilities and discovered, for example, that she could tell time precisely on an analog clock, could recite the multiplication table up to twelve and knew how to use it, and understood how to count currency and make change. But Caitlin spent her time carefully filling in the drawings in coloring books (*never* outside the lines), cutting pretty patterns from construction paper, and generally joining in with whatever activity her classmates pursued. She even lay silent during nap time, although every fibre of her body longed to be up, to be active, to be *accomplishing* something. She was fuelled by an astonishingly rapid metabolism.

If she resented the time spent away from her keyboard, she didn't let it show, but hurried home as quickly as possible after school and disappeared into her own world, that of Dmitry Kabalevsky, Wolfgang Amadeus Mozart, and the mathematically satisfying splendour of Scarlatti sonatas and compositions from the notebooks of Anna Magdalena Bach. She could not remember a time when she did not make music. Although neither of her parents possessed any but very rudimentary keyboard skills, a seven-foot grand piano occupied a place of honour in one corner of their oversized living room. The family numbered among friends and acquaintances several talented players of various instruments, and the house was often filled with live music.

In her rapport with her parents, she was totally secure, although she recognized a distinct difference in the way each of them related to her. She could tell that her mother's love was absolute and unqualified, totally independent of her talent, while her father seemed much more concerned with how her skills were developing, how her academic ability differed from (was superior to) others her age, and especially with what opportunities came her way as a result of her growing reputation. Well before her present age of thirteen, Caitlin could tell that Jessica loved her for herself alone, while her father's affection was more pragmatic.

Caitlin walked at eight months. She was totally irresponsible, fearless—and clumsy. Tiny, slight, and featherweight, she could be tripped by a blade of grass, and in her headlong rush to capture life, she always sported a bruise or two, often in the center of her forehead after a spectacular header from which she would bounce back laughing. She was irrepressible.

Jessica would sit at the piano with the child on her lap, playing one-finger nursery tunes and singing softly. A line in an ABBA tune tells of a child who could sing before she could talk. That was Caitlin, who quickly learned to hum nonsense syllables along with her mother, precisely on pitch. Before long she could crawl up onto the bench unassisted, and not only reproduce the melodies she heard, but also create short and credible songs of her own.

Caitlin was happily exploring the keys one afternoon when Jessica's next door neighbour Alison Maxwell stopped by. In her role as pianist and organist in the United Church, Alison worked with a children's choir. She also volunteered as a teacher's assistant at Bournemouth Elementary, where she was usually co-opted to help in the music room.

Intrigued by Caitlin's attention to the keyboard, Alison found it difficult to concentrate on her conversation with Jessica, and finally abandoned the effort and moved to the piano herself. She scooped the child onto her lap and played a simple melody, the opening phrase of a juvenile Mozart sonata. When she stopped, Caitlin immediately reached for the keys and duplicated the melody, missing only one note, whereupon she played it again and corrected the mistake.

Caitlin was just nineteen months old.

Alison turned her head and gaped at Jessica. "How long has this been going on?" she asked her friend.

"Amazing, isn't it?" Jessica said. "We can't figure out how she does that."

Alison turned back to the keyboard and played the phrase again, but this time she added a simple half note accompaniment with her left hand. Caitlin grinned up at her. "More please," she begged. Alison played it again, and Caitlin watched her with intense concentration. "My turn," she announced, and duplicated the phrase exactly as Alison had played it, two-handed, her tiny fingers barely able to stretch from note to note but somehow managing to put it all together.

Over the next hour Caitlin displayed an unusually long attention span, and when she finally tired and slid from Alison's lap, she had repeated a full sixteen bars of a Baroque two-part invention in the key of G, never forgetting the black F-sharp key.

"We have to have a serious talk," Alison said to Jessica. "Obviously she's too young for lessons, but she needs to hear live music on a regular basis."

"How do we do that?" Jessica asked.

"I have some spare time."

Caitlin couldn't remember anything about those early years, nor the formal instruction that began once it was obvious that she understood exactly what she was doing. By age three she had begun to attract attention beyond the circle of the Sheridans' friends. Alison Maxwell arranged for her to play on a local television program, which led to invitations to perform at public functions. Two professors from Irvine University asked permission to visit, and Russell and Jessica welcomed them, albeit informally, just to observe what the *wunderkind* could do. The verdict: not since Jonathan James MacIsaac had they witnessed such an amazing demonstration of precocity.

Twelve:
Rolf

The day before the cruise I closed out a session at a backwater tavern just shy of midnight, intent on packing a few changes of clothes before taking my boat to a marina that promised tight security. Jenny would be a lonely cat, consigned to a boarding kennel for a week until my return. I could have left her aboard with enough food, water, and litter to last a week, but I was reluctant to risk it. There was always the danger that fate would intervene, preventing me from returning on time.

I was ambivalent about filling in with the Jay Neilson Trio for a confining four-day gig aboard ship. The money was good, however, and the chance to match my skills against two capable entertainers might be worth the effort. I emerged from the kitchen entrance into an alley, having picked up my pay for providing musical ambiance for the dinner crowd. It was the kind of job I like best. It didn't overtax my abilities and was a pleasant way to spend an evening in quiet anonymity. Best of all, the hotel paid under the table, always in cash. The management understood that a long-term commitment wasn't in the cards, and that I might return each successive evening—or not.

The empty back streets were damp and humid from an earlier shower, deserted and poorly lighted. Mackerel clouds concealed the stars and shrouded the moon. Off to the west, occasional stabs of lightning predicted an approaching storm, and I was anxious to get back aboard *Versteck* before it arrived.

I chose a direct route to the deserted cove where my boat tender lay beached, passing through twisted alleys between ramshackle hovels whose inhabitants lived hand to mouth. Often they preyed upon unwary tourists whose appetite for adventure exceeded their common sense, and as I came abreast of a dark passage, two figures stepped out and blocked my way. A tall, lanky Rastafarian in soiled deck pants and a ragged tank top sauntered into the watery moonlight, swinging a fat leather sap. I heard a soft click as a switchblade appeared in his other hand.

His companion, an overweight, bearded white man in heavy boots and a tattered lightweight trench coat, moved ninety degrees to the left—a classic pincer operation. He held a wicked looking ten-inch blade pointed upward in street fighter stance, its tip scribing small circles aimed at my gut. It was a dance I knew well.

Trouble seems to find me; I don't know why. Given my reclusive habits, I should have been left alone. Not that I look like a soft touch; at well above average height, I damn well don't appear helpless. But two guys with knives must have liked their odds.

"Hola, gringo," the black man said, smirking. "Es una buena noche, ¿no?"

"Not looking for trouble," I said calmly, stopping six feet away from them. "Just heading for my boat."

The two men edged forward cautiously, knife hands waving in menace. "Cash, drugs, watch, whatever you got," the fat man said. "Hand it over and you walk away."

I hate knives. In a brawl, the chances of being cut are too great. I would rather have faced almost any other weapon, even a gun. Remembering some sound advice from one of my karate instructors, I decided to end it fast, Marquis of Queensbury rules be damned.

But first I decided to give them a chance to back off. "You sure you want to get into this with me?"

"Two of us, one of you, what you think?" The black man grinned and strode toward me confidently, swinging the sap high. Instead of backing away I ducked under it and stepped into his space. The sap missed my head and bounced ineffectually off my shoulder, and I clasped my hands together in a double fist and slammed upward solidly under his chin, snapping his jaw shut. The man howled and stumbled back, spitting out the severed tip of his tongue and broken fragments of teeth into the street.

His large companion was fast for one so heavy. He lunged forward, knife outthrust, and tore a strip out of the front of my shirt, drawing blood. I spun one-eighty, pivoted on my right leg, and lashed out with my left foot, smashing his kneecap and dropping him backwards to sprawl in the gravel. My teacher's advice echoed in my mind: *Make sure a guy with a knife won't be getting up too soon.* I stomped his knee with my boot, shattering bones and tearing cartilage.

The Rastafarian came at me again, and I fired my right hand edgewise at his throat, hard but shy of breaking the hyoid bone. That would almost certainly have killed him, and I didn't want that on my conscience. He staggered and sat down heavily, clutching his neck and trying to suck in air. His companion lay on his side, grasping his smashed knee and moaning softly.

"Es posible que usted desee pensar considerar otro tipo de trabajo," I told them.

You might want to think about getting into some other line of work.

I turned my back on them and left them in the street to recover as best they could.

Five minutes later I was aboard the tender and rowing out of the cove toward *Versteck*, where she lay secure and hidden in the lee of a headland. I climbed aboard, hoisted the tender onto the stern davits, and retrieved the fore and aft anchors. Despite lightning that danced on the horizon, the air was dead calm as I started the diesel and turned the boat south toward Swordfish Marina, where the management was holding a berth for me.

I stripped off my shirt and found blood oozing from a flap of skin, torn loose by the fat man's knife attack. A narrow bandage would take care of that once I was on my way, but first it was time to get moving. I had a seagoing engagement to play, four fun-filled days of adventure aboard the newest cruise ship to ply the southern seas.

Oh, boy.

Thirteen:
Cruise Port

The motel shuttle threaded its way through a system of security checkpoints in the Fort Lauderdale Cruise Port, dwarfed by hulking vessels bearing the names of Carnival, Norwegian, Royal Caribbean, and Holland America. It finally drew near to a gleaming ship of modest dimensions, its pristine hardware, teak decks and white-painted hull brightly reflecting the Florida sunshine. As the Sheridans waited patiently beside the shuttle's trailer for their luggage to emerge (except for Caitlin, who was spinning around in excitement), uniformed Chilean America crew members stood by ready to take charge of their belongings and direct them.

Despite Caitlin's pleas, Chloe Sharma had not joined them on the shuttle. Her father's team of political advisors had provided a limousine to deliver them to the ship, along with their retinue and two-man security detail. As VIP guests representing a foreign government, the family would not participate in the normal boarding process but would be escorted through the procedure by specially appointed crew members. The girls had made plans to link up just as soon as they could once on board.

Inside the mustering hall, and always eager for new experiences, Caitlin filled out her health disclosure form and proudly presented it to an attendant at the foot of an escalator, along with her passport. As a frequent airline traveler, she was thoroughly at home navigating the intricacies of international transportation and led the way for her parents when they reached the second level. Independence could have been her middle name.

A long line-up waited to check in with a dozen employees behind an elevated counter, where computers, cameras and printers stood ready to record each passenger's coded identity onto stateroom key cards. These IDs were a ticket for leaving the ship and returning when in ports of call. They also allowed the crew to ensure that everyone was aboard before sailing. Caitlin and her parents headed for the end of the line but were stopped by a uniformed attendant who asked to see their boarding passes.

"Welcome to the *Santiago Vagabundo*, Miss Sheridan," the smiling woman said to Caitlin, her accent replete with musical vowels. "We are happy to welcome you and your family to our maiden voyage. This way please."

Her name tag read "Estela Perez" and "C. A. Cruise Lines." She motioned for a colleague to replace her on the line and led the Sheridans to an unoccupied space at the far end of the counter. She handed the boarding passes to a trim uniformed employee behind a computer. "This is the Sheridan family," Estela said to him, "for the Oceanus Suite."

In just a few minutes they were holding personalized key cards bearing their suite number and dining room assignments. Russell also received a folder containing a brief description of the amenities that came with the most luxurious accommodations aboard, including access to private lounge areas and concierge service.

"Boarding begins shortly," Estela Perez told them. "Until then you are welcome to wait in the Executive Lounge. A photographer will be there to take a group picture, a special souvenir of your presence on our first voyage."

In the lounge they discovered a table with drinks and a lunch buffet, and comfortable furniture at the windows overlooking the pier. Below, new arrivals continued to pass their luggage into the care of dock hands.

"Wow!" Jessica exclaimed as Caitlin sprawled in one of the huge chairs. "This is living."

"Pretty special Valentine present from a pretty special girl," Russell said.

"Don't I know it. But it's a shame that Caitlin has to work so hard to pay for it."

"Yeah, right," Caitlin said, "blood, sweat and tears all over the keyboard, and it's all your fault. No sweat, Mom, I knew what I was getting into." She pointed down at the traffic lined up beside the ship. "Look, there's another bunch coming." A driver had just emerged from the cab of a shuttle and was heading toward the back to unload luggage. The passenger side door slid open, and half a dozen young teenagers in tees and shorts spilled out onto the pier.

"Uh, oh," Russell said in mock alarm. "There goes the neighbourhood."

Ignoring her sarcastic father and with her attention focused on the young people, Caitlin had no reason to take notice of several other new arrivals. A taxi discharged Alistair Barclay, Grant Keillor, and Keillor's wife Charlotte, a striking brunette at least ten years his junior, and Archibald MacInnes. MacInnes was dressed in the typical resort style fashion of a Canadian snowbird, that unique breed who regularly flew south to escape the rigors of a northern winter. His dark knee socks and a golf shirt hanging over baggy shorts would attract little if any undue attention.

Barclay looked trendy in trim deck pants and a tee shirt advertising a well-known Canadian beer. Wearing dark, heavy framed glasses, Keillor was sporting newly acquired facial hair, and MacInnes looked somewhat older than expected with dyed streaks of grey topside. Only Charlotte was fashionably dressed for the surroundings, her attractive appearance designed to draw attention away from her husband and his companions. They all believed they would be unmemorable when their mission was completed.

The men hefted their suitcases, ignoring an eager dock worker who was hoping for a tip in return for depositing the luggage in a designated area close by. MacInnes headed inside immediately, but the others held back. From that point on, they would seldom be seen in each other's presence. After they accomplished their objective, it was unlikely that anyone on board would remember them as companions.

Caitlin lost interest in the comings and goings below and joined her parents in perusing some literature that described the ship's amenities. Had she not been diverted, she might have noticed a lean, suntanned man of less than thirty years in khakis and a polo shirt who disembarked from a local bus. His only luggage was a soft-sided carryon slung over one shoulder. Instead of entering the main hall, Rolf Niemand found a door labelled *Staff and Crew*, and presented his ID to the steward guarding the entrance.

Fourteen:
Rolf

I was a bit surprised and moderately pleased to discover that Chilean America Cruise Lines took good care of hired entertainers. Although lacking an ocean view, my Deck One stateroom was relatively spacious and nicely if plainly appointed, with a commodious bed that would not cramp my oversized frame and a private bath with an adequate shower stall. A comfortable-looking faux leather chair squatted beside a coffee table sufficiently large to support a couple of room service trays. A TV, which I would probably never turn on, topped a built-in desk, with a well-stocked mini fridge to one side. A double closet held a complementary robe bearing the cruise line's logo, a pair of one-size-fits-all disposable slippers that almost certainly wouldn't contain my size thirteen feet, and a bright orange life vest.

On the desk I found a stack of information and a copy of the contract for my services, executed on my behalf by the leader of the Jay Neilson Trio. We were to appear every evening in the Dios Del Mar lounge, amidships on Deck Two and just a short elevator ride from my stateroom. I dared to believe that the next four days would be manageable, my privacy secure.

I checked the time—12:50—and left to find Neilson and his bass player. I wanted to get a feel for their style and assess how capable they were. I avoided the elevators and took the stairs up a level, to find Neilson already set up and testing the acoustics in the lounge. I acknowledged his brief nod as he hammered out a riff on his classic Les Paul ax and listened for reverb.

A shiny new baby grand sat at centre stage and a Fender bass lay atop the bench, a stand-up bass on its side on the floor behind it. That was a good sign. I had been expecting an average electronic keyboard, and the presence of an acoustic Kawai suggested that the cruise line was willing to provide quality instruments for entertainment.

An elderly, lanky black man stood to one side leafing through a pile of charts. I pegged him at early seventies, probably old school, which suited me fine. I skirted the piano and extended my hand.

"Rolf Niemand," I introduced myself. We shook—firm hand, quick release.

"Hiram Gaudet," he told me. "Hi for short."

"Nice to know you, Hi. What's your story?"

"I came up through Ontario society bands, regional, nobody famous, but good training. We played dances, coming out parties, bar mitzvahs, whatever paid the freight in those lean times. I depended on after hours in the clubs to feed my artistic soul. Then I teamed up with Jay, and we call our own tune now. You?"

"Just an overgrown kid, bumming around the islands and picking up enough here and there to pay the bills. I'll try to keep up with you."

I could tell by the look he gave me that Hi wasn't fooled, but Neilson walked over right then, so I didn't have to elaborate.

"Glad you could join us," Neilson said, offering a fist bump.

"You use arrangements?" I asked him, nodding toward the music Gaudet was holding in his left hand.

"Just lead sheets for new tunes or unfamiliar requests. I've been with Hi for twenty years, so we don't have to talk much."

"We lean toward the standards," Hi said. "On a cruise ship, it's all just background. Most of the passengers have a lot more on their minds than the music, if you know what I mean. You good with that?"

"Sure. Can I get a feel for your style?"

"Okay," Neilson said. "Want to choose something?"

"Anything. I'll catch up."

He adjusted the volume on his amp, and Gaudet hoisted the acoustic bass off the floor and laid down a short intro outlining the chords from *Yesterday*. I moved the Fender bass onto the floor and sat down as Jay picked up the tune on his low strings, soft and sweet, lingering back-beat on John Lennon's lovely rising scale. I couldn't help smiling; they were the real deal. I gave them some light support, just the basic harmony, and as Neilson wound up the first chorus, he nodded toward me and backed off.

I played the motive ("Yesterdayyyy") over a simple arpeggio figure, and put my own spin on the scale, thirds up, seconds down, thinking how ironic some of the lyrics were in my present situation ("Now I need a place to hide away"). I didn't stray too far from the tune, weaving my decorations in and out around the melody to see how well my band mates would follow. I needn't have worried—they had ears, and on the third chorus Jay cut loose a free-wheeling improvisation, his guitar licks sharp and incisive. We backed off to let Gaudet take the bridge, and he surprised me by grabbing his bow for a lyrical turn in the cello register. Then we rode home to a soft, *sotto voce* coda, unresolved on a tonic major ninth. Leave them wanting more...

"Press that one," Gaudet said to no one in particular.

I smiled at him in thanks. "Guess we speak the same language."

"'Just an overgrown kid, bumming around.' Uh-huh. Gonna be a sweet four days, my man. Welcome."

53

Fifteen:
The Keillors

Grant and Charlotte Keillor parted company with Al Barclay on the lower deck and headed for the central staircase. They would avoid being seen in each other's company as much as possible for the duration of the cruise. Each had specific functions to perform, and they would meet to compare notes only when certain not to be observed.

Charlotte was charged with becoming familiar with the ship as a whole and the habits of their target in particular. She needed to know where and when Vachan Sharma might be at any given time of the day and hoped his entourage might post a printed agenda for the benefit of the media. The Halifax *Herald* had run a feature story outlining the Sharma family's attendance on the cruise, along with a photo of them at the airport. Charlotte memorized the faces of the wife and daughter, as well as the New Democratic Party security personnel who were visible in the background.

Hoping to remain anonymous, the Keillors had not boarded the ship until well after two o'clock. They avoided the photographer who was stationed at the head of the gangway. Souvenir shots of embarking passengers would be printed in the ship's digital lab and placed on display in the gallery, and they wanted no part of that kind of exposure.

Their luggage had not yet been delivered to their stateroom, and the couple took an elevator to the open-air sports venue on Deck Eleven. From there they separated, Grant working his way downward level by level to take note of the major public areas—the specialty restaurants, conference rooms, shops, lounges, a casino, and a large theatre where lavish entertainment was scheduled nightly. He circled each venue on the printed deck plan that came with his stateroom key card.

Charlotte was more interested in locations that would attract

Sharma's wife and daughter, the shops and the teen lounge on the topmost deck. They could be expected to be enjoying the ship's amenities when Vachan Sharma was occupied with publicity shots and meetings with cruise officials and Party members, which meant that his two-man security detail would be divided. It was essential to their plan that the whereabouts of all three family members always be known.

By the time they returned to their stateroom, their suitcases had arrived and there were several pieces of literature on the desk: a welcome from the Captain, a card inscribed with the names of the room stewards, a list of dining options, and a four-page folder identified as "Today on the *Santiago Vagabundo*."

3:00 p.m. Lifeboat Drill, Muster Stations. All passengers must attend.

4:00 p.m. Sail Away Party in the Lido, Deck Nine.

4:30 p.m. Meet the Captain, Main Stage, Decks Two and Three.
Caitlin Sheridan, piano, Art Gallery Anteroom, Deck Three.
Chess Challenge Encounter, all ages, Pelican Library on the Observation Deck.

5:15 p.m. Dinner, First Sitting, Abalone Dining Room, Decks Two and Three.

7:00 p.m. Embarkation photos on display in the Digital Gallery, Deck Two.
Reception, the Atrium, Deck Two, honouring Canadian statesman Vachan Sharma.
Beethoven and More, Caitlin Sheridan, piano, the Mozarteum, Deck Three.

8:00 p.m. The *Santiago Vagabundo* Singers and Dancers, Act I, Main Stage.

8:15 p.m. Dinner, Second sitting, Abalone Dining Room, Decks Two and Three.

9:00 p.m. to 1:00 a.m. The Jay Neilson Trio, Dios Del Mar Lounge, Deck Two.

10:00 p.m. The *Santiago Vagabundo* Singers and Dancers, Act II, Main Stage.

Grant paid particular attention to the reception for Vachan Sharma listed among the events for seven o'clock. He underlined it and located the Atrium on the deck plan just as an announcement concerning the lifeboat drill came over the public address system. The Cruise Director identified herself and explained the system of warning bells that would signify an emergency on board. She outlined the procedures to be followed in case an evacuation became necessary. Charlotte and Grant listened carefully, and five minutes later they heard the signal to move to their assigned Muster Station. They left the stateroom and headed for Deck Three, confident of achieving their goals over the next four days.

Sixteen:
Caitlin

Estela Perez returned to the Executive Lounge shortly before the boarding call and led the Sheridans to their suite on Deck Six. Two of their suitcases were already lined up on the foot of a king size bed in the main room. Vases of flowers stood on flanking end tables, a magnum of champagne was chilling in an ice bucket on the coffee table, and the desk displayed various sorts of welcoming literature. Included were personal letters from the Captain, the Concierge, the Senior Chef, and the Cruise Director. A huge flat screen TV was tuned to the ship's information channel, with the sound muted. A comfortable-looking sofa and two side chairs flanked sliding glass doors that led to a two hundred square foot veranda.

"Looks like a Very Important Person must be staying here," Jessica observed. Caitlin shrugged and set about exploring the spacious suite at top speed. She quickly discovered her own suitcase on a queen size bed in an adjoining alcove. She threw open every closet and discovered a pile of life jackets on a top shelf. She hauled out one labelled "Small" and tried it on, grimacing at her image in a mirror before tossing it back where it belonged. She exclaimed over the whirlpool tub in the bathroom, the wide tiled shower, dual basins, and a huge stack of the thickest towels she had ever felt. Back in the main part of the lounge, she sprawled on the floor and opened the mini bar.

"Off limits!" Russell said sharply, but with a grin.

Caitlin thumbed her nose at him—"There're Cokes in here too!"— then bounced up onto the bed. She found the TV remote control and scrolled through the on-screen menu for a few minutes, exclaiming over the availability of first-run movies she would probably not find time to watch, then checked out the material on the desk. She quickly discovered her name listed twice in the "Today on the *Santiago Vagabundo*" brochure.

"They're putting me to work already," she exclaimed happily. "I'm in the Art Gallery at four-thirty and something called the Mozarteum at seven; that's for chamber music, I guess. I hope someone tells me where to go."

"There's a deck plan in among this stuff somewhere," her father said. "We'll find our way."

"It's a pretty easy schedule," Caitlin said. "Twice a day, three quarters of an hour each, and I get to choose what to play. Light stuff in the gallery, I guess. The email from Mr. Sanchez asked if I knew anything by Beethoven to play the first evening. Duh!"

"How about supper?" Jessica asked.

"I'm off from quarter after five until seven. Where can we go?"

Jessica found the dining information on the desk. "We have a few choices," she said. "This says the specialty restaurants don't open until tomorrow, and they require reservations, but there's a buffet in the Lido and the Abalone Dining Room opens at five-fifteen. Or if you want to be decadent, we can order room service."

"Let's do that," Russell said to Jessica. "We don't want Caitlin to have to rush between her two performances."

"Okay. But if we want something quick, there's also pizza next to the teen lounge, and a burger grill on the pool deck."

"Now you're talking!" Caitlin said. "Can I call Chloe and see if she wants to go with us?" The two girls had not yet managed to find each other on board.

"I'm sure her parents will want her with them the first day," Jessica said.

"We could ask."

"We'll see, but not until after you play your recital. You'll have plenty of time to get together with her over the next few days."

They left the suite and wandered about the ship for close to an hour.

Caitlin was determined to explore every corner and the family took part in the lifeboat drill at three o'clock. The crew member manning their mustering station demonstrated the proper way to put on an adult-sized life jacket, then displayed a smaller version meant for older children or young teens. He drew Caitlin out of the crowd, slipped the jacket over her head, and told her to cinch it up. Painfully shy whenever the centre of attention for anything other than her music (and sometimes even then), she fumbled with the straps and finally managed to get them connected. She wished she could crawl into a hole somewhere.

At five after four the crew cast off the lines, and the bow and stern thrusters eased the ship away from the pier and out into the channel. The three Sheridans joined a crowd on deck to watch a small fleet of pleasure boats escort them toward the open sea. A pair of bottle-nosed dolphins put on an athletic display, leaping playfully just off the port bow, and Russell suggested that they were probably paid by the local Chamber of Commerce. Then they returned to the suite for Caitlin to change clothes and prepare for her first performance.

At four-thirty she slid onto the bench in front of a gold and white Yamaha baby grand in the Art Gallery. The room was deserted except for her parents, who found seats toward the back. She was summery and casual in tailored white Capri pants and a floral-patterned sleeveless top. She surveyed the empty chairs. "Guess I can't compete with dolphins," she said.

She flipped up the keyboard cover, tore off half a dozen breakneck scales to warm up, and launched into a flowing arrangement of Henry Mancini's *Moon River*. Her light and simple accompaniment supported but didn't distract from the lovely melody. After two choruses she improvised a four bar segue into a bluesy D minor vamp, and overlaid it with the short, choppy boogie-woogie phrases that trombonist Tommy Dorsey borrowed from Pine Top Smith eight decades earlier.

There was some traffic up and down the adjoining corridor, and a few people glanced into the anteroom, then reacted with surprise at seeing a child seated at the keyboard. Several stepped inside and took seats— an elderly couple already dressed for dinner and a man and woman with two children, the oldest one sporting a cap with a Canadian flag on the brim. When Caitlin noticed them, she dropped the boogie beat and began pounding out Scott Joplin's *Maple Leaf Rag*. By the time she finished with a quote from *O Canada*, the ten rows of chairs were more than half full, and the room erupted with applause.

Caitlin had a problem with acknowledging praise. She felt embarrassed by the enthusiastic response she invariably received for something that came so naturally, so easily to her. She blushed a modest pink and nodded shyly, then turned back to the keys and played the lovely octave leap that began the theme from *Gone with the Wind*.

When her forty-five minutes were up every seat was filled, and more appreciative listeners were standing at the back. The clapping went on and on, and Caitlin decided that a short encore might let her escape gracefully. She romped through the theme from "Jeopardy" in the dense style of Vivaldi, overlaid it with a jazzy up-tempo take on Debussy's well-known *Clair de Lune*, then took it home on a bouncy two-step that old Claude never imagined. She flipped the cover down over the keys, shrugged as if to say "Twern't nothin', folks," and skipped around to where Russell and Jessica were waiting for her.

And Chloe. The two girls clasped hands joyfully and immediately began making plans to compare notes about the ship over some fast food with their parents, minus Vachan Sharma, who was preparing for the reception the Captain had arranged in his honour.

Seventeen:
Beethoven

By the time they finished dinner (burgers from the grill on the pool deck), word had spread about an exceptional child who had amazed an informal gathering in the Art Gallery before dinner. The velvet-curtained Mozarteum was already overcrowded when Caitlin arrived. At Jessica's urging she wore something less casual, a knee-length lemon yellow sundress with a flared skirt, her tiny waist cinched by a wide white patent leather belt. A delicate gold chain at her throat and dressy sandals completed a sophisticated but youthful style.

With a timid nod she acknowledged a warm reception from the crowd, sat down at the eight-foot grand, and began to play a simple and affecting minuet from the early Classical period. Without pausing for a reaction from the audience, she shifted to early Beethoven, three short movements of an uncomplicated early sonatina—nothing flashy, nothing difficult. Many aspiring pianists her age and younger could have handled those pieces easily.

The applause when she finished was polite but restrained. It was accompanied by a bit of uneasy shuffling among the audience members, who perhaps were wondering if this youngster's advance billing had been exaggerated. Caitlin smiled, dipped her head once in appreciation, and picked up a cordless microphone that lay beside her on the piano bench. She swivelled to face the crowd as a technician at the back of the room switched on an amplifier and adjusted the volume level.

"That first piece was by a very young Wolfgang Amadeus Mozart," she said, "and the second was by Beethoven. Now here's something else from old Ludwig—he was a bit more adventurous when he composed this one."

She turned back to the keyboard, inhaled deeply and blew it out, stretched her fingers once, and plunged into the furious third movement of the *Appassionata Sonata*, its thundering chords filling the room and eliciting gasps of surprise from the listeners. She was a whirlwind, wrenching the magnificent Romantic era harmonies from the hammers and strings with what looked like wild abandon, but was in fact precise and flawless technique. Not a single note fell out of place.

When at last her flying hands raced through the coda to the final chord, the audience sat in stunned silence for several seconds, then erupted wildly. In the front row several jumped to their feet, and the whole room quickly followed suit. Caitlin smiled uncertainly, her mind still elsewhere, entranced by communion with a long-dead master whose scribbled notes never lost the power to enthral her. She rose nervously, bowed slightly from the waist, and quickly sat down again, but the clapping continued and she had to stand once more.

The remainder of the recital might have been an anticlimax, had Caitlin not known how to pace her material to keep an audience interested. Her fingers wandered delicately into the gentle *Moonlight Sonata*, its captivating melody familiar even to the musically uneducated. Barely above a whisper, the deceptively simple motive and its gentle triplet accompaniment spun a web of unsurpassed beauty, uncommon serenity.

Next came Mozart's tender and familiar theme from his twenty-fifth piano concerto that had decorated the soundtrack of the film *Elvira Madigan*. Caitlin finished with one of her favourites from her video audition for the cruise, the haunting *Eighteenth Variation* from Rachmaninoff's *Rhapsody on a Theme of Paganini*. As the last sweet notes died away, her hands dropped to her lap. She closed her eyes and bent her head in personal homage to the genius of the composers.

The audience begged for more. "I'm sorry, I have to go now," she apologized, "but I'll be back tomorrow night. Okay?" The applause nearly drowned out her last word.

Eighteen:
Russell

Talent, skill and ambition were the ruling determinates of Dr. Russell Sheridan's existence. His skill with a knife was surpassed only by an innate instinct for *where* to cut in order to achieve healing results. He possessed an almost uncanny ability to visualize what was wrong within his patients' bodies, to operate with maximum economy and minimal danger to the surrounding tissues, and to know when to *stop* cutting. No one on the staff at Atlantic Regional Medical Centre had a better record for successful surgical outcomes or faster recovery times. His work left minimal disfiguring scars and provided the best prognoses for long term survival. His competence was legendary among the staff, and although it was sometimes difficult for him to rein in his ego, he knew he owed much of his ability to genetics. His sire Orrin was a similarly gifted and highly sought-after artist with a scalpel.

Russell was determined that his own offspring would benefit from the extraordinary attributes of his DNA, and his choice of a mate was driven at least in part by a search for a similarly endowed partner. Not that he didn't love Jessica, wholeheartedly and without reservation, but had she not been his intellectual equal and especially gifted in her chosen field of psychology, he would not have proposed marriage. In his mind, procreation was not to be undertaken haphazardly. He considered it his obligation to pass on his genes for the good of mankind—not just coincidently bolstering his standing in the community.

Jessica's desire for parenthood was more fundamental. She had benefitted from a stable childhood with two relatively strict but loving parents, who nurtured her soul and spirit at least equally with the way in which they ensured the enrichment of her intellect. She hoped she could pass on the same sort of support to children of their own.

When her first pregnancy ended in miscarriage, it was a blow from which Russell was slow to recover, but Jessica took it in stride. They consoled themselves with the knowledge that their childbearing years were far from over and tried again, and for a second time, a spontaneous abortion occurred before the fourth month. Examination of both foetuses indicated the probability of critical birth defects that would have severely limited the babies' physical and mental development, had they survived to term. Fearing that the problem might be genetic, Russell was haunted by a profound feeling of failure and despair. To their credit, however, neither he nor Jessica blamed the other, but accepted their heartbreak together. They determined not to risk a third pregnancy.

Within a few months of the second miscarriage, Jessica tentatively broached the subject of adoption, to which Russell was strongly opposed. He found it impossible to convey to his wife the reasons why he felt that way, reluctant to reveal flaws in his character that he hated to acknowledge even to himself. What if a baby randomly selected for them by an external agency turned out to be *ordinary*? How would such a son or daughter enhance his own standing among his peers, and even worse, how could he relate to a child who was just *average*?

Jessica mentioned the possibility of adoption again several times over the next two months, until finally Russell agreed to look into it. He made inquiries among some of his colleagues and set a few wheels in motion, but aside from some vague promises, he gave Jessica no details.

A year later, Kismet intervened when she found herself two months pregnant with no memory of how or when conception could have occurred. For two medical professionals to fail in something as basic as birth control seemed unthinkable, but biology wouldn't be denied.

They both dreaded the slow passage of days, fearing yet another accident that might dash their hopes once more. Weeks passed, and with the approach of the third trimester they began tentatively to talk about the possibility of success. A second and a third ultrasound predicted nothing abnormal in the pregnancy, and they delighted in watching the electronic blips that outlined a flawless baby girl, fingers and toes in all the right places.

They dared to shop for a cradle for the first few months of infanthood, and a more spacious crib for the child as she grew. They selected a layette, a baby bathtub, an upholstered rocking chair for feeding time, and all the other necessities to outfit a sunny nursery adjoining the master suite. At the end of the seventh month, Russell spent a feverish weekend giving the walls two coats of pale yellow paint and applying luminous silver stars to the ceiling. Baby clothes filled the drawers of a white enamelled chest, along with toys stacked in the corners of the room, most far too advanced for an infant. They even risked choosing a name: she would be Aileen Caitlin, the first in honour of Russell's paternal grandmother and the second a beloved aunt of Jessica's.

Our daughter Ailene, Russell thought but never dared to say out loud, *will make the world sit up and take notice.*

And then came the unimaginable, unbearable terror of a frantic dash to the hospital, and the heroic efforts of a team of specialists to rescue, to stabilize, to *save* what Russell and Jessica had so devoutly believed would be the culmination of their hopes and dreams.

Nineteen:
Rolf

We wound up our first session at one-thirty, half an hour longer than the contract specified. We were pleased to see that most of those in the lounge paid at least partial attention to what we were doing. Jay and Hi packed up their instruments, and Hi, claiming fatigue, took his leave. As Jay and I sat at the bar with nightcaps, he said, "I hate to tell you, but you have competition aboard."

"How so?" I asked.

"There's a forty-year-old midget playing piano in the Art Gallery, pretending she's a kid. She's rather good."

"A midget?"

"Must be. She looks about twelve but plays like Elton John and Liberace combined. She has a serious side too. I caught her second act in the chamber music venue before we went on tonight. I don't know piano literature, the only piece I recognized was the *Moonlight Sonata*, but all of it was a rare treat."

"Another prodigy, I suppose. They're getting to be a dime a dozen. Most of them burn out before they hit twenty." *They end up like me*, I thought, *playing for peasants in the vast wasteland of failed ambition.*

"Even so," Jay said, "you ought to go hear her. She's listed on the ship's program every day at 4:30 and 7:00. Before the *Moonlight*, she played this gigantic sonata that damn near destroyed the keyboard. I've never heard anything like it."

"More Beethoven?"

"That's what she said. I don't remember what she called it, just that it was the *presto* movement of something. It started out with a massive, sustained chord, then a series of rapid fire repetitions, and after that her little hands were an absolute blur on the keys. It was intense."

"The *Appassionata*, maybe. Although I've never heard of a child who could play that one." *Except one*, I thought.

"What's the *Appassionata*?" Jay asked.

"I'll show you." I put down my drink and moved to the piano. I hadn't played Beethoven's masterpiece in years, but it still lay fresh in my mind. I hammered out the opening statement.

"That's it!" Jay said. "My God, Rolf, you're just full of surprises."

"I had a good teacher. But are you sure that's what she played? For one thing, it's exhausting."

"It sure sounded like what you just did."

"And she's only twelve?"

"That's just a guess. She wasn't even breathing hard at the end. I'm telling you, you have to see it to believe it."

"What's her name?"

"Caitlin something."

"I'll check her out tomorrow."

Twenty:
New Friends

The *Santiago Vagabundo* anchored off Caracola Cay shortly before eight the next morning, the harbour being too shallow to allow a liner to dock at the pier. Along with Chloe and her mother Elizabeth, Caitlin and Jessica gazed out toward the low-lying shoreline while lingering over breakfast on the Lido deck. Russell had already left in order to get a better view from the observation deck. Chloe's father was off somewhere being a politician.

Caitlin had become a celebrity overnight and was the subject of interest from some of the other passengers, which made her uncomfortable. A family of four across the aisle stared at her openly. One woman was gesturing in her direction, but quickly dropped her hand when Jessica caught her eye. At a table close to the exit, a man wearing heavy horn-rimmed glasses was looking casually in their direction. A thick growth of stubble covered his chin and jowls.

A slender, brown-skinned man in a bright flowered shirt approached their table, stopping directly behind Caitlin's chair. His round-faced features evoked Pacific Ocean heritage. "I'm sorry to disturb you," he said to Jessica, "but may I ask you something?"

"Of course," she replied.

He waved a hand toward the aisle where a child of about eight clung nervously to the hand of a woman sporting a necklace fashioned from tiny shells. The girl wore a halo of delicate blossoms woven into her jet-black hair.

"My wife and child heard your daughter perform last evening," the man said to Jessica, "and... Well..."

Caitlin swung around in her chair to face the youngster. "Hi! What's your name?"

The girl smiled sheepishly, and her mother encouraged her to move closer to the table. "Manamea," she said, barely above a whisper.

"Wow, pretty name. Is that Hawaiian?"

"We're from Samoa," the girl said.

"We moved to Florida last year," her mother added.

Caitlin leaned forward conspiratorially. "And I bet you play piano, right?" The child nodded. "Hard work, isn't it?" The girl grinned. "It's worth it, though. Once you get past all the exercises, it gets to be more fun."

"I like it," Manamea said, then dropped her eyes shyly. "I can play the first one that you did last night. The Mozart."

"Hey, that's great. Tell you what, why not come down to the Art Gallery this afternoon around four, and we'll play it together. If you want, I can teach you some other stuff too."

The child's mouth dropped open, and her father said, "We couldn't possibly take up your time like that."

"I'm not doing anything else then," Caitlin said to him, "just getting ready to play for the passengers." Then to Manamea: "Hey, I know. This is my friend Chloe." Chloe smiled at the youngster. "She's coming to hear me play too, and you can sit next to her in the front row and be my special guest."

Caitlin glanced at her friend as if to ask *Okay?* Chloe grinned at Manamea. "You bet. We'll have fun."

"And dress up a little," Caitlin added. "Lots of people will see you there."

Manamea's mother promised they would attend, and as the family walked out of the dining area, the child was bouncing on her toes, excitedly stretching up to whisper in her mother's ear.

"She's shy," Caitlin said to her mother.

"Like someone else I used to know," Jessica said. "You were good with her."

"I remember what it was like. I still feel like that sometimes. Lots of times, in fact."

Chloe looked over Caitlin's shoulder. "You're about to have more company," she said. "I know these two, met them last night up in the teen club. They're okay."

Caitlin turned around again and saw two girls about her age edging their way toward the table, looking nervous but brave enough to break the ice.

"Hey, Chloe," a chunky red-haired girl of about fourteen said.

"Hey."

The newcomer turned to Caitlin. "Piano girl, right?"

"Guilty," Caitlin said.

"My Mom and my sister heard you play last night. They said it was cool. You going ashore this morning?"

"I guess so."

"Anyway, I'm Hannah and this is my sister Emily." She indicated a younger version of herself, who looked to be eleven or twelve.

"Hey," Emily said, then to Caitlin, "You play really well."

"There's supposed to be a pink sand beach here, all soft like talcum powder," Hannah said. "Our room steward told us they imported it from Australia or someplace. I think he was kidding, you can't ship a whole beach halfway around the world, can you? Anyway, can you two swim?"

"Sure," Caitlin said, but Chloe just dropped her eyes toward her plate.

"The steward said this is a private island. The cruise line owns it or leases it or something. He says they've got a barbeque set up, and you can, like, rent bikes and snorkel masks and paddle boards. They've even got a bunch of those cool jet skis. Want to go with us?"

"I guess so." Caitlin glanced at Chloe, who was still looking down. Then she turned to her mother, who nodded slightly and smiled.

"Cool," Hannah said. "We're gonna catch an early tender. Give me a call when you're ready, and we'll meet you at the gangway. Me and

Emily are on Deck Seven, seven-one-oh-four. You know how the phone system works?"

"I'll figure it out," Caitlin said.

"Cool. Remember, seven-one-oh-four."

"Got it."

"Well, see ya." Hannah spun around and headed for the elevators, her sister falling in behind, shepherd and sheep.

"Cool!" Caitlin said with a giggle.

"Cool!" Chloe echoed, then both girls in unison, "*Cool!*" They burst out laughing.

Caitlin turned to her mother. "What just happened?"

"I'd say you've been accepted," Jessica said.

"She sure talks fast. The other one, Emily? She didn't say much, couldn't get a word in edgewise I guess." Then she turned serious. "They don't even know me. They wouldn't want me to go with them except for… You know."

"You don't have to go if you don't want to. But I think it was nice of them to include you. You know how some people are too intimidated to talk to you after they know what you can do. It must have taken some courage for them to come over."

"I really hate that. I'm nothing special. So I can play the piano, so what? Big deal! Other kids do neat stuff, like dance or play baseball or whatever. People tiptoe around me like they're stepping on eggshells. Makes me really uncomfortable."

Jessica reached across the table and squeezed her hand gently. "Go be a kid. Make friends. They'll soon forget to be impressed by you. Just have fun."

"I guess so." Caitlin looked at Chloe. "What do you think?"

"You can go if you want to," her friend said. "I think I'll stay on board here."

"How come?"

"I can't swim."

"Hey, that's not a big deal. You don't have to go in the deep water. I bet there's a lot of other stuff to do on the island."

Chloe looked toward her mother. "May I go?"

"Of course. Just check with Jacob."

"Do I have to?"

"Sorry, dear, but you know your father's rules about security."

Chloe sighed, then giggled. "Jake'll look pretty funny on the beach in his suit and tie."

Elizabeth stood up. "We'd better go find your father and let him know what you'll be doing. He has a full day, lunch with the Captain and a couple of meet-and-greet things with the senior crew, so I'm sure it will be okay with him if you go off with your new friends."

"I'll call you," Caitlin said to Chloe.

"Cool! Hey, maybe I'll make that my new word this trip."

"Spare me. Later, 'gator."

"Soon, balloon."

After Chloe and her mother left the Lido, Caitlin sat toying with her napkin. "She's really nice," she said to Jessica. Then, "Getting to know new people makes me nervous."

"You've met famous conductors and all kinds of singers and instrumentalists—even TV talk show hosts and reporters. They don't scare you."

"That's different. They're... They're in the business. They know what it's like."

"You're pretty good at hiding your prodigy side when it's necessary," her mother said.

"Whatever that is," Caitlin murmured. Then: "Thanks, Mom. You're the best."

"Yeah," Jessica said, "I am, ain't I? And if you're going to take the first tender ashore, we better get going."

As they headed for the elevators Jessica looked back over her shoulder, just in time to see Grant Keillor in his horn-rimmed glasses and beard rise from his chair and head for the opposite end of the Lido.

Twenty-one:
MacInnes and Keillor

S harma wasn't at breakfast with his wife and kid," Arch MacInnes said.

"Did anyone recognize you?" Grant Keillor asked.

"Not likely. I can't even recognize myself. Looking in the mirror this morning was like looking at my future, the grey hair and all. Where's Al?"

"I told him to keep track of Sharma's kid. So far she's almost never where her father is. It needs to be that way when we make our move."

Keillor leaned against the aft rail on the sports deck overlooking the sundeck below, comfortable in board shorts, sandals, and a tee shirt. MacInnes stood a couple of yards to his left, hoping to be unmemorable in a monochromatic polo shirt and deck pants in the unlikely event that someone aboard had dealt with him in the past. Neither man looked toward the other, keeping their voices low. In an age of electronic surveillance, they had agreed to talk in a sort of code, avoiding details of their plans.

"Did you hear from Carman?" Keillor asked.

"He gave me a buzz on the satellite phone last night," MacInnes said. "He found a perfect spot to anchor at the far end of the island, a deep-water strait behind some sand dunes where nobody's likely to see the boat. He'll be here when we need him. How about Charlotte?"

"She's going to spend the day cozying up to the staff."

"How's she going to work it?"

"She'll find a mark, that's what she's good at."

"What's her cover story?"

"I didn't ask. You can trust her to come up with something that sounds innocent."

"And how's the bribe going to work?"

"Half up front, the other half when the job's done."

MacInnes nodded. "Are you straight with what you have to do today?"

Keillor counted off on his fingers sarcastically, annoyed by his partner's lack of faith in him. "Stick with Sharma, stay out of sight, get hold of the man's schedule if I can. Try to find out if he's ever out of sight of the security detail. So far that's never happened."

"Make sure of the 'stay out of sight' part. We don't want the crew paying any attention to either of us. When the shit hits the fan, we lay low. You know how the electronic key card system works, right?"

"It tells the crew which passengers get off and when, and records when they get back aboard. The ship won't leave until everyone's accounted for."

"So as long as Sharma is separated from his family when we make our move, there won't be any chance of interference. You and I hang out in one of the lounges and sit around with a couple of drinks. Separately, of course. You can bet there'll be one hell of an uproar when it's time to leave, and we don't want anyone focusing on us." MacInnes checked his watch. "You better check on Al, then stick with the wife. Try to keep a low profile."

"On my way."

Keillor pushed back from the rail and took the outside stairs down to the Lido. MacInnes watched him go, then scanned the stretch of water separating the ship from Caracola Cay. There was little wind, and the first of the Chilean America Line tenders had cleared the end of a distant jetty and was making its way toward the ship.

This will work, he thought to himself. *Sharma won't know what hit him.*

Twenty-two:
Jessica

Shortly after nine o'clock, the ship's PA came to life with an announcement by the Cruise Director: transportation to the island was ready for departure. Caitlin and her friends were among the first to reach the exit on Deck A, followed by their mothers. A large double-deck tender approached the side of the ship and tied up, and crew members deployed a gangway.

Jessica watched the children present their key cards to be scanned before lining up to board. She and Elizabeth introduced themselves to Hannah and Emily's mom, Deanna Watkins. There was no doubt about her children's heritage. The woman's grey-tinged red hair and pale freckled skin shouted Irish.

"Your children look like you," Jessica commented.

"Edgar's ancestors came to the US from Dublin during the great potato famine in the middle of the nineteenth century," Deanna said. "My roots are in County Cork, and we both have the same colouring. The poor kids couldn't have escaped looking the way they do. Edgar's my husband, nineteen years and counting."

"Is he on the cruise too?

"No, he's with NASA. This week he's addressing a technical conference in Boston, something to do with research funding. The physics department at MIT is touting a revolutionary new alloy that holds some promise for lighter weight and more effective heat shields, and he's checking it out."

"Sounds impressive."

"Yeah, well, he was supposed to be here with us, damn it. But the government cancelled his leave at the last minute, claiming he's the best man to evaluate the project." Deanna was watching the girls with obvious unease as they lined up to board the tender. "Do you think it's okay for them to go off on their own?" she asked the others.

"I called the Cruise Director before we came down," Jessica said. "She told me that the whole area is fenced and supervised, with four lifeguards on duty. It should be fine. Caitlin was very definite about leaving me behind, although she said I can join them for lunch later. Glad to have you too if you want."

"Don't worry about your kids," Elizabeth said. "One of my husband's associates is going ashore too. He'll keep track of all of them."

"How old are yours?" Deanna asked.

"Mine just turned thirteen in January," Jessica said, "but she thinks she's all grown up. I expect her to grow horns and a forked tail any day."

Deanna laughed. "I know what you mean. Hannah's driving me crazy too. Her favourite phrase is, 'Oh, mother, *really!*' Nothing I tell her makes any impression."

"Chloe's thirteen too," Elizabeth said, "and I'm beginning to see the signs of rebellion." Then to Jessica: "I didn't want to say anything at breakfast, but your Caitlin knocked my socks off last night. That Beethoven sonata was amazing."

"She scares me sometimes," Jessica said modestly. "She learned that one all on her own, after she fell in love with a recording by J. J. MacIsaac. Have you ever heard of him? He came from our town."

"I don't think so. I don't know much about classical music. Is he famous?"

"He was just beginning to make his mark when he vanished, only in his early twenties at the time. No one knows what happened to him. Anyway, Caitlin ordered the sheet music over the internet without telling us and taught herself to play it. Then she surprised her teacher with it at a lesson."

"I don't understand how she could do that all by herself," Elizabeth said.

"Neither do I. Her brain just seems to soak up music, and she's a natural mimic. She listens to recordings and imitates what she hears, the style and the tempo—the speed—and everything else. Then she puts her own special spin on it. Once she's got it, she never forgets."

"You and your husband must be very proud."

"Well, yes and no. Caitlin wants to experience everything the world has to offer, all at once, and doesn't realize how dangerous it can be. It's as if she were twins, all business at the piano and a reckless little hellion the rest of the time."

"Really?" Deanna said. "Hannah and Emily told me she seemed shy when they saw you at breakfast. But I'll bet Hannah made up for her. She's not exactly inhibited."

"Maybe I'm exaggerating. Caitlin hangs back in new situations. She has trouble making friends. I was really glad that your kids approached her, and I'm hoping she'll loosen up even more once they're on the beach. Do you know what time they have to be back on board?"

"Two-thirty, for a three o'clock departure," Deanna said. "She'll be sunburned and worn out by that time if she's anything like my two. Is she going to play in the Art Gallery again today?"

"You couldn't keep her from it. She has an informal agreement with the ship. She contacted the cruise line herself with the help of her grandfather and wangled an invitation to perform in return for free passage; a Valentine's gift for her father and me. Hard to believe, but it worked."

"Wow! That doesn't sound like shy to me."

"When she sets her mind on something, she can be really pushy."

"That's not necessarily a bad thing," Deanna said, "what with all the competition kids face in this day and age. Will she be up for playing after spending most of the day on the beach?"

"Why don't you come and see? Your daughters too if they'd like to."

"Emily already asked about hearing her again."

After the tender departed, Jessica and Deanna took an elevator back to their staterooms. Elizabeth was scheduled to join Vachan at yet another reception and headed for the Atrium instead. Had she looked behind her, she would have seen Grant Keillor keeping tabs on her progress.

When the elevator reached Deck Six, Deanna asked Jessica if she had time for coffee. "I'll just stay a few minutes." she said.

"Sure," Jessica said. "What's up?"

"I think I know something you might be interested in."

"Some juicy gossip about the Captain, perhaps? Talk about a hunk."

Deanna laughed. "If only. No, it's just that I picked up a copy of the Sun-Sentinel in the Lauderdale airport when we arrived. I always like to get a feel for a new place that way. Then when I met Elizabeth and her daughter, I recognized them from a photo in a feature article on the back page. It seems her husband is a really big deal back in Canada."

"He is indeed," Jessica said. "Hoping to be the next Premier of Nova Scotia."

"Do you know the family well?"

"We just met them yesterday, at the Best Western in Lauderdale."

"So you don't know about their daughter?"

"What do you mean?"

"She's something special," Deanna said.

"Now I'm intrigued," Jessica said. "Come on down to our stateroom and fill me in."

Russell was lounging on the veranda when they arrived and came inside to be introduced. He found some coffee pods in a drawer and started the brewer, and the three of them spread out on the sectional sofa.

"Some spiffy digs your kid cooked up for you," Deanna observed. "And she's something else at the keyboard. That's what I wanted to talk to you about. She isn't the only prodigy aboard this ship."

That caught Russell's attention as he dealt with the coffee machine. "You want anything in yours?" he asked Deanna, indicating the cup. "And who's the other hothouse plant? Not another piano player, I hope."

"Just a little sugar, please. It's Chloe, your daughter's new friend. Your wife told me you just met the family."

"That's right."

"There was an article about them in a Lauderdale newspaper, mostly about the father's political career, but it mentioned Chloe too. She's some kind of math whiz, and she won her first junior chess championship before she was eight. Haven't they told you?"

"Not a word."

"Then I suppose I shouldn't be saying anything. Could be they guard their daughter's privacy."

"We can identify with that," Russell said as he handed Jessica her coffee. "It's hard to make sure a kid has a normal childhood when they're in the public eye."

"I just thought you'd be interested. The article said Chloe's dad was a math major in university, and he taught her to play chess when she was five. Can't beat genetics, I guess. How about you? Is the rest of your family musical?"

"We're consumers only," Jessica said with a smile. "We love all sorts of good music, but no one else in the family performs. Caitlin's talent is all her own."

"Well, wherever it came from, she's a treasure."

* * *

As the ship's tender approached Caracola Cay, the girls climbed to the top deck and clung to the rail overlooking the bow until a crew member asked them to find seats—for safety, he said, until they were securely tied up. Caitlin listened to the others' happy chatter and tentatively joined in, becoming more at ease as Hannah and Emily accepted her as an old friend.

After ten minutes they slowed to enter a narrow channel between a jetty and a rock-bound shore, where seabirds pecked among mounds of shells that were caught in seaweed left behind by the receding tide. Behind the rocks, scrub-covered dunes stretched away toward stunted pines and dwarf palms. The channel ended at a substantial pier, and the tender coasted in close. A crew member lowered a broad gangway that spanned most of the front of the bow, allowing the passengers rapid access to a spacious boardwalk.

Ahead lay a wooden pavilion and a plaza lined with kiosks selling tee shirts, ball caps, and island jewellery and souvenirs. A maze of concrete paths branched off toward cabanas, a seaside bar in the guise of a pirate ship, a cabin where recreational equipment could be rented, and a covered barbeque complex surrounded by several dozen picnic tables.

Jacob Shaffer watched as the girls found a sign that pointed to the beach and took off at a run. He waited until most of the passengers were ashore before following along. He had promised Chloe to be as inconspicuous as possible and had abandoned his suit for shorts and a collared sport shirt, suitably subdued in a medium blue. The girls had ignored him on the shuttle, nor were they aware of a tall suntanned man who stood just behind them as the tender docked, listening to their conversation. Last to disembark was Alistair Barclay, intent on his own mission of surveillance.

Twenty-three:
Rolf

I was feeling confined and restless next morning and decided to go ashore. I hadn't exercised much in several days and was looking forward to finding a secluded area to run and swim a few solitary kilometres.

The first tender was almost full when I reached the gangway, and pulled away from the ship as soon as I was aboard. I sat on the starboard side and watched a handful of gulls and terns performing an aerial ballet above our wake. As we approached the jetty, I moved toward the bow to be among the first off and found myself behind a quartet of young teen girls excitedly leaning over the rail. I picked up the name Caitlin from their chatter—not a particularly common name, although not unique.

Could this be the whiz kid Jay Neilson told me about, the girl who surprised him with her skill at the piano? It hardly seemed likely. She was slight and unexceptional, with light brown hair and eyes so pale as to seem almost colourless, although her slender arms were defined by taut muscles just below the surface. My gaze naturally drifted to her hands—small, but with finely tapered fingers and neatly trimmed, unpainted nails. A pianist's equipment? Hard to tell. But it was her face that arrested me. Her features were arranged in a familiar pattern that I couldn't quite place, as if she resembled someone from my past. I detected a definite east coast Canada tone and rhythm in the vowels and cadence of her speech.

The minute the mooring was secure, the girls went racing for the shore. I turned in the opposite direction and set out at a slow jog down a path toward the heart of the island to undertake my exercise plans. Somewhere in the back of my mind I filed away the image of young

Caitlin, last name unknown, and resolved to be in the Art Gallery by 4:30 to see if she and the child who had so impressed Jay Neilson might be one and the same.

Twenty-four:
The Beach

The girls dropped their backpacks, stripped off shorts and tees, and chased each other into the surf, their bright swimsuits flashing in the sunlight. Caitlin executed a neat surface dive and swam strongly toward a row of orange floats strung on a rope that defined the limits of the swimming area. She pulled up and looked back, surprised to see Hannah right behind her.

"Wow, you're hard to catch," Hannah exclaimed. "Are you on the swim team at your school? I am."

"We don't have a team. I do gymnastics instead. But Dad got us a Sports Plex membership, and they have an Olympic-size pool."

"Where are you from?"

"Nova Scotia, a little place called Bournemouth." Seeing Hannah's puzzled expression, she continued, "Canada? East coast? Northeast of Maine?"

"I'm a southern girl. Atlanta. Geography isn't my thing. Pretty cold up there, right?"

"You can't imagine. Nine months of winter and three months of poor skiing." Hannah gaped at her, and Caitlin laughed. "Old joke, except Mom told me that years ago, people would sometime drive across the border in June with skis strapped to the roof, expecting to find snow. We're not much different from New England, except spring is wet and comes late. Our four seasons are summer, fall, winter, and mud."

"Now I know you're putting me on."

Caitlin scanned the shore and saw Emily and Chloe tossing a Frisbee in hip-deep water. Hannah followed her gaze. "Chloe doesn't swim," she said. "She told me she hates getting water up her nose."

"Think we could teach her?"

"Can't hurt to try. Race you back!"

Hannah bolted up onto the sand, only a step ahead of Caitlin, and the others abandoned their game and joined them. "You guys swim good," Emily said. "Want to see if we can rent some paddle boards?"

"Gotta teach Chloe to swim first," Hannah said.

"No way," Chloe protested. "I'll just watch."

"Nope." Hannah hauled Chloe to her feet, and with help from the other two she dragged her into the water, kicking and screaming in mock terror.

"Don't duck her," Caitlin said. "Show her how to breathe first."

"That's easy enough. I taught Emily."

Her sister nodded, grinning. "It's easy."

"Look, Chloe," Hannah said, "all you have to do is keep your mouth shut and breathe out through your nose whenever your head goes under. Breathe *out*, get it? That keeps the water out."

"I'll drown!"

"Watch me." Hannah lowered her face into the water and blew bubbles out through her nose. She came up laughing. "See? Like that."

Caitlin stayed out of the boisterous lesson, still surprised at how easily the others had accepted her and not wanting to do anything to upset that particular apple cart. Her middle school experience with cliques, intrigues and petty jealousies hadn't prepared her for the kind of easy give and take that turned these strangers from diverse backgrounds into fast friends. She wondered how each of them coped in their own schools. And she was afraid things might change between them if they came to hear her play in the Art Gallery. *Is this the real me, here on the beach? Will they understand that there are two of me, and that the other one isn't real?*

Chloe's swimming lessons were only moderately successful, but she gained enough confidence to sit clinging to a paddle board while the other three dunked each other in pretend combat. They finally quit in exhaustion and climbed back onto the beach, where they spread out towels and slathered themselves in sun block.

"Want to try the jet skis next?" Emily said. She pointed toward the jetty, where people were lined up to ride one of the cruise line's half dozen Kawasaki three-passenger watercraft. Five of the machines were out in the bay, and as the girls watched, a sixth one roared away from the shore, spraying a plume of water out the back. Two young boys in life jackets hung on behind a driver in board shorts and a Chilean America ball cap, screaming in delight.

"Looks scary," Chloe said.

"My Dad says they don't rent to anyone under sixteen," Hannah said. "If you're younger than that you have to go with a crew member."

"Gotta try it!" Caitlin exclaimed. "Let's go."

The more adventurous three ran off, and Chloe followed them at a distance. She sat down on a piling while Hannah, Emily and Caitlin lined up. When their turn came, the sisters climbed aboard the machine and clung behind a handsome twenty-something crew member in a ball cap and a *Santiago Vagabundo* tee shirt. Caitlin shared the next ski, sandwiched between the pilot and an older boy, slender and muscular, bare-chested in board shorts and a slouch hat.

They were soon well out into the cove, both craft bouncing over the waves and cutting broad circles that soaked the riders with spray and made them scream with pleasure. When they finally returned to shore, they tumbled off and splashed happily to the shore. They ran up to Chloe. Caitlin's face glowed with a soft pink blush.

"See?" Hannah said to Chloe. "Perfectly safe."

"And so much *fun!*" Caitlin said.

"Caitlin has a new boyfriend," Emily said.

"Give me a break!"

"He's pretty cute. Bet you got his name."

"Michael Griffin, smart alec, and he's fifteen. Want to know any more?"

Emily laughed. "You get his stateroom number?"

Caitlin blushed again. "Of course not!" she lied.

"Anyone know what time it is?" Chloe asked.

Hannah dug a watch out of her backpack. "Quarter to twelve, and I'm hungry." She scanned the beach in the direction of the pier. Deanna and Jessica were walking along the path that skirted the beach. "Here comes my mom, and yours too, Caitlin." "Let's see if they know where the barbeque is."

The girls gathered up their belongings and hurried to catch up with the adults. They found a sign directing them to the food pavilion and took a lunch break, then decided to explore the island by themselves. Jessica reminded them not to be late for the last tender, and she and Deanna headed back to the plaza for a little souvenir shopping.

Jacob Shaffer followed the girls at a discrete distance, and if Chloe noticed him, she gave no sign. The security guard took his assignment seriously.

As they boarded the shuttle to take them back to the ship, Jessica and Deanna compared notes about their respective offspring. Jessica marvelled at the change in her daughter, at the layer of social confidence she seemed to have acquired. The girls had bonded quickly, but she wondered if Caitlin's transformation from reticent to outgoing in new situations would be permanent.

Time will tell, I guess.

Twenty-five:
Aboard

Arch MacInnes and Grant Keillor arranged to meet in the usual place, the sports deck aft, late in the afternoon and this time with Al Barclay. MacInnes took notes as the others replayed the morning for him, the who, what and where that they had observed.

"Sharma's days are full," MacInnes said. "Everyone wants a piece of the man. You have to give him credit, he puts on a good show. The luncheon went on for over two hours, and he was always at center stage, but he seemed just as fresh afterward as if he'd just arrived. The smile never slips, and that voice? If he were back in India, Bollywood would love him. There's a CBC stringer following him around, and it looks like he's filing a series of stories. This is going to do a lot for his rep back home. Which is a big problem for us."

"How often is he alone?" Keillor asked.

"Never, at least not so far today. Pelletier is always somewhere close by, unobtrusive but alert." Darryl Pelletier was Chief of Security for the New Democratic Party when its principals were travelling, and Jacob Shaffer's boss.

"How about the family?"

"The wife is quiet, but she comes across as supportive. She's by his side whenever he needs her, and she's articulate. Good looking for a slant-eye, too."

"And the daughter?"

"She spent most of the day on the island with the kids you saw at breakfast," Barclay said. "Shaffer kept track of her."

"Anybody else from Sharma's team on the island?" MacInnes asked. "If we're going to pull this off, we have to know where everyone is when we make our move."

"Should be okay. He hasn't gone ashore yet. Too busy with the meet-and-greet."

"We can waylay Pelletier if we have to," Keillor said, "but the wife may be a problem. She stayed with her husband all afternoon when she came back from the beach. The kid went to a concert of some sort by herself about an hour ago."

Al Barclay nodded in agreement. "We have to figure out how to break them up if we're going to get away with this."

"We'll cross that bridge when we come to it," MacInnes said. "How did Charlotte make out?" he said to Keillor.

"A-one. She buttonholed one of the crew while he took a break and made up to him. The poor fool fell for her story hook, line and sinker."

"But will he do what we want?"

"Charlotte says he agreed. 'As long as no one gets hurt,' the guy told her, and she assured him it was all just in fun. Charlotte said he seemed a little worried about losing his job if his boss finds out. She thinks he's a bit naïve, but he's blinded by the easy money. She's sure he'll do as he's told."

"He's the key to making everyone on board accept what happens," MacInnes said. "I wish we could have used one of our own people."

"You know that's not possible," Keillor said. "It would give us away if anyone connected to the Freedom Party was involved. In any case, this guy won't be in a position to rat Charlotte out when it's all over."

"Yeah." MacInnes fixed Keillor with a hard stare. "See to it."

"No sweat."

"Can Carman handle things by himself afterward?"

"He'll be okay."

MacInnes took a deep breath. "I don't like it. There are too many ways it can go wrong."

"Relax," Keillor said. "No one's going to figure it out. It's foolproof."

"I hope you're right."

Twenty-six:
The Art Gallery

Manamea and her mother, Masina Tanielu, were waiting in the Art Gallery when Caitlin arrived at four. The child looked younger than eight, tiny in a short pink sundress that set off the flawless warmth of her milk chocolate skin tones. Her thick black hair was tightly braided, exposing dainty polished shell earrings hanging from her delicate ears.

The gallery anteroom was empty except for a few art lovers browsing among the paintings. Caitlin's performance was not scheduled to begin for another half hour. She had applied sun block much too late while on the beach, and her forehead glowed pink in the overhead lighting. Her reddened arms and shoulders, bare in a white sequined tank top that clung softly above fancy black tuxedo pants, predicted a day or two of discomfort ahead for her. But she didn't care, still riding an adrenalin high after spending time with her new friends.

"Let's see what you can do," she said to the girl.

Manamea had brought a stiff bolster cushion from her stateroom. She placed it in the center of the piano bench to sit on, which raised her high enough to reach the keyboard easily. "I use a thick book at home," she said.

"I did that when I was your age," Caitlin said. "Ready to play the Mozart for me?"

Manamea began the opening motive of the minuet hesitantly and missed a few notes as she fought her way through the first phrase. But as she got into it, the rhythm smoothed out and the errors disappeared. By the time she reached the repeat her concentration kicked in, and she made no mistakes from that point on. She finished strongly and was greeted with a round of applause from a handful of people who had paused to listen. Chloe had arrived and sat down in the front row.

"That was really good," Caitlin said. Manamea thanked her timidly and started to get up. "Hang on," Caitlin said. "I've got an idea. Are you up for trying a little experiment?" The child nodded uncertainly. "Scootch over some and let me sit down too. Now, let's start at the beginning. We'll see what we can do to spice this piece up."

* * *

The audience began to arrive around four-twenty, and Manamea took her seat between her mother and Chloe in the middle of the front row. Caitlin tucked the cushion behind the piano and left the gallery in search of Jessica. Part way down the corridor she found her mother talking with Deanna Watkins. "Mom, I need some advice," Caitlin said.

"I'll go on ahead," Deanna said to Jessica. "Save you a seat."

"What's up?" Jessica asked her daughter.

"I just heard Manamea play the Mozart. Remember her? The little one at breakfast? She's okay, pretty good in fact. Do you think the Cruise Director would mind if I let her play it for everyone?"

"I don't know. It would be nice to include her, but the people come to hear you."

"I don't think that will be a problem. I messed around with Mozart a little, made it into a duet. They told me I could choose my own repertoire, right?"

"I guess so."

"I just want to give her a chance to shine. It might build up her confidence."

"Are you sure she can do it?"

"If she doesn't get too nervous. Anyway, I'll be right there to bail her out if she needs it."

"Okay, I trust your judgment. I hope whatever you have in mind will come off okay."

"Thanks, Mom." Caitlin wheeled off and entered the gallery, the seats now full and people finding places to stand at the back. She spotted Hannah and Emily and tossed a wig-wag wave in their direction, just as Elizabeth Wu entered from the back, followed by Chloe's dad and Darryl Pelletier.

The applause started as Caitlin took her place on the bench, and she smiled at the crowd and plunged into an elaborate medley of songs made popular by Karen and Richard Carpenter in the 1970s: *We've Only Just Begun*, *Mister Postman*, and her personal Sesame Street favourite from when she was two, *Sing*. She followed up with John Lennon's *Ebony and Ivory*. She had promised her friends to throw in a couple of Adele tunes, but that was for later. She picked up her microphone and waited for the applause to die down.

"I want to introduce you to someone," she said as the room quieted. "I only met her this morning, and I discovered something important about her—she plays the piano too, and we both love Mozart." She motioned the child to her feet. "This is Manamea. She's eight, from Samoa, well, she lives in Florida now, but anyway, we cooked up something special for you a little while ago. Want to hear it?"

Caitlin's friends led the clapping as she retrieved the cushion for Manamea to sit on. "Mozart made up this song on his father's harpsichord when he was younger than Manamea," she told the crowd. "I think you'll agree it's a pretty good composition for a little kid." She put the microphone aside and sat down to whisper in Manamea's ear. "You start, just like we practiced."

The girl nodded, placed her hands on the keyboard, and began to play. The lovely little melody spun out into the hall as Caitlin sat motionless to her right, hands in her lap. Manamea reached the end of the opening theme and began the repeat, and Caitlin joined in with a soft obbligato an octave higher. Her simple arpeggios in 18th century style decorated the minuet without obscuring it. When the second theme began, Caitlin reached around behind Manamea's back and improvised a soft bass line at the low end of the keyboard, then switched back to the high notes to play a graceful, flowing countermelody. For the last sixteen bars she duplicated Mozart's theme an octave higher to finish off, a happy collaboration between an old master and two very young, like-minded souls.

Twenty-seven:
Rolf

The Dream came back. I should have known better than to fall asleep in the afternoon. That's when it most often happens, when I'm tired and my mental defences are at their lowest ebb.

I had returned to my room after hearing Caitlin play in the Art Gallery. I found her last name, Sheridan, in the "Today on the *Santiago Vagabundo*" information brochure, but it didn't ring any bells. I was out of touch with up-and-coming talent, having been hiding out in the Caribbean for more than seven years. Except for J. J. MacIsaac, that is; I knew exactly where *he* was.

The girl was very impressive. Although the afternoon performance was relatively lightweight, it was obvious that she'd been well taught. She compensated for her small hands with lightning speed, and in addition to the classics she seemed at home with various styles of pop, Broadway and even country. Her underlying, instinctive understanding of the jazz idioms she inserted into the selections was equally impressive in the casual riffs she laid down among the inner voices.

The duet with the little Samoan girl intrigued me, and I suspected that Mozart would have approved of the improvised accompaniment Caitlin played to showcase the child's performance. There was a keen mind behind the mechanics of her playing. I considered speaking to her afterward, but she was immediately surrounded by others her own age. Besides which, I needed to rest before dinner if I was to be on top of my game later that evening. My muscles felt pleasantly loose after exercising on the island, and when I stretched out on the bed, my eyes closed involuntarily.

The atmosphere in the small sanctuary is oppressive, lighted only by a few candles burning in sconces on either side of the altar. A massive crucifix looms above me, its stylized Christ figure shedding copious blood from wrists and abdomen, a bizarre snarl of hate twisting his lips. He wears an incongruous clerical collar. I know that face; not Jesus, but...

I can't recall his name.

A grand piano sits silently in one corner, oddly shrunken, the keys too small for my fingers, although I knew I had spent many hours, many days, many weeks, labouring over it.

Someone speaks my name. A woman's voice, no, a girl's; soft, compelling.

Another voice, male, severe, commanding...

I'm afraid.

I rise and move toward a door, a solid oak barrier that moments before defined my prison but now melts away to reveal a vista both beautiful and frightening. Dark, brooding hills define the far horizon. Ahead stretches a blood-red sea on which a solitary raft rocks in the current, gentle wavelets rippling toward the pure white sand and lulling me in tempting invitation. I step aboard, and suddenly she is there. Her huge dark eyes lock onto mine, loving me.

She is smiling.

She is crying.

I love her.

Surrounded by a halo of stars, the Man in the Moon hovers above me, beside me, beneath me, a sombre, tear-ravaged face with trembling lips that call me to my destiny. The piano keyboard appears and I reach out to caress the keys, silent ivory and black rectangles as soft as her skin, beckoning, compelling, begging me to bring them to life. There is no melody, only that insistent rhythm, ancient and unrelenting and as compelling as the pounding of the drums inside my head, the blare of brass. I sink into depths of overwhelming fear and excitement and misery and longing and...

And I jolted awake, bathed in sweat as always after The Dream, momentarily confused and disoriented. It always ends the same way. I threw off the sheet that covered me, achingly engorged. Unable to resist, I suffered a painful, unbidden release brought on by haunting images that never change, never lose their power to shame me. I swung my feet over the side of the bed and staggered to the bathroom to deal with the aftermath, then sprawled in the chair to wait for my racing heart to slow to normal.

What brought it on this time? And why?

Twenty-eight:
Carman

Three weeks earlier, The Spider sat in a booth in a nondescript lounge not far from Everglades City, adjacent to a part of the Everglades in south-western Florida known as the Ten Thousand Islands. The area's name may have been an exaggeration, as many of the hundreds of islets were actually no more than mangrove swamps, although some larger ones had been home to native populations thousands of years earlier. Most were now deserted, and except for limited tourism from Everglades National Park and the Wildlife Refuge, visitors rarely penetrated far into the twisted waterways. The tiny cays offered the exact kind of isolation that was needed to support the latest project of Canada's clandestine white supremacy movement.

The man was a prominent member of that organization's inner circle, his identity carefully guarded to preserve his ability to navigate Nova Scotia's political scene in secrecy. The nickname "The Spider" derived from his associates' vision of him as the central figure in a vast web of conspiracy theorists whose efforts had done much to further the movement's objectives. Skilled in disguise, he was unrecognizable whenever pursuing the illegal and often terror-oriented activities that threatened the stability of his country's society.

There were few others in the lounge: two at the bar, fishermen perhaps, and two rough looking middle-aged thugs playing pool. A couple oblivious to their surroundings held hands across one of the free-standing tables. The Spider hadn't been told the identity of his contact, nor what he looked like. He knew only that someone would meet with him, a man recommended by criminal associates as the sort who could provide the services the Freedom Party required.

He had been waiting over an hour and was about to abandon the quest when one of the patrons at the bar rose abruptly and headed for the door, after which the bartender emerged from behind the counter and slid into the booth.

"You're Spider?" he said softly.

A nod.

"That your real name?"

"Does it matter?"

"Guess not. The guy you need to see is named Carman Russo. He's something of a recluse, had plenty of run-ins with the law."

"Where can I find him? What's he look like?"

"Ex-military, neck bigger around than his head, built like a fire hydrant and just as tough. Not someone you'd want mad at you, but he knows this area better than anyone else, and he can probably tell you where to find what you're looking for."

"Sounds like just the guy I need."

The bartender shook his head. "Not if you cross him. Don't say I didn't warn you. He keeps a fifty-three-foot trawler down at the Glades Isle Marina. Make sure he sees you coming from a distance. He's always armed, and he doesn't like surprises."

* * *

The next morning The Spider scouted out the modest marina and found Russo lounging on the afterdeck of a sleek, well-maintained vessel. He waved and pretended to move on, then paused, looked back, and said, "Nice looking boat."

Russo shrugged.

"What is she?"

"Trawler."

"Doesn't look like a fishing boat to me."

"You ain't a sailor, are ya?" Russo said.

"Afraid not."

"This here's a cruiser. Deep keel, big gas-powered V-8, long range tanks. Tough enough to hold her own in almost any kind of sea."

"Is she fast?"

"Fast enough, and she can ride out anything short of a hurricane."

"Can I see below?"

"What for?"

"Just curious."

Russo shrugged again and headed for the companionway, gesturing to be followed aboard. After a tour below decks and some small talk, The Spider explained his objective. He needed access to a hidden island with some sort of building on it where he could set up shop for a few months with little likelihood of interference.

"What're you gonna do there?" Russo asked. "Smuggling? Bootlegging?"

"Do you have to know?"

"Not unless you want my help. There's less than half a dozen islands suitable for what you're talking about, and you'll never find one by yourself. 'Course, if I know what I'm getting into, I might just help you out. Depends on what's in it for me."

For the next twenty minutes The Spider talked about his objective, the nature of the crime he and his associates were about to commit, and the fact that his clientele was not averse to skirting the law if necessary.

"Too risky," Russo said. "That kind of thing will bring the feds down on your head real fast, and they've got the clout to smoke you out."

"Not if they don't know where to look. This deal has international connections. If they look anywhere, it'll be in Canada, and if we play this right, no one will know our location except you and me. We're prepared to pay you enough to keep you on our side."

Russo stood up and looked out over the stern rail, deep in thought. Long moments passed. "What's my cut?" he said at last.

The Spider knew he had sunk the hook. All he needed to do was reel it in.

* * *

Later that afternoon and using a shallow draft skiff, Russo showed The Spider a suitable site in a nearly impenetrable part of the island chain, two acres surrounded by mangrove trees where a fenced-in, flat-roofed building lay hidden from passing watercraft. Once used as a fishing cabin, it had been abandoned and forgotten for years.

"I use it myself sometimes when I need a place to lie low," Russo said. "It's got five rooms, a well, propane hookup for the stove and a working generator in a lean-to out back. Not in great shape, but for what you want, it's perfect. Nobody could escape from here without a boat 'cause the mainland is too far away. The fence keeps the 'gators out, and you could top it with barbed wire so no one can climb over."

Ownership of the deserted island was not an issue. The Party had no intention of buying or leasing the property, which would involve documents with names on them. As long as no one discovered them over the summer, and given the location that seemed improbable, the site was ideal.

The two men struck a deal and money changed hands, with more to come at regular intervals. Russo would be in charge of transportation to and from the island and would see to security. Over the next two weeks he would stock the cabin with supplies and make certain modifications to the structure to ensure the expected occupant—read "prisoner"— would be unable to escape.

The Spider was on the first plane back to Canada the following morning, pleased with his success.

Twenty-nine:
The Band

Caitlin wound up her evening performance with George Gershwin's three jazz-infused *Preludes* and started back to the suite to change into a swimsuit. She'd promised to meet Hannah at the pool to help give Chloe a second swimming lesson. As she exited into the corridor, two oddly dressed twenty-somethings and an older man caught up to her.

"You got some chops, babe," said a rail-thin guy with spiky blond hair.

Caitlin frowned at him. "Uh, thanks… I think." She blinked at his sleeveless tie-dyed tee shirt and baggy plaid shorts, outrageous in shades of red, purple and orange. His runners were pink with green-striped laces, untied.

"I'm DeeZee," he said. "This is Mouse, she channels Janis Joplin"—he pointed to a blue-haired girl in a skimpy latex halter and black dancer's tights—"and this senior citizen here is Bazoo. We're the evening entertainment. You catch our act on stage last night?"

"Sorry."

"No sweat. You jam?"

"Do I what?"

DeeZee grinned at his band mates. "Ninety-degree angles on this one," he said. Caitlin turned away and headed for the elevators. "Hey, wait up," he called after her.

She glared at him. "I know what 'square' means," she said.

"Whoa!" the one called Bazoo said. He was about fifty, an aging rock star in grunge gear, his head shaved. "Don't pay any attention to the Deeze. He's obtuse. Let's start over, okay? Do you play the charts? Like, top forty?"

"Why do you want to know?"

"You got *technique*, babe," DeeZee put in. "Attitude! We groove on that."

"Shut up!" Bazoo said. Then to Caitlin, "What we need to know is, are you a page-turner, or can you do the head thing?"

"I have no idea what you're talking about," Caitlin said.

"He means do you need printed music to play from," Mouse said. Her voice was soft and low, a mellow contralto. Caitlin found it hard to believe she could imitate the frenetic Joplin.

"We don't read," Mouse continued. "I mean, we can, but we don't, you dig? Like, we play what we hear. That's called a head arrangement."

"If you play something for me, I can usually pick it up. Is that what you mean?"

"Righteous!" DeeZee said. "Okay, there's this magician dude doing his thing in the theatre tonight from eight to nine, again from ten to eleven. In between his two acts we do a session for the *cognoscenti*, if you know what I mean. We've got a spare keyboard with nobody on it. It's yours if you want it."

"You mean play with you? On stage? When do you rehearse?"

"We don't. We jam," Bazoo said. "Quarter to nine, come one, come all, do your own thing."

"I guess I can't," Caitlin said, although she was intrigued. "I'm on my way to the pool to teach somebody how to swim, and Mom wants me back in our room after that."

"Bring her along," Bazoo said. "Does she blow a mean chorus?"

Caitlin laughed, caught up in the jargon and high spirits. "Look, I'll talk to her. If she says I can do it, where do I meet you?"

"On stage, like ten to nine, soon as the magic dude *disappears*." He laughed at his own joke.

"Okay, I'll try to be there. Later, cats."

Mouse grinned at her. "Be cool, babe," she said. "No one says 'cats' anymore."

Thirty:
Caitlin

Caitlin burst into the suite, grabbed a bikini from a drawer, and disappeared into the bathroom to change. She called out through the closed door: "Mom, can I play with the ship's band at nine? They invited me."

"What's the ship's band?" Jessica called back.

"Part of the entertainment, I guess. You wouldn't believe it, there's this skinny guy with hair standing straight up, and a bald guy, and a girl they say sings like Janis Joplin, only I won't believe it until I hear it, and they want me to 'jam' with them, which I think means improvise."

"Sounds like fine, upstanding folks," Russell observed quietly.

"Hush!" Jessica whispered. Then louder: "When do they want you to come?"

Caitlin burst out of the bathroom, belting a gauzy cover-up over her swimsuit. "Between the two stage shows. There's a magic act at eight and ten, and the band gets together in between to like, mess around. Rock and stuff, you know."

"Rock? And you really want to play with them?" Russell didn't try to hide his scepticism and disdain for the state of popular music in the new millennium.

"Come on, Dad, you're always telling me to look for new experiences. It'll be fun."

"How old are these musicians?" her mother asked.

"Don't know. Older than me, I guess they're pros, and Bazoo looks even older than Dad."

"Bazoo?" Russell raised one sceptical eyebrow. "What are the others called?"

"The young guy's DeeZee and the girl is Mouse."

"I think you better just come back here after Chloe's swimming lesson," Russell said.

Caitlin's shoulders slumped. Faced with one of her father's protective moods, she frowned, scuffed her feet on the tile floor, and turned to leave.

"It's just that we don't know these people," Jessica said, "How about if your Dad and I come along too, just to keep an eye on things. We'll sit in the balcony and people won't know we're with you."

Caitlin spun around, daring to hope. "I thought you hate that kind of music."

"That's not the point. You're allowed to make your own choices about what to play and who to play it with. But you're only thirteen, and we'd be irresponsible if we let you hang around with an older crowd without some strict guidelines. That includes chaperones."

"I'm okay with that. So can I go?"

"Not in that bikini," her father said.

"Relax, Dad. I'll come back and change first."

He grinned weakly at her, and Jessica said, "Go. And don't let Chloe drown."

Caitlin whirled and ran for the door.

* * *

She reached the theatre ten minutes before nine. DeeZee was setting up his drum kit while Mouse fiddled with a stubborn mike stand. An acoustic guitar hung around her neck. Bazoo was tuning his Stratocaster, and a rail-thin girl in huge round glasses stood in the wings fingering Paul McCartney licks on a mahogany Ibanez bass. Stacked electronic keyboards and amps filled the left side of the stage, where a straight-looking dude in khaki shorts stood twisting some dials. Caitlin thought he looked to be about her own age, but she knew he must have been older if the ship hired him. She introduced herself.

"Name's Jason," the boy told her. "You're the Beethoven chick, right? Bazoo says you'll probably want the grand." He motioned toward a small Baldwin piano on the other side of the drums. "It's miked. You'll need it, 'cause we get kinda loud. Amp's underneath it. Use the pedal to crank it."

The theatre was nearly empty, most of the crowd having left after the magic act. Caitlin figured that those who remained had probably been invited. She glanced up and saw her parents enter the lower tier of the balcony. They chose seats in a shadowed corner, unobtrusive but with full view of the stage. A bit intimidated by the other musicians, Caitlin felt reassured by their presence but nervous too, not sure what kind of contribution she could make to an ensemble far different from what she was used to. She didn't want to embarrass herself.

The bass player hauled an amp in front of the Baldwin and offered a fist bump when Caitlin sat down on the bench. "Caught your scene in the gallery this aft," she said. "I'm Lynx."

"I'm Caitlin."

"I know. Gonna play with us, you need a new moniker. How about we call you 'Jailbait'?"

Caitlin laughed. "My Dad would love that."

Bazoo joined them as the others took their places, ready to begin. "You know the Randy Racoons' chart *Kilauea Kickass*, babe?" he asked Caitlin.

"I'll lay out the first chorus to get the changes."

"Radical."

Bazoo struck an A major chord, DeeZee ticked a four-beat on the hi-hat, and Jason played a vamp into a bluesy rock tune, vaguely Hawaiian but mostly generic pop. Caitlin tuned in, picking up the chord progression from Mouse's rhythm guitar, and by the time they reached the bridge she was comping, soft and easy, getting a feel for the shape of the melody. When they swung into the second chorus she cranked her amp, echoed Bazoo's guitar line for four bars, then played fill-in licks to back him up.

The band caught fire, jiving on the newcomer, and on the third go-around Bazoo backed off and gave her the nod. She stayed close to the tune at first, filling out the harmonies in a rolling left hand, and at the bridge they all dropped out except for DeeZee's drums to let her do her thing. After sixteen bars she caught Bazoo's eye and played a two-bar minor-third lift into C major. The band followed her lead and grabbed the spotlight again. DeeZee took an eight-bar solo, and they rode the final chorus to a raucous major seventh climax.

By that time a few hundred newcomers were in the hall. Lynx leaned over and whispered in Bazoo's ear, and he high-fived her and walked around the piano. He raised his mike. "How about that?" he said to the crowd. "We've got a newcomer tonight." He motioned Caitlin to her feet. "We found this little doll hangin' out with Bach and Brahms and all those other old-time dudes. Give it up for Jailbait!"

Caitlin cringed as some cheering broke out, fully expecting her father to jump to his feet and drag her off the stage. Her face flamed, and she dropped down on the bench, trying to hide.

"Got something special for you now," Bazoo told the crowd, which continued to grow as people checked in to investigate the sounds that had blasted out of the theatre. "Our own Mouse—that's her name, not her species—she writes songs, and she's got a new one for you, calls it *Midnight Solitaire*."

Mouse shrugged off her guitar and took over the mike, moving it a few feet forward. She had swapped her tights and halter for a diaphanous white lace dress that skimmed the tops of her boots and left her shoulders bare. The techie on the lights dropped a halo spot on her, and the effect was magical; an angel risen from ashes.

Lynx laid down an eight-bar bass line, Jason joined in halfway through, and DeeZee traded his sticks for brushes. Caitlin listened as a sweet, light rock ballad played out, Mouse's Karen Carpenter contralto low and pure.

Janis Joplin, Caitlin thought. *Right!*

Jason's accompaniment was thick and ripe with tremolos, and Caitlin had the chord changes down by the end of the first verse. Bazoo cued her to take over behind the vocal, and she thinned out the harmony with eighth note decorations in the right hand, triplets in the left: Mozart meets Mancini meets Neil Young. Between phrases a pleased Mouse smiled at her over her shoulder.

And the beat moved on.

Thirty-one:
Rolf

I could hardly believe what I was hearing. This tiny fugitive from a middle school sock hop was a chameleon. An hour earlier she'd been showing the world how to give Shostakovich and Copland a fresh new sound, and letter perfect besides. Rarely had I heard such precision, such accuracy, even from professionals many years her senior. And now came a whole new dimension of her talent, an intuitive feel for improvisation that made her at home at the heart of a rock band. After pulling out all the stops in the first number, she was laying down a soft and graceful foundation that complemented the singer's phrasing perfectly—all, I could tell, made up on the spot.

I was due to play with Neilson and Gaudet in the lounge, but having overheard the band members invite this child to join them, I wanted to hear what she could do. Jay said they could do a twosome until I got there, and I wasn't about to let her get away without finding out where she came from. As the band wound up its session with a rousing, irreverent romp through Elton John's *Crocodile Rock*, I was already in the wings, ready to buttonhole her as she came off stage.

"Caitlin Sheridan?" I called out to her.

She turned. "That's me."

"Did you rehearse with these guys before going on stage?" I asked.

"Nope. Didn't have time. We just winged it."

"Do you have any idea how few people in the world can do what you just did?"

She blushed prettily. "I was just filling in."

"Sure. I heard you in the Art Gallery this afternoon too, and later in the Mozarteum. You have a rare talent."

"It's no big deal. Are you a musician too?"

"I play a little keyboard," I told her.

"Cool."

"I'm with the trio in the lounge on Deck Two. If you have the time, maybe…"

"I gotta go," she said. "My Mom and Dad are waiting for me." She hopped down off the stage and headed for the center aisle.

"Where are you from?" I called after her.

"Nova Scotia. Bournemouth." She grinned. "Bet you never heard of it."

"I know it well."

"No kidding? What's your name?"

"Rolf."

"Nice to meet you, Rolf, but I really gotta go. Parents, you know."

She waved toward a couple standing in the balcony, then spun around and raced up the aisle.

Thirty-two:
Caitlin

Back in the suite, Caitlin was figuratively bouncing off the walls. "They want me to join them for the stage show tomorrow. We go on twice, at eight and ten. Some of it's just to play for the singers and dancers, but we get solo sets too. The Cruise Director okayed it, even though I'm not on the payroll, and Bazoo says I get to do a solo chorus in two of the songs. Lynx says she'll help me put on some cool makeup." She prowled around the room. "What am I gonna wear?"

"How about you settle down a little so we can talk about this," Russell said.

"You're not gonna tell me I can't do it, are you? Didn't you hear me tonight? I can *do* this stuff, Dad. It's fun, and DeeZee says I should kiss Beethoven goodbye and run away with him."

"That's what I'm afraid of."

"I'm *kidding*. Come on!"

"Jailbait?"

"It was just a joke!"

"In poor taste."

"Okay, I get that, but what did you expect them to call me? They're *rockers*."

"And you're too damn young for sex, drugs and rock'n'roll."

"Time out," Jessica said. "I think both of you are overreacting just a bit. Sweetheart, I'm glad you had fun tonight, but don't forget why you're really on this trip. And you," she said, turning to her husband, "stop taking this so seriously. You're always harping on the fact that she needs to fit in more. Now when she does, you're playing the heavy. Lighten up."

"These so-called musicians…"

"Are pretty darn talented," Jessica finished for him. "Okay, they may be too caught up in projecting an image, but that's what sells these days. Maybe when you get to know them, they're Boy Scouts in disguise."

"Spaced out gang bangers, more likely."

Caitlin's head swivelled back and forth between them. "So I can't do it?"

Russell caught his wife's disapproving eye and threw up his hands in surrender. "Your mother's right, as usual. They just put me off, especially with that 'Jailbait' line, but I have to admit, you did all right. As long as they treat you with respect, I guess you can be in the show. But I'll be watching."

Caitlin grinned. "And can I go live with DeeZee after the cruise?"

"I'll lock you up in a nunnery!"

Thirty-three:
Prodigies

Early the following morning, Chloe played four simultaneous chess games in the Pelican Library. Two of her opponents were amateurs. An intense young woman in her mid-twenties played too quickly and sacrificed pieces to gain temporary advantage without grasping the long game. The youngest, a ten-year-old with a startling blue-black complexion and exquisite features, was much more controlled. She studied each move carefully but lacked the experience to keep track of her opponent's underlying strategy. Chloe decided to go easy on her and give her a chance to learn from her mistakes. But she planned to finish off the brash older gal in short order.

Her third opponent was Michael Griffin, the teenager who had shared a jet ski ride with Caitlin. It was clear to Chloe that he knew the game well. He didn't rush but seemed to have an internal clock, as if obeying a tournament timer. He employed a routine Scandinavian Defence, and Chloe treated him with respect, studying the board an extra minute or two before making each move.

"I saw you on the beach yesterday," Michael said. "How come you didn't ride the ski with your friend? She told me her name, but I've forgotten."

"Just not in the mood," Chloe said. "That was Caitlin."

"Oh, yeah. She was nice." He paused, studying the board. Then, softly: "I have a girlfriend back home."

Chloe looked up impishly. "What happens in the Caribbean, stays in the Caribbean."

Michael laughed. "Not my style," he said.

"Too bad."

A few minutes later the woman resigned first, blitzed by Chloe's attack on both her knights and not waiting for the inevitable checkmate. She knocked her king on its side, stood up abruptly, and left the library without a word, as if resentful at having lost to someone half her age.

The fourth player was an elderly gentleman, no pushover, and Chloe suspected he had probably been a worthy competitor in his younger days. He shook his head sadly at the woman's abrupt, rude departure, then seemed distracted. He hung in for three more moves before finally giving up both bishops, a knight and a rook and letting his queen get trapped in the back row. He resigned gracefully, stood up and bowed to Chloe, and thanked her. "You brought back a lot of memories," he said. "I won a regional championship when I was twelve, a high point in my life. It was an honour to face someone like you across the board again."

"The honour was mine," Chloe said sincerely.

The ten-year-old was frustrated. "I don't know what happened," she said, staring at a choice between losing a rook and putting her queen in jeopardy—mate in three, either way.

"What's your name?" Chloe asked.

"Ngoni," she replied. "But everyone just calls me Nan."

"Are you from Africa?"

"Nope, San Francisco. My Mom and Dad moved there from Zimbabwe before I was born. Mom was a chess champion there."

"She taught you well. Do you want to play this out, or shall we back up a few moves so I can show you what would have worked better?"

"Let's go back, please," the girl said, and they reset the board. Step by step, Chloe took her through half a dozen moves that would give the child a mate against a less skilled player. When they were finished, the girl circled the table and gave Chloe a big hug in thanks.

Slow and deliberate, Michael survived the longest. "You've got me," he finally admitted, laying his king on its side before Chloe could make her final move. "Thanks for a great game."

"You play in any tournaments?" she asked.

"I made the Connecticut finals when I was eleven and came in second at Tri State two years ago. But it's intimidating, facing all you pint-sized geniuses who hardly look things over before you move."

"You pushed me pretty hard," Chloe said graciously.

"Thanks, but I know better. I've given up competing, just play for fun. Want a rematch sometime?"

"Call me. I'm in six-oh-one-seven."

With Jacob Shaffer following at some distance, Chloe headed down to the aft pool and found Caitlin at her hyperactive best in the water. She was burning off excess energy by racing back and forth close to one side, where she wouldn't collide with some children playing in the shallow end. Chloe called out to her, and she did a somersault and came up sputtering.

"Where've you been?" Caitlin asked.

"Playing chess in the library. I ran into your ski ride partner yesterday."

"Michael?"

"One and the same." She tilted her head to one side, affecting a mocking, sad look. "He has a girlfriend."

"Shit," Caitlin murmured.

Chloe barely suppressed a giggle. "I'm starved. You had breakfast yet?"

"Nope. I've been in here since six-thirty. Give me five to get dried off, and we can go to the Lido." Caitlin levered herself out of the pool and headed for the changing rooms.

Chloe turned toward Jacob Shaffer, who had sunk into a chaise a few meters away. "Hey, Jake, we're gonna go eat in the Lido. Want to hang with us?"

"I'll cramp your style, squirt," Shaffer replied.

"Don't be a stuffed shirt. Come on. Give us a chance to pick on you."

The three of them were soon at a window table, sharing an assortment of food. Caitlin claimed the lion's share, needing to fuel her galloping metabolic rate. They discussed their plans for a shore excursion on Grand Turk later in the day. Chloe and Emily were booked for a trail bike expedition, and Caitlin and Hannah were looking forward to a boat ride. Shaffer sat listening in amused silence, surprised to have been included in their breakfast plans.

He wasn't sure it had been a good idea to accept their invitation.

Thirty-four:
Ashore

A huge Carnival Lines ship towered over the *Santiago Vagabundo* at the pier on Grand Turk. Russell Sheridan walked down the long promenade toward shore holding a disposable waterproof camera, angling to get a photo that would highlight the differences between the two boats. After clicking off two exposures, he entered the gathering hall and found the line-up for his trail ride excursion. He turned in his reservation card, then struck up a conversation with a fit-looking teen who introduced himself as Michael Griffin, and who was also signed up for the horseback tour.

Arch MacInnes disembarked carrying a golf bag, although playing a round was merely a cover for a meeting with his two associates and Carman Russo. They wanted the privacy of the links while making plans.

Chloe and her mother approached a tour guide who was holding a sign for an Eco Kayak Safari, Elizabeth's choice for the day's recreation. Using all her powers of persuasion, she had talked her husband into taking time off to join her, although Vachan Sharma seemed self-conscious and uncomfortable in resort clothes. Jacob Shaffer was still on the clock to keep track of Chloe. Uncharacteristically, Sharma had dismissed his Chief of Security, Daryl Pelletier, thinking the man was entitled to some time to himself. They handed in their tickets and joined the queue for a bus to take them to the Safari site.

Chloe watched anxiously for Emily to arrive, then spotted Michael and waved. She left her parents to go and talk with him. Caitlin and Hannah came running down the pier, followed a long way back by Jessica and Deanna. The two women were primed for some shopping on shore and a tanning session on the beach, and the two girls were eager to experiment with some underwater photography while snorkelling over a reef. They found a woman who was holding a sign for their expedition. Hannah waited there as Caitlin ran to her father on the opposite side of the hall to collect the camera. She slid to an abrupt halt when she noticed Michael and Chloe standing next to him.

"Hi." She almost stuttered.

"Hi yourself," Michael said.

"You know each other?" Russell asked.

"We shared a jet ski ride yesterday," Michael told him. Then to Caitlin: "Catch you later, back on the ship?"

"Maybe after I play."

"Play what?"

"Caitlin entertains in the Art Gallery every afternoon," Russell said.

Michael gaped. "You're her? The piano player everyone's talking about?" Caitlin blushed and couldn't answer. "Holy sh... cow!" he continued. "Okay if I catch your act?"

"I guess," Caitlin said.

"Great. See you then."

"See you."

Emily came running up next to Chloe, who said goodbye to Michael, breaking the tension. They set off in search of the queue for the trail bike ride and found it already heading for the buses in the parking lot. Jacob Shaffer looked resigned as he followed along. Caitlin started toward the line-up for snorkelling and suddenly realized she had forgotten the camera. She ran back for it, ignoring her father's raised eyebrows and sidelong glance toward Michael.

Grant Keillor and Al Barclay walked up to the golf kiosk and joined MacInnes. It was a rare occasion when the three would be seen together in public for any length of time. Barclay and Keillor refused an offer of rental clubs. Keillor explained to the agent that he was the designated caddie. MacInnes paid for the use of a powered golf cart, and they left the hall and found the kiosk where the carts were stored. There they found Carman Russo already waiting for them, a rented golf bag at his feet.

Deanna checked in with Elizabeth and her daughter Emily, where the line-up for the Eco Kayak Safari adventure was already moving toward their bus. Satisfied that everything was under control, she found Jessica and they left the pier to scope out the shopping possibilities.

Just another carefree day in paradise.

Thirty-five:
Planning

Carman Russo teed up on the par four ninth hole and hooked an errant shot into the rough. He swore, and Grant Keillor barely managed to stifle a laugh. They began walking toward the green. Arch MacInnes followed in the motorized cart. He coasted up to his ball and climbed out to take his second shot, landing just inches short of the hole for a kick-in birdie.

Carman's second attempt found the fairway, but his third, with a nine iron, rolled a dozen yards past the green on a downhill slope. MacInnes carded a birdie three and waited while Carman fumbled his way to a double bogie. They all climbed into the cart and pulled to one side of the green, waving for a foursome behind them to play through.

"Sharma's on his own today," Keillor observed. "His security chief didn't go with him. Wish we'd known that would happen."

"Probably just as well," MacInnes said. "It's too soon. Did you talk to the crew member that Charlotte found?"

"Caught him on his way to supervise the Sports Deck. Seemed like an okay guy for a black boy, a Jamaican. Charlotte chose well. I'm almost sorry for what's going to happen to him."

"Can't be helped. Did you give him half the money?"

"Yes, and I went over everything we need him to do. He asked a few questions and said that Charlotte had been a little vague about what would happen later. I managed to reassure him, especially the part about no one on the ship finding out he was involved."

"He's the weak link," Barclay observed.

"Relax," Carman said. "Leave him to me. I'll take care of him, and we'll all be in the clear."

"What if he gets cold feet?"

"Won't happen," Keillor said. "I told him he was in for an extra bonus in addition to what Charlotte promised him if everything goes smoothly. It's a sure thing."

"Grant, you're a babe in the woods," MacInnes said. "Nothing's ever a *sure thing*. It's the human element that's likely to rear up and bite you in the ass in a deal like this. Okay, forget it! Look, I've decided to stay in my cabin while it all goes down. It's best if no one sees me. You two have to go to ground before noon, too."

"I don't see why," Barclay complained. "Everyone will think it was an accident."

"You better hope so. But a hundred things could go wrong, someone in the wrong place when it happens, the security guy, Pelletier, does something unexpected, or someone spots Carman's boat. We can't let anyone connect us to what's gonna happen. Now how about the timing? Noon, right?"

"The ten o'clock video conference is the most important event on Sharma's schedule," Keillor said. "All the media reps will be in the big dining hall, and everyone has to clear out in time for lunch to be served at twelve fifteen. If Sharma follows his usual routine, he'll take a break then. That's when it goes down."

"And if he doesn't? What if he decides to leave the ship and join the family on the beach?"

"He won't get off. I'll be at the departure ramp to make sure."

"How about Pelletier, the security guy?"

"Ten to one, Sharma will let him go to lunch. That's been the pattern every other day."

"Are you sure the wife and kid will be on the island then?"

"That's my job," Barclay said. "I'll see to it tonight. I've already made up the invitations."

MacInnes turned to Keillor again. "Are you sure we can depend on the Jamaican dude to do what he was told?" he said. "And Carman, you have to be far away before anyone in authority gets there to investigate."

"No sweat," Carman said. "My boat's plenty fast."

"Let's run through it again. Start with when you anchor on the other side of the island."

For the next ten minutes the men picked at the details of their plan, looking for weak spots. "All right guys, it should work," MacInnes said at last. Another foursome was approaching the tee, and he put the golf cart in motion. "Nine holes enough for you? I'm a little bored, given such pathetic competition."

"Up yours," Carman muttered. They headed for the club house.

Thirty-six:
Friends

Almost everyone was back on board by mid-afternoon. Michael Griffin attended Caitlin's four o'clock performance in the Art Gallery, making her uncharacteristically nervous. As sometimes happened with new acquaintances, she feared her display of talent might scare him off, but she needn't have worried. When the session was over, they wandered off to the upper deck for a snack, and to formulate some plans for that evening, following Caitlin's gig on stage with the ship's band.

* * *

Caitlin was almost late for supper. The Sheridans, Elizabeth and Chloe met up with Deanna Watkins and her daughters in the Lido. As usual, Vachan Sharma was needed elsewhere. They found a table large enough for eight and compared notes on the day's adventures. Over dessert the conversation shifted to Caitlin's experience with the ship's band.

"What kind of music are you going to play tonight?" Deanna asked.

"Rock, mostly," Caitlin said. "I'm finished in the Mozarteum at quarter to eight, and I'll invite everyone to go to the auditorium before I leave. That'll be a shock to the straight crowd."

"*Straight* crowd?" Russell said. He turned to Jessica in mock alarm. "I told you she'd go over to the Dark Side, didn't I?" Then to the others: "The stage name they gave her is *Jailbait*."

"Relax, dear," Jessica said.

"My Dad thinks I'll chuck the classics now," Caitlin said. "I keep telling him that I'll go back to them, after DeeZee and I shack up for a few years."

"Caitlin!" Russell was apoplectic, and his wife and daughter both burst out laughing.

"She sure knows how to push your buttons," Elizabeth said.

"When this cruise is over, she's off to convent school," Russell muttered. "In Siberia."

Deanna said, "If that's the worst you ever hear from her, you'll be lucky." She looked pointedly at her daughters, and Hannah blushed. Emily, still a bit naïve, just grinned.

"I have to run, get ready to play for the seven o'clock crowd," Caitlin said, getting up. She called back over her shoulder to her Dad as she escaped into the corridor. "The band goes on third, about eight-twenty, so be sure you aren't late. I'll just have time to change first… into my red bikini."

Thirty-seven:
Russell and Jessica

Caitlin's parents stood close to the back wall in the upper balcony, far enough behind the box seats to allow quiet conversation without disturbing anyone. Below them on the brightly lit stage, four couples engaged in sensuous, complex choreography to the rhythm of a guitar and bass duo. In the foreground the charismatic DeeZee delivered rapid-fire hip-hop lyrics to the delight of the crowd. Russell was apprehensive, given the often pornographic content of the genre, although to that point the entertainment had been strictly vanilla.

The number concluded and the dancers became stagehands, helping to bring the band's equipment front and center. The musicians' costumes were eclectic, ranging from Bazoo's grunge persona to the bass player's ragged skinny jeans and dangerously low-cut tank top. Jason seemed comfortable with his preppie look, but it was Mouse and Caitlin whose entrance attracted the most attention.

"Oh my God," Russell murmured. "Did you know about this?"

"I had nothing to do with it," Jessica said. "But what's the problem?"

"The *problem* is her *age*! She looks like she could be walking the streets."

"You're exaggerating," Jessica said. "It's just show biz."

"So you're okay with this? Where did she get that stuff, anyway?"

"She told me the band has a costume trunk, and asked if it was okay if she, quote, 'went a little wild.' What was I supposed to say?"

"You could have said *no*!"

Jessica laughed. "Stop acting like a father."

Mouse and Caitlin might have been sisters, both in brief denim cut-offs over distressed metallic fishnet tights. Caitlin's sleeveless top was cropped to within millimetres of her diminutive breasts. Her hair was tossed in a wild mop; dark black makeup surrounded her eyes and black lip gloss completed the look. They took their places, Mouse at stage center and Caitlin at the piano to the left, side on to the audience with her sleek, slender legs too much on display for Russell's comfort.

"*Jailbait!*" he grumbled. "I'm *so* not ready for this."

Bazoo stepped up to the microphone. "Y'all having a good time out there?" he bellowed into the mike, and the younger members of the crowd cheered. "We're 'Cinnamon Skin,' and I'm Bazoo, chief skinhead."

Russell wondered if the man was conscious of the current neo-Nazi connotation associated with his assumed nickname.

"Behind me on the drums," Bazoo continued, "is that legendary Neanderthal, DeeZee, with Jason and his nimble fingers on the synthesizer. Lynx gets down on the bass… (she nodded and struck a raucous chord) …and up front we have the inimitable Mouse, she of the velvet voice. Over on the grand and fresh from Carnegie Hall, that's our newest member, Jailbait. Kick it off, sweetheart."

Caitlin smiled and launched into eight bars of the well-known "Ode to Joy" theme from Beethoven's Ninth Symphony, in elegant early nineteenth century style. Drowning out her last chord, the band blasted the theme back at her, fuzz guitar and DeeZee's fortissimo rock beat filling the hall. Bazoo soloed first, then Jason poured fistfuls of chords into the high register. DeeZee took a four-bar break to set up for Caitlin.

Russell watched his diminutive daughter in startled amazement as she wove Beethoven's classic theme into an inventive jazz-rock solo that raced up and down the keys for sixteen bars. Then, at a signal from Bazoo, the band gave her free reign for another sixteen, and the audience roared.

"She looks so tiny," Jessica said to Russell as the entire band came together again.

"How does she do that?" Russell said. "She's making it up as she goes along, isn't she?"

"You know I don't understand her gift. She *hears* it first, I guess, inside her head. She's always been a perfect mimic, only now it's more than that. I asked her teacher about it once, and she told me that improvisation is just instantaneous composition. Not only jazz and rock players can do it, but Mozart too, Leonard Bernstein, Andre Previn—and other serious musicians whose names I can't remember."

The band finished the Beethoven pastiche and began their featured slow ballad, *Midnight Solitaire*, with Mouse on the vocal and Caitlin painting a gentle frame around the lyric at the low end of the keyboard. Jessica motioned for Russell to follow her out into the hall where they could talk more easily.

"She's growing up so fast," she said. "Isn't it time for us to tell her?"

Russell sighed. "We've been all over this, more than once."

"It just seems wrong to me. She has the right to know the circumstances of her birth."

"She knows that she was born in Ontario while we were on a trip. She knows that's why her birth certificate reads Toronto. She knows about the emergency. What else could we possibly tell her?" His eyes shifted toward their daughter. "We agreed to keep the rest to ourselves."

"I know. But she's been asking questions about why she has this special talent when the best you and I can do is pick out one-finger tunes. One day I found her researching genetics on the internet, half a dozen sites about how talent is passed down in families, like Mozart's father being a composer. Bach came from a long line of professional musicians too."

"And Leonard Bernstein's father was a businessman who didn't want his son to study music. Stephen Sondheim's dad was a dress manufacturer, and his mother was an interior decorator. I looked them up."

"Try to tell Caitlin all that."

"Next time she brings this up, you let me know, and I damn well *will* tell her. Are you suggesting that we should have ignored her talent just because it doesn't run in our families?"

"No, of course not."

"Even though she isn't interested in going into medicine, she's everything I ever wanted in a daughter, smart beyond measure and already a world class performer. And she's no prima donna. Look how she hides her talent from her friends, afraid they'll think she's stuck up or something. She does everything she can to seem normal—or what she thinks is normal, anyway."

"You're right. She's a great kid, a little too hyper maybe, but with a good set of values. And she's dedicated to using her talent in all the right ways."

"Until tonight, maybe," Russell said.

"This won't do her any harm. She's just having fun, and it's good for her. I can't believe that being a pop musician would be enough to satisfy her in the long run. She loves serious piano literature too much."

"All the more reason not to bring up the past," Russell said. "Why rock the boat?"

"Last month she asked if she could see her birth certificate."

"And?"

"I dug it out her and showed it to her."

"Did that set her mind at ease?"

"I doubt it. She didn't say anything, but I could tell the wheels were turning in her head. I'm sure she knows that words on a piece of paper can sometimes hide the facts."

"Jessica, don't make a big thing out of it. If we tell her what happened now, it could lead to all sorts of problems."

"I can't help it. It just seems wrong."

The band wound up the ballad and launched into a heavy metal wall of sound, as subtle as a nuclear explosion. Jessica and Russell re-entered the theatre and watched their daughter rocking along with her new friends, clearly having a ball. In her outrageous outfit she was the center of attention, having found a whole new avenue for communicating with youngsters her own age and loving every minute of it.

She's happy, Jessica thought. *But what if she finds out the truth by herself?*

* * *

Caitlin vanished following the performance and didn't return until nearly midnight. Armed with cold cream and infinite patience, Jessica faced her in the suite's bathroom, transforming her daughter from a rock star into a pretty young teen once again.

"Where did you disappear to?" Jessica asked.

"I met up with a friend. I told Dad. He said it was okay."

"I know that much. He told me. But just exactly who is this friend, and where did you go?"

"Dad met him. His name is Michael, and we went to the Teen Deck, that's all. Did you hear the song Mouse wrote?" Caitlin said to change the subject. "*Midnight Solitaire*? It's a great melody, and the words are *deep*, you know? All about love and loss, and about having to live with the decisions you make. I have thoughts like that sometimes, only I can't express them like she did."

"She has a really nice voice," Jessica said.

"Yeah, but her *song*... What she *wrote*. That's like... It's like Mozart's fortieth symphony, his next-to-last one, and it makes me so sad whenever I hear it. It doesn't have words, but it sounds just like he knew he'd die soon, with too little time for everything he wanted to say with his music. It... He..."

Jessica tilted a hand mirror so Caitlin could see her face, now devoid of the heavy makeup. "There's my beautiful girl again."

"Thanks," Caitlin said. "So, what did you think of Mouse's song?"

"Very pretty."

Caitlin tilted her head to one side and stared fixedly into her mother's eyes. Jessica realized she had said the wrong thing, her understanding of the music and of Caitlin's reaction to it sadly inadequate. She didn't know how to remedy her gaffe. But Caitlin's quizzical look melted into a tolerant smile and she wrapped her arms around her mother's waist and hugged her.

"Thanks, Mom," she said. "For everything. Especially for getting Dad to let me play tonight."

And so to bed, anticipating the last full day of the short maiden cruise of the *Santiago Vagabundo* and a return to Caracola Cay—the site of Chloe's first swimming lesson, and the promise of another delicious beachside barbeque.

Thirty-eight:
Invitations

Robbie and Claire Hadley were climbing into bed when their mother returned from an impromptu bridge game in the Pelican Library. She plucked a small envelope from the information slot beside the door and carried it inside. She opened the envelope and discovered two complimentary invitations for a jet ski ride, leaving from next to the pier on Caracola Cay at one o'clock the following afternoon.

Robbie sat up in bed, eyeing the envelope. "What's up, Mom?"

"Looks like you and your sister get to ride one of the jet skis tomorrow. Interested?"

"Oh, boy, you bet!"

* * *

Spencer Haas gripped his invitation tightly. "Can I go? It says one o'clock on the island."

"Aren't those things dangerous?" his mother asked her husband.

"The invitation is signed by the Captain," Spencer's dad Jeremiah said. "I'm sure it's okay."

"I watched the skis when we were on the island a couple of days ago," Spencer said. "They give you a life jacket, and you sit right behind the driver. Anyway, I can swim good." He turned to his father. "Can I go, Dad?"

"Don't see why not. Is it okay if your mother and I come along and watch?"

* * *

Fourteen-year-old Jeff Danker went to bed at ten-thirty, his jet ski invitation tucked under his pillow. He was looking forward to being on Caracola Cay well ahead of the one o'clock appointment. His parents had okayed the excursion, mainly on the strength of the wording contained in the invitation: "... piloted by an experienced Chilean America staff member."

* * *

Ramona Vicario had just managed to put her nine-year-old twins, Juanita and Diego, to sleep in their stateroom when her husband Aarón arrived back from the Fitness Center. He was carrying a small envelope.

"Found this by the door," he said softly to his wife, so as not to wake the children. He sprawled on the settee and put his feet up on the coffee table. He tore open the envelope and drew out two cards. "It's a couple of complimentary tickets for the kids to ride a jet ski."

"We have reservations for the glass-bottom boat at ten," Ramona said.

"This is for one. We'll be back in time."

"How about lunch?"

"We can eat before or after. The barbeque stays open until two-thirty, and the ride can't be that long."

"They must be inviting every kid on the ship," Ramona said. "That'll be a mob scene."

"I don't think so." Aarón passed the cards to her. "See, it's handwritten on the ship's stationery and says *Special Invitation Just For You* at the top."

"Why us? We're not VIPs. In fact, I heard one of the dining room waiters call our deck 'steerage,' and it didn't sound like a compliment."

"A lottery maybe? Whatever, let's let the kids do it. Diego wanted to when we were here the first time, but the lines were too long. Maybe that's why they're using invitations now."

"Anything you say, *querido*. Just don't try to get *me* on one of those things."

* * *

"Did you arrange this?" Elizabeth Wu asked her husband, showing him the invitation. He had just returned to their suite after a marathon session with a news anchor from the CTV network.

"What's it say?" Sharma asked.

"It's for Chloe, a ticket to take a jet ski ride tomorrow."

"I don't know anything about it. But when we boarded the ship, the Excursion Director asked if there was anything she could set up for us. I told her it wasn't necessary, but maybe she took it on herself to come up with this. I doubt that Chloe will want to go, though. She loves our boat, but avoids anything scary to do with being *in* the water."

"Her new friends have been helping her learn to swim. Maybe she'll risk it."

"You should go with her to make sure it will be safe."

"How about your interview?" Elizabeth said. "Jacob will keep an eye on her."

"Do you really want to sit through another boring media scrum?" Sharma asked. "It'll be the same old hype that you've heard dozens of times. You deserve some time off. As long as you and Chloe are beside me for the closing banquet tomorrow night, that'll be good enough. Where is Chloe, anyway? It's after midnight."

"In the library, playing chess with a boy she and Caitlin met," Elizabeth said. Sharma raised his eyebrows. "Relax," she continued, "Jacob is there too, and I met the boy. He's a couple of years older, but very polite. I got the impression he's in awe of her. He's won a few championships himself, but she's skunked him twice so far. I think she might have a crush on him, but he treats her a bit like a little sister which annoys her, so she doesn't cut him any slack."

"Did you give her a curfew?"

"An informal one, one o'clock at the latest. After all, the cruise is almost over. I'll tell her about the ski ride when she gets back."

Thirty-nine:
One More Day

The final day of a cruise is bittersweet. There is still much to do for diversion, tailored to those who seek the excitement of interesting excursions. Others simply wish to soak up the ambiance of a tropical paradise by lounging about in surroundings far different from home turf, trying to forget that in less than twenty-four hours it will all be over.

The Cruise Director assembles the entertainment staff, who spend the afternoon in rehearsal for an evening extravaganza on stage. The chefs and kitchen crew go all out to produce an incomparable menu for a gala evening meal. Flyers appear in staterooms, touting wonderful end-of-journey bargains to be found in the shops during the final sprint to home port. The crew members responsible for shore activities gird themselves for their busiest day.

Children awake early, determined to wring every second's worth of enjoyment from the remaining hours of their adventure. Parents fret over finding time to pack, and how much gratuity to leave for the cabin stewards.

Last day.

* * *

Caitlin, Hannah, Chloe and Emily reached the Lido Deck early, impatiently awaiting the first breakfast call. When the blinds around the buffet went up, they loaded their plates, found a table, and exchanged plans and gossip and whispered giggles about the cute boys they hoped to encounter on the beach; one cute boy in particular. The adults were more relaxed, anticipating a relaxing day in the sun or last-minute sales in the onshore kiosks. For the more adventurous or physically inclined, a wide variety of expeditions beckoned on the island and in the surrounding water.

Two of the passengers had a more specific agenda to follow, some split-second timing to arrange, and some details to attend to. Arch MacInnes was apprehensive, Grant Keillor less so. He had been in similar situations before. With one minor reservation, he had confidence in his compatriots' ability to carry out their assignments. He anticipated complete success before the ship re-boarded for the overnight return to Fort Lauderdale. He knew, however, that the trip was sure to be delayed, the captain having to deal with officialdom who would be called in to investigate events involving VIP passengers from Nova Scotia while they were anchored near beautiful Caracola Cay.

By nine o'clock Caitlin and her friends were clustered near the stairway leading to the exit. They were determined to be first aboard the tender, first on the beach, first into the water. They revelled in their freedom, parents left behind in staterooms or lingering over extra cups of coffee or tea. The adults were anticipating time on their own, content to consign their offspring to the safety and supervision of the ship's crew and recreation staff.

* * *

Before the first tender arrived on Caracola Cay, Akoni Clarke, a shaved-head young black man wearing a monogrammed cruise line tee shirt and ball cap, met with the crew assigned to operate the fleet of Jet Skis. "The boss told me to give you guys a hand," he told them. "A bunch of kids have special invitations for rides at one, and I'm supposed to take up the slack. Anybody want to take an extra long lunch break?"

The crew members grinned at him. "How about all of us?" one said.

Clarke laughed. "Work it out among yourselves. I'll be here about twelve thirty. Make sure the gas tanks are full, okay?"

"You've got it, m'man. Have fun."

* * *

On board the ship, the last of the breakfast crowd exited the main dining room to make way for the arrival of media technicians and their bank of cameras and microphones. Vachan Sharma arrived with his Chief of Security, Darryl Pelletier, for his most important interview of the cruise. It would be streamed live to his home Province and rebroadcast nationally on the evening news of the three Canadian networks, CBC, CTV and Global.

The opening topic would be a glowing review of the accommodations aboard the *Santiago Vagabundo*, a gratuitous tip of the hat to give the cruise line free publicity in return for the hospitality the politician's entourage had enjoyed. It was sure to increase the company's profile in a northern country where large numbers of the population regularly sought escape from winter weather on the high seas. But the main purpose was to enhance Sharma's image on the national stage of Canada, for the man's ambitions extended beyond his east coast constituency. He believed that the office of Prime Minister of Canada was not out of his reach at some point in the future.

Minutes before the interview was to begin, Sharma called Pelletier to his side. "Darryl," he said, "I think we'll be safe in keeping this as informal as possible. I don't need you here. Why don't you take off now and have a cup of coffee? You deserve some time to yourself, and I'll be perfectly safe." He smiled, a trace of fatigue veiling his eyes.

"Where will I find you?" Pelletier asked.

"I'll need some quiet time back in the suite when this is over. The family is heading for the island, and I might even sleep for an hour or so. I'll call your stateroom when I need you again."

"Okay, if you're sure. I'll be ready any time." Pelletier gathered up his clipboard and left the room.

Last day.

Forty:
Ashore

The ship's tenders plied back and forth, disgorging vacationers onto the pier where they hurried off in search of sea and sand. Boisterous water games echoed joyfully among the palms. At the near end of the beach, younger children scampered up the ladder of an impressively tall and twisty water slide and screamed delightedly as they plummeted into three feet of water under the watchful eyes of lifeguards. Snorkelers cruised back and forth among the rocks and pilings of the jetty, and inexpert beginners fought to remain upright on paddle boards near the ropes that defined the swimming area.

At ten o'clock, members of the Jet Ski crew began firing up the fleet of green and black machines, and children lined up for rides. The crew distributed life jackets, ensured that the children strapped them on correctly, and invited them aboard, two kids behind each of the pilots. They were soon racing up and down the curved coastline, back and forth between the pier and a headland that marked the limit of the cove. The skilful pilots executed sliding turns, bounced over each other's wakes, and generally gave the riders the kinds of thrills they would remember as a highlight of the cruise.

At twelve-thirty the public address system announced the opening of the barbeque, which triggered a gradual exodus in that direction. Laura Hadley and her husband Brent were at the far end of the beach, watching Robbie and Claire build sandcastles in the shallows.

"Let's go eat, kids," Laura called out.

Robbie jumped up and ran to them. "What time is it?"

"Twelve-thirty," his mother said.

"We won't have time before the ski ride!" Robbie said excitedly. "And if Claire eats before we go, she'll throw up."

"I will not!" Claire shouted, close on her brother's heels.

"He has a point," her dad said to her. "Remember last summer at Canada's Wonderland, when you had a hot dog just before getting on the roller coaster? *Très embarrassant.*"

Robbie laughed and Claire pouted.

"The lines stay open long enough," Laura said. "We can eat when the kids get back."

"Where's my reservation?" Claire asked.

"You probably left it back in our stateroom," Brent said.

Claire's face fell, and Laura poked her husband in the ribs. "Stop teasing the child." Then to her daughter, "I've got them in my backpack. Grab your towel and let's get going."

When they reached the pier area, most of the Jet Skis were out on the water, and the line-up of children awaiting turns was relatively short, many having headed to the barbeque pavilion. Akoni Clarke stood next to a large sign that advertised *Reservations*. He wore khaki shorts and a tee shirt sporting a handwritten name tag that identified him as Captain of the Watercraft Crew. One of the ship's souvenir ball caps perched on his head.

The Hadleys approached him. "Are we in the right place for the ski rides?" Laura asked.

"Names?" Clarke said cheerfully.

"Robbie and Claire Hadley."

"Put on your life vests," he said to the children. "We have to wait for the others to arrive."

Over the next five minutes, Jeff Danker, Spencer Haas, and the twins, Diego and Juanita Vicario arrived. Clarke handed out life belts. Chloe was last to appear, leading a reluctant Caitlin in her wake. Russell, Jessica and Elizabeth found places to stand under a sun umbrella nearby, accompanied by Jacob Shaffer, who had a medium-sized backpack slung over one shoulder.

Clarke counted heads, then took roll and collected the tickets.

"Should be just seven of you," he said, looking at Caitlin, who did not have an invitation.

"Told you," Caitlin said to Chloe.

"I can't go then," Chloe said.

"What's the problem? Clarke asked her.

"I don't swim so good. This is my friend Caitlin. I need her to go with me."

"This line is for special invitations only. Don't you want to go?"

"Not by myself."

"I'm sorry." Clarke picked up a whistle and blew it sharply. He held up four fingers, and four of the jet skis turned toward shore. When they coasted in close, their passengers got off.

Clarke glanced at his clipboard. "Robbie and Claire Hadley?" The two children stepped forward. "You two are going with Mateo on this one." He indicated the first ski in line, and the children scampered into the shallows where the crew member helped them to board the idling craft. Clarke sent Jeff Danker and Spencer Haas to the second ski and the Vicario twins to the third one. When all were aboard he called out, "You're good to go!" The three drivers powered up and turned toward the bay. They were quickly performing turns over each other's wakes, giving the children an exciting ride. Their parents moved closer to the shore to watch the fun.

Clarke turned toward Chloe. "You're supposed to go with me," he said.

"Thanks anyway, but no," she answered.

"I don't know what to do with you," he said. "I have my orders, invitations only."

Elizabeth approached him, and Jessica and Russell followed along. "What seems to be the problem?" she asked.

"I'm only supposed to give this one a ride," Clarke said, pointing to Chloe. "Invitations only," he repeated.

"She doesn't swim. She's nervous. Surely there's room enough on your machine for her friend to go too."

"That's not the issue."

Russell stepped forward and pointed at the man's name tag. "Mr. Clarke... Akoni, may I call you that? This says that you're in charge of this whole operation, is that right?" Clarke nodded. "Surely you have the authority to bend the rules a little. I believe the ship's captain would want you to keep all of the children happy."

Clarke looked uncertain. He glanced down the beach toward the far end of the island, shrugged, and came to a decision. "Grab your life belts," he said to both girls, "and climb on."

As Caitlin and Chloe cinched up their flotation devices and splashed toward the ski, Jacob Shaffer approached Elizabeth. "Ms. Wu," he said, "Darryl... uh, Mr. Pelletier said you'd be okay here with your friends while Chloe is out on the water, and that I could get some lunch at the barbeque now. Is that okay with you?"

"Of course, Jacob, we'll be fine. Take your time."

"Thanks." Shaffer crossed the sand and climbed the low rise that separated the beach from the concrete paths leading to the pavilion. He found a sign that pointed toward the barbeque area. With a quick look behind him, where Elizabeth and the others were watching activity in the cove, he turned and hurried off in the opposite direction.

With Chloe and Caitlin securely on board, Akoni Clarke put his machine in gear and moved out from the shore, then turned parallel to the coast and advanced the throttle. The ski reared up and spouted a tall plume of spray into the air. It sped off in the direction of the headland, threading among the other craft that were doing manoeuvres in the bay. Clarke cut a series of figure eights and drew parallel to Mateo's craft, and the two raced away side by side, criss-crossing back and forth to bounce over each other's wakes.

When they reached the open sea off the end of the island, all four skis turned and came roaring back at high speed, not slowing down until they neared the pier. Caitlin and Chloe wore happy smiles on their faces as the machines settled low in the water and came around abreast. Clarke raised one hand high in the air, then chopped down sharply in a prearranged signal, and the machines dropped to idle, rocking in the waves.

Elizabeth Wu and Caitlin's parents sat watching, side by side on pilings next to the pier.

"She's not a little girl anymore," Jessica observed.

"Neither of them," Elizabeth said.

"Can't stop time," Russell agreed. "She's always in such a damn hurry, wants to try everything and do it *now*."

"I'm so glad you convinced the driver to take Caitlin too," Elizabeth said. "Chloe was too timid to go without her. She looks like she's having a wonderful time."

"I'm so glad," Jessica said. "Caitlin's fearless. I guess I told you that she engineered this whole trip as a present for us. With a little help from her grandfather Orrin, that is."

"Speaking of Orrin," Russell said, "I wish he had come along too."

"You know he wouldn't leave Marjorie for that long." Jessica turned toward Elizabeth. "That's his wife, Caitlin's grandmother. She's essentially helpless after a series of strokes."

"She doesn't even recognize him anymore," Russell said, "or know who's taking care of her. And the nurse, Ms. Hulse is it? She's wonderfully capable. He could have left her in charge for a week."

"He'd have been worried sick."

"He needs to get away once in a while. I'm not sure he's looking after himself as well as he should."

With their skis still out of gear, the drivers blipped their throttles, announcing the next phase of the adventure. The children, Chloe included, were waving toward shore wildly, eyes alight with excitement as the pilots manoeuvred into a single row, side by side.

"Everybody hang on tight!" Akoni Clarke shouted. "Here we go, one, two, *three!*" The engines roared and the bows came up as the pilots leaned forward to bring them up on plane. They took off back the way they came, racing each other, then peeled off to weave in and out like military jet aircraft. They formed a single line and disappeared behind the distant headland. When they fell quiet and didn't reappear immediately, Russell stood up and moved to the edge of the water. He shaded his eyes against the glare of the sun.

"Where'd they go?" he said.

"Behind that hill," Jessica said.

"But I can't hear them anymore. Why'd they slow down?"

Just then the engines roared to life once more, and the first of them emerged, racing into the cove. Russell relaxed and sank back on his piling.

Forty-one:
Jet Skis

The children screamed in pleasure. Leaving the beach area behind, the skis flew toward the far end of the island, where they executed a series of intricate turns that soaked the riders and left them breathless. They coasted around the end of the island, out of sight of the beach. The drivers throttled back and formed up once more, this time single file about twenty meters apart. Clarke eased up beside Mateo's craft.

"Got a problem," Clarke told the other man. "She's idling rough, trying to cut out. Think I've got some dirty gas."

"What you gon' do, mon? Mateo said.

"The rest of you go back. I'll pull in close to shore and try to clear the line. If I'm not back in ten, send the launch." Akoni Clarke shoved his ski away and signalled the others, and one by one they reared up and sprinted for the return trip.

When the third ski cleared the headland, Clarke turned his ski abruptly and steered in the opposite direction.

* * *

Back near the pier, Russell spotted the second of the Jet Skis emerging from behind the headland, and then the third, but when the fourth didn't follow along, his face creased in a frown.

"Which one's missing?" he said.

"Can't tell," Jessica said, but as the three skis neared the pier, it became apparent that it was Akoni Clarke who hadn't returned.

"What's going on?" Elizabeth said.

Russell waded out into the surf as the three machines coasted toward the shore. "Where's the other one?" he called out to the closest driver, Mateo.

"He have engine trouble, mon," Mateo answered in his rich Jamaican accent. "They not come soon, we send a launch, bring your kids back. No worries."

The pilots helped the rest of the children down from the skis, and they ran onto the sand, exhilarated by their adventure. Mateo secured his craft. "Got to get m'radio," he said. The others shut their engines off and the three men crossed the sand and headed for the reception centre that stood among the kiosks that lined the plaza.

"I don't like this," Russell said. "Why didn't they go back with skis to get them?"

"I'm sure it's okay," Jessica said. "These people all seem very professional."

"I sure as hell hope so." He walked a few paces down the sand and was straining for any sight of the missing ski when the dull thump of a massive explosion split the air. Smoke and debris erupted from behind the headland, and Russell took off running down the beach toward a flame-tinged cloud of smoke that billowed into the sky.

Forty-two:
Aftermath

ONE DEAD, TWO MISSING IN
VACATION ISLAND TRAGEDY
Jeffrey Dahl, The Associated Press

FORT LAUDERDALE, Florida – A massive explosion that rocked a Bahamian island Friday afternoon has claimed the life of a Chilean America Cruise Lines crew member, tentatively identified as a Jamaican national. The body has been recovered, along with the remains of the Kawasaki Jet Ski he was operating. A spokesperson for the Coast Guard reported that two children who were riding behind the pilot are missing and presumed dead.

The two-thousand-passenger ship Santiago Vagabundo was anchored off Caracola Cay on the final day of its maiden voyage. Authorities have withheld the identities of the missing children at the request of their families. The ship was delayed for several hours before returning to port in Fort Lauderdale following the tragedy.

* * *

MYSTERY DEEPENS OVER
JET SKI EXPLOSION
Jeffrey Dahl, The Associated Press

FORT LAUDERDALE, Florida – An official representative of Chilean America Cruise Lines has identified the employee who was involved in an apparently accidental explosion of a Kawasaki Jet Ski on a private island in the Bahamas. "His name is Akoni Clarke," said Enrico Sanchez, Human Resources

Director for Chilean America, who expressed condolences to the man's family. The company has also sent regrets to the families of the second and third victims, two as yet unidentified young girls who were riding on the machine at the time of the mishap. Their bodies have not been recovered.

* * *

DAUGHTER OF NS POLITICIAN
MISSING IN CRUISE SHIP DISASTER
Megan Rumboldt, The Canadian Press

FORT LAUDERDALE, Florida – Authorities have released the names of two children presumed dead off the coast of the Bahamian island of Caracola Cay. Chloe Sharma, daughter of Nova Scotia Provincial NDP leadership candidate Vachan Sharma and his wife, Elizabeth Wu, is missing after a watercraft on which she was riding exploded, killing the operator. The second child is identified as Caitlin Sheridan, daughter of Russell and Jessica Sheridan of Bournemouth, Nova Scotia. Caracola Cay is a private resort leased by Chilean America Cruise Lines. The company has promised a full investigation into the tragedy.

Chloe Sharma was a middle school student in her hometown of Bedford, well known as a championship chess competitor. Her father is considered the front-runner in a bid to become leader of the Provincial New Democratic Party. Polls suggest that due to his popularity with the voters, he would be favoured to lead the Party to success in the upcoming election.

Caitlin Sheridan was well known to the Canadian arts community, a promising young pianist whose talent first came to public attention when she was just five years old. Thirteen at the time of the tragedy, she made her Carnegie Hall debut in New York at age nine, and subsequently appeared with the Toronto and London Symphonies.

* * *

LOCAL GIRL VICTIM
OF TERRORISM

Margaret Wilson, The Bournemouth Bugle

FORT LAUDERDALE, Florida – Caitlin Sheridan, daughter of Dr. and Mrs. Russell Sheridan of Bournemouth, has died after a terrorist attack on a remote island in the Bahamas. Caitlin, well-known to local residents as a wizard of the piano, was competing in the International Festival of the Cays when a band of mercenaries stormed a local beach and set off a series of violent explosions. The perpetrators of the crime have so far eluded police.

* * *

JET SKI OPERATOR
HAD VIOLENT PAST

Jeffrey Dahl, The Associated Press

FORT LAUDERDALE, Florida – The operator of a Kawasaki Jet Ski that exploded off the coast of Caracola Cay in the Bahamas had a criminal record, according to investigators. Omario Lewis, a Jamaican national who worked under the alias Akoni Clarke, served a total of five and a half years in prison for drug possession and related offenses until his escape in 2016. His whereabouts were unknown until fingerprints taken during the autopsy of his body revealed his true identity.

Caracola Cay is leased by Chilean America Cruise Lines as a private destination for its Caribbean passengers. The company denies any knowledge of Lewis's earlier involvement with the law and reported him to be a capable and diligent employee. The watercraft on which he and two young passengers were riding has been recovered. It is the subject of a forensic examination to determine the cause of the explosion.

The bodies of the missing children have not been recovered.

* * *

CHRONICLE HERALD OBITUARIES
Halifax, Nova Scotia
SHERIDAN, Caitlin Aileen—

Age 13, of Bournemouth, Lunenburg County, daughter of Russell and Jessica Sheridan; from accidental causes. There will be no visitation and no funeral by request of the family. A Celebration of Life will be held in the Irvine University Convocation Hall at a later date.

Forty-three:
Logbook, *Versteck*

March 08, 15:47:53 G.M.T.
Position: 26° 17'52" N 85° 39'27" W
Fuel Reserve: 7/8
Seas calm, winds southwest and light, skies cloudy.

A beautiful, promising light has been extinguished. What a waste! Any death is a tragedy, but for one so young to be the victim of such senseless catastrophe is unthinkable. Caitlin Sheridan was so alive, so vital, and had so much to offer. What possible twist of fortune could have conspired to snuff out all that potential? What treasured performances might she have offered the world, had she not been taken away so needlessly?

Mortality: momentous on an individual level but commonplace and universal in the overall scheme of existence. Worldwide, more than a hundred and fifty thousand people pass away each day, perhaps a staggering sixty million annually, only to be replaced by well over twice that many live births. Some consider humanity's unchecked fertility to be a plague that threatens irrevocable damage to the viability of the planet.

But these are just statistics. Life goes on, even if individual lives do not. Death is imponderable, while just to be alive, to be here in the midst of so much wonder, tempts one to ask the ultimate question.

Why does anything exist?

If there is an answer, a purpose to it all, it has escaped the world's greatest philosophers thus far. And so, we invent a reason. Many call it God, known by whatever name one's culture assigns, or perhaps "prime mover" and even "the Big Bang," but simply assigning a name to something does not explain it.

Consider the suffix "–ology" that we attach to denote a field of learning: biology, the study of living organisms; geology, the investigation into the history and structure of the earth; psychology, the exploration of the human mind and behaviour.

Theology, the study of... what? In purely academic terms, it is an examination of religious practice. Fair enough. But in more common usage it is the study of the Divine, or God in his (her, its) various incarnations.

We may study biology, because we are surrounded by living things, concrete and available for inspection. We may study geology because the earth beneath us is accessible for scrutiny. We may study psychology, in the knowledge that there must be influences and reasons for why people act the way they do.

But to study theology in the specific context of the Divine is to assume that the Divine exists, without a shred of concrete evidence to support it. For example, do we accept as fact those ancient and contradictory texts, in all their multiple and questionable translations, that tell us who or what god (God) is? Is the Bible the indisputable word of some anthropomorphic creator? (It must be, because it says it is, right?) Are we to trust those erudite scholars who, in the late fourth century, gathered at the Council of Hippo? Were they celestially motivated when they compiled the western world's most revered religious book? (They must have been. They said they were.)

Imagine instead that when they met to debate which texts were worthy of inclusion in The Good Book, they were merely politicians, and for personal reasons were determined to include, for example, the Book of Revelation, but not the Gospels of Thomas or Nicodemus or (shudder) Judas. Maybe those learned sages were simply intent on preserving their own fundamental biases as to what constitutes Truth.

Were their beliefs inspired by personal contact with the Divine, or merely propaganda, disseminated by self-appointed prophets with agendas of their own? Risking a charge of heresy, only the brave would dare to suggest that those thinkers were campaigning for acceptance of the party line as handed down by their mentors, who in turn were following their own agendas, similarly handed down by others who came before them in order to achieve whatever goals would benefit them the most. And so on, and so on... Thus do personal beliefs become universal myth.

What texts did these learned men reject, and on what basis? If theology seeks answers to questions such as these, it is indeed a worthwhile pursuit. But if it presupposes that the solution to the fundamental question of our existence is "God," that forestalls any further investigation. We have the answer; why should we look further?

Once having lived, we find it hard to conceive of the universe continuing without us after we're gone, and yet we know that it does. Out of this inescapable certainty comes the widespread faith in, the hope for, an afterlife. It is a cornerstone of the vast majority of religions, despite no verifiable confirmation of spiritual continuity.

Our species is not unique; we share all basic characteristics with every other beast on the planet, down to the cellular level—including and especially our mortality. The human embryo in its early stages is virtually indistinguishable from that of a porpoise, a penguin, a puppy. That can't be an accident. Those who reject the concept of evolution are simply determined to ignore overwhelming evidence of the unity of life.

Once born, like other creatures we eat, we procreate, we defecate... and we die. And when life departs, our bodies decay into component chemical parts, akin to every other being on the planet. We are not different in that respect. But because we also think, *and can contemplate our existence on a level that we suppose to be superior to every other living thing, it is tempting to accept that we are imbued with something exceptional. Call it a spirit or soul or whatever; it supposedly takes us, and us alone, to some higher plane for all eternity after our bodies fail us.*

That is a comforting thought, one to which I wish I could subscribe. But it is wholly at odds with the sure and certain reality that everything dies eventually, including our planet itself. Why should we, an insignificant biped whose primary accomplishment is incredible fecundity, be different? Although the universe is thought to be unimaginably ancient—some say eternal—for all we know it too will eventually cease to exist. Eternity is the most callous of all myths, especially in its promise of heavenly reward.

We would like to be immortal, but believing we are does not make it so. Scientists cannot demonstrate survivability in any form, corporeal or spiritual, beyond death; neither can all the sermons in all the churches, temples, and mosques throughout the world. These institutions promise us an unlikely scenario of everlasting bliss in Paradise as a reward for our piety and service to the Divine.

It is a haven (Heaven) where we will live forever, in what must be mind-numbing boredom. Would I even have access to a piano to help me fill those empty hours in the Great Beyond? Imagine doing nothing but singing endless psalms in praise of a supposedly supernatural being that created us, year after eon after ever! That is not a credible answer to the most basic question that all thinking persons must entertain.

Why?

How much more realistic it is to accept that we are here for a finite time, and that our individuality is of no value other than our contribution to the totality of existence and its continuation. Only then will a piece of ourselves, our reason for being, live on in our influence over those who come after us. To cite just one example, does not a gifted teacher achieve the only true measure of immortality through the achievements of those students who carry on his or her legacy?

But who am I, Rolf Nobody, to speculate on such matters? I may be totally wrong. Is our world fundamentally purposeless, a simple accident in an unbelievably remote corner of the vast universe, and totally without meaning?

Or perhaps some extraterrestrial being is, at this very minute, shaking his (her, its) ancient head at the sin implicit in my lack of faith.

And does it matter?

—*Rolf Niemand, Captain*
SS Versteck

Forty-four:
Post-mortem

The four thousand square foot home at 34 Chestnut Street in suburban Bournemouth was unchanged on the outside, while to the Sheridans the interior was either claustrophobic or almost unbearably empty. Jessica requested indeterminate leave from the mental health clinic, while by contrast, Russell plunged into his normal routine at the Medical Centre immediately and avoided being at home any more than absolutely necessary. Day after day the couple awaited news that never came: the recovery of Caitlin's body. They retired each night unable to decide whether to be relieved or devastated. Until they knew for sure, they could hold out hope, however slim, that their beloved daughter had somehow escaped death and would be returned to them.

Their personal relationship deteriorated. It was as if they had lost the glue that cemented them together. They tended to communicate in meaningless monosyllables or not at all, and as a psychologist, Jessica was well aware of how often the death of a child resulted in divorce. Since their return from Florida, they had tried just once to experience intimacy. Having failed, they were both afraid to try again.

After the first few days, the investigation into the Jet Ski accident went nowhere. Forensic analysis identified C-4 plastic explosive as the cause, and the melted remnants of a miniature circuit board suggested what may have triggered the blast. Nevertheless, there seemed to be no possible motive for the crime, if indeed that's what it was.

Inquiries into the background of the ski driver, Omario Lewis, AKA Akoni Clarke, were similarly inconclusive. His parents had died on the highway when the boy was seven, and his subsequent shuffle through a series of substandard foster homes had done little to build his character.

After dropping out of school on his sixteenth birthday, he attached himself to the only family that would accept him, a Kingston, Jamaica street gang called *Santos Salvajes*, the Savage Saints. That was where his true education began.

He started his criminal career as a runner, a sacrificial lamb his compatriots set up to take the fall in the event a robbery or assault went wrong. Either by luck or circumstance, he survived long enough to be promoted up the ranks by El Padre, a putative Fagin who organized the troops and reaped the spoils of their raids. By the time he was nineteen, Omario had graduated to head a lucrative protection racket promising immunity for commercial establishments that coughed up a substantial percentage of their revenue at the end of every week.

His advancement through the ranks might have continued unimpeded, had not a rival gang member riddled his abdomen with buckshot in a territorial dispute. After recovering from his injuries while in police custody, he was convicted of enough charges to merit twenty-five years in jail. Lewis was no fool. Following a spectacular jail break he fled the country, changed his name, and used his native charm and a false ID to secure a position with Chilean America Cruise Lines. There he hoped to amass enough savings to enable him to return to his former profession, a sadder but wiser career criminal.

Falling under the spell of a beautiful woman named Charlotte Keillor led to his downfall before he could realize that dream.

Forty-five:
Rolf

I'm disoriented, restless, and without purpose. Day after day the earth rotates beneath me, relentless, uncaring, unstoppable. A fraction of a degree at a time, the northern hemisphere tilts more and more toward the sun, and as the average daily temperature rises, vacationers and snowbirds head back to Canada, to more temperate climes where they can escape the southern summer heat.

Life persists, unmindful of what has been lost.

After leaving the cruise ship there was nowhere I wanted to go, but nothing to keep me in Florida either. After a few days of aimless ennui, I'm now heading north up the west coast of that strange, flat, wet, elongated state, much of which the rising seas of climate change may soon render uninhabitable. After leaving the *Santiago Vagabundo*, I reclaimed my yacht and little Jenny and headed for Key Largo, where I bought provisions before rounding Cape Sable to drift out into the Gulf of Mexico. In no hurry, it took me several days to reach Everglades City, but there was nothing to keep me there either.

For the past seven years I haven't allowed anyone to get close to me. And now a pint-sized *wunderkind* has wormed her way under my skin, only to be taken away far too soon. It's an unimaginable loss; humanity will be the worse for it. And for some reason I can't banish her from my mind.

Gnothi Seauton, the ancient Greeks advised, echoing the inscription said to have been emblazoned on the Temple of Apollo at Delphi. *Know thyself.* I thought I did. Grief and loss are no strangers to me. I mourned my father's passing less than a year ago, news of which reached me via the internet when, through force of habit, I scanned the on-line obituaries from my hometown newspaper. But he has never haunted my dreams as Caitlin Sheridan does. I can't identify or explain the host of tiny details that call her to mind, as if I'd known her not for a couple of days, but forever.

Her voice is familiar, although I don't know who she reminds me of. Her shy dismissal of her incredible talent is more than simple modesty. She is truly humble, reminiscent of someone I think I should recognize but cannot. She is empathetic, an emotion I seldom feel but understand, having experienced it in abundance in the home of my parents and grandparents. Her lust for life inspires everyone fortunate enough to encounter her.

Or so it once did. I still can't convince myself to stop thinking of her in the present tense.

Who was she, really?

After leaving Everglades City I found the weather favourable and the winds light, with *Versteck* making a leisurely three knots up the coast off the Ten Thousand Islands. The autopilot managed the steering, leaving me free to attend to housekeeping duties topside—polishing the bright-work, sewing minor rents in the mizzen and spinnaker, and replacing several worn sheets, those stout ropes that connect to a boat's control systems.

Anything to keep busy; a yacht never leaves you alone. The sea and salt air constantly abrade the varnish and leave spots of corrosion on the cleats and winches. It won't be long before I have to haul her out to have the hull scraped and painted, forcing me to find land-based lodging until the work can be completed. My sea-loving cat will hate that.

I enjoy my solitude. I've spent far too many nights ashore, and a healthy store of cash on board from performing in coastal lounges and on the cruise has bought me an extended period of economic freedom. I have no desire to seek employment. I'll no doubt end up somewhere on the southern shore of the Florida panhandle, possibly Wakulla Beach or St. Teresa. Or if the unpredictable spring winds take me farther northwest, I might pull in at a major venue such as Pensacola, or even Mobile, Alabama. I haven't thought ahead any farther than that, not even to how long I might stay—a month or more, possibly a side trip to the Yucatan, then wherever. These decisions will be made by whim, of little import in the overall scheme of things.

* * *

The wind dropped off, and after leaving behind the larger islands north of Highland Point I encountered almost no seagoing traffic. The sails lay slack, and I allowed *Versteck* to drift close to the smaller mangrove swamps where I could watch for great blue herons, loggerhead turtles, and various species of migratory birds. I was hoping they might offer some distraction from my gloomy thoughts. Wildlife of all kinds are my preferred companions on a solitary voyage—plus Jenny the cat, of course.

With little to disturb the serenity of the scene, I was relaxing by the starboard rail with a thermos of coffee when I spotted a grey shape just below the surface, a manatee almost stationary in the shade cast by my boat. The large female's back was scarred by an encounter with a hull or propeller, but she seemed otherwise healthy. I couldn't help but wonder whether her existence was more satisfying to her than mine was to me.

A vast diversity of life pulses in the waters just beneath my keel, unaware of my presence as I am of theirs, except as an abstraction. In the overall scheme of things, marine life has nothing to do with me, other than providing an occasional meal when I bother to cast a baited line in my wake. As a solitary predator, I'm little threat to the survival of any species of fish, although I've lately come to regret that as a member of the greedy and uncaring human race, I'm part of the mass extinctions that continue to ravage so many parts of the globe.

I was nearly becalmed, and noticed that a second, somewhat

smaller and probably male manatee had come to lie almost motionless beside the first—a docile pair of gentle vegetarians, accustomed to dining on mangrove leaves, shoal grass, and other saltwater plants. Unlike my own kind, these placid giants were no threat to any ecosystem.

Upon closer inspection I could see a calf between them, shielded from possible shark attack by its parents' more massive bodies. I wished the youngster safe travels and a long, long life—a future denied to Caitlin Sheridan, the victim of whatever chain of events placed her on that doomed watercraft.

The sound of an engine echoed from the northeast, and presently a substantial trawler emerged from one of the narrow, twisted waterways that weave among the mangrove islands. As soon as the boat reached open water, the helmsman advanced the throttle and carved a sweeping turn south. His wake rocked my yacht but didn't disturb the manatees, and I was thankful that they stayed close until that lethal spinning prop was far away.

I was puzzled by whatever reason the boat's owner might have had to risk grounding in the shallow water between those islands. I knew from previous experience that there was almost nowhere a large boat could go in there. Perhaps he had anchored to spend a quiet night or to repair some engine malfunction; maybe fishing or simply napping. Given the depth of his keel, it was unlikely that he could have penetrated far into the maze of swamps and islets that kept this part of the Ten Thousand Islands uninhabited and mostly unvisited by tourists or sportsmen.

I decided to enter a waypoint on the GPS. If I were to come this way again, I might decide to lower the dinghy and explore the channel where the trawler emerged. If not, perhaps the manatees would find me again.

Around noon the wind freshened out of the south, and I cranked up the main and raised the spinnaker. The yacht began to make reasonable progress, averaging five and a half knots on a steady north by northwest heading without much of my attention to the helm. I felt sorry to leave my aquatic friends behind, but such is the life of a seagoing nomad, especially one with an aversion to permanence or social entanglements.

The future would take care of itself.

Forty-six:
Recovering

Boredom. I decided to go back to work, even though I didn't need the money. I'd been anchored fore and aft on the south side of Santa Rosa Sound for more than a week, restless and distracted. I had occupied my time trying to get back in shape, and between working out with free weights, long runs on the beach, and hours of swimming to near exhaustion in the warm waters of the strait, I was feeling better physically but still mentally adrift. It was time to shake it off, go ashore, and check out the local action.

I looked in at several bars in the downtown district before finding a dimly lit cellar where a small combo played cerebral jazz to a mixed crowd of well-dressed professionals and folks in yachting clothes. I found a table near a back wall where I would attract no attention and nursed a virgin drink for which I was charged the full alcoholic price.

The saxophone player had a sweet, mellow tone and a restrained approach that reminded me of the Dave Brubeck/Paul Desmond alliance, and I wasn't surprised when they wound up their set with a smooth, gentle reading of *Take Five*. Amid warm applause the musicians announced a break and disappeared into a back room.

Caitlin Sheridan had played that clever composition the last time I heard her aboard ship. How long would it be, I wondered, before every piece of music, everything I played, would somehow stop reminding me of her. Would anything ever erase the inexplicable sense of heartbreak I felt whenever a vision of that lovely child's face crossed my mind?

Why such a connection with this poor, lost kid? Why did I care?

Once my drink was gone, I wandered to the stage and sat down behind the piano. I planted my left foot firmly on the soft pedal to reduce the volume and began Errol Garner's old standard, *Misty*. It calmed me but left me feeling depressed, so I segued into a Frank Sinatra classic in a gentle swing tempo, *You Make Me Feel So Young*; wishing that were true. Lost in my own world, I was surprised to hear some sporadic applause when I finished. Then I discovered the band members had returned and were grouped behind the bench.

"Sorry," I muttered, and stood up quickly to get out of their way, but the sax player stepped up with his hand extended. We fist-bumped.

"Union member?" he asked. I nodded. "I'm Quinn," he said, with a slight Scottish lilt reminiscent of Sean Connery. He was broad, beefy and placid in appearance, nearly equal to my six-foot-three in height and with a reddish beard and deep green eyes. "Want to sit in on the grand? Barney says he'll take the Roland." He nodded toward the electronic keyboard, where a nearly bald, five-by-five elf was already climbing onto a custom-built stool with the instrument's pedals attached.

"Thanks," I said, "but I might cramp your style."

"Not from what I just heard. Let's give the room a treat."

I shrugged and sat down again. A tall, slender black man in a three-piece suit picked up the bass, and a Gene Krupa lookalike slid in behind the drum kit, relaxed and casual in jeans and tee shirt.

The foursome became a quintet. As sometimes happens in such situations, the combination jelled. We explored the Brubeck catalogue, stole a few pages from Chick Corea and Miles Davis, and did a set of movie soundtracks.

Time flew. We played until three in the morning and promised the crowd a repeat the following day. I made my way back to *Versteck* under scattered clouds that drifted across a three-quarter moon, feeling satisfied and at peace for the first time since leaving the cruise ship. Checking my watch—three-fifty-five—I sprawled in the cockpit. Jenny rose from her accustomed spot under the canopy and stretched, then dropped to the deck, took three quick hops, and landed in my lap. She ran her rough tongue part way down her spine and settled in. Relaxed but unable to sleep after a stimulating evening at the keyboard among talented, simpatico professionals, I sat stroking my little buddy's fur, enjoying her company and the satisfaction of a night well spent.

Forty-seven:
Russell and Jessica

Dr. Rothstein's receptionist ushered them into his office, and the marriage counsellor invited them to sit across from his desk. When they were settled, he asked, "How can I help you?"

"I'm not sure you can," Russell said. "Our daughter was killed in an explosion down in the Bahamas a few months ago. Caitlin is… was our only child."

"I'm very sorry for your loss," Rothstein said. "When I saw your name on my appointment list, I thought it seemed familiar, and I looked up the news stories. A tragedy like that can be difficult to deal with."

Both Russell and Jessica stared at the floor, reluctant to meet the doctor's eyes. After a few moments he said, "I suspect you've been having some personal problems."

Russell looked up. "Jessica blames me for what happened. And she's right. It was my fault."

"I don't think that," Jessica said softly.

They fell silent again. Presently Rothstein said to Russell, "I understand that what happened was an accident. Why do you think you're to blame?"

"It's complicated."

"Tell me about your relationship with your daughter, then. Both of you, please."

"I loved her," Jessica said softly.

Russell stared at her. "I loved her too," he said defensively. Then to the doctor, "You see, that's part of the problem. Jessica thinks I… that all I cared about was… was her talent, and how it reflected on our family. But that isn't true. We got along well. We had fun together."

"I didn't mean to suggest you didn't love her," Jessica said. "I know you did. But did *she* know it? *Really* know it?"

"What more could I have done? I gave her everything, every opportunity, the best teachers and every chance to perform that came along. She was famous by the time she was eight."

"And you were her father!" Jessica sat up straight, animated. "Every time Caitlin played in public, your name was in the paper too, the 'noted cardiac surgeon' whose amazing daughter was the youngest child ever to solo with the Toronto Symphony. As if she was a, a *trophy!*"

Russell sighed and slumped back in his chair. "I didn't care about that."

"Stop kidding yourself. Why else did you push her so hard? You never turned down a single invitation for her to appear."

"She always wanted to."

"*You* always wanted her to."

Rothstein made a few notes on a yellow pad centered on his desk. He looked up. "Did Caitlin do well in school?" he asked.

"She was an honour student," Russell replied. "She inhaled schoolwork like a vacuum cleaner. She was speaking three languages fluently by the time she was ten, and she researched composers' lives in *German*, for God's sake. We had tutors come to the house three times a week to challenge her in all her subjects. Not that she needed it. She was curious about everything, and nothing was too hard for her to tackle on her own."

"Did you consider home schooling her?"

"She *wanted* to go to school," Jessica said softly.

"They told us she could skip grades," Russell said, "but Jessica wouldn't... We wouldn't allow that."

"Why not?"

"She had trouble making friends," Jessica said. "I thought it was best for her to stay with her own age group. You see, other children were in awe of her, and the way they treated her made her feel lonely. It was partly all the attention she received, the famous people she met; television shows, interviews."

"How did you handle that?" Rothstein asked.

"We didn't. *Caitlin* did. She built a shell around her talent, would never play the piano when there were any other youngsters in the house. She never told anyone when she was going to be on radio or TV."

"I didn't know," Russell said.

"Of *course* you didn't. You were never home during the day. I had to deal with all that. I was the one who came home early so she wouldn't be alone in the house and had to work weekends to make up the time."

"Did she have any close friends?" Rothstein asked.

Jessica smiled. "Not at first, but eventually, yes. She was a chameleon. She could be talking to Ellen or Oprah under all those lights, holding her own in the most adult conversations. Next day she'd be up in her room playing Barbies with the neighbourhood kids, or when she got older, giggling with them about the boys in her class."

"Did you think that was abnormal?"

"She was faking it. She had figured out how to get along, and she played the role, but it wasn't good for her. She was too focused on hiding her talent, always afraid that it would get in the way and... I don't know, spoil things for her somehow. That's what she used to say: *spoil*."

"So, you think she didn't want to perform?"

"Oh God, no! I didn't mean that. She *loved* it! It was her life! On the cruise she'd be playing Bach and Bartok for the passengers, absolutely in her element. Then half an hour later she'd be on the big stage, the center of attention in a rock band and fitting in." Agitated, Jessica fumbled in her purse for a tissue to blot her eyes. "Fitting in," she whispered.

"You couldn't keep her away from the keyboard when the time and place were right," Russell said softly. "But I didn't realize until right this minute what it must have cost her." He sat quietly, lost in thought. He wanted to reach out to Jessica, to touch her, console her, but was afraid to try, afraid of rejection.

"Tell me how this equates with you thinking you're responsible for what happened to her," the doctor said to him.

Jessica interrupted before Russell could reply. "It doesn't. I see that now. I thought that if we hadn't been on the cruise ship, it never would have happened, but that wasn't my husband's idea in the first place. In fact, he was against the whole thing."

"How so?" Rothstein said.

Jessica explained how Caitlin had engineered the trip as a surprise for them both. She lapsed into silence, not looking at Russell, a figurative brick wall still towering between them.

"Our time is about up," Rothstein said. "I would like to see you both again, perhaps separately next time. Are you agreeable to that?"

"If you think it will help," Russell said.

"I don't work miracles. You have to decide for yourselves where to go from here. All I can do is help you to understand and deal with your feelings and learn to cope with your loss. But I think you've made some progress today."

Jessica stood up. "Thank you, Doctor," she said, and turned abruptly toward the door, leaving Russell behind. He hesitated as if to offer to shake Rothstein's hand, then seemed to think better of it. He paced to the door, head lowered, and followed his wife from the room.

Forty-eight:
Rolf

I was becalmed and drifting slowly, at least four hundred nautical miles southeast of the Florida panhandle, after enjoying and being nurtured by a solitary passage across open water. Following several weeks among crowds in the Pensacola area, I'd taken advantage of a local shipyard to have *Versteck*'s hull hauled, scraped, and painted below the waterline. The crew did a mediocre job, but good enough to keep the bottom from getting fouled for awhile.

Quinn and his band mates were gone, packed up and on the way to whatever bookings their agent had lined up for them in the Virgin Islands and points south, and later the glitter of Las Vegas. I reluctantly turned down an offer to go along, having appreciated performing with them, but I'd had my fill of civilization for the time being.

The charts told me that there was plenty of water below the keel, and I stuck close to shore, well out of the way of commercial traffic. The mangrove islands on the port side looked inviting, and I set the anchors and assembled a survival backpack filled with necessities. I tossed it into the tender and rowed east, hoping to catch sight of a loggerhead turtle or two.

The sun hung just inches above the horizon and the wind had risen once more, clouds scudding away to the northeast to leave the sky clear. Early evening is a special time on the water. My plans called for a bit of exploring, happy to have no one to answer to, no destination in mind.

Memories of the Caracola Cay tragedy no longer haunted me, except late during those nights when sleep eluded me. I was mostly at peace, content and anticipating a prolonged period of solitude and reflection.

With full dark approaching, I debated returning to *Versteck* but was tempted to wander awhile longer. I found a wide inside passage heading east and began to row away from the Gulf. In about ten minutes I came upon a promising island that stood high and dry, and beached the tender and stepped ashore. Nothing stirred among the trees. A bull gator grunted a long distance away. Something splashed nearby.

Time passed, the light faded, and I felt no impulse to leave the little islet. The wind, so brisk and variable when I landed, disappeared along with the daylight, and stars emerged in dramatic display, having no competition from manmade illumination. But then the mosquitoes found me, and I had to move on. I sprayed some repellent, re-launched the tender, and drifted west again, but before I covered a hundred yards a low-riding inflatable dinghy came around a spit of land and struck me amidships. Someone screamed.

I back paddled to a halt and could just make out two small figures scrambling to steady their craft. Above me the gibbous moon was mostly obscured by leaves and branches overhead, and in the near darkness the inflatable seemed no more than ten feet in length, far too small for safety in the Gulf waters. I wondered if the occupants had come from another yacht that had anchored near my own. I couldn't imagine what they were doing in such an isolated and potentially dangerous location.

"Who's out there?" someone called out. It was a young girl's voice, scratchy as if her throat were sore. When I didn't answer, she followed up with "Is that your boat out there? *Versteck*?"

I dipped my left oar and swung around parallel to their tiny boat, then reached out and pulled it in to lie against my gunwale. I opened my backpack and began searching for a flashlight. The two figures backed away from me and huddled in the stern.

"Say something!" the girl shouted, sounding frightened but defiant. "Do you speak English? Was machen Sie hier? ¿De donde eres?"

"What are you saying?" another young voice whispered.

"Maybe he doesn't understand English," the first girl hissed. "His boat's got a German name, so I tried that. Spanish too."

These kids were just full of surprises. Given the girl's excellent accent, I decided to answer in kind, that *Versteck* was indeed mine. "Das ist mein Boot dort draußen," I said, and then to reassure her, "Du brauchst keine Angst zu haben."

You don't have to be scared.

"I'm not afraid of you. Bist du Deutscher?"

Are you German?

"Österreicher," I said. "Austrian."

I found the flashlight and played it over them. One girl sat crouched in the far corner of the stern, arms tightly crossed in front of her chest, knees drawn up and pressed tightly together, her face a frightened mask.

But the other one! It wasn't possible! A huge wave of relief washed over me. I laughed aloud.

"Caitlin Sheridan, how in the name of Bach, Beethoven and Brahms did you end up way out here in the middle of alligator country? Everyone thinks you're dead."

PART TWO

Forty-nine:
The Cruise, Last Day

On Caracola Cay, Akoni Clarke (Omario Lewis) swung behind the headland beyond the cove and twisted the ignition key, his hand out of sight of his passengers. The engine died. He started it again, quickly shut it off, then brought it back to life once more.

"What's wrong?" Caitlin shouted to him.

"Don't know," Clarke said. "Keeps quitting on me. We better get some help." He pointed to a trawler, anchored fifty yards up a strait. He moved toward it, barely above an idle, and drifted to where Carman Russo stood on a swim platform at the stern. He shut the engine down.

"Having trouble?" Carman asked.

"Dirty gas, maybe. Won't keep up to speed. How about giving the girls a ride back to the cove?"

"Sure. Send them aboard."

"I'll stay with the ski. Maybe I can fix it."

"Come on up, kids," Carman said with a smile. He held the ski steady for Chloe and Caitlin to get off and pointed to a short ladder hanging over the stern. They clambered up happily, a new adventure in the offing, and headed for the companionway leading to the cabin.

Carman moved close to the ski. "Where the hell did the second kid come from?" he growled.

"I couldn't help it," Clarke answered. "The Sharma girl was scared. She wouldn't go with me without her friend."

"Jesus, what a screw-up."

From inside the boat, Caitlin screamed.

"Shut up in there!" Carman shouted. "Scream like that again, and I'll dump the two of you overboard and drown you."

"What's going on?" Clarke said. "This is a birthday surprise for the girl, isn't it? That's what the woman who hired me said."

"The less you know, the better. You're getting paid well enough to keep your mouth shut."

"Jesus, this'll get me fired. I've got a record. They'll slap me in jail again."

From beside the console Carman produced a backpack that Jacob Shaffer had dropped off earlier. "There's enough dough in this bag to set you up for a long time, asshole. Just take the ski around the far side of the island and make yourself scarce."

"Listen mon, they're gonna want to know what happened to the kids. I'm responsible."

Carman produced a pistol from his waistband behind his back. "Take the money. Sneak back aboard the ship and find somewhere to hide until she sails. Unless you want me to shoot you right here."

Clarke shrank back, then reached out tentatively and took the backpack. Without a word he fired up the engine, spun the ski around, and aimed it out into the channel.

Carman reached into his pocket and hauled out a device with a numbered keyboard, half the size of a cell phone. He watched until the ski was abreast of the headland and keyed in a three-number code. The machine erupted in a massive blast, hurling Clarke's shattered body into the sea.

Carman hurried into the cabin. A dark-skinned Latino in a striped tank top and three-quarter pants stood over Caitlin and Chloe, who were sprawled on the deck with their wrists bound behind their backs by nylon cable ties.

Caitlin glared at Carman. "My dad's gonna kill you."

"Your dad will never see you again, or me either." Then to the rough-looking man: "Shut them in the berth, and if they open their mouths, slap them silly. Don't let them look out the porthole."

When the girls were shut away, Jacob Shaffer emerged from the head, wearing only swim trunks. "The bomb worked, I take it?" he said softly.

"Damn straight," Carman whispered. "Plastic explosive is great stuff. The detonator did its job too."

"Damn shame we had to off him. Collateral damage always heightens the risk."

"It's better this way. He'd be a loose cannon. The cops would sweat him until he ratted out Charlotte and the whole deal."

"You're right. Probably too damn stupid to follow orders. In any case, when they find his body they'll assume the girls died in the blast too. They won't even think about a kidnapping. But the second girl complicates things."

"Couldn't be helped. Might even work out okay. Having a friend with her might make the Sharma kid easier to handle, until The Spider forces her father to do what he wants."

"I hope you're right," Shaffer said. "I've got to get back and put on an act. They'll put me through the wringer for not keeping the girl safe, but her mother okayed me going to lunch. I'll come out of it all right."

"Tell Keillor I'm on schedule."

"Right." Shaffer dove over the side and swam toward shore as Carman started the trawler's V-8. He strode to the forward berth and opened the door. The girls were huddled against the hull, securely tied. He motioned to the swarthy man and they returned to the main cabin.

"Good work, Alonzo," Carman told him. He produced a wad of bills and gave it to the man, who counted the money and smiled. They high-fived. Carman hauled up the anchors and was quickly under way, heading north before anyone from the cruise ship reached the scene.

Fifty:
The Cabin

Caitlin awoke dizzy and disoriented, unable to make sense of unfamiliar surroundings. She swung her legs over the side of a low cot and sat lethargically, taking in a room sparsely furnished with nothing but a small table, two straight chairs, and a low chest of drawers. Chloe lay unconscious on a second cot beside a double casement window that admitted scattered sunlight through mixed vegetation outside. The walls held no decoration except a silver-encrusted mahogany cross that hung opposite the door.

Caitlin blinked her eyes and stood up unsteadily. She made her way to the windowsill to find a large grassy yard outside, enclosed by a substantial chain link fence that was topped by coils of barbed wire. She turned a crank and half of the window rotated inward, exposing a thick-mesh aluminum screen. She pushed against it and it gave slightly under pressure. She wondered if she could break it if she tried hard enough.

Near one corner a narrow door stood slightly ajar. Caitlin pushed it open to reveal a compact bathroom with a basin, toilet and a makeshift stall with a simple pipe and shower head near the ceiling. Bath and hand towels hung from a bar mounted on one wall, next to a shelf containing paper cups, toothbrushes, toothpaste, soap and shampoo, as well as a small hand mirror.

Feeling faint, her throat raw and dry, she moved to the basin and tried the faucet. A thin stream of water dripped out, and she captured it in a cup and drank. She backed out into the main room again and dropped into one of the chairs. She rested her head in her hands and stared toward Chloe's unmoving body. Memories surfaced: the Jet Ski ride; engine trouble; climbing aboard a large boat. She bolted upright.

The image of a man named Carman jumped into her mind, and the other one who tied her hands behind her back and shoved her painfully into a berth at the bow. Alonzo, Carman had called him. She looked down at her wrists and found them chafed and red.

She fought back panic. Her head was clearing, and she recalled being given something sour to drink, and then feeling very sleepy. After that she didn't remember much, just muffled voices that she couldn't understand. She recognized Chloe's name, but nothing else made sense.

She examined the room more closely. Unfamiliar clothing hung on hooks in one of the corners; they looked to be her size, and Chloe's. She got to her feet and realized for the first time that her swimsuit was gone, and the white cotton nightgown she was wearing was not her own. Chloe was similarly dressed.

A wide, heavy door across from the foot of the bed was topped by a narrow horizontal transom. Faint light flickered through the filthy glass, and she dragged a chair over and climbed up. Standing on tiptoe, she peered out and discovered she could see part of a larger room on the opposite side.

"Hey!" she called out. "Anybody there?"

"I'll be along to speak with you shortly," a woman's voice came from somewhere near the ceiling, and Caitlin, startled, whirled and hopped off the chair. She backed up and dropped onto the edge of the cot. She spotted a small speaker in the corner above the door. When she heard the sound of a deadbolt turning in the door, she was determined to stay cool until she found out what was going on.

The door swung inward, and a medium tall, muscular woman in a white nurse's uniform stepped inside and locked the door behind her with a key. She appeared to be in her mid to late thirties, with medium brown hair, a somewhat square face suggesting Teutonic ancestry, and a stern unsmiling expression. She crossed to the table and pulled out a chair. "Let's get acquainted, Caitlin," she said.

"Who're you? And how do you know my name?"

"You may call me Shelagh."

"Which means that's not really who you are, right?"

Shelagh smiled. "They warned me you'd be difficult."

"Who did? Where am I?"

"Come and sit down. I will answer all of your questions in time. But first you need to hear the ground rules."

Caitlin glanced toward Chloe and was surprised to see her friend's eyes open. "Why am I here?" she said.

"You don't need to know that right now, except that there's no way out of here. We're a long way from anyone who can help you escape, so get that out of your head. Now come and sit. Please."

Caitlin grimaced, shrugged, and with one more look toward Chloe, motionless on her cot but looking alert, she retrieved the second chair and sat down. She leaned back and crossed her arms over her chest, defiant. "You're gonna be in a lot of trouble when my dad finds us," she said.

"He won't find you. No one will. Anyway, nothing bad is going to happen to you as long as you cooperate. You aren't even supposed to be here, just your young friend, but that's water under the bridge. If you behave yourself, you'll go home eventually. The food here is good, and you'll even be able to go outside sometimes."

"So like, I'm in prison, right?"

"Not exactly. We aren't monsters. We'll take good care of you. But you have to stay here for now. Elsewhere on the island there are dangers that could result in your death."

"My death? Somebody's going to kill me?"

"Not as long as you follow the rules."

"This is an island?"

"Yes."

"And what's to keep me from just swimming away?"

"A fence, for one thing. And there's nowhere for you to go. We're a long way from civilization, and if you didn't drown, you'd soon be attacked by something. Alligators, sharks… These waters are very dangerous."

Caitlin stood abruptly and strode to the door. She hammered her fists on the heavy wood, then turned and glared at her captor.

"That was mature," Shelagh said. "Once you calm down, I'll explain the rules you need to follow to get along here."

"I don't care what you say! I'm not gonna do anything you tell me to."

Shelagh regarded her placidly. "Yes, dear. You will."

Fifty-one:
Captivity

Not trusting Carman Russo completely, The Spider had more confidence in Rose-Ellen Foster to manage the day-to-day operations at the cabin. Known to her charges by the alias Shelagh, she was a registered nurse and a committed adherent to fundamental Christianity; also a sadistic, unrepentant sociopath. Foster enjoyed her role as disciplinarian to her charges.

The remainder of the staff consisted of Anna, a housekeeper who doubled as cook, and a Brazilian maintenance man named Alonzo Cardoso, whose native Portuguese was little better than his awkward Spanish. His command of English was minimal. The cabin was stocked with enough supplies to last up to six months. Should they be required to remain longer, Carman Russo would bring them anything they might need in his trawler.

The island was a natural prison, with no access to the distant mainland. Snakes and alligators were a constant threat, and Rose-Ellen frequently mentioned them to the girls. To the west the open ocean was a similar barricade, difficult to reach and home to four dozen species of sharks.

A week after the girls were captured, The Spider flew into Southwest Florida International Airport and rented a car to drive to Everglades City. Russo picked him up in his trawler at the marina and took him to the island. He and Rose-Ellen met outside the cabin at mid-afternoon, out of sight of Chloe and Caitlin, who were locked in their room. It was important that the girls be unable to describe him, if and when they were released and returned to Nova Scotia.

"So, you have *two* girls to look after," The Spider said. "Sorry about that. It couldn't be avoided. Did the drugs wear off okay?"

"It took a long time. What did you use, Rohypnol? Whoever dosed them used too much. Otherwise they seem all right. The smaller one, Chloe? She knuckled under pretty fast, docile and cooperative."

"She's the important one."

"Ransom?"

"Not for her," the Spider said. "The main reason we kidnapped her was to force her father to drop out of an important political race in Canada. We haven't told him she's alive yet. We'll let him grieve awhile, then let him know and give him his marching orders if he ever wants to see her again. How about the Sheridan kid?"

"That one!" Rose-Ellen shrugged. "She's a handful. I haven't been able to break her yet. She even tried to bust out through the window, fortunately without success."

"Carman says those screens are tough, made of stainless steel. She won't get out that way. We're going to ask for a fortune to send her back to her parents. She's something special. Her IQ is off the charts, and you should hear her play the piano."

"She's bright, all right. She knows their room is bugged, and she probably suspects we can see her too. I watched her trying to find the hidden cameras. Most of the time she just sits, looking grim, or exercises like a track star. She does dozens of sit-ups, push-ups, even isometrics in the bathroom doorway until the sweat pours off her. She runs back and forth across the room, bouncing off the walls, over and over again. She won't undress in the room. She goes in the bathroom and shuts the door. She must think there's a camera in there too, because she leaves the light off. Her latest ploy is a hunger strike. When I bring her dinner, she overturns the plate on the floor and just stands there glaring at me."

"She'll soon get hungry enough to stop that."

"I suppose. But she'll think of something else."

"What do you suggest?"

"Let me turn up the heat." Rose-Ellen's eyes gleamed in

anticipation. "Corporal punishment will bring her around."

"All right, if you keep having trouble with her, you can spank her, but nothing worse than that. And be careful of her hands and arms. The kid's an incredible musician, and once the ransom is paid, I want to send her back to her parents undamaged."

"She has to learn that I mean business."

"Listen, Rose, you have to keep yourself under control. This is a valuable piece of merchandise, and if the father pays up and she goes home unhurt, I think he'll suck up the loss and move on. But he has a reputation for being a hard ass. If we ruin her talent, he might never stop looking for us."

"I won't injure her."

He studied her face carefully, doubtfully. "Okay. But I'm warning you…"

"You can depend on me."

"I hope so."

Fifty-two:
Caitlin

Rose-Ellen Foster ("Shelagh") made little progress in overcoming Caitlin's hostility. The girl ignored even the most routine requests, and although she had abandoned her hunger strike, she refused to keep her surroundings in order. She exercised obsessively and was aggressively hostile. Chloe by contrast was meek and obedient, and almost obsessively tidy. She kept the clothes provided for her hung up in good order or stored neatly in a drawer in the chest. She followed orders and made no demands, although she did ask if someone could bring her a chess set. Foster promised to radio someone on the mainland to have one delivered.

Early on the morning after The Spider left the island, Foster entered the girls' room carrying a single breakfast tray and a slim canvas bag. She set the bag on the floor and let the door swing shut behind her, leaving it unlocked. She placed the tray on the table and motioned to Chloe, who sat down uncertainly to eat. She was fully dressed, while Caitlin was still in her nightgown.

"Why didn't you bring *me* some breakfast?" Caitlin said belligerently.

"So you can throw it on the floor again?"

Caitlin shrugged, turning away. "Whatever."

"This little war you're conducting is getting old," Foster said. "You aren't going to win a power struggle with me, not now, not ever, and you may as well get used to it. How about we start over?"

"Like how?"

"Life will be easier for all of us if you decide to cooperate. You won't be here forever, and you won't be able to leave any sooner if you keep acting up, so why not just calm down and, as they used to say, go with the flow."

"Why am I here? Tell me what's going on. Am I being held for ransom?"

Foster sighed. "You may as well know, we didn't expect you to get caught up in our plans. If Chloe hadn't insisted that you ride the ski with her, you wouldn't be here. So yes, now that we're stuck with you, your folks will have to pay to get you back."

"Chloe too?"

"Not exactly. She's here for a different reason. And we can't have a little shit disturber like you getting everyone riled up until this is all over. You just have to follow the rules, try to be pleasant, and get along."

"And if I don't?"

"Caitlin, do you know God's word? Do you read the Bible?"

"Sure. I've read the whole thing twice. The language is beautiful, just like poetry, but it's a mess. It contradicts itself all the time. Like in the Book of Exodus the Ten Commandments says, 'Thou shalt not kill,' and then God himself goes rampaging around wiping out all the enemies of the Jews. A real hypocrite, right? And how about that nonsense in Joshua where the sun stops moving through the sky for a whole day? If that's really the word of God, and he made the whole universe himself, wouldn't you think he'd know the sun is stationary and it's the earth that revolves around it? And if the earth suddenly stopped moving, we'd all fly off into space. It's obvious that Joshua was written by someone who didn't know anything about physics or astronomy."

Foster reached forward and slapped Caitlin sharply across the face. "Blasphemy!" she said. She raised her hand again, and Caitlin skipped back out of range.

"You're nuts!" Caitlin shouted. "Use your head. *People* wrote the Bible, not some god, and some of it may be history, but a lot of it is myth."

"You're wrong, and I'm going to educate you," Foster said. "First, you are going to accept Jesus as your personal Saviour. And then you will do exactly as you're told and not interfere with our glorious plan until all the world recognizes that white people like us are destined to inherit the earth."

"Holy shit! What are you, some kind of racist?"

"You'll wish you hadn't said that. As you must know from your extensive reading, the Bible instructs us that children need discipline in order to enter a state of grace. Young sinners like you must be punished before you recognize the evil within you and cast it out."

Foster's words hung in the air. Caitlin glared at her, then turned away abruptly and stared out the window. "I'm not afraid of you," she said softly.

"I've been very patient so far, and you've caused me nothing but trouble. It's time to make up your mind. Either shape up right now or suffer the consequences."

Caitlin's eyes flashed. "Go straight to hell!" she said evenly.

Shelagh levered herself out of the chair. "What did you say to me?" she said quietly.

Caitlin was trembling but defiant. "I *said*, go to hell!"

"So be it. You've made your choice." She turned to Chloe, who had not yet finished eating, frightened and caught up in the confrontation between her friend and their captor. "Chloe," she said, "take your tray and go outside. You can finish eating there."

"What are you going to do?" Chloe whispered.

"That isn't your business."

"Don't hurt Caitlin. Please?"

"Outside! Now!"

Chloe stood and edged toward the door, leaving the breakfast tray behind. When she was gone, Foster turned the key in the blind dead bolt, then walked to the window and drew the shade to prevent anyone from looking in. She retrieved the canvas bag and drew out a substantial hardwood paddle. She twisted Caitlin's arm roughly behind her back and threw the child face down on the cot. She yanked the back of the girl's nightgown up to her shoulders.

Fifty-three:
Aftermath

After a restless, tortured night, Caitlin awoke before dawn and saw that Chloe's cot had not been slept in. She hadn't seen her friend since the previous morning. She struggled into the bathroom to relieve herself and sat uncomfortably on the toilet for a long time, head cradled in her hands. She was sorely tender after three intense beatings the previous day, and angry and embarrassed at being handled and punished so easily. She was more determined than ever to resist whatever was in store for her.

Eventually she returned to the cot and crawled back under the covers but was too uncomfortable to fall asleep again. Time passed slowly. At five after ten the door opened, and Foster entered with a generous breakfast tray: scrambled eggs, orange juice, and toast with marmalade. A bowl, a small box of corn flakes, and a pitcher of whole milk completed the meal.

"Good morning," she said. She set the tray down, arranged the silverware, and opened the cereal box. She dumped the contents into the bowl.

"It's a beautiful day," she said. "Would you like to go out in the yard? Chloe's been asking about you."

Caitlin ignored her.

"You'll feel better once you have something to eat. Sit up here and I'll teach you how to ask the Lord to bless your food. It will help you begin to know him."

"Stick it up your ass," Caitlin muttered.

Foster sighed and looked toward the ceiling. "Oh, sweet and gracious Jesus, hear my prayer. Help me to lead this child of Satan into your holy light. Teach her the way to redemption, that she may learn the power of your love. And guide my hands, oh Lord, to do what is necessary to overcome her resistance to thy glorious truth."

She strode to the cot, threw back the blanket and sheet, and hauled the girl to her feet. Caitlin grimaced. She leaned back and spat into the woman's face.

* * *

The next day Caitlin was too stiff and bruised to get out of bed. When Foster arrived with a tray, she pretended to be asleep, her face buried in the pillow.

"I know you can hear me," Foster said as she arranged the dishes on the table. "Are you ready to be more cooperative?"

"So you're stronger than me, so what?" Caitlin muttered. "Big deal."

"My strength is that of ten, for it cometh from the Lord."

"You're crazy! And I'm not gonna do anything you tell me, so you can just go ahead and beat me to death."

Foster sat down beside her. "You'll survive. You're obviously a tough kid, and I respect that. But I'm in charge, and unless you want to wake up every morning feeling like you're a hundred years old, you have to face facts."

Caitlin rolled over to stare at her tormentor. "Such as?"

"This is where you'll live for the next few months, maybe longer if your father doesn't come up with what we want. We don't demand much of you, and you might even get to like being here. Your friend can move back in with you. Why not give it a try?"

"I want to go back to my family *now!*"

"You know the answer to that."

"And I guess you know *my* answer, then."

* * *

186

Caitlin gave up the following day. Her back was a mass of angry welts and bruises from shoulders to knees. Only her arms and hands had been spared. When Foster entered the room and touched her, she flinched and startled awake. "Don't hit me again!" she cried out.

"Are you ready to do as you're told?" Foster said.

Caitlin sobbed. She curled into a ball, knees drawn up to her chest, every movement a torment. "Whatever," she whispered.

"Good. Get dressed. From now on you'll take your meals in the other room with Chloe and Anna and me. I'll be back later to get you."

Foster left the room. After half an hour she returned to find Caitlin still in her nightgown, huddled on the floor under the window. "You aren't dressed," she called out from the doorway. "You've already missed breakfast, but Anna will make you an early lunch."

"I don't want any," Caitlin said softly.

"You have to move around some. If you don't, it'll take a lot longer to recover. You need to get up and stretch, maybe do some of your exercises again. You'll feel better after a few days."

Caitlin rubbed her swollen eyes. "I can't," she said, barely above a whisper. "You broke something."

"Not likely. I'm an expert at this sort of thing, and even though you don't believe in the good Lord, I asked him to protect you. But if you don't come around soon and stop being difficult, he might change his mind about that."

"Are you gonna hit me anymore?"

"That's up to you. Are you going to get dressed?"

"I hurt too much."

"Then I'm going to punish you again and again, starting right now, and it will go on and on and on until you start doing as I say."

Caitlin drew in a deep breath and struggled to her feet. She shuffled awkwardly to the dresser and shrugged off her nightgown, not caring about privacy. She struggled into a long-sleeved cotton tee shirt and a pair of Capri pants that hid the bruises on the backs of her thighs. She located her sneakers and put them on, wincing as she bent to tie the laces.

"That's better," Foster said as she turned to leave. "Come out whenever you're ready. You can go out in the yard with Chloe if you want to." She left the room.

Caitlin lay back on the cot once more and tried to go to sleep but couldn't. Boredom soon set in, and she rose to her feet. Through the window she could see Chloe near the fence at the far side of the yard. She wandered into the next room and shuffled outside, stepping into the sunlight for the first time in almost two weeks.

Fifty-four:
Together Again

Caitlin and Chloe sat silently at a table in the main room while Anna served lunch. Chloe stood up and headed toward the bedroom when she finished eating, but Caitlin said, "Wait. Let's go outside again."

"Why?" Chloe asked.

"You know." And of course she did. Before the beatings started, Caitlin had discovered a listening device taped to the underside of one of the chairs.

"You okay?" Chloe asked once they were out in the yard.

"I'm so damn mad; that miserable bitch! I thought she was gonna kill me. And she enjoyed it, I know she did, kept smiling and humming to herself the whole time. She said she'd keep on hitting me every damn day until I promised to cooperate, and I believe it. Okay, if it's a war she wants, that's what she's going to get, only I have to be a lot sneakier about it from now on. Are you with me?"

"What can we do? Listen, Caitlin, I'm getting really scared. I overheard something I wasn't supposed to. Shelagh was talking to that woman who does the cooking. They didn't know I was just behind the door. They said some really mean things about me and my parents."

"Like what?"

"Shelagh kept calling us 'mongrels.'"

"Yeah," Caitlin said, "it's because your mom and dad are two different kinds of Asian."

"What do you mean?"

"Shelagh's a racist, and a religious fanatic too. Probably *all* the freaks who kidnapped us are too, white supremacists. She kept quoting the Bible while she was beating me, and mostly getting it wrong. She thinks white Christians are God's 'chosen people', doesn't even know that's what the Bible calls the Jews."

"Do you think they'll ever send me back home?"

Caitlin looked at her sadly. "Not until they get whatever they're after. I think you're the key to getting your dad to do something for them, but I don't know what."

"They're gonna kill me. I know it."

Fifty-five:
Chess

Carman Russo delivered a folding portable chess set to the cabin a few days later. Foster made a big deal out of presenting it to the girls, and to Chloe it was. They took it outside and sat down under the shade at the north side of the cabin.

"Can you play?" Chloe asked.

"Never learned," Caitlin answered.

"It isn't hard, at least in the beginning. It's an analogy of war, and all about strategy. The object is to trap your opponent's king so he can't move without being captured. That's called checkmate."

"'Off with his head!'" Caitlin quoted.

Chloe grinned. "That's the spirit." She set up the board and identified the various pieces. She explained how each of them moved, and Caitlin caught on quickly.

"Seems easy," she said, "like checkers, so I must be missing something."

Chloe smiled. "It's a lot more complex than checkers. You have to plan a whole bunch of moves ahead. Look, the best way to learn is to play a game. Every time it's your turn, you make whatever move you want, and I'll explain what's likely to happen next, and what would work better. That way you'll get the whole picture. Okay?"

"Whatever you say. There's nothing else to do in this damn jail."

"I'm white and you're black, so I start." Chloe moved the pawn in front of her king two spaces forward. "That space is called 'e4' because on the white side, the ranks are lettered from left to right, 'a' through 'h'. A rank is a row of spaces from side to side, so 'e' is the fifth space. The ranks are numbered one through eight. On your side, the letters go from right to left, so our 'e' pawns face each other. I moved my pawn to the fourth rank space, so 'e4'. Get it?"

"Duh. What do I do next?"

"The most common move is to do the same thing, move your 'e' pawn two spaces forward."

Caitlin moved her piece. "So now they face each other. Are you gonna capture my pawn on your next move?"

"I can't. Pawns only capture diagonally," Chloe said.

"Oh, right, I remember."

"Now I'll bring my bishop to 'c4' like this. Bishops can only move diagonally, and they capture that way too." She moved the piece. "Now you have to figure out what I might do next, and counter it."

"Tell me again how all the pieces move. How about the horse?"

"The knight. Good choice. He can skip over other pieces in an "L" shape, one square in one direction, two in another."

"Like this?"

"You've got it. Now here's why that was a good move."

For the next three hours Caitlin struggled to absorb the intricacies of the game, likening it to the organization of a sonata or symphony. Chloe avoided any advanced moves and corrected her friend's obvious mistakes, and Caitlin stored the information away in her prodigious memory. By the time they decided to take a break, she was already learning terms such as "King's gambit" and "Sicilian Defence." The coming days promised to be less boring for both of them.

Fifty-six:
Rebellion

Rose-Ellen Foster had zeroed in on Caitlin's essential personality trait with uncanny accuracy. The defiant child could be a world class shit disturber, although after repeated beatings she was clever enough to go underground and pretend to be cooperative. But she needed her friend's help to come up with a workable plan. She had to shake Chloe out of her submissive state and force her to think about escape.

In a particularly spirited chess game a week later, Caitlin had her opponent on the ropes a couple of times before losing her queen to Chloe in a spectacular pincer move; mate in four. Afterward they folded the board and moved to the most distant point in the yard, where they were sure not to be overheard.

"Tell me about your dad," Caitlin asked. "Besides being a doctor."

"Well," Chloe said, "he's active in the New Democratic Party. He's probably going to lead the Nova Scotia branch after the convention."

"Does that have anything to do with why you're here?"

"I can't see how."

"Shelagh said they aren't asking any ransom for you, so there must be something else they want from him. I don't follow politics; no offense, but it bores me stiff. What does he stand for?"

"Social justice, mostly," Chloe said. "And diversity. He's really high on immigration, says we need talented people to grow the economy, no matter where they come from. And he hates discrimination of all kinds. He says it's a major cause of poverty among minorities."

"All I remember about the New Democrats is what we learned in school about Tommy Douglas, and how he promoted universal

Medicare. And my dad's always talking about somebody he admired named Jack Layton."

"He was the national NDP leader way back when. He died of cancer around twenty-eleven, I think, after leading the Party to a huge win in Quebec and Official Opposition nationally. His wife was a member of Parliament too, Olivia Chow. She came to Canada from Hong Kong."

"You see a pattern here?" Caitlin said.

"I'm beginning to. Racism."

"These white supremacist jerks must hate the New Democrats. If your dad becomes the leader and the NDP wins the election, he'll be Premier."

"That's how it works. That would drive people like Shelagh nuts. It's like when the United States elected President Obama. The far-right wing couldn't stand having a black man in the White House, no matter how capable he was. It's the old 'Master Race' thing. It dates all the way back to Plato's *Republic*."

"And Adolf Hitler in Germany, too," Caitlin said. "He was such a hypocrite. Master Race: tall, blond, athletic, super smart, all that? How did that short, dark, dumpy loudmouth think he could be a part of that?"

"Say what you will about him," Chloe said, "but he was clever and compelling. He told the big lie, and the more and louder he repeated it, the more people began to believe."

"Why?"

"Because they wanted to, so they could feel superior to everyone else, everyone who was not like them. Hitler gave them an excuse. Donald Trump pulled the same crap when he was president, and it still goes on in Africa and even Europe, like in Armenia and what used to be Yugoslavia."

"I never thought that kind of thing could happen in Canada," Caitlin said, "but Dad once told me it's going on right now. It hides behind labels like nationalism and populism, but that's just another way to justify getting rid of people who are different. Muslims, blacks, Hispanics, they're all targets. Like your family."

"Uh-huh. Anyone who isn't what they consider 'white'. But if that's why they snatched me, what do they expect to gain?"

"Want me to take a guess?"

"Sure."

"It'll scare you."

"I can't be any more scared than I am already."

"Okay," Caitlin said, "I'll bet whoever did this told your dad they won't turn you loose unless he quits politics. They want a white guy to be elected."

"So what'll they do to me if he refuses?"

"What do you say we don't hang around to find out? We have to find some way to get out of here. And I'm gonna start by figuring out how to get that heavy screen off our window. Are you with me?"

"I guess I'd better be. Besides, I'm to blame for getting you mixed up in this, making you go with me on the Jet Ski, so I have to help."

She'll stick by me, Caitlin thought, relieved. *She has the most to lose.*

Fifty-seven:
Facing Facts

The girls began by assessing their situation, the weaknesses of their captors and their prison if any, and how to protect themselves if they manage to get off the island. The fence was the first problem. It stretched well above their heads, and the coils of barbed wire appeared impenetrable. The gate was equally formidable, heavy and secured by a huge padlock. But even without the fence, the island itself was an effective jail, surrounded by a vast swamp filled with predators. Given her championship form in the water, Caitlin might be lucky enough to reach some other islands without being eaten, but Chloe could barely dog paddle.

It was hard to tell how much of a threat the cook, Anna, might pose. Her last name was unknown to the girls; she spoke with a typical southern drawl. She was brusque and intimidating, obsessed with order and cleanliness, and Caitlin suspected she would be happy to see the last of them. She wondered if the woman might be co-opted to help with their escape but decided against asking her, doubting that she would care one way or the other.

Mostly, the cook seemed indifferent to them, as was Alonzo Cardoso, the maintenance man. He was a sullen loner, muscular and slow-witted and firmly under Shelagh's thumb. In a crisis, Caitlin thought he would be subservient to the woman's demands, and no doubt incapable of independent initiative. He would simply follow orders. He took little notice of either of them and didn't seem to understand anything they said to him. Shelagh was another matter. Obviously a true believer in the political as well as the religious sense, she was too powerful to oppose directly.

Carman Russo rarely visited the island, at most once a week when a delivery was needed. Caitlin knew they would have no chance against him. He was powerful and quick, and based on their experience on Caracola Cay, Caitlin and Chloe were determined to give him a wide berth. Even more than Shelagh, he was most likely to frustrate their plans.

Rather than discouraging her, these obstacles just made Caitlin more determined to contact the outside world. If possible she wanted to be the instrument by which the hated Shelagh would pay for the beatings she'd meted out. The first step was to find a way to escape from their room when it was locked at night, which proved to be easier than expected. With a thin-bladed knife filched from the dining room, she and Chloe managed to pry most of the screws out of the window frame. They left only two at the top to keep the screen in place until they needed to break free. They hoped the slow-witted Alonzo would not discover what they had done.

Fifty-eight:
Developments

Vachan Sharma dropped the phone and shouted, "Liz! Where are you?"

"In the kitchen," his wife replied. "What's wrong?"

"Phone call! She's alive!"

Elizabeth Wu dashed into the study, where Sharma was poised beside his desk, his face ashen, his hands trembling. "Who are you talking about? Chloe?"

"She didn't die! She was kidnapped!"

"Who told you? Was it another prank call?"

"I couldn't recognize the voice. It was distorted, one of those voice-altering things, I guess. But he knew what happened on the cruise. He knew so much; it must be true. We can have her back in a week. If…"

"If what? Ransom?"

"No. Come, sit down. I'm feeling light-headed." He eased himself onto the sofa and she sank down beside him. He drew in several deep breaths and wiped sweat from his forehead.

"It's the leadership convention," he said, his voice shaky. "That's what this was all about. The election."

"What about it?"

And he told her.

* * *

SHARMA QUITS NDP LEADERSHIP RACE
Megan Rumboldt, The Canadian Press
HALIFAX, Nova Scotia – In a stunning announcement delivered on the steps of the Provincial Legislature this morning, Vachan

Sharma, candidate for the leadership of the Nova Scotia New Democrats, officially ended his campaign to take the Party into the next election, which is widely expected to be called in late summer. Sharma gave no reason for his decision, other than to cite personal reasons.

Until recently Sharma was believed to be strongly favoured over incumbent Douglas Kauffman, the interim leader who has held the post for the past eleven months. Recent polls indicate that the Party under Sharma would easily defeat both Liberals and Conservatives in the election. Pundits suggest that Sharma's withdrawal, coupled with widespread public dissatisfaction with old-line politics, might work in the Freedom Party's favour by allowing them to attract a substantial protest vote to form the next government.

Speculation about Sharma's reasons for abandoning the leadership race centers upon his sadness over the loss of their daughter, Chloe, in a tragic accident while on vacation in the Caribbean in February. When contacted at home, his wife, novelist Elizabeth Wu, declined to comment.

* * *

Carman Russo picked up his cell phone on the third ring. Jacob Shaffer's voice came over the line: "It's over."

"No shit!" Russo said.

"He made the announcement this morning. The CBC is already suggesting the possibility of a Freedom Party minority government in the fall. All we have to do now is push the envelope hard enough to squeak out a majority."

"Does Sharma suspect you?"

"No chance. I used a voice changer when I called. He was in some shock, let me tell you, practically crying. He folded fast."

"Now what?"

"I told him she'd be back home in a week. We have to check that with Arch."

"You know what he'll say. Get rid of both kids. It's gonna be hard enough to explain how Sharma's daughter survived the explosion. Toss the Sheridan girl into the mix, and the RCMP will be all over it, probably the FBI too, considering that the cruise originated in Florida."

"Bad idea," Shaffer said. "When Sharma doesn't get her back, he'll go public. He'll probably contest the leadership again and set the Mounties on us anyway. And that'll get him the sympathy vote. We'll be worse off than before."

"Jesus," Russo said. "Screwed both ways. I'm glad I'm not in your shoes. Listen, let me know what the boss wants me to do, okay?"

"Keep your phone charged."

* * *

Late that evening, The Spider flew into Southwest Florida International and called Rose-Ellen, telling her that Russo would be dropping him off early the following afternoon. She was instructed to lock the two girls away before he arrived. The next day dawned overcast and windy, and Caitlin knew something was about to happen when Anna served lunch half an hour early. She and Chloe weren't surprised when they were confined to their room. Because of the hidden microphones, they decided not to talk, but just to wait and see what would happen. An hour later they heard the sound of Carman's outboard through the open window, then the squeak of the gate opening, and finally the footsteps of more than one person coming in the door.

"I bet they stay inside because of the rain," Caitlin whispered. "I'm gonna see if I can hear what they're saying."

She lifted a chair, carefully so as to make no noise, and placed it next to the door. She stood up just below the transom so she wouldn't be seen, hoping that the voices from next door would be easier to hear through the thin pane of glass.

At first the voices were muffled and inaudible, but as the conversation continued, the people in the main room seemed to forget that the girls were close by and grew louder. Caitlin could pick up an occasional word or two, then whole phrases, just clearly enough to recognize individual voices. She heard the hated Shelah, of course, and Carman's rough, somewhat louder sentences. A third voice dominated the discussion but was unfamiliar to her. She suspected that whoever he was, he was in charge. She concentrated hard, using her musician's ear to pick up the rhythm of the man's speech and his tone.

The meeting continued for three-quarters of an hour, and Caitlin strained to hear every word. The snatches of conversation that she picked out worried her. It seemed as if they were planning to return Chloe to her family, but her own fate was the subject of argument. She caught the word "ransom" and Carman laughed. "Who needs it?" he said. "I vote we toss the little bitch to the 'gators."

Shelagh suggested coffee, and when the trio left the room to go to the kitchen, Caitlin climbed down and sat on her cot. "I think you're going home," she told Chloe, whispering in case someone was listening through the hidden microphone, her voice unsteady. "Carman's coming back to get you in three days."

"Really?"

"I think so. That's what they were talking about. And from what they said, I sort of know where we are. Someplace on the west coast of Florida. They're gonna take you to someplace called Tampa first."

"How about you?"

Caitlin looked down, and Chloe could see she was trembling, and that tears had welled up and stained her cheeks.

"What!" Chloe said. "Tell me!"

"They're keeping me here."

"To hold you for ransom?"

"Maybe. But Carman wants to kill me."

They sat in frightened silence for several moments, and Chloe moved to the cot and wrapped her arms around her friend in a fierce hug. Then Caitlin stiffened her spine and sat up, fire in her eyes.

"I'm getting out of here, damn it! I'll find some way. And when I do, I'll find the asshole who did this to us."

"How'll you do that?"

"I memorized his voice, and I'll never forget it. If I ever hear him again, I'll know it, and I'll tell my dad. He'll make sure the bastard goes to jail. Or worse."

Fifty-nine:
Opportunity

It was Chloe who engineered their escape from the island; quiet, obedient Chloe, whose meek and retiring acquiescence tended to make Foster and the others pay little attention to her. She kept her mouth shut, her eyes and ears open, and missed little of what was going on around her. Paying close attention to the rhythms by which the cabin operated, she knew exactly when their captors were most likely to be asleep. With the window screen loosened, she was able to slip outside and snoop around at will when least likely to be discovered.

Two days later, an hour before dawn, she left Caitlin asleep and climbed out into the yard. She was prowling along the fence, looking for a place where the barbed wire might be breached, when she heard the soft purr of an electric outboard motor approaching the island. She backed away and hunkered down among some shrubbery, and presently an inflatable dinghy coasted into view, with Carman Russo at the tiller.

Chloe could see him clearly in the moonlight as he shut off the motor and hauled the lightweight boat halfway up onto shore. He tied it to a mangrove root and approached the fence, walking unsteadily. When he reached the gate, he drew a hip flask from his back pocket, unscrewed the cap, and took a deep draught. He wiped his mouth on the back of his hand and retrieved a key from the pocket of his shorts. On the third try he managed to insert it in the padlock that secured the gate. He lifted it from the hasp and swung the gate open, the hinges squeaking sharply. He stumbled into the yard and lost his balance, falling heavily to the sand. The lock fell from his hand.

Russo swore softly. He took another drink from the flask and sat with his back against the fence, coughing and gasping for breath. After several minutes he climbed to his feet again, closed the gate behind him, and walked unsteadily toward the cabin. He raised his hand to pound on the door and lost his balance once more, falling to the steps. He shook his head, upended the flask into his mouth and, finding it empty, tossed it into the bushes. He leaned back against the door and closed his eyes.

Chloe huddled absolutely still, watching the man closely through the dense foliage that concealed her. After what she estimated to be about ten minutes, during which time Russo began snoring, she crept out and circled the cabin, careful to stay in the shadows. She reached the bedroom window and boosted herself inside.

Caitlin stirred and opened her eyes when Chloe touched her shoulder gently. "What?" she murmured.

"Shh," Chloe cautioned. "Get dressed. The gate's unlocked."

Caitlin's eyes widened. She threw back her blanket and gathered up her clothes, and a few minutes later the girls were out the window and peering around the corner of the cabin where Russo was slumped sideways against the door jamb, snoring heavily. Chloe motioned toward the gate, and they crept across the yard and lifted the latch. When they pulled it open, it emitted a piercing squeak, and Russo's snoring abruptly stopped.

The girls looked back toward the door and froze in place. Russo stirred and rubbed his eyes, looked around briefly as if trying to understand where he was, and fumbled for his back pocket. Not finding the flask, he swore, coughed, and tried to stand. When he couldn't get his feet under him, he gave up the effort and collapsed onto his side, facing away from the gate. A few minutes later he was asleep once more.

Sixty:
Escape

Faint traces of dawn appeared in the east as the girls pushed the dinghy into the water and climbed aboard, Caitlin shaky and unsteady, Chloe anxious and in a hurry. She hauled two short oars from under the midship thwart and fitted them into the oarlocks.

"You know how to row this thing?" Caitlin whispered.

"Piece of cake," Chloe answered. She sat facing the stern and dipped the blades, swinging the bow around and pulling out into the stream.

Caitlin managed a weak smile. "Apparently you've done this before," she said. "Should we try the motor?"

"Not yet," Chloe said. "Let's not take a chance on someone hearing it."

"How did you get the gate open?"

"I didn't. Carman was so drunk when he arrived that he dropped the padlock, then forgot about it. When Shelagh sees the gate standing open, they'll come after us."

"How can they? We've got his boat."

"They have another one, a wooden one. I discovered it when I was snooping around the yard."

"Can we take that one too?"

"It's chained to a pipe stuck in the ground, in the lean-to with the generator and the propane bottles."

"Shit!"

"That's not our biggest problem," Chloe said.

"What is?"

"Look." Twenty meters ahead the narrow creek split into three. "How'll we know which way gets us out of here?"

Caitlin peered ahead in the dim light, just able to make out masses of mangrove roots thrusting out of the water. "Damned if I know."

"Listen," Chloe said, "you heard someone say we're on the west coast of Florida, right? So if we head west, we'll end up in the Gulf of Mexico."

"Which way is west?"

Chloe pointed toward the predawn light. "Sun comes up in the east, so we go the opposite way."

Caitlin examined the little electric outboard and traced the cables that connected it to a bulky battery under the aft seat. "We must be far enough away by now. How's this thing work?"

"Can't be too hard. The long handle on the front is the tiller. Push it right and you'll go left, and vice versa. Is there a key somewhere?"

"How do you know all this stuff?"

"Dad's got a motor boat, keeps it in Bedford Basin," Chloe said.

Caitlin found the key and turned it, but nothing happened. "How do I start it?"

"There should be a control knob at the base of the tiller."

"This thing?" Caitlin twisted a dial and the motor purred to life. The little boat surged forward. "All right! Now we're getting somewhere." She reversed the dial and the motor slowed down. "You're the expert. You want to steer this thing?"

Chloe shipped the oars and the girls traded places. Caitlin settled in the bow. Faced with three route choices, she said, "We still don't know which way to go."

Chloe waved a hand behind her where the shapes of trees had emerged from the nighttime shadows. "The sun's coming up that way, so we just have to keep it behind us." She increased speed and picked the middle stream, and a few minutes later they bottomed out where the channel ended in a shallow quagmire. She reversed and headed back to where the routes divided.

"Okay," she said, "that didn't work. Left or right?"

"Eenie meenie."

For the next half hour they threaded their way among the islets, backtracking when necessary but always trending west. In full daylight they found it easier to pick a route, and finally discovered a small lagoon.

"Is that what I think it is?" Caitlin said, pointing excitedly.

"Carman's trawler," Chloe said.

Sixty-one:
The Cabin

Rose-Ellen Foster awakened late. She padded out of the bedroom she shared with Anna into the main room and looked through the window. She spotted the massive gate gaping wide in the sunlight.

"Son of a bitch!" she exclaimed aloud. She threw open the cabin door and Carman, who had been sleeping against it, fell backward into the room. She dragged him far enough inside to close the door, then hurried to the girls' room, unlocked it, and burst inside. The screen hung loosely from the window. The cots were empty.

It took three cups of coffee before Carman was coherent enough to explain what he was doing there. The Spider had called his cell and ordered him to fetch Chloe and take her to Tampa a day earlier than originally planned. Carman was already half drunk at the time, and it was well after dark when he arrived at the lagoon where he anchored his trawler before heading for the island. He had finished off a bottle of rum and fallen asleep, and it was hours before he managed to inflate his dinghy and navigate the confusing channels to the island.

"You miserable idiot," Rose-Ellen shouted at him. "You've compromised the whole operation."

Carman sat with his face buried in his hands. "I'll get them back," he said. "They'll get lost out there for sure."

"And if they don't?"

"Nobody can find a way out of here without a chart, especially two dumb kids."

"*Dumb?*" Rose-Ellen snorted. "That Sharma kid's got brains like Einstein, the other one too. Get your sorry ass out on the water and *find them!*"

Carman shuffled to his feet and left the cabin. He uncovered the wooden tender in the lean-to, unchained it, and dragged it through the gate to the water. He returned for a little three-horse outboard and mounted it on the stern. He gassed it up and shoved the boat through an expanse of partially submerged sea grass into the stream. The engine caught on the first pull of the cord and he aimed toward the southwest.

Sixty-two:
Caitlin and Chloe

A rising wind nudged the inflatable dinghy up against the port side of the trawler, and Chloe grabbed a cleat and tied it off. They climbed aboard and found the big boat deserted. Chloe located the control panel, but there was no key in the ignition.

"How far do you think we are from the Gulf?" Caitlin said.

"Has to be close, 'cause this boat needs deep water. Anyway, there's no way to start it without a key, and the dinghy's real slow. We'll never get away if Carman comes after us. He's probably on the way here right now."

Caitlin considered. "Think we can disable this beast?"

Chloe looked around. "We can't get at the engine," she said. "It's under the floorboards, and they're bolted down. We could smash our way in, but we don't have any tools." She frowned. "I don't know anything about engines anyway."

Caitlin stared at the wheel. "How about the steering? Can we screw that up somehow?"

"Same problem, no tools. Nothing to smash it with."

"Must be something we can do."

"Let's haul her anchors and see if she'll drift aground." Chloe mounted the gunwale and ran to the bow. She grasped the forward anchor line and tugged on it and the boat moved a few feet, but the anchor wouldn't break free. "Try the back one!" she called out.

"Got a better idea!" Caitlin shouted. "I found a knife under a seat."

Chloe hurried back to the cockpit where Caitlin was sawing away on the aft anchor line. It took her awhile to sever the stout rope, but eventually it parted and the stern began to swing with the current.

"Nice work," Chloe said. "Give me the knife and I'll get the front one. Go untie the dinghy so we can get off quick when she starts to move."

Within minutes the girls were seated in the dinghy, watching the ponderous trawler as it floated toward a tangled mass of mangrove roots. The bow struck and the hull canted to starboard and continued on its way, driven by an increasingly brisk wind. The trawler spun around stern first and rammed into another stand of mangroves. It broke free and rotated on its axis, then ground to a halt with the keel buried in the seabed.

"Tide's on its way out," Chloe said. "When he gets here, he won't be able to get her off the bottom for hours."

"You know a lot about this stuff," Caitlin said.

"My Dad's a boat nut. I've been going out on the water with him since before I can remember."

"But not *in* it. How come you never learned to swim?"

"Get off my back." Chloe grasped the outboard's tiller and pointed the dinghy into the wind. They rounded the nearest island and found a narrow waterway that branched off in two directions, north and southwest.

"Take the left one," Caitlin said.

"Why?"

"That puts the wind behind us. If we get to open water, that'll give us more speed."

"We don't even know where we are."

"Doesn't matter, does it? Anywhere is better than here. The farther we get away from those crazy bastards, the better."

Chloe took the left channel, and within fifty yards they entered a broad bay beyond which the Gulf of Mexico yawned invitingly. They cheered and headed toward open water, but as they cleared the last of the coastal islands the motor faltered, and the boat slowed.

"Now what?" Caitlin said.

"Battery's nearly dead, and there's no spare."

"We can't quit now. Want to teach me how to row?"

Sixty-three:
The Lagoon

Carman reached open water and slowed the outboard to idle. He couldn't see the trawler and throttled up again to circle north, finally spotting the stranded craft where it lay canted to port in the receding tide.

"Son of a bitch!" he muttered. "I'm gonna kill those snot-nosed brats!"

His cell phone chimed. He turned it on and Rose-Ellen bellowed in his ear. "Did you find them yet? Where the hell are you?"

"In the lagoon," Carman said. "The trawler's aground. I can't move it until the tide comes back in."

"And when is that?"

"Late afternoon, maybe."

"How'd it happen?"

"Looks like the little bastards set her adrift."

"The two you called 'dumb kids,' right?" she said sarcastically. "So where are they?"

"Not here. Probably still lost."

"More likely out in the Gulf and on their way to the cops. I told The Spider you'd screw this up somehow!"

"Listen, Rose, they can't get far in the inflatable. The motor will quit soon and there's no spare battery."

"Suppose someone picks them up?"

"Okay, what do you want me to do?"

"The Spider called. He said if you haven't found them by tomorrow morning, we're to pack up and get out. Abandon the site."

"What's the rush? Nobody knows these islands like I do. It'll take days for the Coast Guard to find us."

"You jackass, how about thermal imaging? They'll fly a copter over the area and pick up our heat signature."

"That doesn't mean they can get to us."

"Don't be stupid. Air boats, survey maps, local guides? We'd be sitting ducks. We're out of here at dawn. We take what we can and torch what's left. We can't risk leaving anything behind that might lead the cops to us."

"Okay, start packing. But I'll have the trawler back in service before sunset and run a few miles up and down the coast. If I find the kids, I'll call you. If not, I'll be back for you by midnight."

"Stay out of the bottle!" Rose-Ellen said. "That's what got us into this mess in the first place."

Sixty-four:
Rowing South

"Are you okay?" Caitlin asked Chloe. It seemed to her as if her friend had been rowing for hours. She looked exhausted. "Want me to take over again? I'm getting good at this rowing business."

The sun was falling toward the horizon, and they still hadn't passed a single sign of civilization. Nor had any other boats passed within hailing distance. They tried several times to penetrate the mangrove swamps, looking for a passage to the mainland, only to be forced out by narrow, shallow straits.

Chloe shipped the oars and leaned back, stretching her cramped muscles. "What about your hands?" she asked.

Caitlin examined her red, blistered palms. "I'll be fine."

"You're gonna bleed all over your piano," Chloe said.

"I might never get to play again unless we find someplace to land soon. And why the heck didn't we think to bring some water? I am so damn thirsty. I must have an albatross hanging around my neck."

"What?"

"Coleridge? *The Rime of the Ancient Mariner*"?

"Oh, right, I hate that poem," Chloe said. "You think you're cursed like that sailor?"

"*We drifted o'er the harbour-bar, and I with sobs did pray—O let me be awake, my God! Or let me sleep alway.*"

"Thanks. That really cheers me up."

Caitlin laughed. "You look half dead anyway. Come on, let me row awhile."

They switched positions, and Caitlin dipped the oars and pulled. The wind had dropped, no longer helping them along, and they were moving slowly just a dozen meters offshore.

"What's the tide doing, oh master mariner?" Caitlin asked.

"Past high," Chloe said. "You thinking what I am?"

"Carman will get his boat off the bottom and come after us. We should've tried to sink it."

"Maybe he'll go north instead."

"Can't count on it. How about we hide in among the islands?"

"And by morning we'll be dead from thirst."

"Nah, people can live a week or more without water."

"You call that living?" Chloe said. "Anyway, you're wrong. You can go that long without food maybe, but three days is about the limit without water before you either croak or go nuts and try to drink sea water. And that'll kill you quicker."

They passed a wide island that projected out into the Gulf, and as they came around the end, Chloe sat up straight and pointed excitedly. "Look!"

Caitlin stopped rowing and swung her head around. Tucked in close to shore, a substantial yacht lay quietly at anchor, stern on toward them. The sails were down and no one was in the cockpit.

"What do you think?" Chloe said.

"Can't be Carman. Even if this were his boat, which isn't his style, he couldn't get ahead of us without us seeing him. Let's take a chance." Caitlin leaned hard on the oars, oblivious to her sore hands, and within a few minutes they were close to the big yacht's stern.

"It's either a yawl or a ketch." Chloe said.

"Y'all sure of that, honeychile?" Caitlin said in a broad southern drawl.

"That's a stupid pun."

"What's a yawl, anyway?"

"A boat with two masts. A ketch is, too. I always get them confused. Dad would know. It has something to do with whether the mizzen is before or after the rudder. I think this one might be a ketch, only there's no jib. That's weird!"

Caitlin swung the dinghy parallel to the stern. "Yawl? Ketch? Mizzen? Jib? What language is that?"

"Sailor talk, you landlubber. And this thing is huge. I wonder how big a crew she carries?"

"See anyone yet?"

"Looks deserted. There's a name on the stern, only I don't think it's in English."

Caitlin looked over her shoulder again. "German: *Versteck*. It means 'hiding' or 'hideaway.' Strange name for a boat." She dipped the oars and they pulled alongside.

Chloe vaulted onto a narrow platform at the stern. "Anyone here?" she called out. There was no answer, and she tried again. "May we come aboard?"

When there was still no reply, she shrugged and tied the dinghy to a cleat. She and Caitlin climbed the ladder and peered over the stern rail to find the entry to the cabin closed and padlocked.

"Nobody here," Chloe said. "It's got a security system, and it's armed. See the green light beside the hatch?" She looked around, then stood on a seat so she could see from stem to stern. "No tender hanging in the davits, so whoever owns it must be over among the islands."

"Can we get inside? I really need some water. My throat's on fire."

"We'd have to break in, and there's a big lock on the hatch. Take a look under the seats and see if there's anything there to drink."

Caitlin rummaged around and came up with a can of ginger ale. She popped the tab and they shared it gratefully.

"Warm but good," Caitlin said. "That helps a little. Now what'll we do?"

"We sit and wait, I suppose." Chloe was leaning over the port rail, trying to see in among the mangroves. "Or we can row over and look for them."

Caitlin didn't answer. She was staring rigidly back the way they had come, where the distant shape of a motor vessel had just appeared some distance off shore.

"Is that Carman?" Chloe said softly.

"Too far away to tell. But we better not hang around to find out."

The girls climbed over the stern rail, and two minutes later Chloe was pulling hard toward the swampy inlets.

Sixty-five:
Carman

"I know where they are," Carman said into his cell phone. His trawler lay dead in the water, the engine idling. "There's big yacht anchored about a mile south, close to shore. I checked it out with my scope and spotted them in the cockpit. They just rowed in among the islands."

"Did they see you?" Rose-Ellen asked.

"Not unless they've got binoculars. I'm too far away."

"So go get them!"

"I can't. I left the tender back in the lagoon. They're in my inflatable, and I can't take the trawler in there. But there's nowhere they can go. They have to come out eventually, and I'll grab them and bring them back."

"You damn well better," Rose-Ellen said, "and in one piece, too. Don't forget why The Spider's crew snatched the little mongrel in the first place."

"I could drown the other one. You said she's no good to us."

"Better not. Somebody might recover the body, and they'd know she didn't die in the explosion. You have to bring her back too."

"Yeah, well, I may wring her scrawny neck first."

"Wait until you get back here. We can stash her under some mangroves and let the 'gators have her. But first you have to catch them. What makes you think they'll show their faces if they see your trawler?"

"I'll stay out of sight until dark. Somebody'll show up sooner or later, either the yacht's crew or the kids, maybe together. I'll wing it from there."

"Don't screw this up, damn it! You're armed?"

"You ever know me not to be? Relax. I'll have the rotten kids back to you long before sunup. And if I have to, I'll deep six the yacht's crew and set her adrift."

"Why not just sink it?"

"If I scuttle her in this shallow water, she'll be too easy to spot, especially from the air."

She sighed. "Carman, you better not screw this up. The Spider will deep six *you* if he loses his leverage over the kid's father. You keep in touch, you hear me? I want to know the minute you have them."

"Take a Valium, Rose. I'm on this. I'll call you as soon as the brats are aboard."

Carman disconnected and thrust the phone into his pocket. "Stupid bitch," he grumbled. He throttled up and moved behind the nearest island, where he anchored with his lights off and settled down to wait for full dark.

PART THREE

Sixty-six:
Rolf

Caitlin Sheridan, how in the name of Bach, Beethoven and Brahms did you end up way out here in the middle of alligator country? Everyone thinks you're dead." I could hardly believe it, finding her alive and well in a dinghy off the Florida coast after months had passed. But more surprises were to come.

"Who are *you*?" she said, blinking and shading her eyes. I turned the flashlight on my face. "I know you!" she said. "You talked to me on stage after the concert. Wie heißen Sie?"

What's your name?

"Little girl," I said, "I'm impressed. You speak German like a native, and Spanish too. My name is Rolf Niemand, and my English is fine."

"Your name is *Nobody*?" Caitlin said incredulously.

I ignored that and nodded toward the other girl. "Is this your friend from the Jet Ski accident?"

"I'm Chloe," she said. "If that's your boat out there, where's your crew?"

"Just me," Rolf said. "She's cat rigged."

"What's that?"

"No jib, and the mast is stepped close to the bow. All the sheets and halyards lead to the cockpit, so I don't need a crew."

"That's hard to believe."

"Maybe I'll get a chance to show you. Now how about we start over and get to know one another. How did you two get here? Are you lost? In trouble? Brauchst du Hilfe? ¿Necesitas ayuda?"

"Need help?" Caitlin sighed with relief. "Do we ever! Somebody is chasing us."

Twenty minutes later I was trying to make sense of everything the girls told me, a wild tale of kidnapping and imprisonment, hidden islands, a sadistic bitch named Shelagh, and someone called Carman who was following them. Unbelievable—but I couldn't imagine why they would make up such an implausible story, and what else would explain the presence of two supposedly dead young teenagers in a tiny dinghy so far from the mainland?

"We have to call the police," Caitlin insisted. "You've got a radio on your boat, right?"

"Of course."

"Well, let's *go!* Now that they know we're gone, who knows what they'll do? We need the Coast Guard or the Navy. Somebody has to stop them!"

"One of you come over here. I need you to hold the flashlight so we can find our way out of here in the dark."

Caitlin scrambled into my bow and took the light from me.

"What about me?" Chloe said.

"I'll tow you. You sit at the oars and help out as much as you can."

"What if that freak Carman is out there waiting for us?"

"How would he know you're here? You said he didn't see you. If you spot his boat, we'll hide out in here until he's gone." I dipped my oars. "Here we go."

The wind had risen again, stirring up a light chop in the Gulf, and the inflatable wallowed in my wake as we approached *Versteck*. The nearly full moon cast a warm glow on the water to improve visibility, and there was no other boat in sight. My hull loomed above us, and as I swung to come alongside the stern platform, a bulky figure rose up in the cockpit and pointed a shotgun at us.

"Tie up," he ordered.

"Shit!" Caitlin whispered. "That's Carman."

If I'd been alone, I'd have had a reasonable chance of disarming the man once I reached the cockpit, but I had two other lives to consider. I wrapped my tender's painter around a cleat on the platform to keep it in place.

"Send the brats up first," the man said.

"Do what he says," I whispered, "but try to stay away from him."

They climbed out, crept up the ladder, and stepped over the rail. Carman reached out and slapped them both. Caitlin sprawled backward on the deck. Chloe dropped to her knees.

"Don't move!" he growled at them. He turned and looked toward me again. "Keep your hands where I can see them and get up here." He stepped back.

I climbed into the cockpit. Carman levelled the shotgun at my gut, his finger inside the trigger guard. I glanced over the starboard side and discovered his trawler tied up to seaward in the shadow of my hull, fenders squeaking as it shifted in the chop. My cabin had been breached. Beside the companionway the red security lamp was blinking. The hasp hung open and the padlock lay on the sole next to a bolt cutter, its shank in pieces.

"Sit!" Carman said, and I obeyed. "You two, over the side into my boat," he told Caitlin and Chloe.

Caitlin struggled to her feet and looked toward the starboard rail. It was a short drop to the deck below. She stared at me, panic in her eyes, and I nodded reassuringly. "Do as he says," I told her. "It'll be all right."

"You think?" Carman laughed. "I should toss these brats to the sharks right now."

"You do that and Shelagh will kill you," Caitlin muttered.

"Shut up! I can handle that bitch."

"*Sure* you can."

Carman reached out to slap her again, and she ducked and swung her feet over the rail. She dropped out of sight, landing lightly on the trawler's deck. Carman motioned to Chloe. "You're next, mutt."

Chloe edged around him toward the rail and followed Caitlin. Once she was out of sight, Carman spun to face me. I was still hoping for a chance to overpower him, but the gun never wavered.

"Keys," he ordered. I dug into my pocket and produced the Styrofoam float attached to the yacht's ignition key. He grabbed it from me, then reversed the shotgun and slammed the stock into the side of my head. My cheekbone shattered in a spray of blood. I collapsed onto the deck, and he stooped and boosted me over the rail and dropped me into the sea.

Sixty-seven:
Carman

Carman vaulted over the stern rail and slid down the ladder. He untied the inflatable and sat on the middle seat to row around to the trawler. Once aboard, he found the girls cowering in the galley.

"In there!" he snarled at them, motioning toward the forward berth. Caitlin and Chloe stumbled through the door and he slammed it shut behind them. He threw a bolt to keep them inside and returned to the deck.

He stood on the gunwale, reached up and caught *Versteck*'s rail, and hauled himself aboard. He retrieved the shotgun, ejected the shells, and lowered it carefully down to the trawler. The stern anchor of Rolf's yacht came free of the bottom easily, and Carman hauled it aboard. He ran forward and raised the bow anchor, then returned to the cockpit and started the engine. He pointed the prow due west and aligned the wheel to leave the rudder straight.

He cast off the trawler's forward line and loosened the aft one, then reached for the control panel and put the yacht in gear and advanced the throttle to a modest eight hundred rpm. He released the trawler's stern line and dropped quickly over the starboard rail onto his boat's deck. As the two craft drifted apart, he fired up his engine, turned north, and pulled out his cell phone.

"Rose?" he said when the call went through. "Call off the evacuation. I'm on my way home with a full cargo and no loose ends."

Sixty-eight:
Caitlin

A s soon as Carman bolted the girls in the forward berth, Caitlin began looking for a means of escape. She pried at a stubborn latch on the starboard porthole.

"What're you doing?" Chloe said.

"We're getting out of here. If I can get this thing open, we're skinny enough to squeeze through."

Chloe looked panicked. "I can't! I can barely swim. You know that."

"It's our only chance. You can make it if I help you. Once Carman leaves, we'll get aboard the yacht and radio the Coast Guard."

"Where's Rolf?"

"I don't know."

When the latch gave way, Caitlin swung the porthole open and squirmed through feet first. She flipped over on her stomach and slithered all the way out, dropping into the sea. She surfaced and waved to Chloe. "Come on," she called out quietly.

"I can't. I'm too scared. I can't touch bottom out here."

Caitlin heard the sound of the yacht's diesel starting up. "Okay, Carman probably won't check on you before he takes off. By the time he knows I'm gone, I'll already have the Coast Guard on the way. They'll come and save everyone."

"Suppose Rolf's gone. You don't know how to sail his boat. Or how to use a radio either, do you?"

"How hard can it be?" They heard Carman's footsteps on the trawler's deck. "I'm outta here," she said softly, and swam toward the bow as the yacht started to move. She stroked hard and caught the edge of the stern platform, and found Rolf's inert form hanging halfway over the edge.

Sixty-nine:
Rolf

The impact and shock of the cold water jarred me awake. I fought my way to the surface, sucked in a deep breath, and turned over to float on my back under the curve of the hull. I lay there semi-conscious, some instinct keeping me on the surface, until I heard Carman moving around the deck, dealing with the anchors. The big boat shifted with the current. Then the diesel came to life. I struggled toward the stern and hooked one arm over a cleat and hung on.

When I heard the transmission drop into gear, I heaved myself halfway up onto the platform and clutched the slats of the drainage grate. The hull began to move and my mind clouded, my eyes closed, and the next thing I knew, Caitlin was shouting in my ear, begging me to wake up. She was tugging on my belt to keep me from slipping into the sea. My arms and legs felt leaden and my stomach contracted, spewing gouts of brine over the side.

My head cleared slowly and I blinked my salt-stung eyes, hardly able to see in the cloud-shrouded moonlight. Instinct took over again, and I tightened my grasp on the slats and inched forward. With Caitlin's help I managed to get completely out of the water.

"You're bleeding!" she cried. I raised my hand to my face and discovered torn flesh and a deep depression where my cheekbone had been. Congealing blood oozed thickly from multiple cuts.

"Are you gonna be okay?" she said. Her voice was a salt-ravaged croak. "I need you!"

"What happened?" I asked her.

"I escaped from the trawler. Carman locked us up and I got out through a porthole. I had to leave Chloe behind. She can barely swim and was too scared to come with me."

"We're moving? What's happening? Is Carman aboard?"

"He started your engine and then went back to the trawler and took off. We're heading away from shore, out into the ocean."

"We better get to the controls." I rolled over onto my knees and grasped the ladder, but my legs buckled when I tried to stand and I fell back, dizzy. I couldn't catch my breath.

"I'll do it," Caitlin said. "Tell me how."

"Control panel," I told her, gasping for air. "Find the gear shift. It's marked FNR, for forward-neutral-reverse. Move it to the letter N and we'll stop."

"You gonna be okay if I leave you?"

I managed a sour grin. "Por supuesto," I said in Spanish.
Of course.

"Natürlich." Caitlin managed a weak grin and scooted up the ladder. "Found it!" she called out to me. I heard the transmission drop out of gear and could feel the boat begin to slow.

"The lever on the right is the throttle," I called out. "Pull it all the way back." She did, and the diesel slowed to idle. I got to my feet, grasped the ladder, and moved upward one hesitant step at a time.

"Don't let go!" Caitlin said, alarmed, reaching out to grasp my shoulder.

"I'm okay. Thanks to you." But as I half stepped, half fell over the rail, everything turned black and I collapsed onto the deck.

Seventy:
Carman

Back in the lagoon, with the trawler's anchors lying somewhere on the bottom after the girls cut them loose, Carman dug a spare line out of a storage bin and secured it to a bow cleat. He climbed over the rail and rowed the dinghy to shore, where he tied the line to a mango root.

He rowed back to the trawler and opened the forward berth, where Chloe cowered on the bunk. He looked around for Caitlin, puzzled at first, then spotted the porthole hanging open. "Christ on a crutch!" he groaned. He pulled the cell phone out of his pocket and called Rose-Ellen Foster.

"I'm back in the lagoon," he said when she picked up.

"Good. Get the kids up here."

"Problem," he said. "I've got the mutt, but the other one jumped ship."

"How the hell did you let that happen?"

"I locked them in the forward berth. The skinny bitch pried the porthole open and got out. But she must've drowned. I sent the yacht off under power, aimed at Yucatan. Even if she managed to swim to the islands, there's nowhere she can go. A 'gator'll get her if a shark doesn't first."

The line stayed silent.

"Rose?" Carman said. "You still there?"

When she spoke at last her voice was flat, cold and dead, without inflection. "You haven't lost the tender, have you? Bring the mongrel back here."

"I tell you, the operation's safe. There's no way the other kid ain't dead by now."

"I'll see what The Spider says." The line went dead.

Carman glared at Chloe. "When did she go overboard?"

"I don't know," Chloe lied.

"What do you mean, *you don't know!* You were right here!"

"I fell asleep."

"You friggin' bitch, you better be tellin' the truth." He grabbed her arm and dragged her out to the deck. He pointed to the seat by the port rail. "Sit there and don't move!" he ordered. He climbed down and hauled the tender close to the swim platform and started its engine.

"Let's go," he shouted above the noise. Chloe climbed over the rail and stepped into the tender. Carman slapped her backhand across the face and she tumbled backward across the stern seat. "I should've drowned you when I had the chance. Sit down and keep your goddamn mouth shut. I'm gonna find some way to make you pay for this."

He untied and throttled up to head for the island.

Seventy-one:
Aboard *Versteck*

When I came around, Caitlin was bathing my face with a damp cloth, washing away the dried blood from my flattened cheek. She helped me to my feet, but I had to lean on her for balance. I braced myself behind the wheel, turned the boat east again, and throttled up, keeping *Versteck* to a safe four knots. The depth gauge showed plenty of water beneath the keel, and we were close to the islands before the bottom rose up to just a few fathoms. Then I slowed and hove to.

"You have to help me put the anchors down," I told her. "We can't risk running aground in the night."

"Tell me what to do," she said.

With Caitlin moving from bow to stern to toss the big hooks overboard, I edged *Versteck* back and forth and soon had them set securely. Another bout of vertigo hit me, and when I tried to enter the companionway to go below, I stumbled on the ladder and sprawled on the sole of the galley. Caitlin helped me onto the port bench and I lay back, still trying to catch my breath.

A quick glance toward the chart table confirmed my worst fears. The communication equipment was smashed, the wiring torn loose and hanging out, the circuit boards crushed beyond repair.

"Carman did that?" she asked.

"Who else?"

"The radio's dead?"

I nodded. "Looks like he trashed the EPIRB too."

"What's that?"

"Emergency Position-Indicating Radio Beacon. It sends out an automatic signal when a boat is in trouble. When it's working."

"How about your cell phone?"

"Never needed one."

"So we can't call the Coast Guard or the Navy? What'll we do?"

"We're on our own, at least until we can get help somewhere. I have to do something about my face first. See that overhead bin behind the table? There's a first aid kit in there. Haul it down, okay?"

Caitlin stood on the bench and found the kit. She handed it over.

"Grácias, bella dama," I said, hoping a light tone would help set her mind at ease.

"De nada." She looked down at her shorts and tee, soaked and ripped after her escape from the trawler. "Thanks for the compliment, but I'm not too beautiful right now. At least you haven't lost your sense of humour."

"Just testing you. To see how good your Spanish really is."

"Cállate, hombre," she said with a smile.

Shut up, man.

"Think you can bring me a mirror? There's one in the head."

"Head?"

"Badezimmer. Baño. Badkamer. *Waschraum*, for Pete's sake! Take your pick."

"Okay! Enough! I've got it!" She looked relieved. "You're feeling better."

"There's a blacksmith forging horseshoes in my brain. How about finding that mirror?"

She located the head, and I could hear her rummaging around in the cubby beside the shower stall. She brought the mirror out and handed it to me.

"Danke," I thanked her.

"Bitte." She shook her head, smiling, but I could tell from her expression that she was still concerned. I hoped I could convince her that I would be all right.

As I sorted through the contents of the first aid kit, she cast her eye around the galley. She spotted something familiar in the aft compartment, my Roland keyboard mounted in a gimballed rack, headphones draped across it.

"You have a keyboard back there?" she asked. I was staring in the mirror, probing the bone fragments in my cheek, and waved her off without speaking. She entered my seagoing studio and began examining the equipment I had installed seven years before. She turned her attention to the huge mixer and recording deck, then noticed what I knew would surprise her: a cloth-covered piece of furniture that had no business being aboard a yacht. She lifted one corner of the cover.

"Holy cow!" she exclaimed. "You have a *piano* in there! A *real* one!"

"Just a small spinet. This isn't exactly Carnegie Hall, you know." My face throbbed and the shattered chunks of cheekbone scraped together as I worked antiseptic into the torn flesh.

"How do you get someone to tune it?" she asked.

"Do it myself."

She whirled around, whipped the cover off, and dumped it in a corner. She tried to pull out the bench and couldn't move it. She looked at me with raised eyebrows.

"Had to bolt everything down in case of rough seas," I told her.

She sat and stretched her feet out toward the pedals. "I can hardly reach," she complained.

"It fits me. I don't usually have a runt like you on board."

"Yeah, yeah, I've heard that line before." She dismissed me with a wave and examined the blisters on her hands. She flexed her fingers, and I could tell from her grimace that she was stiff and sore. I could almost read her mind: *What the hell, they can't feel any worse.*

She plunged into a series of four octave scales at breakneck speed, all around the circle of fifths; a bit ragged but smoothing out as her hands loosened up. She hammered out a favourite Hanon exercise, played "shave and a haircut, two bits," and jumped directly into the principal theme and cadenza of the *Emperor Concerto*. The spinet's little soundboard did its best to reproduce Beethoven's early Romantic tour de force.

"Oh, man, am I ever rusty," she muttered as the last chord died away. "But that felt so good."

She stood up hesitantly and padded back into the galley, looking self-conscious. "Sorry about that. I guess I got a little carried away. You okay?" she asked.

"You're back," I said, eternally grateful to whatever gods or demons had wrought this miracle. "I was sure you were gone forever."

Seventy-two:
Recovery

Caitlin was anxious to find a Coast Guard station, but I convinced her that waiting until morning wouldn't make any difference. I didn't feel confident to be travelling at night in my weakened condition. I checked the time—past one a.m.—and tried to sleep, but Tylenol barely touched the pain in my face. Caitlin was wide awake, stimulated by her narrow escape. She dug through my cabinets and made sandwiches for us both, which helped relieve my headache somewhat.

She was curious to know why a sailor had such an elaborate music studio on board.

"I told you I was a musician when I talked to you on stage," I said.

"Yeah, I remember. 'I play a little keyboard,' you said. "Define 'a little' for me, will you? And why don't you keep all this stuff at home? Where do you live, anyway?"

"You're looking at it. I just bum around the islands, picking up gigs here and there."

She looked puzzled. "Rock?"

"Sure. Or jazz, blues, even country if I have to. Whatever pays the freight. For myself, I play the classics."

"Wow! Know anything for four hands?"

"I might be able to recall the Mozart *C Major Sonata*."

She grinned. "That one's neat. My teacher used to play it with me when I was eight."

When you were eight, I thought. *Right!* "I don't have the score. Do you remember it?"

"Duh," she said. "Come on. You do the *Primo*."

"You know the second part too?"

"You can't play the top if you don't understand the bottom."

Out of the mouths of babes.

"Let's give it a try."

I was a little unsteady as I left the galley but beginning to feel alert again. I sat at the right side of the keyboard, Caitlin to my left. After a couple of false starts our memories kicked in, and we were off and running. Then we switched places and tried the same composer's *Fugue in G minor*, Caitlin on the top part, myself *Secondo*.

"That's enough," I told her finally. "The blacksmith is back rampaging around in my skull." I made my way stiffly into the galley and downed more Tylenol, then sank onto the port bench. Caitlin followed along and plopped down beside me.

"That was fun," she said, grinning widely. "You're really good!"

"I'm out of practice, but you are incredible. You haven't played that sonata since you were eight?"

She shrugged. "I missed a few notes."

"Yeah. Probably two."

"How long are we gonna stay here? I'm really worried about Chloe."

"We'll get under way at first light."

"My parents must think I'm gone for good."

"You said you're from Bournemouth, in Nova Scotia?"

"Uh huh. Not much of a town, except there was another piano player who came from there, way better than me. I only know about him from what I've been told. He was a genius. I think he must be dead now, 'cause my mom says he dropped out of sight years ago, just suddenly stopped performing and recording. No one knows why. He was young, like twenty something."

"J. J. MacIsaac?"

Her face lit up. "Did you know him?"

"I did. A long time ago."

235

Seventy-three:
Underway

After too little sleep we were up before dawn, having an early breakfast in the galley. "Are we gonna go somewhere to call the Coast Guard now?" Caitlin asked.

"Not until we see if the people who held you captive are still around. By now your old buddy Carman knows you escaped, and he'll be afraid you'll blow the whistle on them. It's my guess they'll bug out as quickly as they can."

"He's not my buddy, that's for sure. And if they leave, I may never see Chloe again. Something awful could happen to her."

"That's why we have to try to find them."

"How'll we know where to look? All those islands look alike to me. I'll never remember how to get back there."

"I'll show you." I carried our dishes to the sink. "You want to brush your teeth first?"

"Sure, why not? Nothing as important as good oral hygiene, right?"

"I can do without the sarcasm. You'll find a couple of fresh brushes in the right-hand drawer in the head."

Caitlin went in search of one, cleaned her teeth, and came back two minutes later. "Sure wish I had a change of clothes," she said, pulling at her salt-encrusted top that had dried stiff and probably itchy.

"I think I can find you a pair of size thirty-six shorts."

"I'll pass."

"You can go topside. I'll be there in a minute."

Once she was up the ladder and out of sight, I found a small Ziploc bag and walked down to the head. I picked up her toothbrush with a tissue and dropped it into the bag, then returned to the galley and placed it in the chart table.

"So, what's this magic of yours that'll help us find them?" she asked as I climbed out of the companionway. She was haloed by light from the rising sun that filtered through the mangroves, looking alert and eager to get moving despite her bedraggled clothing.

I took the cover off the GPS and booted it up, relieved to find that Carman hadn't touched it. "Take a look." I pointed to the chart that appeared on the screen, showing a dot and some numbers. "See this? It's called a waypoint. When I sailed north last spring, I stopped and watched some manatees for awhile. Fascinating creatures. They hung out next to the hull for half an hour, two big ones and a baby."

"Fascinating," Caitlin said impatiently. "So what?"

"I entered a waypoint so I could look for them again the next time I came this way."

"What good does that do?"

"I'm getting to that. I also saw Carman's trawler that day. I didn't know who he was at the time, of course. He was coming out from among the mangroves and passed right by me. All we have to do is sail to the waypoint and look for an inlet that's wide enough for a boat that size."

"Holy cow! That's amazing! But it's a long way inland to where they kept us locked up, and really confusing. How'll we find Chloe? Carman took the inflatable, so even if we could find the cabin, your boat is too big to go there."

"They have to come out some time."

"But what can we do? You're hurt, and I'm just a kid."

"Let's cross all those bridges when we come to them," I told her. "I'm feeling better, and I'm not exactly helpless. If we can locate the right island, even if we can't rescue your friend ourselves, we'll know how to tell the Coast Guard where to find her. And we better get going. We're farther down the coast than I thought." I started the diesel.

"I'm scared," Caitlin said. "But I trust you."

That surprised me, and I looked at her curiously. I hadn't thought that would be an issue. "Thanks for the vote of confidence," I said. "Even though you hardly know me."

"I know you're an awesome piano player, even if your Mozart is a little shaky. Musicians have to stick together, right?"

"Right."

Some people can make you smile, just by being themselves. Caitlin Sheridan was a charmer. Then she surprised me again. "How about showing me how to drive the boat?" she asked.

"You don't 'drive' a boat. You *sail* her. That's what you say, even when you use the engine. It's like when a diesel-powered ship *sails* out of port. Not *drives*. That's for cars."

"Okay, okay, enough lectures. Just show me how it works."

"Do I have a choice?"

"Nope."

Seventy-four:
The Cabin

Carman arrived back at the island with Chloe before midnight, towing the inflatable behind the gas-powered tender. Rose-Ellen Foster was incensed and nearly out of control. She dragged Chloe to a utility room at the back of the cabin and locked her in. She moved on to the children's room to empty it, and in a frenzy, she dumped all of Chloe's clothing into a garbage bag, along with anything that might identify her if anyone searched through the wreckage after they left.

She and the staff worked through the night, destroying everything inside the building. Although Rose-Ellen believed that burning the cabin would destroy all traces of their presence there, she wasn't about to take any chances. The Spider would make her pay if she left anything incriminating. Anna and Alonzo gathered up whatever they thought they would need and took it outside. Then they made one last round of the building, searching for anything they may have missed.

At first light the exodus began. Carman refilled the little outboard's gas tank, then carried the fuel can back to the cabin and set it inside the door, prior to pouring it around the foundation. He put a fresh battery in the inflatable, then returned to find Shelagh pacing around the main room.

"Ready to go," Carman told her. "Where's the kid?"

Foster ignored the question. "Tell Anna to stay here with me," she said. "We'll come along in the inflatable after I set the fire. Is the battery charged?"

"I just put in the spare. It's only about half charged, but that'll get you to the lagoon."

"You and Alonzo get aboard your tender and be ready to go. I have a loose end to take care of. Don't leave until I tell you."

* * *

Chloe huddled miserably in the closet, hungry and thirsty and desperate for a toilet to relieve herself. Rose-Ellen had left the light on, a bare bulb in the ceiling, but bright enough so that Chloe slept only fitfully under its glare. Finally unable to control her bladder, she urinated in a corner. Terror faded to resignation as she awaited whatever fate was in store for her. She had no idea what was happening to her friend Caitlin, nor whether she and Rolf were still alive. She had no hope that they could help her. She searched the room, hoping to find a way to escape, and pried ineffectually at the door's hinges, but couldn't drive out the pins without a tool to loosen them.

She knew she was about to die. They had no use for her. She had overheard the women talking on the other side of the door. "What do we do with the mongrel?" Anna had said, and "We should have gotten rid of her when she first arrived."

A mongrel, they called her, racially impure, not *white*—damned pious, sanctimonious "Christians" with their grandiose plans for enslaving or annihilating the world's coloured populations. Chloe knew it was the same sort of hatred and insanity that had wiped out huge numbers of European Jews in the war all those decades ago. And now the damning fact of her parents' mixed Asian ancestry guaranteed her own death.

Regrets. She loved her life. Although embarrassed by feelings of hubris, she gloried in the mental prowess that fuelled her curiosity about the world and drove her to explore every new idea that came her way. She loved her family, her friends back home, and her new friend Caitlin, the bravest girl she had ever met—Caitlin, who had escaped from Carman's boat by plunging fearlessly into the sea. *If only I'd had the courage to follow her*, she thought. *But I won't beg for my life when they come for me. It won't make any difference, but it's important to me. They may kill me, but they won't defeat me.*

Sounds penetrated her prison, a door opening somewhere outside, heavy footsteps approaching. The lock clicked and the knob turned, and morning sunlight flooded into the closet from the room beyond. Her tormentor stood in the opening, hands on hips and eyes burning malevolently.

"You're the cause of all this," Rose-Ellen said flatly.

Chloe shrank back in terror, all bravado gone, faced with the inevitable.

* * *

Ten minutes later, Rose-Ellen emerged from the cabin with something wrapped in a heavy quilt slung over her shoulder. She dumped it on top of the baggage amidships.

"Is that…?" Carman began.

"Just leave it be," Shelagh said. "Dispose of it in the lagoon before you leave."

"The Spider's gonna be mad as hell."

"Too bad. He already got what he wanted from the kid's old man. He'll have to figure out how to handle things himself from now on. Get moving. I'll stick around until I'm sure the fire will do its job, and then Anna and I will catch up with you."

Carman started the engine. Alonzo glanced at the motionless quilt and crossed himself. Using a long pole, he shoved them out into the bay, and they turned west and disappeared into the maze of densely grouped islets.

Seventy-five:
Rolf

A soft chime signalled our arrival at the waypoint. I took the engine out of gear and let the boat drift.

"This is it," I told Caitlin. "I saw the manatees here, and then the trawler appeared out from among the islands to the north." I pointed. "Think you'll recognize where you and Chloe came out when you escaped?"

"I hope so," she said.

I throttled up a little and sent *Versteck* forward, barely above two knots, and we examined each inlet carefully. Two looked promising, but when I nosed the bow into them, I could see that they narrowed almost immediately, and the depth gauge sounded a shrill warning. Then fifty yards farther on, Caitlin pointed to an outcropping of mangroves.

"That looks familiar," she said. "If I'm right, you go left behind that swampy area, and there's a lake and then some little islands all bunched up together. After that everything widens out, and that's where we grounded the trawler."

I checked the depth gauge; the bottom was coming up fast. "We can't take *Versteck* in there. Our keel's too deep, but trawlers only draw half as much water, three feet or a little more. Damn, if only that son of a bitch hadn't taken the tenders, we could go aboard and surprise them when they come."

We anchored the yacht fore and aft, then sat down in the cockpit to think.

"There'll be four of them, plus Chloe," Caitlin said. "Too many to handle, right?"

"Doesn't matter. I'm sure there'll be guns aboard the trawler. I

242

could take them by surprise, if only we could get aboard."

They sat in silent thought for a few moments.

"We could swim," Caitlin suggested softly.

"Too dangerous."

"Not if we're quick. We could stay close to the shore and climb out if anything comes after us. I haven't seen an alligator the whole time we were on the island. I bet Shelagh was just trying to scare us."

"Caitlin, this is the Everglades. Everything that lives here is always hungry, and 'gators are as fast on land as in the water."

"It's worth a try, isn't it?"

"Not if you lose an arm or a leg, or your life." I peered in among the mangroves. "See anything?"

Caitlin scanned the roots and foliage. "Nothing's moving."

"How far is it to where he anchors the trawler?"

"Not far. Maybe the length of a football field, with a couple of small islands in between."

"All right," I told her, "I'll give it a try."

"Good. Let's go."

"You're staying here. You can't take any chances. Your parents need you. If you hear any shooting and if I don't come right back afterward, you pull the anchors, just like I showed you, and take the boat north."

I had taught her how to handle the boat from the console when under power. "Find some people somewhere and get help. Go to the Coast Guard and tell them where we are. And you are *not* to try to follow me. Okay?"

"I want to help."

"Promise me!"

"I don't want to lose you."

"You won't. I'll be okay. This is just in case, that's all."

I slipped over the side and swam fifty meters to the first landfall, using a gentle crawl stroke that might not attract a predator. I climbed out and turned to wave to Caitlin, then sloshed through the swampy terrain until I spotted the trawler across the lagoon. It was less than half a kilometre away in a straight line, a quick swim, but if I followed the ragged shoreline it would take a lot longer. Logic told me that 'gators would be more likely to be hiding among the foliage than the open water anyway, and if one came at me, I wouldn't have a chance to outdistance it no matter where we were. My best shot would be to swim directly toward the trawler and hope for the best.

For whatever reason, skill or plain dumb luck, I reached the trawler unscathed and pulled myself over the transom. There was a gun rack behind the chart table, and I identified a twenty-two rifle, a thirty-aught-six Springfield, and a twelve-gauge shotgun. I hauled them down and checked the magazines. I hadn't been there more than ten minutes when I heard the distinctive mutter of a small outboard approaching from upstream. After throwing the guns overboard, I climbed to the flying bridge and flattened myself down low on the sole, where I could watch the lower deck without being seen. The tender came into view, Carman at the tiller and a man I hadn't seen before in the bow. Several duffels, a lumpy quilt, and a couple of black garbage bags crowded the centre seat.

The outboard dropped to idle as Carman eased his tender up to the trawler's stern. He spotted the cabin door standing open. "Something's wrong," he shouted to the other man. He climbed aboard and entered the cabin. The first thing he noticed was the empty gun rack.

"Son of a bitch!" he yelled and rushed outside. "Goddamnit, Alonzo, somebody's been here, maybe the cops. Forget Rose and the others. They're on their own now. We need to take the boat up the Gulf shore and hide out."

From the puzzled look on his face, I suspected the second man understood little of Carman's tirade. He simply stood still.

"Shit! Goddamn stupid Portugee," Carman mumbled. He re-entered the cabin, muttering to himself, sotto voce: "You're on your own too,

Alonzo, you dumb jerk!" He threw off the line that tethered the trawler to the tree roots and started up the steps to the bridge. I waited until he passed my hiding place and then sprang to my feet and launched a vicious kick to the back of his knees.

Carman stumbled and sprawled on the sole. Catlike, he jumped up and dove down the ladder again. He whirled around to face me, fumbling a long-barrelled Colt revolver out of his belt, but before he could fire I caught up with him and landed a solid blow to his gut. He doubled over and I delivered a massive uppercut to his chin that dropped him to the floor. The gun flew out of his hand and slid under the chart table.

Stunned and disoriented but still game, Carman kicked out and caught me just below the left knee. Off balance, I fell sideways, and he scrambled up and dashed out of the cabin. He leapt toward the rail and dove into the lagoon. I followed after him and peered over the side, expecting to see him swimming away, but the man was nowhere in sight. As the ripples died away, I jumped over the stern rail and approached the tender. The man named Alonzo cowered in the bow, brandishing a boat hook. I avoided his swing and caught hold of his ankle, dumping him over backwards. I jumped aboard at the stern, stepped over the bundles in the middle, and pinned him down with one knee to his stomach. Then I reached out to compress the carotid arteries in his neck. He struggled briefly until his eyes rolled back and he fell limp, out cold.

I released the bow line from the trawler's cleat and lashed the man's hands together behind his back with the bow line. As we drifted away in the tender, I started the outboard and headed for the outlet to the sea. I looked back toward the trawler in time to see Carman climbing aboard over the stern. He ran awkwardly into the cabin and disappeared from view. As I throttled up, he reappeared holding the pistol and fired six shots at us in quick succession. I ducked down low and the slugs flew over our heads without hitting either of us. Carman dropped the pistol and turned to the console.

The trawler's engine roared to life, and with a loud *whump* the boat erupted in a giant ball of flame. Debris flew into the air. Shards of decking rained down on sand and roots and littered the surface of the water. A second explosion blew the port superstructure apart, and I caught a momentary glimpse of Carman's body cartwheeling into the lagoon as I dove for cover.

Alonzo came awake at the noise and screamed as burning fragments cascaded down into the tender. Behind us, the trawler's back was broken. It canted far over to starboard, with the hull gaping open and the keel breached beneath the remains of the heavy gas-powered engine. The big boat settled low in the water, coming to rest on the bottom. Thick smoke billowed upward.

I grabbed the bailing bucket and doused the burning debris, and poured some water over Alonzo's scorched and smouldering shirt. I scanned the surface to try to locate Carman and saw him floating face down, his head nearly severed from his body by the blast. Unable to do anything for him, I grasped the tiller and headed out of the lagoon.

Seventy-six:
Versteck

Once clear of the islands, I manoeuvred into the Gulf to find Caitlin hanging over *Versteck*'s stern rail. She scrambled down and caught the line I tossed her as I coasted up to the platform. "What happened?" she yelled.

"Carman forgot the blowers before he started the engine, and the bilge exploded."

"Huh?"

"Gasoline fumes below decks. I'll explain later."

"Where's Chloe?" she asked, looking at the man in the bow. "Where's Shelagh?"

"I don't know. Carman and this guy came alone," I said, gesturing toward Alonzo.

"What's all that stuff in the bags?"

"No idea. They brought it all with them."

She scrambled back up the ladder and I lifted the object in the quilt, preparing to toss it over the side, but the weight surprised me. I folded back a flap and discovered Chloe's battered, bloody face. I pressed my fingers to one side of her neck and felt a weak, uneven pulse.

I heard Caitlin gasp as I carried the unconscious girl up the ladder. I reached the companionway and took Chloe into the cabin and stretched her out on the starboard bench.

"Is she okay?" Caitlin asked anxiously.

"I need the first aid kit," I told her, "and a wet towel. You can get one from the head."

Chloe's face was badly bruised and torn, her left eye swollen shut, her lips split and caked with blood. Her clothing was tattered, evidence of a massive assault. Her breathing was ragged, but when I listened to her chest, her heart thumped slowly, not racing—a good sign.

Caitlin reappeared with the kit. "Will she be all right?"

"No permanent damage," I assured her, knowing it was most likely a lie. I took the towel and began wiping away the dried blood to assess the child's injuries.

"That would have been me too, if I'd stayed on Carman's boat. She wouldn't come with me. I could have helped her swim, but she was afraid."

"That was then, this is now."

Tears ran down her cheeks. "It's my fault." She backed up to give me room and began to cry softly.

After doing as much for Chloe as I could, I covered her with a light blanket and left her sleeping in the berth, deep in coma. Her breathing had eased, however, and she didn't seem to be in pain. I motioned Caitlin up the ladder and onto the deck. I made my way to the stern rail and found Alonzo still in the bow of the tender, trying to free his hands.

"I need information," I called down to him. "How many are left back there?"

The man stared at me blankly.

"Okay, if that's how you want it." I vaulted over the rail and landed on the rear platform. I reached into the tender and hauled him to his feet. I freed the line from the bow cleat, gripped his left arm and the back of his belt, and swung him off his feet. Alonzo screamed. I pivoted as if about to toss him into the sea, and he cried out in fear.

"Ready to talk?" I said.

"Eu não entendo!" he begged!

"Damn!" I recognized his speech as Portuguese but knew only a few words myself; he'd said something like *I don't understand*. I set him down again and tried Spanish. "¿Cuantas personas hay en la isla?" I said.

How many people on the island?

"Dos mujeres," Alonzo gasped.

Two women.

"Caitlin?" I called out. She appeared at the rail. "Is there another power boat on the island?"

"Maybe Carman took the inflatable there. It has an electric motor, but the battery died."

That lessened the threat of interference from the others if they reached the Gulf before we were ready to leave. Alonzo struggled in my grip. He tilted his head toward the east, where two separate plumes of smoke billowed into the sky, one from the remains of Carman's trawler and the other more distant.

"Fuego!" he said. "La isla!"

"I'm sure you'll be happy to tell the Coast Guard all about it," I said. Alonzo cowered at my side and shook his head, not understanding. I dragged him out of the tender and up the ladder. I pointed toward the port locker. "There's rope in there," I told Caitlin. "Think you can truss him up to the rail?"

With his hands still tied behind him, Alonzo offered no resistance. She looped a line tightly around his waist and knotted the ends on a cleat.

I hoisted the tender onto the davits to reduce drag once we were under way and went below to check on Chloe. She seemed to be breathing normally, and I climbed back to the cockpit. Caitlin joined me to help raise the main and mizzen. She knew how to operate the boat from the console when under power, but not under sail, so I showed her how to use the winches and quickly explained the function of the sheets and halyards. She watched me closely, then set to work.

It was still a long distance to civilization and assistance, but my cat rigged beauty was stable and relatively upright at any point of sail. It promised to be a reasonably comfortable trip, easy on my injured passenger. We'd been under way about an hour when Caitlin spotted a pair of Coast Guard cutters making good time, heading south well out in the Gulf and too far away for us to hail them. I hoped they were on the way to investigate reports of fires and explosions among the Ten Thousand Islands. That would simplify explaining what happened when we reached Naples. Caitlin stood at the wheel, following my instructions to the letter, enjoying her status as unofficial First Mate despite her worry over Chloe's condition. Every ten minutes she relinquished her post to check on her friend below.

"No change," she told me each time she reappeared. That didn't keep her from ducking below decks again and again to assure herself that Chloe was still alive.

Chloe slept on.

Seventy-seven: Fugitives

Rose-Ellen Foster arrived at the lagoon in the inflatable dinghy, with the housekeeper Anna at the oars; the electric outboard had sputtered to a stop halfway to the lagoon, its battery undercharged. Their meagre possessions lay scattered below the seats. They were alarmed to discover the trawler's sunken remains and Carman's corpse caught up among some mangrove roots. There was no sign of anyone else.

Their only option was to venture into the Gulf in the tiny boat. They kept close to shore, fearing discovery by Coast Guard vessels, and managed to avoid detection by two police launches, but their most immediate problem was lack of fresh water. Nor had they thought to salvage any food before burning the cabin, expecting to share what Carman and Alonzo had taken with them.

Several hours of travel in the open boat under a blazing sun left them exhausted and desperate. They found several promising inlets that they hoped would lead to solid ground, perhaps a road through to the interior or an isolated cabin where they could beg or steal what they needed to survive. But most of the narrow waterways proved to be dead ends.

As evening approached, they finally discovered what appeared to be an abandoned fishing site on one of the larger islands. They elected to stop for the night and beached the dinghy. As the last daylight faded away to the west, hoards of mosquitoes descended on them, and they covered up as well as they could with the few extra clothes they had brought. Their only respite was a short thunderstorm toward morning that helped sooth their burning flesh. They managed to capture enough water in the dinghy's bailing bucket to ease their thirst, and when the first rays of dawn penetrated the trees, they set off once more in search of the mainland.

Seventy-eight:
Good News

At home in Bournemouth, Jessica Sheridan picked up the phone in the kitchen.

"May I speak with Dr. Sheridan, please," an official-sounding voice said.

"This is Dr. Jessica Sheridan," she said into the phone. "Is it my husband Russell you want?"

"Ma'am, this is Chief Petty Officer Liam Thompson. I'm calling from St. Petersburg, Florida."

Jessica came suddenly alert. "Is there news about our daughter? Has her body been found?"

"Please hold. There's someone here who wishes to speak with you."

A series of clicks and a buzz sounded in her ears. "Russell!" Jessica called out, "There's someone on the line from Florida."

"I'll get on the extension," he called from the den.

The officer's voice came back on the line. "Sorry for the delay, Ma'am. Here she is."

"Mom?"

"Oh my God! Caitlin? Is that really you?"

"I'm okay, Mom. I'm at a Coast Guard station."

"I can't believe it! What happened? Where have you been all this time?"

"It's a long story. Can you come get me? And bring me some clothes too. I'm a mess."

"Where are you? Wait a second, your Dad's on the line too."

"Hi, Peanut," Russell said.

"Dad! You haven't called me 'Peanut' since I was five!"

He laughed nervously. "We thought we'd lost you," he said, his voice breaking.

"Nope. I'm fine. Chief Thompson says you can fly to Tampa International. He'll take me there himself once he knows your flight number. They want a doctor to check me over to make sure I'm okay, but I am, really."

"We thought you died in the explosion."

"I was kidnapped. Chloe too. They hurt her, really bad. She's in a hospital somewhere."

"Who hurt her? Where have you been all this time?"

"Someplace in the Florida Everglades, I think, only we got away, and this amazing guy on a really huge sailboat saved me and Chloe too, and he plays piano, he's really good and…"

"Whoa, slow down," Russell interrupted. "We've been worried sick. Who's this man who saved you? How did he find you?"

"He didn't, we found *him*, Chloe and me, we got away in a dinghy and found his boat. You have to meet him, he was on the cruise too, he talked to me after I played with the rock band, and he remembered me. He's too cool, loves Mozart, and he's even got a real piano on his boat, only I don't know where he is now. The Coast Guard wanted him to stay, but his boat's gone from the wharf, and I don't even know his real name. He called himself Rolf Niemand, but I think that was fake. It means 'nobody' in German."

"Nobody?"

"I know, weird, right? Wait a minute. Chief Thompson wants to talk to you."

The officer came on the line. "Dr. Sheridan, may we have your permission to have our Medical Officer examine your daughter? She's a fully qualified MD."

"Of course," Jessica said. "Is she really okay? I can't make any sense out of what she told us."

"Other than some sunburn and blisters on her hands from rowing a dinghy, she seems fine. We don't have the whole story yet either. She and another girl were out in the Gulf of Mexico in a ten-footer. They must have rowed for miles. That's some feisty kid you've got there."

"We'll book a flight. How do I contact you when we know when we'll arrive? And where will Caitlin stay until we get there?"

Thompson gave her a phone number to call. "We have a room for her, but I suspect she'll be hanging out in the Officer's Club most of the time. She's made friends with just about everyone here. She promised to play piano for us too. Is she any good?"

Jessica laughed in relief. "Wait and see."

* * *

Elizabeth Wu and Vachan Sharma sat quietly by Chloe's bedside, patiently waiting while a nurse checked the girl's vitals. She hadn't awakened since being carried from Rolf's yacht and loaded into an ambulance by paramedics, and was now in an induced coma to speed the healing process. The doctors said they were optimistic, but Chloe's battered face and body, and the tubes and wires that connected her to medication and a variety of monitoring devices, suggested otherwise.

"Give it time," one doctor told them. "She's young and strong. As soon as the swelling in her brain goes down, we'll bring her out of the coma gradually. Until then, we'll keep a close eye on her. Why don't you go back to your hotel and get some rest?"

"Thank you, doctor," Vachan said, "but we're fine here."

He smiled at them both and left the room. Elizabeth placed her hand gently on her daughter's arm, gazed at her closed and swollen eyes, and bowed her head in prayer.

Seventy-nine:
Aftermath

BURNED TRAWLER, CORPSE
FOUND IN FLORIDA LAGOON
Carlos Hernandez, The Associated Press

TAMPA, Florida – Authorities are refusing to comment upon the discovery of the burned remains of a trawler in a lagoon in the Ten Thousand Islands. Civilian reports suggest that the vessel may have been destroyed in a violent explosion, and that the incident is related to recent sightings of Coast Guard vessels in the area. No further details are available at this time.

* * *

MYSTERIOUS FIRE SUBJECT
OF POLICE INVESTIGATION
Chuck Petersen, Coral Gables Free Press

TAMPA, Florida – Spokespersons for the Florida State Police remain silent today over reports of a burned-out cabin located on a remote island off the west coast of Florida. Investigators have sealed the area to search through the rubble. Early indications are that the fire was deliberately set, and that everything inside was completely destroyed. There are no casualties.

* * *

CANADIAN TEEN, CHESS PRODIGY,
IN CRITICAL CONDITION IN HOSPITAL
Jeffrey Dahl, The Associated Press

FORT LAUDERDALE, Florida – Chloe Sharma, daughter of

novelist Elizabeth Wu and Dr. Vachan Sharma of Bedford, Nova Scotia, is resting at Horizon Medical Centre, undergoing treatment for injuries received in a bizarre kidnapping episode deep within Florida's Ten Thousand Islands. The young Ms. Sharma was missing and mistakenly declared dead following an explosion on Caracola Cay, Bahamas, earlier this year. Her current injuries are believed to be the result of a severe beating by person or persons unknown. The US Coast Guard is credited with her rescue.

Chloe Sharma is well known to chess aficionados for the many titles she has won in local, provincial, and international competitions. She has also represented her school in mathematics events, including the Acadia University Team Challenge for middle school students.

* * *

POLICE IDENTIFY SUSPECT
IN GULF COAST KIDNAPPING
Dhirendro Singh, The Associated Press

TAMPA, Florida – Authorities have released the name of Alonzo Cardoso, no fixed address, who is in custody after the rescue of two teenagers under mysterious circumstances from a remote west coast Florida island. Cardoso has refused to admit knowing the people involved in the incident. "I'm just a handyman, don't know nothing about no girls," he is quoted as saying in his native Portuguese. The investigation is continuing.

* * *

CANADIAN PRODIGY RESCUED
FROM FLORIDA PRISON ISLAND

Megan Rumboldt, The Canadian Press
CAPE CORAL, Florida – Caitlin Sheridan, the 13-year-old piano sensation who was declared missing and presumed dead following an accident during a vacation stopover in the Bahamas last spring, returned home to Nova Scotia this week. Ms. Sheridan was rescued from an isolated mangrove cay in Florida, where she had been held in captivity since being erroneously listed as lost in a watercraft explosion in the Bahamas.

Caitlin is the daughter of Drs. Russell and Jessica Sheridan of Bournemouth, Nova Scotia. She and her parents were passengers on the Chilean America cruise ship Santiago Vagabundo at the time of the explosion. The blast claimed the life of Omario Lewis, AKA Akoni Clarke, an employee of the cruise line. Police are continuing an investigation into the cause of that tragedy.

The Atlantic Symphony in Halifax has announced a "Welcome Home" concert, during which Ms. Sheridan will perform a concerto of her own choosing with the orchestra. The date of the performance will be announced.

* * *

TEEN TELLS OF BRUTAL ASSAULTS
IN FLORIDA KIDNAPPING INCIDENT
Carlos Hernandez, The Associated Press
TAMPA, Florida – One of the two girls rescued recently from a clandestine island cabin in southwest Florida has reported suffering severe beatings at the hands of a missing suspect in the case. Known to them only by the name Shelagh, the powerfully built woman spoke with a distinctive Alabama accent. She has medium brown close-cropped hair and dark eyes described as "intense." She was usually seen dressed in a

nurse's uniform.

In addition to one suspect already in custody, the Hispanic handyman identified as Alonzo Cardoso, police are seeking a woman known only to the girls as Anna, who was responsible for preparing their meals while they were on the island. Anna is described as heavyset and in her 60s, with grey hair, pale hazel eyes, and a southern accent. She also looked after cleaning the rooms where the captives were held.

Another suspect, an illegal immigrant from Italy via Nicaragua and Mexico who had lived in Florida for two decades, was identified as Carman Russo. His burned body was discovered near the wreckage of a recreational trawler near the site of the investigation. Authorities suggest that Shelagh and Anna may be travelling together. Anyone sighting them is cautioned not to approach, but to contact the nearest police precinct.

* * *

MYSTERY SAILOR VANISHES
AFTER WEST FLORIDA RESCUE
Jeffrey Dahl, The Associated Press

FORT LAUDERDALE, Florida – Details are emerging about an unidentified sailor whom police now credit with rescuing a pair of girls from captivity on an islet off the Gulf Coast of Florida. He is described as above average height with brown hair, blue eyes, a neatly trimmed moustache, and a severely injured face. His age is estimated as late twenties to early thirties. The name he gave police, Rolf Niemand, is believed to be an alias.

After delivering the rescued teenagers to authorities in Naples, Florida, Niemand failed to honour official requests to remain in the area. "He is suspected of having sailed away on a large two-masted yacht," a spokesperson said. Police wish to interview him, hoping to gain more information about the circumstances surrounding the case. Anyone knowing the whereabouts of Niemand or his vessel, the *Versteck,* is asked to contact any US Coast Guard station.

* * *

INMATE MURDERED IN
PRISON EXERCISE YARD
Dhirendro Singh, The Associated Press

TAMPA, Florida – Police have identified the victim of a jailhouse slaying as Alonzo Cardoso, a suspect in the kidnapping and confinement of two girls on a mangrove island in the vicinity of Cape Romano. Cardoso was allegedly stabbed in the exercise yard of the local correctional centre. There are currently no suspects in the murder.

* * *

WELCOME BACK CAITLIN!
Margaret Wilson, The Bournemouth Bugle

BOURNEMOUTH – Caitlin Sheridan is home again, following a high seas adventure in which she was declared missing in the Caribbean. Bournemouth's favourite star pianist is none the worse for wear after escaping from a gang of pirates who held her for ransom aboard their ship. Caitlin was reportedly rescued following a ferocious battle between the pirates and a lone hero who then spirited her away to safety in his high-powered cruiser. He is described as resembling actor Harrison Ford in the "Indiana Jones" movies. Caitlin was uninjured during the incident. More details will appear in these pages as they become available.

* * *

NEO-NAZI SYMPATHIZERS
DEMONSTRATE IN CAPITAL
Dhirendro Singh, The Associated Press

TALLAHASSEE, Florida – Police dispersed a gathering of white supremacist demonstrators in the Capital Saturday morning, in response to complaints from the public of lewd and aggressive behaviour. The participants resisted arrest, citing First Amendment protection under the US Constitution, and were detained overnight. No charges have been laid. Inside sources suggest that the protest rally was related to allegations that a neo-Nazi organization from out of state was responsible for the kidnapping of two teenagers in a plot to further the concept of Adolph Hitler's "Master Race." No additional details are available.

Eighty:
Rolf

No doubt the Coast Guard has branded me a fugitive. They were too busy looking after my passengers to pay much attention to me when I reached Naples, but told me to stick around. I promised to be available to answer their questions, but that wasn't on my agenda. I slipped away under their noses and sailed out into the Gulf, on a roundabout course toward Key West.

The last thing I needed was a gaggle of reporters poking their noses into my past. I'd worked too hard to hide from the world, and I was not about to submit to an official interrogation that would draw attention to myself, no matter how well intentioned. I didn't feel like a hero. I was just grateful to have been in the right place at the right time to lend a hand, and was already planning to change my appearance and fade back into obscurity.

Among a number of personal concerns demanding my attention, *Versteck* needed a new radio so I could keep track of news about the investigation, and especially Caitlin. I wouldn't rest easy until I knew she was safe at home again. Most of all, I required competent medical attention from a plastic surgeon who could repair the damage from Carman's assault. I didn't want to go through life with a deformity that would cause me to stand out in a crowd.

And finally, I hoped to obtain the services of a reputable laboratory to conduct a certain test for me. Even if what I suspected was true, I had no intention of revealing the results to anyone. But for my own peace of mind, I wanted to know for sure.

Eighty-one:
The Spider

The Spider sat motionless in his office in Halifax, anticipating a text message from Rose-Ellen Foster to his private email account that might never come. The wide screen TV opposite his desk was tuned to CNN, where commentators continued to pounce upon every shred of information coming out of Florida: the kidnap victims, the burned trawler, the fire on an isolated island, and most of all, snippets of news that eager reporters ferreted out from those who had witnessed the mysterious yacht's arrival in Naples.

There had been nothing concrete concerning the search for fugitives, the two women whom the girls identified as among their captors. Anna Tremont was of little concern to him. She was too ignorant of the overall scope of his operation to be able to provide police with any vital information. Carman was dead in the boat explosion and the maintenance man Cardoso had been disposed of while in lockup, the victim of a rogue prison guard and a Nazi sympathizer who was already serving a life sentence and had nothing more to lose.

That left only Rose-Ellen Foster, who had thrown a monkey wrench into his plans by losing control and nearly killing the Sharma child. Even though Vachan Sharma had announced his withdrawal from the NDP leadership race, he might renege and reoffer, and even attempt to pin the blame for the kidnapping on the Freedom Party. But there could be no proof of that. Sharma still didn't know that his own security guard, Jacob Shaffer, had helped engineer the girl's abduction. For all he knew, either the Liberals or the Conservatives could have been responsible.

Foster posed the greatest threat. She knew too much. Should the authorities capture her, he doubted her ability to hold out under intense questioning. If she ended up in custody, he would see to it that Alonzo's fate awaited her too.

And then there was the matter of the Sheridan kid, without whose help Chloe Sharma would not have escaped from the island. But The Spider was not vengeful. In fact, he entertained a certain respect for the little brat, and wished her a long and happy life. Ever practical when things turned against him, The Spider simply cut his losses and moved on.

* * *

Vachan Sharma had decided to move on too. Once assured by doctors that Chloe would recover completely, he began planning their return to Nova Scotia. While he intended to support and contribute to the New Democratic Party, he planned to devote more time to his family, and specifically his relationship with Elizabeth, whom he had neglected in recent months. He planned a few personal appearances on behalf of Doug Kauffman, should he be returned as leader, but he would leave it to others to run the campaign.

Eighty-two:
Official Visit

Early in November, the upstart Freedom Party edged out the opposition parties by the slimmest of margins, gaining just enough seats in the Nova Scotia Legislature to form a minority government. Rumours circulated that the defeated Conservatives would join with them in a tentative coalition to keep them in power, in return for "certain considerations." Newly elected Premier Carter Williams had been much in the news, and his face was seen frequently on television. His personal popularity was widely credited with his Party's victory, however slim.

The Sheridan family paid little attention to the election. They had managed to pick up the pieces of their shattered lives when Caitlin was so miraculously returned to them. With the help of Dr. Rothstein, Jessica and Russell were once again becoming comfortable with each other, especially since Russell had admitted to his obsession with Caitlin's talent as an asset to his standing in the community. He vowed to rectify that, and Jessica believed he was sincere.

Other than suffering occasional nightmares, Caitlin seemed little affected by the trauma of her incarceration and the abuse she suffered at the hands of the sadistic Rose-Ellen Foster. One evening she was leafing through the newspaper clippings that her mother had accumulated since the cruise. She was laughing aloud.

"Old Mrs. Wilson at the Bugle is amazing," she told her parents. "She takes one little fact and turns it into a movie of the week. First, she has me blown up by terrorists, then captured by pirates, and did you read what she wrote about how I got rescued? By Harrison Ford, no less."

"She's in step with the times," her father said. "Fake news, alternate facts, she'll print whatever she thinks people will believe—or want to believe."

"And she never prints a retraction," Jessica said. "I guess she thinks the truth shouldn't be allowed to get in the way of a good story."

The doorbell rang. Caitlin bounced up and hurried to answer it, and found a uniformed RCMP officer and a woman holding an FBI shield standing on the porch.

"You must be Caitlin," the woman said. "Are your parents at home?"

"Wow! Dad, the FBI is here," Caitlin called over her shoulder.

Russell entered the foyer. "May I help you?"

"I'm Special Agent Sophia Thanos, Dr. Sheridan, from the Portland, Maine Field Office of the United States Federal Bureau of Investigation. This is RCMP Sergeant Major Edward Mason. We'd like to ask your daughter a few questions about her kidnapping. May we come in?"

"She already told the Florida police everything she knows. When did your agency become involved?"

"This is an international investigation with a Canadian connection. We've been working with the RCMP since early last month. We have some new information to share."

"All right," Russell said. "Come in then." They stepped inside, and he led them to the living room and invited them to sit down.

"We apologize for this intrusion," Mason said, "but there have been several developments south of the border." He nodded to Thanos, who extracted a photograph from a folder she was carrying. She passed it to Caitlin.

"Do you recognize this woman?" she asked.

"Shelagh!" Caitlin said disgustedly. "She's the one who beat me up."

Thanos nodded. "Her name is Rose-Ellen Foster. I'll need you to sign a statement identifying her as one of your captors. She's now in custody in Florida. She and another woman were found trying to steal a car in Everglades City, and it took some time to connect them to your kidnapping."

"What's gonna happen to her?"

"She faces a number of charges," including the attempted murder of Chloe Sharma, but her lawyer is trying to negotiate a plea deal. If he is successful, she'll serve time for what she did to all of you, but in return for giving evidence against everyone involved, her term will be reduced."

"She should rot in prison forever for assaulting the girls," Russell said.

"We have you and Chloe to thank for exposing what was going on." Thanos said to Caitlin. "She was on the Jet Ski with you, wasn't she?"

"Uh huh. And Shelagh beat her up really bad, worse than me. She was in hospital for three weeks. She's a lot better now."

"Do you keep in touch with her?"

"Sure. In fact, we're gonna spend New Year's Day with her and her parents down in Florida."

Thanos smiled. "I'm happy to hear that she's well again."

"So do you know who was behind all this?" Russell asked. "And why?"

Thanos and Mason exchanged glances. "We're following a number of leads. What we're about to tell you hasn't been made public, and you mustn't reveal it to anyone, at least not until after it comes out in court. Do you agree?"

Jessica and Russell nodded as did Caitlin, not wanting to miss a word.

"As part of Foster's plea agreement," Sergeant Mason said, "she is expected to testify against several prominent Haligonians who were responsible for everything that happened to you. That's the Nova Scotia connection. We don't have their names yet. But even when we receive that information, it may not be enough. We need eyewitnesses who can confirm their involvement. And we don't yet have a motive for the kidnapping. Foster clams up when we ask about that and claims she doesn't know."

"Are they all white supremacists too," Caitlin asked, "like what's-her-name? Foster?"

"What gives you that idea?" Thanos said.

"She was always going on about Jesus and about Christians being God's chosen people—wrong!—and how they were going to take back the country from all the dark-skinned people, like Chloe and her family."

Thanos looked pointedly at Sergeant Mason. "Are that child's parents prominent here?"

"Her father, Vachan Sharma, is a big wheel in one of our political parties," Mason said. "He was in the news some before the election. His wife is the novelist Elizabeth Wu."

"Sharma and Wu," the FBI agent said. "Pakistani and Chinese?"

"He's Indian, I think, but both are Canadian citizens."

"Then that's an angle to look into," Thanos said quietly. "But if taking the Sharma child was somehow racially motivated, we still don't have a reason. What would they have to gain?"

"Vachan Sharma hasn't been any help either," Sergeant Mason said. "We think he knows more than he'll admit to, but he claims otherwise."

"Maybe I can help," Caitlin said softly.

"How, dear?" Thanos said.

"There was this guy who came to the cabin just before we escaped, and I can identify him."

"What did he look like?"

"I never saw him. But I *heard* him."

"That's fine, but I don't think…"

"If Caitlin says she can identify him that way," Jessica said, "you should listen to her. Caitlin is a trained musician, and she has amazing tonal memory. It's a rare gift."

"I don't see how that could help," Sergeant Mason said.

"Look at it this way," Russell said. "Suppose you have a suspect, and you put him in a line-up, and a witness looks them all over and picks him out. Would that hold up in court?"

"It usually does."

"So, what if you put all six in a room where Caitlin can't see them, then have them talk into a microphone. And suppose she picks out the suspect's voice."

The two officers looked at each other. "I've never heard of anything like that," Mason said. "But it might be worth a try."

"You could test me!" Caitlin said excitedly. "Let me listen to someone and memorize his voice, then play a whole bunch of voices back to me, including that one, and see if I can identify him. Wouldn't that prove I can do it?"

"How many voices could we use?"

"I don't care. A dozen? Two dozen? Two *hundred*, if you want."

"You can pick out one person's voice, someone you've heard only once, out of two hundred others?"

Caitlin grinned. "Let's make it two thousand. I have the time if you do. After what those monsters did to us, I want to help. He should have known better than to mess with me."

Eighty-three:
Rolf

It's amazing what a skilled plastic surgeon can do. It took two operations, but my face is symmetrical again, the scarring minimal. I recuperated on the island of St. Croix, working on other changes in my appearance in the hope that no one who knew me as Rolf Niemand will recognize me. I'll be Juan José Gomez from now on, a unilingual Spaniard. My dyed black hair has already grown to twice its former length, and my moustache is luxuriantly bushy. I'm sporting a Che Guevara ear-to-ear beard. Except for very faint traces of the surgery, nearly hidden by all that hair, there's nothing left of my former persona.

I also consigned my boat to Felix van der Westhuizen's gentle ministrations again, excepting the electronics, which I wanted to install myself. *Versteck*'s formerly grey hull is now shiny white with pinstriped trim, and she sports a pair of deep red sails, custom ordered from a firm in Charleston, South Carolina. I'm hoping the changes are enough to conceal her former identity.

In addition to multi-band radios, I installed redundant GPS systems, a new and more sensitive depth sounder, and a robust autopilot. New additions include radar and a thermal night vision camera, all of this to increase my margin of safety and provide advance warnings of most of the perils that can befall sailors. With a new name painted on the stern, *Escondite Encantador*, I can go back to my former pattern of living—nomadic, carefree, and anonymous.

Jenny has been restless during this time. She may be suffering from "land legs," sensitivity to the lack of motion beneath her paws that is a constant component of living aboard a yacht. Nor was she pleased with being indoors, having always been allowed to roam the deck at will. My cramped motel room gave her little room for exercise or exploration, but I couldn't let her wander freely in strange surroundings. I detected an expression of reproach on her normally beautiful face whenever it was necessary to leave the room without her.

With little to fill my time while work on the boat was underway, I leased a local studio and returned to practicing with a vengeance. I was stung by Caitlin's reference to my rendition of Mozart being *shaky*. It wasn't my musical memory that had slipped, but too many hours devoted to hotel lounge music had dulled my classical technique. I vowed not to let that happen again, despite the fact that I never plan to perform on the concert stage. It's not only a matter of pride. I have simply forgotten how much pleasure there is in more serious repertoire, even when played only for my own enjoyment, and I'm fussy enough not to tolerate deterioration of my skills.

I devoted early mornings to keeping in shape: lifting weights, running several miles daily, and challenging myself to swimming a minimum of two nautical miles each afternoon. When the foreman at the marina called me to report that the boat would go back in the water "on the morrow," I was feeling fit and eager for the sea.

There remained a question of whether to do anything about the report from the lab that conducted a biological analysis for me. But that would be a decision for another day.

Eighty-four:
Sadness

Marjorie Sheridan succumbed to her illness in the early morning hours of December first. Two days later, his final reason for living fulfilled, Orrin Sheridan followed her into the great beyond, or into oblivion, depending upon one's view of the workings of the universe. Orrin had contributed much to his native Province, and to countless numbers of patients who had benefitted from his medical expertise, his skill as a surgeon, and especially his kindness and counsel. The couple's bodies were cremated, their ashes intermingled and cast into the sea off Bournemouth as per their wishes.

Caitlin was inordinately sad over their passing. Her grandfather had loomed large in her life, his love and guidance an ever-present rock in the shifting sands of her unusually complex childhood. Jessica's parents had died in a plane crash a year after the child was born, and Caitlin knew how lucky she had been to have two remaining grandparents. Now she had none. She felt a strange and debilitating emptiness inside, especially as she realized how close she might have come to losing her own life.

Jessica and Russell debated cancelling their plans for a winter vacation but decided to go ahead. They had both loved the old couple and owed them much, but there were others to consider now. Caitlin needed distraction from grief, and a chance to reconnect with her friend Chloe, with whom she had survived such a harrowing experience. They all deserved time in pleasant surroundings to come to terms with a capricious future that once had seemed so predictable.

Christmas in the Sheridan household was a quiet affair, with a modest tree and gifts as usual but lacking the joy of previous years. The absence of Orrin and Marjorie was as tangible as their presence had ever been. Russell spent much of the day on call at the Medical Centre, dealing with minor complaints and such serious emergencies as a burst aneurism, an aortic bypass, and various injuries suffered by victims of a multiple-vehicle accident on Highway 103. Jessica and Caitlin were busy packing for the trip on Saturday.

Time passed slowly.

Eighty-five:
Friends

Chloe and her mother had already been vacationing in Florida for a week when they greeted the Sheridans in the arrivals area of Fort Lauderdale-Hollywood International Airport a few days after Christmas. Vachan was to arrive January first, after attending a series of fund-raising dinners for the NDP in widely spaced Canadian cities.

It was a happy but tearful reunion. Caitlin hadn't seen her friend since she disappeared into the back of an ambulance at the Coast Guard station. She thought that Chloe looked pale and underweight, but her broad smile seemed to suggest full recovery from her injuries. The two girls embraced, as did Jessica and Elizabeth, mothers sharing a single emotion: what was feared lost had been returned to them.

Russell took charge of the luggage. They climbed into a shuttle and set off for a trip to Hotel Camelot, a boutique establishment that was advertised as private and intimate. Traffic on the fifteen-mile journey was moderate, and within the hour they were checked into their rooms. The girls hit the beach while Elizabeth, Jessica and Russell found a table on the patio overlooking the sea.

"I didn't want to ask you with Chloe in the van," Jessica said, "but how is she? She looks so thin."

"The doctors say we have nothing to worry about," Elizabeth said. "She's tough."

"I'm so glad."

Elizabeth was watching the girls playing in the surf. "Caitlin seems like her usual bouncy self."

"She's carrying a load of guilt," Russell said. "She thinks it's her fault that Chloe was injured, that she shouldn't have left her alone when she escaped from that criminal's boat."

"If Caitlin hadn't gotten away, they'd still be at the mercy of those… those terrorists. She did the right thing."

"She'll drive your daughter crazy until she learns to swim better," Jessica said. "She told us that was why Chloe wouldn't go with her, afraid she would drown."

"It doesn't matter now," Elizabeth said. "That's all behind us. Have you heard any more about the investigation?"

"Not since the FBI came to the house. How about you?"

"Nothing, except that even though we never received a ransom note, the RCMP haven't ruled that out as being at least part of the motive."

"Some people think having enough money can justify doing anything," Russell said ironically, avoiding his wife's eyes. "I've been guilty of that by times."

Elizabeth regarded him curiously.

"Let's not go into that," Jessica said. "This is supposed to be a happy occasion, seven days with nothing to do but enjoy the warm weather and watch our kids get past what happened to them. How hot is it anyway? It was seven degrees below freezing when we boarded the plane in Halifax."

* * *

Caitlin badgered Chloe until she agreed to another swimming lesson, and they left the beach and rinsed sand off in the outdoor shower before entering the pool.

"You have to get better at this," Caitlin said. "Next time we get kidnapped by pirates, you have to be ready to escape with me."

"Pirates?" Chloe said.

"You wouldn't believe it, we have this pathetic little weekly newspaper, the Bournemouth Bugle, and all it ever has in it is gossip and what it calls 'social news.' When we were kidnapped, Mrs.

275

Wilson—she's this goofy columnist, thinks she's on the Toronto Star or something—she wrote that we were blown up by terrorists. Later she reported that we were rescued by Harrison Ford from pirates who were holding us for ransom."

"The actor?"

"Or someone who looks like him. That must have been Rolf."

"That's nuts."

"She's a nosy busybody. That social column of hers is full of stupid news about who's hosting what party, what the women's bridge club is doing, how 'Dr. and Mrs. Sheridan and their daughter will be spending New Year's Eve at Hotel Camelot in Miami Beach.' Mom never says anything, but I know it annoys her, that 'Dr. and *Mrs.*' business. As if her Ph.D. wasn't worth her being called 'Doctor' herself. Even Dad couldn't laugh that off. Mrs. Wilson got your name wrong too, when she wrote that you and your mom and dad were joining us. Said you were Cleo."

"Does she ever get anything *right*? Pirates! Did anyone believe that?"

"I don't know. Lots of gullible people in the world, I guess. Dad says you can't trust anything you read these days; you have to check everything out for yourself. 'Fake news, alternate facts, it's all bullshit,' he says. He tells me that whenever I read or hear anything that sounds wrong, I'm supposed to ask myself why some person telling me this. What do they have to gain?"

"That's like what my mom says too, I guess," Chloe said. 'Think for yourself,' she's always telling me, and 'If it sounds too good to be true, be suspicious.' Half the time I don't know what to believe anymore."

"I know one thing," Caitlin said. "If you hadn't been awake the night that Carman got drunk and left the gate open, you'd be who knows where by now, and I'd be shark food."

"That was mostly luck. You get most of the credit."

"Not me. It was Rolf. And he took care of you after Shelagh beat you up so bad. He gave you first aid and made sure the Coast Guard took you to the hospital first thing."

"I don't remember that," Chloe said. "I wish I could thank him, but the police said he disappeared, and the Coast Guard can't find him anywhere."

"I know. I wonder why. It's really strange, but Mom and Dad think he's just modest and doesn't want any credit. I guess that explains the name he was using: 'Nobody'."

"Do you suppose he's some kind of criminal?"

"Maybe, but I don't care, not after what he did for us. He's a hero, and a hell of a piano player, too."

"He's what?"

"I guess I never mentioned that. He has a music studio on board his boat, with a real piano. We played duets that first night before we came back and he rescued you. See, if you weren't so scared of swimming, you'd have been with me. So let's get to it."

And the swimming lesson began.

Eighty-six:
New Year's Eve

Some sad news awaited Elizabeth and Chloe when they entered their room to get ready for the evening celebration. The light on the telephone was blinking, and when Elizabeth listened to the message from her husband, her face fell. A massive snowstorm blanketing the Prairie Provinces threatened to continue for at least another twenty hours. All airports were closed from west of Toronto to Eastern British Columbia. Vachan could not hope to get out for a day or more, and it made no sense for him to fly to Florida only to have to turn around again immediately. He would see them when they arrived home.

Dinner was a semi-formal affair, jackets and ties on the men, the sky's the limit for women. Russell wore a tuxedo and both Jessica and Elizabeth were beautiful in elegant cocktail dresses. Caitlin and Chloe looked cute in slightly-too-short, bare-shouldered versions of their mothers' style, thinking themselves very grown up. After an excellent meal, the adults lingered over coffee. The girls enjoyed virgin mai tais—pineapple and orange juice with grenadine syrup, minus the rum.

"Chloe and I are winter widows," Elizabeth told the others when they were seated. "Vachan left me a voice mail. Much of the West is snowed in. I called him back, and he said it's still coming down, and everything in Alberta is shut down."

"I'm so sorry," Jessica told her.

Elizabeth shrugged. "I should be used to it by now, I guess. Except ever since he quit running for the NDP leadership, I was getting used to seeing more of him. He wasn't even scheduled to attend these fund-raisers, but Doug Kauffman came down with the flu and twisted his arm to fill in. Now I wish he'd turned him down."

"Is he coming later?" Russell asked.

"Not much point. Even if they get Edmonton International opened up again tomorrow, he might not get a flight. In any case he wouldn't get here until just before we're booked to go home." She sighed. "You two were smart not to get involved in politics."

During the meal they were entertained by a thirty-something vocalist with an imitation Jo Stafford contralto. Her repertoire suited an older crowd, dating from well before the new millennium. She had a gift for intimate communication, making every diner, most especially the men, feel as if she were singing just for them. But Caitlin was more captivated by the accompanist, a rough-looking light-skinned Hispanic with a gentle touch whose appearance was at odds with his style.

A server came around with drink refills as the singer closed out her signature piece, a mellow version of Hoagy Carmichael's late 1920s classic, *Stardust*. She left the stage but the pianist remained. He eased into a delicate and lilting arrangement of *The Girl From Ipanema*, and Caitlin's attention strayed from the table conversation to the soft strains coming from the Baldwin grand. She excused herself and approached the piano.

"You play beautifully," she said softly.

"No hablo Inglés, chica," the man replied without missing a beat.

"What's your name?" When the man didn't reply she continued in Spanish. "¿Como se llama?"

"Soy Juan José Gomez."

Intrigued and suspicious, she switched back to English. "How did you learn to play so well?"

He ignored her. She slid around into the curve of the piano's case where she could see his face more clearly. She studied his features and spotted a faint surgical line that disappeared into the beard below his left cheekbone. He continued to pay no attention to her. She leaned forward, bracing her elbows on the crossbar, and cupped her chin in her hands.

"¿Qué tal un poco de Mozart, Guapo?"

How about a little Mozart, Handsome?

He looked up sharply.

"¡Vete, niña!"

Go away, girl!

"Why the disguise, Rolf?"

"Get the hell away from me!" he whispered hoarsely. He dropped *Ipanema* and broke into a spirited version of the *Mexican Hat Dance*.

Stunned, she backed away, mouth agape. He refused to meet her eyes. She fought back tears, confused by his rejection, and made her way to the table.

"That man plays well," her mother said.

"You don't know the half of it," she muttered softly.

Russell was deep in conversation with Elizabeth. Chloe leaned toward Caitlin. "That's him, isn't it?" Caitlin nodded.

"That's who?" Jessica asked.

"The man who saved us," Chloe said. "His name's Rolf."

"Not anymore," Caitlin said. "He was speaking Spanish, and he said he doesn't know any English. Then he swore at me, told me to back off—in English!"

"Swore at you?" Jessica said.

Chloe's brow furrowed. Then she brightened. "He's hiding, isn't he."

"Huh?" Caitlin was confused.

"It's *Versteck* all over again. Mom said he disappeared from the Coast Guard station right after he took us there. He didn't want them questioning him. He's 'nobody,' remember? That's how he wants it."

"I guess you're right."

Caitlin finished her drink. She sat silently for five minutes, thinking. She frowned, then came to a decision. Her eyes flashed.

Chloe watched her friend's face shift from hurt to annoyed. "What're you gonna do?" she whispered.

Caitlin stood up abruptly. "Watch me!" she hissed.

Eighty-seven:
Rolf

I spotted Caitlin and Chloe the minute they entered the dining room, the worst kind of bad luck. There wasn't much I could do about it, being under contract to entertain all throughout dinner, and I hoped neither of the girls would penetrate my camouflage.

I should have known better. Caitlin watched me closely, intent on my playing, and after a few minutes she approached the piano and complimented me. I pretended ignorance and tried to ignore her, but she must have spotted the scar and called me by name. It pained me to do what was necessary, but I chased her away with a soft but angry curse and she returned to her table.

I hoped that would be the end of it, but she and Chloe had a whispered conversation, and presently she approached the piano again, looking determined. I was well into a lyrical rendition of *Besame Mucho*, and she perched on the right end of the piano bench and hip-checked me gently.

"I know this song," she whispered. "What are you gonna do, shove me off on the floor in front of all these people?"

She began to weave a clever upper register obbligato to decorate the tune. I tried to ignore her and she stepped up the pressure, spinning a couple of rapid arpeggios against my three-to-the-beat melody. She looked left and grinned at me, and I gave up and eased over to give her more room. We ended the song early, and I played a fancy tremolo on a G dominant ninth chord and plunged into the *Secondo* part of Mozart's four-hand sonata. Caitlin quickly caught up on the *Primo*, and the exquisite music filled the room.

"You've been practicing," she whispered as we cadenced the second theme.

"Shut up," I growled, and she smiled cutely, eyes on the keyboard, smug and self-satisfied.

When we finished the diners broke out in enthusiastic applause, redoubled when Caitlin stood up and they realized how young she was. She took hold of my hand and pulled me to my feet to share the praise, then led me to her table. I tried to resist, but she held on tight and I decided not to make an issue of it.

"This is Rolf," Caitlin said as she drew out her chair for me to sit down. "He's the man who saved us, Chloe and me."

"And you've just blown my cover, *diabla*."

"I'm a devil, am I?" She giggled. "I like that. And you only had half as much hair back then, and no beard. Rolf, this is Chloe's Mom, Ms. Wu." She waved toward Elizabeth. "The other two are my mom and dad."

"Jessica," her mother said, rising slightly and extending her hand. I took it. "I'm so pleased to meet you," she said, "and so grateful for what you did for the girls."

"That goes double for me," Caitlin's father said. "I'm Russell. You gave us back our life, in more ways than one."

"Not really," I said. "Caitlin was already doing a pretty good job of looking after herself."

Elizabeth stood up and offered me her hand too. "That's not the way my daughter tells it," she said. "My name is Elizabeth, and I understand you gave Chloe first aid and made sure she received proper attention from the Coast Guard. Thank you."

"I'm glad I could help."

Caitlin poked me gently. "Wo hast du denn deinen deutschen Akzent verloren?" she teased.

Where did you lose your German accent?

I shook my head, smiling. "Soy Juan José ahora, ¿recuerdas?"

"A thousand pardons, Señor Juan José. I won't forget again. And aren't you supposed to be playing for the crowd?"

"Come on, *mocosa*, we may as well do this together."

She bristled. "I'm not a brat!"

I left the table and she danced alongside me as we returned to the keyboard. We sat side by side.

"Know any Lady Gaga tunes?" she said.

* * *

Caitlin was riding an adrenalin high when we wound up the last set shortly after ten. "That was so much fun," she said. "Are you through for the night, Rolf?"

I didn't answer as we walked back to the table. I turned to face her directly, staring intently into her eyes.

"What?" she said, alarmed.

"I'm not Rolf. And I'm not Juan Gomez, either. You've put an end to it, you little monster."

"How did I do that?"

I pulled out a chair and sat down heavily. I reached out and gathered up her small hand in mine.

"When I left you with the Coast Guard, I convinced myself I could just disappear and forget all about you. But according to Chinese tradition, when you save someone's life, you're responsible for that life forever. You *think* I saved your life, and I suppose I did to some degree, so I guess I have to step up."

"You're scaring me," Caitlin said softly.

"I can help you. With your career, I mean. And I'm going to do it."

"Why?"

"You deserve to know who I really am. Or maybe you already know."

"I have no idea what you're talking about."

"What would you think if I told you that when your vacation is over, I'm moving to Nova Scotia?"

"Wow! That would be great! But why?"

"Caitlin…"

"What? Tell me!"

"I'm just tired, I guess. I want to stay in one place for awhile. Maybe forever. It's time to go home."

"Home?" She looked puzzled.

"I was born in Nova Scotia, in Bournemouth in fact. You were too young to know me when I was there last, but when I shave off my beard and moustache, people in town will remember me. They used to call me J. J., but he's someone I want to forget, so I'm going to be Jon from now on."

"You're… You're J. J.?" Caitlin said in amazement.

"Yes. Jonathan James MacIsaac."

Eighty-eight:
Escondite Encantador

W hat does she draw, Jon?" Russell asked me as we cleared the final harbour buoy.

"A little over two meters at the keel. Close to seven feet."

We were seated aft in the cockpit, watching Chloe at the wheel. She was nervously guiding the big yacht well off the wind, the sails filled but not driving hard on a safe broad reach, starboard tack. Her eyes were glued to the compass. Every few minutes her hand strayed to the pull tab on her lightweight inflatable life belt, as if ensuring that it was still there if she needed it. She had told me that she loved to pilot her dad's power boat, but that sailboats made her nervous, the way they leaned way over to the side when going fast.

"Speed?" Russell asked.

"Just shy of eight knots max. I can push her harder if I have to, but too much canvas makes her a bit wild."

Jessica and Elizabeth climbed out of the forward companionway. Jessica carried a tray of sandwiches and drinks and skirted around Chloe to take a seat with us.

Elizabeth stopped beside the wheel. "Having fun?" she asked her daughter.

"I'm working," Chloe said seriously. She pointed to a dial. "Jon wants me to keep the compass right on sixty-five degrees."

"Where's your buddy?"

"She got bored with watching me steer and abandoned me."

Caitlin was sprawled atop the cabin below the main. She had shucked off her life belt and was soaking up the sun. Jessica called to tell her that lunch was ready, and she skipped back along the gunwale and dropped into the cockpit.

"Slow down!" her mother said. "You're going to fall overboard one of these times. Where's your life belt?"

"Wrong color. Doesn't match my bikini."

"Caitlin…"

"I know, that was rude. I'm sorry. But honestly, Mom, it's not as if I can't swim."

"I may toss you over the rail myself," Russell said.

"I'll help," I told him. "We can practice a 'brat overboard' drill."

"Whee! Let's do it!" Caitlin crowed.

"Nah, too much trouble. I don't want to turn my boat around to pick you up. If you fall in, you can just float around for a couple of hours until we come by this way again."

"This is so great. I never want to go back."

"We have to. You promised to help me entertain the crowd in the dining room tonight."

"Yeah, well, there's that." She chose a sandwich from the tray. "You get to sail every day, don't you?"

"When I want to."

"Wish *I* could."

"You'd get tired of it soon enough."

"Never! Hey, Chloe, want a sandwich?"

"Sure. And something to drink."

Caitlin picked out a ham on rye and a can of root beer and delivered them, then came back to stand beside me.

"Jon, can I ask you a question?"

"Na sicher."

Of course.

"Why don't you want to be called J. J. anymore?"

"Don't you like my name?"

She looked at me quizzically. "My grandfather once told me everybody has a right to be called whatever they want. I agree with that, but I'd like to know why you want to change."

"Change is good," I answered. "I'm carrying around too much excess baggage, and if I'm going to make a success out of returning home, *mi nombre viejo* has to go."

"Why is your old name excess baggage?"

"Not something I want to talk about."

By three o'clock we were heading southwest, myself at the wheel and close hauled, beating hard. The girls were forward, clinging to the deck side by side and watching the approaching coastline, with Elizabeth nearby. They glowed pink from the sun. After sleeping in the forward berth most of the day, Jenny had emerged to the delight of them both, and was curled up between them.

Jessica and Russell sat in the forward end of the cockpit. It occurred to me that the time might be ripe for some serious talk. I decided to approach it by first talking about the unusual incidence of multiple piano prodigies coming from the same small town.

"There's something I think I should tell you while the girls are up front," I said to them. "Do you know the Dickenson family, from back in Bournemouth?"

"The preacher?" Jessica said.

"Everyone knew Joshua Dickinson," Russell said. "He's dead now, and his church disbanded. That cult of his was the talk of the town for years. Holy rollers, the gossips called them."

"That was hardly fair," Jessica said. "They had some unusual beliefs and practices, I suppose, but they kept to themselves. There was never a hint of any trouble, and the children in the community seemed to be well taken care of; although they didn't go to school, which was the source of some of the stories about them."

"They were home schooled in a way," Russell said. "Or maybe privately schooled is a more accurate description. The authorities had to allow it, because Dickenson had three degrees himself, a B.A., a Doctor of Divinity, and a Ph.D. in Education. A professor from the university and a couple of retired schoolteachers were church members, and all of them tutored or met with small groups. The children wrote standardized exams every year, and most of them excelled."

"It was so sad what happened to his daughter," Jessica said. "I think her name was Sabrina. Apparently she just disappeared one day. No one ever knew what happened, or at least they never told anyone."

"Did you know she was an excellent pianist?" I said.

"The daughter? Really?"

"That's amazing," Russell said. "You, Caitlin, the Dickenson girl; all that talent coming from Bournemouth?"

I made a small correction to the wheel to line up my approach to the harbour. "Caitlin knows she's adopted, doesn't she?" I said.

"What?" Russell snapped angrily.

His reaction surprised me, and I fell silent. I checked the GPS and brought the boat five degrees to port. I let the mainsail run a bit as we slowed to approach the marina. If Caitlin's origins were a point of contention, I had to tread lightly.

Jessica allowed a little time to pass, then said quietly, "Russell..."

"Never mind, Jess!" he said shortly.

"But there's no point in..."

"I said, drop it! Please!"

"I'm sorry," I said. "I thought it was common knowledge, especially since Caitlin herself told me that musical talent doesn't run in either of your families."

"What gave you this idea?" Russell said.

I shrugged. "Her appearance, I guess. Those very pale blue eyes and light hair. You both are darker, and your eyes are brown, Russ. Jessica's are blue, but a deep shade."

"That doesn't mean anything. Lots of children have light hair when they're young. It darkens later. Children aren't clones of their parents. People's genes can combine in all kinds of differing ways."

"Granted. But the tendency toward light blue eyes is a recessive gene."

Russell glared at me, his lips a thin, rigid line, warning me to back off.

"I'm sorry I mentioned it," I said, and turned my attention to the wheel. I was almost certain I knew the whole truth by that time and that Sabrina Dickenson had been Caitlin's birth mother. The clues were piling up, but given Russell's evident denial of the obvious, I wanted to do a little more research to be absolutely sure.

We arrived back at the hotel at four-thirty, in time to grab quick showers and change for dinner. The children were effervescent, still stimulated by a tiring but exciting day on the water, and Elizabeth was relaxed and content. Caitlin's parents, however, were tense with each other and very short with me.

Russell cornered me once the others had entered their rooms. "You seem to think that there's something sinister in our daughter's background," he stated bluntly. "Well, I'm telling you, you're wrong."

"I didn't mean that. I just thought that if you adopted her, you might want to know where she came from."

"She's ours, and that's all you or anyone else needs to know."

He wrenched open the door to his room and slammed it behind him. His anger was all out of proportion to what I had said to them, and I feared what his response might be if and when he learned the results of the DNA test I had ordered. I had the last piece of an important puzzle, and in all fairness, sooner or later Caitlin had a right to know.

Eighty-nine:
The Hotel

Caitlin and Jon were banging out a lively four-hand version of *Maple Leaf Rag* in the dining room in honour of a table full of northern snowbirds who, judging by their accented French, were part of the seasonal influx from Quebec. At the end of every chorus they traded major third lifts, B-flat to D, then a wicked F-sharp major, and back to B-flat again to finish up. Caitlin bounded off the bench, laughing at their clever inventiveness, and joined the others at the table.

"That was a workout," she said happily. "Jon has some ear. Did you order yet?"

"Chicken Kiev and a virgin mai tai for you, right?" Jessica said.

"Yup, thanks. Gonna go back. Call me when it's all here." She returned to the piano where Jon had already begun a medley of Beatles tunes, and entered in mid phrase with an improvised countermelody to *Eleanor Rigby*.

"You'll never get her to sleep tonight," Elizabeth said.

"She'll be hyper at first, then all of a sudden she'll crash," Russell said. "I've even had to carry her to bed sound asleep sometimes. Something to do with a rampaging up and down metabolism."

"How do they play all those songs without sheet music?"

"I sort of understand how it works," Jessica said, "but it still amazes me. Music to her is simply another language, like English is to us. Just as we can pick out whatever words we need to express ourselves verbally, she commands a huge vocabulary of notes and chords. And with her incredible memory, if she hears a melody once, it's hers forever."

"Just like Mozart," Jessica said softly.

"That's what we've been told," Russell said. "One in a billion."

Their meals arrived, and Jessica waved to Caitlin. She and Jon finished *Hey Jude*, did a quick first four bars of *O Canada* doubled in octaves for the Québécois, then a raucous thirty-two bar canon on "Shave and a haircut" in three keys, grinning broadly at each other. She headed for the table amid strong applause, and Jon brought the temperature down with the intro to *Moon River*.

"Now take your time," Jessica said. "You have all evening to play. If you eat too fast, you know what happens." Caitlin was well-known for a touchy stomach.

"Can I stay up until the lounge closes? Jon plays until then tonight."

"What time is that?"

"Ten plus three," she said between bites.

"No matter how you say it, that's one o'clock in the morning, right? That's pretty late."

"But we're leaving tomorrow. It's my last chance to play with him. I can sleep on the plane."

"You'll probably fall asleep at the keyboard. But we'll see."

Despite her mother's warning, Caitlin downed her dinner twice as fast as the others. She swallowed her mai tai in four gulps and hurried back to the piano. She settled in with a slow decorative obbligato to Jon's gentle version of the old standard, *Someone to Watch Over Me*. Every time they played the part of the melody that fit the title lyric, she stared hard at him, eyes shining. Jon smiled at her gently. They bumped shoulders. Their bond would be hard, maybe impossible, to extinguish.

Ninety:
Jon

The following morning I found Caitlin having breakfast alone on the hotel patio. "What time are you heading for the airport?" I asked her.

"Mom says we have to be there three hours before the flight, and dad says that's ridiculous, that they won't leave without us, so they compromised on two. The plane leaves at three-ten. You're still coming to Nova Scotia, aren't you?"

"Soon. As I told you, I want to see my family again, and I'm getting too old to be bumming around the Caribbean."

She laughed. "Oh, yeah, you're *so* ancient. I'm getting old, too. I have a birthday coming up this month, the eighteenth. I'll be fourteen."

"Practically a senior citizen."

"Yeah, right." She took a few more bites of her breakfast. "This hotel is going to miss you. I heard one of the waiters say they've doubled their business since you started playing here. So listen, tell me why you left Canada and stopped performing. Your recordings are great."

"Just needed a change." I wasn't about to tell someone so young what had happened to me when I was a teenager, and how I had never been able to come to terms with it.

Caitlin pushed away the remains of her eggs and toast and sat back. "I had a lot of fun on your boat yesterday. I'd love to go sailing with you again."

"We don't have time. You need to get packed, don't you?"

"Or..." she began.

"What?"

"Are you gonna fly to Nova Scotia, or sail there?"

"That depends," I said. "I haven't decided what to do with the boat. Maybe sell her. The sailing season in Nova Scotia is pretty short. On the other hand, I invested a lot of money in her to repair all the damage that Carman did, and I'm kind of attached to her. If I take her up north, I can always spend summers there and sail back down here each winter."

"I don't like the name you chose, *Escondite Encantador*. 'Charming Hideaway.' Too… too prissy, and you're not hiding out anymore, anyway. She shouldn't be *Versteck* again either, for the same reason."

"Maybe I'll call her *Österreichischer Stolz*. She was the real hero of your rescue."

"Austrian pride, huh? Nah. Pompous. And you've already changed it several times. Isn't that bad luck?"

"That's an old wives' tale. It's best if a boat's name means something important to the owner."

"If you come to Nova Scotia, you could give her a good old Canadian name."

"She might like that."

Caitlin stared out to sea, lost in thought. "There's nothing to keep you here, is there? I think you should sail her north. Soon."

I finished my breakfast and gathered up our plates into neat piles, making it easy for the server to collect them. Compulsive tidiness is a habit I've developed from living alone in the below-decks confines of a seagoing abode.

Caitlin seemed distracted, examining the beach, the surf, and the snowbirds inert in lounge chairs, tanning safely in the early morning sun. She fidgeted with the hem of the tablecloth and rearranged the condiments and salt and pepper shakers into neat rows and geometric patterns.

"You could go right now, couldn't you?" she said in a tiny voice, looking down at her hands. "If you need help, I could go with you."

"You wouldn't like it, especially this time of year. Once past the

Carolinas, it's bitterly cold out in the Atlantic."

More silence. She still didn't look up. "You could teach me how to sail, *really* sail, all the fine points of how the ropes and winches work. The electronic stuff, too." She dipped her head, a sly smile on her lips. "And I could teach you to speak better Spanish."

"Hey! Mi Español es excelente."

"Sorry, but your accent is terrible, and sometimes you screw up the word order. You talk like a transplanted Burgomeister, a Chicano in lederhosen. An Austrian…"

"Stop! I get the point. Look, Caitlin, your folks wouldn't let you come with me. They'll want you with them."

She bristled, eyes flashing. "Let's add up the score here. I'm kidnapped on a cruise with Mom and Dad, that's minus one. Jon MacIsaac saves me, one point for you. Carman grabs Chloe, and Shelagh beats the crap out of her. Jon MacIsaac to the rescue again, two points. Just exactly who am I safest with?"

"Don't you ever say anything like that to your folks! It would hurt them."

"I won't, but that's how things came down, right? Anyway, if you're gonna sail all the way to Canada, I can steer while you take naps, and help you cook and stuff. Feed your cat, even clean the kitty litter pan if I have to. And we'll have time to play lots of duets."

She looked down. "I really like hanging out with you," she said softly. "After my Granddad died, I haven't had anyone to talk to about… You know, important stuff."

"I was sorry to hear that your dad's father passed away. It sounds like he was a wonderful man."

"I loved him."

"All right," I said. "You may come with me if they say it's okay. But they won't."

"I'm gonna ask anyway. Maybe I can convince them." She paused, grinning. "I'm pretty good at that."

* * *

Although I hadn't told Caitlin, I was already planning to abandon Florida and head north the following afternoon. I was below decks, running a check of all the electronic gear, when I heard a strident voice call my name. I climbed to the cockpit and discovered Russell and Jessica standing on the dock, the former glowering and his wife looking confused and uncertain.

"Did you tell our daughter she could sail to Nova Scotia with you?" Russell challenged.

Here we go, I thought. "That's not exactly what happened."

"And just exactly what *did* happen?"

"Come aboard and I'll explain."

The couple stepped over the gunwale and into the cockpit, and I waved them to seats. Jessica lowered herself to the starboard bench, but Russell remained standing, poised as if for battle.

"I did tell her she could go…" I began.

"You had no right!" Russell leaned forward aggressively, his anger boiling to the surface.

"…with a very big *if*," I continued. "I made it absolutely clear. She had to have your permission, and I also told her that I was sure you wouldn't allow it."

"All she told us was that you invited her to go."

"Of course she did. She's thirteen," Jessica said softly. "You know what she's like when there's something she really wants. Can we just talk about this calmly for a few minutes?"

Russell threw up his hands, shook his head, and collapsed down next to his wife, and Jessica seized the advantage. "Jon, there are a number of issues here. First of all, how safe would this trip be? I know you're a very experienced sailor, but I've heard the Atlantic can be treacherous in the winter."

"You're right," I said. "Cold and stormy and plenty rough."

"That settles it," Russell said. "She flies home with us."

"How long would it take for you to reach Nova Scotia?" Jessica said.

"Jess, you can't seriously be considering this!"

"Just bear with me, dear. What happens if a storm comes up, Jon? How much advance warning will you have?"

"You've seen my electronics," I told them. "Whenever I'm at sea, I monitor the weather constantly. If the forecast looks bad enough, I'll head for the Intracoastal Waterway."

"What's that?" Russell said.

"Protected waters, mostly between the coast and a string of barrier islands. It's a system of bays, rivers, canals and such stretching all the way from Florida to Maryland. After that there are some additional sheltered passages all the way north to Boston."

Jessica leaned forward, as if searching my face for the truth. "And is that how you plan to go?"

"No. It would take forever. There are well over a hundred swing bridges, lift bridges and bascules that have to open to let a tall boat go through. The wait can be interminable. And I wouldn't dare navigate such close quarters at night. Lots of twists and turns to slow me down, especially with my long waterline. Offshore I can sail twenty-four hours a day, full speed ahead. Some of the canals have locks, meaning more delays, and with my deep keel there are places I can't go, such as the Great Dismal Swamp."

"The *what!*" Russell exploded.

I couldn't help smiling, although from the look on his face, that infuriated him. "It's an area bordering parts of Virginia and North Carolina. It has a canal, but I'm not sure it's deep enough for my boat to pass without going aground. I would have to put out to sea at least part of the time. In any case, using the Waterway could take months."

I was exaggerating, but not much. "By going off the coast, I can easily be in Canada in a couple of weeks, maybe less, and I can always find shelter when necessary. Not only that, I can hitch a ride part way on the Gulf Stream. That's good for three knots added to my overall speed."

"How can you possibly sail all day and night, day after day?"

"I can't if I'm alone. That was one of Caitlin's arguments for coming. She wants to learn all about sailing, which would let me take naps during the day."

"She knows nothing about boats."

"Not true. She learned the basics during our escape last summer, and she's a quick study. Give her a couple of days of instruction and lots of practice, and she could be a pro. But look, I understand your reservations, and I don't need a juvenile crew member. I have an autopilot and can always heave to when I need to sleep. I tried to discourage her."

"You could simply have said no!"

"Russell, we've talked about this," Jessica said. "You know why he couldn't do that." She turned to me. "She thinks you're Superman. She has a massive crush on you, and we wouldn't be responsible parents if that didn't worry us."

I started to object, but she waved me away. "I'm sure you would never do anything to hurt her. If it weren't for you, we'd have lost her. But two weeks alone with you on the boat, she'll be dealing with some very adult emotions."

For the next twenty minutes we explored the problem, while I stressed my honest reluctance to have Caitlin join me on the voyage. Russell remained vehemently opposed, but Jessica took the bit in her teeth, refusing to make a decision until she had talked to Caitlin further. In the end, nothing was resolved.

Ninety-one:
Going Home

Russell changed their airline reservations to the following day, and he and Jessica talked far into the night, torn between trepidation over letting Caitlin sail north through the frigid Atlantic and her almost desperate need to assert her independence.

"It's an adventure," Jessica had said, "a wonderful chance to explore who she really is. Should we deny her that?"

"It's too soon. She's a *child*," Russell had said. "I know she seems much more mature than her age would suggest since surviving the kidnapping. But we don't know anything about this man, not really. I'm sure he's a fine sailor, he proved that when he rescued the girls, but her crush on him worries me."

"I know. And let's face it, it's more than a crush. It's deeper than that. She's grown to love him, and in some strange way, I can tell he loves her too. But I believe it's in a healthy way. Almost like…"

"Go ahead, say it. Almost like a father." Russell couldn't deny pangs of jealousy over the way their daughter had bonded with this virtual stranger.

"I trust him," Jessica said. "He's kept her safe so far, and I'm absolutely convinced that he would never do anything to betray her faith in him."

"He knows something. I don't know how, but all his talk about her being adopted hits too close to home. Suppose he says something to her? And how about Sabrina Dickenson? There can't be any connection, but suppose he thinks…"

"That isn't an issue. We were in Toronto when…"

"Uh, huh, except Canada can seem like a very small country sometimes."

"We should let her go with him," Jessica said firmly. "After all she's been through, she's earned the right. We might alienate her if we try to tie her too closely to us now. I know the dangers she could face, both physical and emotional, but that can't be worse than what she suffered at the hands of those kidnappers. I believe, I *know*, that Jon MacIsaac is a good man. He *will* bring her back safely to us, in every way that matters."

* * *

The next day, Russell and Jessica stood on the dock at the marina with Elizabeth and Chloe, where a taxi waited to take the four of them to the airport. Their luggage was stowed in the trunk. With her own suitcase and backpack already aboard the yacht, Caitlin could hardly contain her impatience to be underway.

"How long will it take you to get to Nova Scotia?" Russell asked her.

"Jon says that if we have good weather and sail around the clock, we could probably do it in eight days, but he doesn't want to push it. He says we'll have to stop off somewhere to get heavier clothes and take a break or two from the sea to stretch our legs. Maybe see some sights. What's today, the fourth? So even if it takes two weeks, I'll still be back in time for my birthday."

"You should be in school before then."

"Dad, give me a break. I'll learn a lot more on this trip than I ever could sitting in a bunch of boring classes."

"You have your passport?"

"Duh!"

"How about Jon?"

"I asked him. He has a Canadian passport, with two years to go before he has to renew it."

Russell looked toward the yacht, where Jon was coiling lines on the forward deck. His beard was gone, his hair neatly trimmed. The dark hair dye would take time to grow out, but Juan José was gone forever. As was Rolf.

"Sweetheart, I'm just worried about you, that's all," her father said.

"You heard what Jon said at breakfast. We won't go anywhere near the shipping lanes, and help is always close if we need it."

"What kind of help might you need?" Jessica asked uncertainly.

"I don't know, if we hit an iceberg maybe, or an alligator stows away in the bilge. Or suppose a giant ten-armed kraken comes over the rail and grabs me. Everyday stuff like that."

"You're too tough," Chloe said. "Any overgrown squid that dares to take you on had better watch out."

"I guess you'll be all right," Russell said. "I looked up the design of his yacht on the internet. It has a great rep, able to handle the worst kind of weather, and Jon says he has just about every safety device you can buy. But anything mechanical is subject to problems." He smiled weakly, trying to ignore his own second thoughts.

The yacht's diesel was rumbling softly and Jon stood by the console, ready to take to the sea. He had said his goodbyes before going aboard, after offering his assurances that the trip would be an easy one, that they would keep in close touch.

Caitlin embraced Elizabeth and stretched up to kiss her cheek, then wrapped Chloe in a long, fierce hug. "You're all coming to my birthday, right? It's the eighteenth. And you have to talk your dad into it too. I hardly got to meet him."

"It's already on our calendar, dear," Elizabeth said.

"Don't forget, you're to call us every night after supper," Jessica reminded Caitlin.

"And if you want to come home earlier," Russell said, "Jon promised to stop somewhere and take you to an airport. You just have to call and give us your flight number so we'll know when to pick you up."

"You won't have to," Caitlin said. "I'm going all the way."

"You know it'll be really cold and probably stormy once you get north of Virginia."

"Dad, the boat has a *heater*, for Pete's sake." She looked toward the cockpit. "And the world's best captain."

"Okay. Just saying."

She pulled him down and buried her face in his shoulder. "You're so great! Thank you for letting me do this."

"You're welcome, Peanut. Just stay safe. Wear your life belt, and don't run around on the deck, especially if it gets icy."

"I promise." She kissed him hard and turned him loose, then hugged her mother. "I'm off! Cast off for us, okay?"

She scrambled over the side onto the boat and joined Jon in the cockpit. Russell moved to the bow and released the spring line. Jessica did the same at the stern, and *Northern Passage* eased out into the channel, her new name and home port—*Bournemouth, NS*—proudly displayed on a temporary board hanging from the stern. The Canadian Maple Leaf fluttered on the aft flagpole. Caitlin waved to them from the rail until they were well out into the bay.

"I'm still not okay with this," Russell said to his wife.

"We have to be," Jessica said. She turned to Elizabeth. "Would you have let Chloe go with him if she asked?"

"In a heartbeat," Elizabeth said. She wrapped her arm around her daughter's shoulders and drew her in close. "If not for him, we wouldn't have her back. I admit, there's something strange about him, so secretive, and I suspect his past haunts him for some reason. But like you, I trust him. And I think Caitlin needs this time to heal after all that's happened to her, just as Chloe does."

"She still has nightmares," Jessica said. "I've heard her crying in the night. In some ways she's still a little girl."

"This trip might help with that. I'm sure she'll be tired enough to sleep soundly. I talked with Jon for awhile while you two were packing.

He's promised to make a seasoned sailor out of her. It will give her new confidence."

"Everyone says the North Atlantic can be violent this time of year. I still can't help worrying."

"She's with an expert," Elizabeth said. "They'll make it through."

Ninety-two:
Airport

Chloe and her mother wandered about the kiosks next to the departure lounge while Jessica and Russell sat near the gate.

"One thing still bothers me," Russell said. "Do you suppose he might let something slip about suspecting that she's adopted?"

"He promised me he wouldn't."

"What? You didn't confirm it to him, did you?"

"I had to, Russell. I don't know how, but he figured it out, and if he could, others will too. All these secrets have to end."

"Jess, I can't believe you told him! You should have cleared it with me first!"

"And you would have tried to talk me out of it." She stared out at the tarmac, where an Air Canada 737 was pulling into the gate. "She has to know eventually. The longer we put it off, the harder it will be."

"I don't know how she'll react when she finds out."

"I think she'll be angry that we waited so long, at least at first. Before we tell her, we ought to dig into her background ourselves. The way she came to us, we don't know a thing about her, nothing about who her biological parents were except that they were supposedly healthy and smart. Jon is right about her talent, how rare it is, and she could be related to someone famous. She deserves to know."

"What are you suggesting?"

"A DNA test, maybe?"

"What good would that do? Without anything to compare it to, it wouldn't give us any more information. It would just confirm that she isn't biologically ours."

"There are companies who can do a search and put you in touch with others who have matching or similar DNA."

Russell was becoming agitated. "That's what I'm afraid of. What if they locate some blood relations, maybe even her birth parents? What if she wants to meet them?"

"Don't you think she has that right?"

Russell shrugged and slumped back in his seat.

"Anyway," Jessica said, "we'll cross that bridge later. Right now, I really think this trip is the best thing for her. She's entitled to explore her relationship with Jon, and they have so much in common. He bought some new piano literature before we left, mostly duets. She'll have a wonderful time."

"I'm just afraid," he said. "I can't help it. We came so close to losing her."

"If we try to wrap her in cotton wool, she'll rebel and be gone for good."

PART FOUR

Ninety-three:
Jon and Caitlin

As we headed north off Florida's east coast, a surprise weather window brought a stiff southeast wind that drove us strongly under dense, heavy air and brilliant sun. I let the autopilot do most of the work, for an honest eight-and-a-half knots under a single-reefed main, plus the added boost from the Gulf Stream for twelve overall. With little else to do, I lounged in the cockpit while Caitlin roamed the boat in a bikini, as if reluctant to let go of her warm weather vacation any sooner than necessary.

I could hear her poking into all the hidden cubbies and stores below, familiarizing herself, she told me, with the location of everything she supposed we might need. I insisted that she always wear her life belt when on deck, clipped to a lifeline in rough seas—"I promised your Dad"—and she grumbled but complied.

When we entered the waters off Georgia, a front moved in with an expected drop in temperature. The wind came around to the northwest and dropped, requiring us to work the sails to keep our speed up. Eager for the promised sailing lessons, Caitlin switched to shorts and a tee shirt, then added a ball cap and a light windbreaker when the sun slipped behind a cloud bank. With the autopilot off she stood the helm and set about learning the points of sail—"Wind on the bow is a close reach, right?"—and how to shake off a reef when things calmed down. She had to practice that several times.

With her prodigious memory she quickly understood the principles of navigation, how to read the instruments, and how the wind powered the sails, no matter which direction it was coming from. We practiced tacking endlessly until she could bring us about almost as fast as I could.

"Let's see how much you remember," I said to her one afternoon. "What happens if you raise the traveler?"

"She'll heel over," Caitlin said, studying the sails, "and we'll pick up half a knot."

"Let's see if you're right."

She hauled on the sheet and the hull canted. The knot meter jumped. She grinned and we shared a high five. She returned her attention to the compass, corrected our heading, and trimmed the mizzen smoothly, with no wasted motion. With a light hand on the wheel, she lapsed into uncharacteristic silence.

"Something on your mind?" I asked.

"Dad sounded concerned when I called home last night," she said. She had mastered the VHF radio and promised never to forget to check in with Russell and Jessica each evening. "He still calls me Peanut when he's worried about me. He asked me twice if I wanted to get off and fly home."

"He loves you very much. I can tell."

"Yeah, I guess he does. I haven't always thought so, but he's changed."

"Maybe you have, too."

"After what happened to me this summer? Duh! But I survived. That's mostly thanks to you, I know, but Chloe and I escaped by ourselves the first time. I'm sort of proud of that."

"You're entitled."

"And that tells me I'm ready to do more things on my own now. Make my own choices."

"I think your dad recognizes that. Otherwise, you wouldn't be here now. He really didn't want to let you come with me. It's hard for parents to let go, to allow their children to take risks. People learn how dangerous the world can be as they grow older."

She thought that over. "My granddad told me that making mistakes can be the best way to learn. He used to say, 'Kids who are overprotected grow up without the tools they need to keep themselves safe.' And if he thought I was about to do something really stupid, like when some of my friends started smoking, he never told me not to. He'd just give me the pros and cons and say, 'Think it over carefully,' and let me decide for myself."

"He was a wise man."

"Should I cut my nervous old dad some slack, then?"

"'Think it over carefully,'" I quoted.

She poked me in the ribs. "Ho, ho."

"Coming about!" I said.

* * *

When the weather was right, the autopilot was our friend. We stayed well outside the shipping lanes, but far enough offshore to avoid casual traffic. With the new radar installation, it wasn't necessary to keep deck watch around the clock. We played intense games of cribbage, and Scrabble in three languages at once. In a locker she discovered my ancient chess set, which hadn't seen the light of day since I left home all those years ago. Chloe had taught her well.

We spent hours together at the piano keyboard.

Despite the close quarters, we quickly became completely at ease with one another. Caitlin was obsessively neat, which suited me fine. She took over the chore of feeding and cleaning up after Jenny. She tried to entice the old girl into playing with a wad of paper on the end of a string, but my furry senior citizen preferred to sleep, either in the forward berth or curled up in the sun at the stern.

"Aren't you afraid she'll fall in?" she asked me.

"She did once, in the harbour the first week we moved aboard. A seagull landed on the tender and she leapt after it. She misjudged the distance and overshot, plop, right into the water. By the time I fished her out, she was more embarrassed than hurt. I had to bathe her to get the salt out of her fur, and she hated that."

"Cats can swim?"

"They can, but they don't like to. Ever since then she's been more careful."

I soon found I could trust Caitlin to keep watch for traffic during the day, to check the autopilot, and to adjust the sails without my input in response to changing wind and weather conditions. That allowed me to catch enough sleep in the daylight hours to stay fresh. But she was no help with the boat at night. She burned energy like a blast furnace from sunup to sundown and crashed every evening by ten. She simply couldn't stay awake longer than that.

She quickly learned to cook simple but nourishing meals to sustain us, and I explained to her the military approach to taking a shower to conserve water—get wet all over quickly, shut off the tap, soap up and scrub, then rinse off fast. She sluiced the salt off the decks each day and polished the brightwork. Between us we kept the cabin in perfect order, everything in its place.

Each evening she filled her parents in on all the exciting events of the day: the gigantic tankers and container ships that sometimes crossed our path on the way into port; the seabirds that hitched a ride and always seemed to arrive when there were food scraps left over from dinner; the sudden squalls that sent us dashing under the canopy.

The fun.

As she had predicted when we were in Florida, she was never bored by the yacht. By the time we left the shores of North Carolina behind and came abreast of Virginia, she was a seasoned sailor.

Ninety-four:
Stopover

I chose the port of Newport News to spend a day and a night ashore. We used the better part of the afternoon to shop for warmer clothes and foul weather gear, anticipating the colder climate that we were already beginning to encounter. We found a quiet oceanfront restaurant and had our first land-based meal since leaving Florida.

"Want to fly home from here?" I teased her as we lingered over dessert.

"Just try to get rid of me. I'm having a ball."

"Miss your folks?"

"Well, sure. But you know something strange? I don't think I need them so much anymore, not like I used to. I know what you're gonna say, 'don't tell them that,' and I won't, but it's true. Guess I'm growing up, huh?"

"I envy you. I haven't seen my family in years. I left Nova Scotia without telling them, and I'm sure they think I'm dead."

"Why did you do that?"

"It's a long story. Something happened to me when I was not much older than you, and I had to go away to put it behind me. Someday maybe I can explain it to you."

"So, have you called them? Do they know you're coming?"

"No..."

"Why not?"

"My Dad is dead. My mother is probably okay, but my grandparents could both be gone by now. Anyway, I'm not sure they'll be glad to see me after all this time. It's like I abandoned them, and I'll never be able to tell them why."

"Wish you'd tell me."

"Someday."

* * *

We took a two-room suite for the night in a motel near the harbour, and after she turned in I sat up reading at one end of the sofa, a light blanket draped from my shoulders to the floor. The door between our rooms was open a crack, and around two o'clock I heard her cry out. A few minutes later she pushed the door open and looked in.

"I saw your light" she said. "Want some company?"

"What are you doing awake?"

"Nightmare."

"Come on, then."

She perched beside me, kneeling, feet tucked beneath her and peering past my shoulder. "What's the book?"

"Joshua Slocum's *Sailing Alone Around the World*. I reread it every few years. I always find something new to learn from it." I set the volume aside. "Slocum wrote it more than a hundred years ago. He circumnavigated the earth in a thirty-six-foot sloop called 'The Spray,' smaller than mine and no one else on board. As far as anyone knows, he was the first person ever to do that. Pretty gutsy for those times."

"Must've been a Nova Scotian."

"Right you are. He was born on the North Mountain, overlooking the Bay of Fundy. Had salt in his veins, I think."

I told her more about that epic adventure, and we discussed the next day's route until her eyes began to droop. She looped her hand around my arm and snuggled in against my side. Her speech slurred, then faded away as she dropped into deep sleep. I spread the blanket over her and picked up Slocum's book again, but a few pages into it I realized I wasn't retaining anything I read. I closed my eyes, just for a moment, and the next thing I knew, bright sunlight was shining into the room.

Caitlin lay prone beside me, knees drawn up, her head resting on my thigh and one arm tucked in behind my back. I stroked her hair gently and she roused.

"Hi," she said shyly.

"Hi, yourself."

"What time is it?"

I glanced at the clock radio across the room. "After nine."

"Wow! Late." She uncurled and sat up.

"No more nightmares?"

"Nope. I'm safe again."

She's finally beginning to feel secure, I thought. But I was more and more convinced that she should know the truth about her background. I had promised Jessica to keep my own counsel, at least for now, but if the secret were to come out the wrong way, it could devastate her.

What to do…

Ninety-five:
Sightseeing

The days passed quickly, and Maryland, Delaware and southern New Jersey fell away behind us. Caitlin begged to see the New York City skyline, and we sailed up the harbour as far as Liberty Island. *Northern Passage* drifted slowly past the impressive statue that had once symbolized freedom and opportunity for many immigrants and refugees—an image tarnished in recent years by shifting political tides. Caitlin delighted in the view of the city, standing a long time at the bow in an icy January wind that blew down the Hudson River.

The next day brought a surprise change in the weather, an almost tropical breeze from the south that followed us along the southern shore of Long Island and past Block Island on the way to New England. It was a welcome respite that allowed us to do some housekeeping topside in relative comfort. We passed up the Cape Cod Canal in favour of seeing Martha's Vineyard and Nantucket, but as usual in those latitudes, the warm spell didn't last long. We were well out in the open Atlantic abreast of Provincetown when the temperature plummeted under a lowering sky, presaging a long haul across a stormy Gulf of Maine.

We checked in with Canada Customs, Immigration, and Border Security at Yarmouth. I suggested to Caitlin that she call home to let her parents know we were back in Canadian waters, but she kept putting it off, reluctant for some reason. A cold front moved through, and when we set sail again we found ourselves fighting a turbulent headwind—Force Six on the Beaufort Scale. *Northern Passage* took the twelve-foot waves in stride with the main double reefed, but it wasn't comfortable.

"Not exactly a fast way to travel," I told her as we tacked for the fifth time. We hadn't made much progress since turning northeast. "If it gets much rougher, we can pull in somewhere and wait it out."

"You said we can't sink, right?" Caitlin said nervously as the boat pitched and yawed in a sudden crosswind. The mainsail luffed and roared, and I spun the wheel to correct.

"I think I said *wouldn't*, not couldn't. Any boat can sink, given the most difficult conditions. But she's weathered much worse than this down south. I got caught once when I ignored a storm warning. The Caribbean looks calm most of the time, but when a tropical front blows through, or a full-fledged hurricane, you better head for shelter."

"If we keep going, when will we get there?"

"The forecast says things will settle down soon. We'll be ahead of time. It's still a couple of days until your birthday if that's what you're worried about."

"Where do we tie up?"

"The manager at the Bournemouth Marina is expecting us. His name is Bill Palmeter. I radioed our position yesterday, and he agreed to give me a sheltered slip on their permanent dock until he can have her pulled out of the water for the rest of the winter. They have only a skeleton crew this time of year, so I have to wait my turn. When we get close you can call your mom and dad to meet you and take you home."

"Where will *you* live?"

"On board at first."

"How about later?"

"I haven't figured that out yet."

Nova Scotia lies midway between the Equator and the North Pole, and winter days are short. With the sun dropping near the southwest horizon, nearly invisible behind clouds and fog, the light was fading rapidly. But the approaching cold front brought the wind around to a favourable point of sail, and we picked up a few knots. Two hours after sunset we were getting close, and I pointed out the first of the buoys that defined the channel into Bournemouth Harbour. I let *Northern*

Passage fall off the wind.

"Time to go below and call home," I said.

Caitlin hesitated. "Let's just turn around."

"What?"

"Turn around. Go back. I don't want this to be over yet."

I smiled at her. "'You may delay, but time will not.'"

"Is that a quote?"

"Benjamin Franklin said it, and he was right. People are waiting for you, expecting you. They *need* you, and you may not think so, but you need them too. It's best to let them know you're okay."

"I suppose so. But this has been so much fun."

"We'll do it again."

"Promise?"

"Por supuesto, niña linda. Por supuesto."

Of course, beautiful child. Of course.

* * *

Two hours later I stood uncertainly on the old familiar porch and rang the bell, expecting to find strangers living in the house where I grew up. Presently the door opened. *She looks just the same*, I thought. *A few more wrinkles, maybe a bit more stooped. But the same.*

"Come in out of the cold," Becky MacIsaac said, holding the door open wide.

"Mom, it's me. J. J."

"Of *course* it's you. Don't you think I know my own son? I always knew you'd come back some day."

Ninety-six:
Home

Life returned to normal, at least as normal as possible with a renowned prodigy and a recently resurrected world-class artist concertizing together. Caitlin celebrated her birthday with an impromptu dual performance in a packed-to-overflowing Baxter Hall at Irvine University, the Sharma family in attendance. She and Jon each soloed, and after telling the audience a humorous and sanitized version of how they found each other in the Gulf of Mexico, they finished together with the Mozart *C Major Sonata*. Their encore featured five minutes of improvisation on *Maple Leaf Rag*, blended with quotes from *The Nova Scotia Song*.

The months melted away. They performed together in Halifax, Montreal and Vancouver, with several stops at smaller venues in between, while the crew at Bournemouth Marina undertook minor improvements to *Northern Passage*. They launched her on June thirteenth. In spite of her long absence from school the previous year, Caitlin completed her final exams with honours. The school again raised the issue of letting her skip grades, but she refused, not wanting to be separated from her friends.

* * *

July arrived, warmer than usual. Just when the events in Florida had receded far back in memory, Sergeant Major Edward Mason of the RCMP made an appointment to meet with the Sheridans at home to give them an update on the investigation. One Friday morning he arrived shortly after ten-thirty, and the family invited him into the living room. Caitlin sat on the edge of her chair, anticipating good news, but the Sergeant disappointed her.

"I'm sorry to report that we are still no nearer to identifying the rest of the people involved in the kidnapping," Mason began. "Rose-Ellen Foster, the woman you knew as Shelagh, Caitlin, was charged with a number of offenses, including multiple assaults on you and the attempted murder of your friend Chloe Sharma. Her trial was scheduled for next month, but the Tallahassee District Attorney's Office decided to offer her a plea deal in return for the names of everyone involved. It looked like she might accept, but all she would tell us at first was that the person who planned the whole operation called himself The Spider. She wanted to consult with her lawyer before she said anything else."

"What happened?" Russell asked.

"That meeting was arranged for the following day, and she was returned to prison overnight. There was an altercation in the cafeteria and Foster was stabbed to death by another inmate. I'm afraid she was our last hope of finding out who was behind what happened."

Caitlin sank back into her chair. "So that's it? Whoever was behind it gets away with it?"

"We have our suspicions, and we're pretty clear as to motive, thanks to Vachan Sharma. As you know, he dropped out of contention for the leadership of the New Democratic Party, under threat of Chloe's death. We don't know for sure whether they intended to release her after her father acquiesced to their demands."

"Not a chance!" Caitlin said. "We heard them talking. The Foster woman was planning to kill her all along. She hated Chloe, called her a 'mutt' and a 'mongrel', and that guy Carman would have killed us both if Jon hadn't saved us."

"You must have some suspects," Russell said, "someone connected with or working for the Freedom Party. No one else had anything to gain by what they did."

"I'm sure you're right," Mason said, "but without any witnesses, it doesn't look good. Unless we can put together an airtight case against someone, it's unlikely we'll ever be able to bring charges."

"Is Caitlin still in danger?" Jessica asked.

"We don't think so. The only faces she ever saw were Foster, Carman Russo, Anna the housekeeper and Alonzo Cardoso. Those four are all out of the picture, so the rest have no reason to think she's a threat to them."

"Unless I hear that voice," Caitlin said. "The guy who I heard in the next room of the cabin. If I ever hear him again, I'll know."

Ninety-seven:
A Witness

Seven of the eight Executive Members of the Freedom Party met with Premier Carter Williams at their favourite restaurant in late July, sequestered in a private room where they would not be overheard. They were joined by Jacob Shaffer, who still served as security for Vachan Sharma. He continued on the Freedom Party's payroll as a mole within the New Democratic Party to report back on the Official Opposition's plans and strategies.

"What's on the agenda?" Grant Keillor asked when the men had finished their dinner and lingered over wine and cocktails.

"We have a resignation," Arch MacInnes told them. "You've noticed that Al Barclay isn't with us this evening. He's stepping down, resigning from the Legislature. His wife has cancer, and he says he wants to spend as much time with her as possible."

"Goddamn!" Keillor said. "We have a razor thin edge as it is. The NDP and the Liberals have already ganged up to block some of our bills, and they're hinting at a Motion of No Confidence to bring down the government."

"So, do we call a by-election?" MacInnes asked.

"We need to take a poll first. If the opposition parties get together, we could lose. I wouldn't put it past the Liberals to decide not to field a candidate. They know they can't win, so they might step aside and let the NDP walk off with the seat just to screw us. We need to improve the odds. Any chance we can put some pressure on someone, like we did with Sharma?"

"We could snatch his kid again," MacInnes said. "Force him to give up his own seat to get her back."

"That won't work twice," Keillor said. "We're already under

suspicion. That would bring the Mounties right to our door."

Shaffer spoke up for the first time. "You wouldn't have a chance to get near her anyway. I was lucky to keep my job with them after supposedly going to lunch when the kid got on the Jet Ski, and they keep really close track of her ever since."

"Okay," MacInnes said, "let's take a few days to assess our options. We can meet again on the weekend and woodshed it. Dig up whatever you can find on anyone in the Legislature who might be vulnerable to attack. Look for any kind of scandal, some hint of corruption, even if we have to invent it. We need to bump at least one opposition member out of the House, maybe two."

The discussion continued for another half hour with no clear path toward solidifying the Party's hold on Province House. The men adjourned to go home, and on the way to the parking lot, Shaffer caught up with the man who called himself The Spider and joined him in his car.

"We have a problem," Shaffer said quietly.

"Now what?" The Spider said.

"How are your legal problems working out?" Shaffer asked. "Have the Mounties tied any of you to this mess in any way?"

"Ralph Pickett is the Party's lawyer. He's damn good. He says that with Rose-Ellen Foster dead and buried, there's no connection to us whatsoever."

"Except for the fact that no one outside your group had any motive for what happened. Does Pickett himself suspect anything?"

"I think I've convinced him that the Party had nothing to do with the kidnapping, that it must have been some rogue outsiders who pulled it off."

"How about if a second witness shows up?"

"*What?*"

"I overheard a conversation between Sharma and his daughter. When you were at the cabin the last time, the Sheridan kid heard you

319

talking to Rose."

The Spider frowned. "I don't see how. It was raining that day, so we couldn't go outside, but the girls were locked away in their room."

"Apparently the Sheridan kid could hear you through a transom. According to Chloe, she memorized the sound of your voice, and she's sure she'll recognize it if she ever hears it again. If you give any interviews on CBC, eventually that'll happen."

"Remember my voice? What are the odds of that? It was months ago."

"According to Chloe, the girl has what she calls 'tonal memory'. It's something to do with her musical ability. She swears she can pick your voice out of a crowd."

"I've never heard of this 'tonal memory' shit. I'll look into it. If there's any truth to it, we'll find a way around it."

"You want my take on it? Eliminate the kid now, before it's too late."

The Spider sat thinking for several moments. "Jake," he said, "you've just earned yourself a bonus. Leave this to me."

Ninety-eight:
Jon

Near the end of July, Jessica and Russell Sheridan asked to see me. We met in an outdoor location, the park adjoining the Bournemouth Marina. They explained that they had finally told Caitlin about her adoption, and it hadn't gone well. I decided it was time for me to come clean about the DNA test that was performed on Caitlin's toothbrush, and what it had revealed about her ancestry. The explanation took a long time, leaving both of them shocked and afraid of having to tell their daughter what they had learned.

They asked me to come to their home the next day, and I seated myself on the piano bench in the living room. They wanted a witness, and possibly an arbiter, during the uncomfortable conversation that was to come. But I was determined to be more than that. I would be an advocate for Caitlin, who was understandably angry. Trying to deal with her parents' deception and its implications had caused a major upheaval in her self-concept.

Caitlin chose an armchair at the far side of the room, her face a mask of brooding contempt. It was plain that she wanted nothing to do with a mother and father who supposedly loved her, but who had lied to her for her entire life. It looked as if she didn't want to have much to do with me either. She seemed to see me as in league with the enemy.

Russell and Jessica sat on the sofa facing her. "This is going to be hard, sweetheart," Russell said, "but we know more today than we knew yesterday, and I promise to tell you everything, and answer any questions you have."

"Just get on with it," Caitlin said quietly, her tear-reddened eyes burning like hot coals.

"You already know that your mom lost two babies by miscarriage.

After the second one, we believed it was probably best not to try again, and we also decided not to adopt. At least that was what I decided. Your mom was open to the idea."

"You'd better tell her why you felt that way," Jessica said.

"I knew there would be no guarantee we'd get the kind of child I… That we wanted."

"And what kind was that?" Caitlin said.

"Someone who would fit in well with our family."

"So, no little kid from Africa, or some poor country in Asia or Central America. Right?"

"You know we aren't racists, Caitlin."

"Maybe. Anyway, go on. What happened?"

"This is the hardest part to explain," Russell said. "You have to understand, I have a lot of professional contacts through the hospital. I thought that if I put the word out and let my colleagues know what we were looking for, someone might be able to help us."

"What exactly *were* you looking for?"

"We had a lot to offer, your mother and I, and I wanted a son or daughter who would be able to take advantage of… Who could…"

"What your father is trying to tell you," Jessica said bluntly, "is that he wanted a guarantee that any baby we adopted would be extra smart. Talented. Perfect in every way."

I watched a pained expression cross Russell's face, and hoped that he was able to accept what I suspected was the truth behind his wife's bitter words.

Caitlin turned to her mother. "Is that what you wanted, too?"

"I just wanted a child to love," Jessica said sadly. "I had already lost two. But at the time I didn't know what your dad was going to do."

Caitlin focused on Russell again. "Is Mom telling the truth?"

"Yes," he said. "She would have been happy with an international adoption, mixed race, whatever, as long as she could have a newborn."

"But you were looking for a designer baby! And it's pretty damned obvious that you found one."

Russell sighed. "If you'll just hear me out, maybe you'll understand. After we exhausted all of the conventional routes to adoption, a classmate of mine from medical school suggested I look on line. Do you know what the dark web is?"

"Hidden sites, extreme porn, terrorism, snuff films. That kind of thing."

"Well, yes, but a lot more. It's a source for many different kinds of criminal activity. My friend showed me how to access a site that offered what was called 'specialized adoption services,' and told me it was probably what I needed. He helped me set up a meeting with some people connected with the site."

"An *illegal* adoption site," Jessica added.

"I'm not proud of it now, but it looked like the answer to our dreams. They claimed to provide superior children, born to young, highly intelligent parents who for some reason couldn't care for them. We could even specify their background—academics, sports, artistic talent, whatever we wanted."

"At great cost, I found out later," Jessica said.

"Yes, it wasn't cheap, but at the time I didn't care. I paid the deposit without telling your mother. I knew I was breaking the law, but at that point I was willing to risk it."

"Because *you* wanted the perfect child," Caitlin said.

"I told you I'm not proud of how I felt then, and I'm not making excuses now. It's hard for me to admit it, but I promised to tell you everything."

Russell stood and turned his back to stare out the window. When he began to speak again, his voice trembled with emotion. "They promised delivery within two years, a baby almost certain to be healthy and gifted and talented and, God help me for asking for this, beautiful and physically perfect."

"Made to order," Caitlin said disgustedly. "Like choosing furniture out of a catalogue. So what happened?"

"The following year we discovered we were pregnant again," Jessica said. Her eyes filled, and she turned away and blotted her cheeks with a tissue.

"We were frightened," Russell continued. "We even considered terminating the pregnancy, rather than go through the sorrow of another miscarriage. But that had to be your mother's decision, and she couldn't face having an abortion. She kept hoping that this time, everything would work out all right."

"I was wrong," Jessica said quietly.

"You couldn't have known that then, especially after the first six months. The doctors kept telling us that all the signs were good, everything was fine, that you were well past the time when you lost the first two."

He turned to Caitlin again. "We began to relax. Around the middle of December, we took a trip to Toronto. I was scheduled to speak at a medical symposium, and your Mom wanted to see a couple of shows. Her gynaecologist said it would be perfectly safe to travel, so we took a chance. Everything was fine until the night before we were to head for home."

"I already know about that," Caitlin said, watching her mother's stricken expression. "Mom began to bleed, and you called the paramedics, and they took her to a hospital where the doctors stopped the bleeding. After that everything was okay until I was born."

"Not you," Russell said, barely aloud.

"Surprise, surprise," she said sullenly.

"The doctors managed to deliver the baby that night, a beautiful little girl, but she was a month premature and had trouble breathing. For some reason she couldn't seem to digest your mom's milk. Baby formula didn't work either, even after they inserted a feeding tube. They put her in intensive care and told us they would do everything they could for her, but she went downhill rapidly. I called the Medical

Centre back home and arranged for a leave of absence without telling anyone what was happening. We took turns, your mother and I, keeping vigil in the hospital. We named her Aileen Caitlin."

"My name backwards."

"Uh huh."

"But it wasn't me."

"No, sweetheart, it wasn't you. Little Aileen lived only six days."

The room was silent for several long minutes, each of them lost in thought. I rose from the bench and walked out of the room. I already knew the rest of the story, having heard it the previous day, and I didn't want to witness Caitlin's reaction when the whole truth came out. I lingered in the hall, however, where I could be available in case I was needed.

"What did you do next?" Caitlin asked.

"We were devastated by that time," Russell said. "I secretly called my contact in the illegal adoption operation. That was when I first met a lawyer named Thomas Curtis. He agreed to see me at a downtown location."

Ninety-nine:
The Solution

—December, fourteen years earlier, Toronto, Ontario.

Russell was seated in a booth at the back of a Yonge Street coffee shop when Thomas Curtis arrived, wearing a two-thousand-dollar suit and carrying a monogrammed calfskin attaché case. He scanned the room, spotted Russell, and made his way to the booth.

"Dr. Sheridan?" he said. Russell nodded nervously.

"My name is Thomas Jamieson Curtis, an attorney. My associate told me of your call and explained the situation to me. It's possible we can help you. May I sit down?"

Russell nodded again, unable to speak, not daring to hope that this man might offer them relief from their sorrow.

Curtis slid into the booth opposite him. "First, I'm deeply sorry for your loss. However, your file with us is still active, and having paid your deposit you are in good standing and still in the queue for delivery of a child."

"That was explained to me on the phone," Russell said.

"Good. Tell me, how is your wife holding up after your misfortune?"

"As well as can be expected, I guess. She doesn't say much."

"Does she know you are meeting with me?"

"I didn't tell her where I was going when I left the hotel or why, and she didn't ask. I didn't dare say anything that might get her hopes up."

"Have you told anyone else about the death of your daughter? Anyone back home?"

"No." Russell swallowed hard. "All of our friends have been so happy for us, and I haven't had the heart to let them know what happened."

"How were the remains handled?" Curtis asked.

"Aileen was cremated here in Toronto."

Curtis sat back and folded his hands in his lap. "How soon do you have to return to Nova Scotia?"

"We're not expected back until next week."

"Can you stay longer?'

Russell sat up straight. "What are you suggesting?"

"Dr. Sheridan, we may be able to solve your problem in a way that will fulfill your contract with us and simultaneously bring you and your wife a great deal of happiness. We are presently awaiting what the poets call a blessed event. In mid-January. The timing is serendipitous."

"Are you saying you have a baby for us?"

"A little girl is expected. Her background is perfect for you, both parents healthy, highly intelligent, and with no history of drug or alcohol abuse. The only problem is, the infant has already been promised to another couple."

Russell leaned back, deflated. "Why are you telling me this, then?"

"We might be able to come to an arrangement."

* * *

Jessica was sobbing quietly, huddled in a corner of the sofa. Caitlin sat poised on the edge of her chair, hanging onto her father's every word.

"What did that man tell you?" she asked.

"He said the baby could be ours, and that if we elected to stay in the city until she was born, we could claim she had been born to us. He would provide an official birth certificate naming your mom and me as parents. If our Aileen had come to full term, she would have been born about the same time as this baby was due. We made plans to take an extended leave from our jobs and stayed in Toronto."

"When did this baby come?"

"January eighteenth."

The room was still. "My birthday," she whispered.

"Yes," Russell said.

"That baby was really me."

"Yes."

"What was it like? I mean, *buying* a baby like that. I want to know!"

One Hundred:
Blessed Event

—Fourteen years earlier, Toronto, Ontario

The delivery was relatively easy and uneventful, due to the newborn's diminutive size. She needed no assistance to begin breathing and voiced an immediate healthy cry. The midwife severed the umbilical cord and whisked her away to a receiving table to be cleaned up and checked for abnormalities; there were none. She wrapped the baby carefully and placed her in a bassinet. An attendant wheeled the mother to a recovery room. She would return to her home province, never again to see the child she bore.

For the next four days, staff members monitored the infant around the clock. At the end of that time, the baby was declared fit to travel and was soon to be on her way to the adoptive parents who had placed an order with the organization.

The transaction was scheduled for ten o'clock on the morning of January 26th. Barrister and solicitor Thomas Curtis, LL.M, J.D., welcomed a visibly apprehensive Russell and Jessica Sheridan through the rear entrance of a law firm in downtown Toronto. He led them to an elegant consultation room and ushered them into chairs drawn up to a ten-by-twelve eighteenth century mahogany conference table. No one else in the building witnessed their arrival.

Curtis sat opposite and produced a folder from his embossed leather attaché case. He opened it and extracted a thin sheaf of documents but did not yet pass them across the table. "I believe you will find everything in order," he said.

"When can we see her?" Jessica asked eagerly.

"As soon as we complete the necessary details to finalize transfer of ownership," Curtis said. "First I must ascertain whether either of you are experiencing second thoughts about the responsibility you are about to assume. Do you understand that from this day on, you will be the parents of a child who, in the eyes of the legal system and the public at large, is your natural progeny? Flesh of your flesh, so to speak."

"Of course," Russell replied. "That's how we want it."

"And do you further understand that you may not contact our organization again? Unless at some time in the future you decide to make an additional purchase, that is. In that case you go through the same channels that led you to us this time."

"Just to clarify," Russell said, hoping to take some measure of control over the proceedings, "the baby is guaranteed to possess superior genetic heritage, right? With above average intellectual potential and talent that will set her apart from the general population. She has to be equipped to profit from the advantages we are able to provide. If this should prove not to be the case, what recourse do we have?"

"Dear," Jessica began tentatively, "I don't think…"

"Your choice of the word 'guaranteed' is inappropriate," Curtis said, but not unkindly. "We can make no such promise. As I explained last week, the baby was exceptionally alert at the moment of delivery. We believe her background to be a perfect fit for your family. The mother was a healthy sixteen-year-old who excelled in her high school studies, especially mathematics and languages. She was also an accomplished pianist. We found her in a shelter for unwed mothers and arranged to have her tested. The results indicated an IQ of 165. She was strong and fit, athletically inclined, with no history of either drug or alcohol abuse. Also, with such a small baby, labour was of short duration and unusually free of stress for both of them. The Apgar score was a perfect ten."

He paused and leaned forward in emphasis. "We are proud of our reputation. You are paying a substantial premium for our service, and we have expended considerable effort to fulfill your exact requirements. We have every reason to believe that your daughter—*your* daughter—will exhibit superior intellectual traits, but we cannot ensure this. There may be factors, biological or otherwise, that mitigate against such an outcome. But the same would be true if she were the product of your own efforts at procreation. Healthy, normal people may bear less than perfect children, and if I understand correctly what led you to seek our assistance, such was your situation."

Jessica wiped away an unbidden tear, sad to be reminded of her inability to bring a healthy baby to term.

"We are convinced," Curtis continued, "that the daughter you are about to receive is as vital and flawless as any that has ever been born."

"Like buying a car," Russell muttered, "but without a warranty." Then more forcefully: "So you're saying we'll have nothing in writing to fall back on if you have misrepresented this arrangement in any way. Is that correct?"

"Nothing but my word, I'm afraid. I'm sure you can understand, given the laws of this country with regard to such an unconventional covenant, that we cannot afford to leave behind any documentation that might pose difficulties later on. That is for our mutual protection."

The couple looked at each other. Jessica was visibly tiring of the legalese, and of the delay in achieving what they came for. "It doesn't matter," she said to her husband. "None of this matters, except that we're here to pick up our baby. *Our* baby. This is the child we are destined to have. I really believe that."

Russell shrugged and turned back to face Curtis again. "I think we should be allowed to see her before we have to make a final decision. Or at least a photo."

"No such photo exists," Curtis said, "nor anything else that might someday lead someone to question our role in this matter. I feel confident in saying that the child is as beautiful as any infant who ever passed through our care, but even if that were not the case, I understand physical appearance is not your primary concern. Isn't that correct?"

Russell sat back, feeling defeated and impotent when confronted by a man who held all the cards. What choice did he have but to agree to whatever terms were offered to them?

Curtis leafed through the papers and handed one across the table. "We have taken the liberty of drafting a birth announcement for you to publish in your local paper when you return home. We recommend that you do not alter it in any way. The printed word tends to take on a life of its own. The least suggestion as to your daughter's true origin, no matter how inadvertent or obscure, could cause difficulties at some point."

He handed them another sheet. "This is your baby's birth certificate, dated January 18th, Toronto, Ontario, along with the name you chose for her. Both of your names appear as parents." He smiled at Jessica. "This document is as real as if you had spent half a day in the delivery room."

"How did you get this?" she asked.

"Anything is possible, given access to someone in a position of authority, and provided one is willing to pay for it."

"Please," she said, placing her hand over her husband's. "Let's just do this."

Russell sighed and lifted his briefcase onto the table. From within he removed a number of certificates authorizing the transfer of currency, bearer bonds and real property as previously agreed upon, to a total value of one hundred and fifty thousand Canadian dollars. "It's all here," he said as he passed it across the table. "I assume you will want to have these documents verified before we take possession?"

Without examining them, Curtis placed the papers in his attaché case and closed the lid. "Given the reputation you both enjoy within your professions, I'm sure that won't be necessary. I am also sure that you know the consequences that will result, should you default on our agreement or disclose today's transaction to any third party or institution. Do you agree?"

"We do."

"Congratulations on the birth of your daughter," Curtis said as he pressed a buzzer on the underside of the table. Half a minute later the door opened, and a woman in a nurse's uniform wheeled a bassinet into the room.

One Hundred One:
The Final Piece Of The Puzzle

Caitlin began to cry. She stumbled from the room, passing through the hall without noticing me, and ran up the stairs to the second floor.

"You didn't tell her the rest," Jessica said to Russell as I returned to the living room.

"She doesn't need to hear that," Russell said.

"You *promised* her! *Everything*, you said."

"It's too much. We should let her get used to what I just told her first."

"Was a hundred and fifty thousand the going rate for an illegal adoption?" I asked. "You didn't mention that yesterday."

Russell turned toward me, his face a tortured mask of guilt and shame. "There was a deposit of fifty thousand up front, non-refundable, against a total fee of one-fifty. At our first meeting, Curtis said that was also what the other couple had agreed to pay, and he had a prior obligation to them. I figured our meeting was over, but he made no attempt to leave. For an additional fifty thousand from us, he said, he would find a way to stall them until another baby was available."

"Unbelievable," I said. "What kind of world is this where you can buy a helpless human being for that kind of money?"

"Wouldn't you say she was worth it?" he said to me. "In any case, what we were really paying for was anonymity, a secret that we thought would never come out."

"Caitlin will probably need therapy for a long time to get over this," Jessica said. "It's a lot for her to take in all at once."

"That's why I don't want to tell her what you found out," Russell said to me. "At least not yet."

"No!" Jessica said firmly. "We have to finish this. She has to know the whole truth, sooner rather than later. I won't let you hide this any longer." She looked directly at me. "Jon, she has to know that you're her biological father."

In the silence that followed, Caitlin crept out from where she had been hiding around the corner in the hall. "You're my real father?" she said to me. "How can that be?"

One Hundred Two:
The Explanation

I've already told your parents enough to satisfy them that you truly are my daughter," I told Caitlin, "but you all deserve to know more—the whole story of what happened. It began when I was fifteen. I was already making a name for myself. I'd played in Carnegie Hall twice and soloed with the Montreal Symphony, Winnipeg too. But I was desperately unhappy. I had no friends at school. They thought I was strange, and I guess I was. I was no good at sports, and always knew all the answers in class, which made me a constant target of bullies. They thought I was some sort of freak. I just couldn't take it, so I ran away."

"Why didn't you tell your parents?"

"Let me tell it my own way, Caitlin. You need to see how it was, and then you'll understand better why I chose to leave home later and go to sea." I tried to continue, but the words caught in my throat. I stood up and walked over to look out the window. Once I was sure I could speak without my voice breaking, I tried again.

"I met a girl. She was fifteen like me. She was beautiful. Her name was Sabrina."

Expectant silence settled over the room. I turned to find Caitlin staring at me fiercely. I returned to my seat and took a deep breath to steady my pounding heart.

"She was an outcast," I said, "just like me, a misfit. The other children called her 'the brain,' and to make matters worse, she played piano too, really well. She lasted in public school only until grade six, when her parents pulled her out. She was home schooled from then on."

"How did you meet her?" Caitlin asked.

"In church. Her father was the pastor in a country parish, and I was looking for some place where I might be accepted. I started sneaking away Sunday mornings to attend services. When my mother asked where I'd been, I just said 'Out for a walk' or something like that. She never questioned me about it. The people in the church treated me well. They never asked me about my family, just told me that everyone was welcome in the House of God."

"What about the girl?"

"She played for the services. They didn't have an organ, so she played piano for the congregation to sing hymns. The third or fourth time I went there, I hung around afterward to talk to her. That was how it started. Only there was a problem."

"What happened?"

"Her father discovered we were hanging out, and he forbade her to see me. He was some kind of Puritan, with all kinds of rules that every member of the church had to follow. One of the rules was that none of the teens in the community could date. Boys and girls could only see each other in the presence of an adult. They weren't allowed to go to public school but were taught by Sabrina's father, an Irvine professor, and a couple of old women. I was told that as an outsider I was welcome to attend services, but I couldn't see Sabrina at all unless I joined the church. I went home that day really confused, and the next week at school was awful. I got beat up twice, and that was the last straw. The next Sunday I went to the preacher and told him I wanted to stay. I told a bunch of lies about being an orphan and living with a mean old aunt who didn't care where I went."

"That must have been awful," Jessica said.

"It worked out okay. Sabrina's father arranged for me to stay with a nice older couple who had no children. They treated me well. The church provided me with clothes and everything else I needed, and I started attending classes with the other kids. I was allowed to practice on the church piano, and I could see Sabrina as long as I followed the rules. Only I didn't. *We* didn't, I mean, Sabrina and me."

"What do you mean?" Caitlin asked.

"We sneaked around. We got really good at hiding out together, and we didn't get caught for months. But we made a big mistake."

"What?"

"Caitlin, you have to understand, I was only fifteen, and not having any friends, I didn't learn much about life the way other kids do. Sabrina knew a lot more than me, only she didn't know how to protect herself. She knew about birth control, I guess, the pill and all that, but didn't know how to get them."

Caitlin's eyes grew wide. The room was absolutely still.

"Before long," I continued, "you were growing inside her."

We all sat in silence for what seemed like hours but was only a few minutes. Then Caitlin turned to her mother and said, "Did you know about this?"

"Not until yesterday, when Jon told your father and me."

Caitlin stiffened, under rigid control, her mouth set in a firm straight line. "Go on," she said to me.

I explained that Sabrina managed to hide the pregnancy by always wearing oversized sweatshirts and a loose coat whenever she was required to wear a dress, such as for church services. She walked slouched over and got away with it for a long time, until finally the pregnancy became obvious to anyone who looked at her. Her father was furious, but he wasn't a violent man. He simply ordered me from the community immediately. I had to leave behind everything they provided for me, and could only wear my summer clothes, the ones I had arrived in the previous spring. I nearly froze going home and wouldn't tell my family where I had been all those months."

"What happened next?"

"That was soon after Christmas," I said. "I went back a week later, hoping to talk with Sabrina, and one of the other boys saw me hiding in some bushes and stopped to talk with me. He told me that the preacher had sent her away, and the rumour was that she wasn't allowed to return. Ever. The church had rigid rules, and if you broke them, you were cast out. It didn't matter who your family was; the rules applied to everyone."

"How could a father do that to his own daughter?" Caitlin said.

"Some religions are like that," Jessica said. "Jon, you may as well tell her the rest."

"I learned this just recently. Sabrina was lucky, at least at first. She went to the Principal of the local school, who helped her to get into a home for unwed mothers. A dishonest one, it turned out, that turned you over to the illegal adoption ring. I didn't know any of this until I got the DNA test results back and tracked her down. She had died of an aneurism just a few days after you were delivered."

"So I can never get to meet her," Caitlin said quietly.

"I wish you could. Your birth mother was a wonderful person."

"Did you love her?"

"Of course. Very much."

"It's okay, then. Everything." She looked toward her parents sadly. "Only you should have told me about this a long time ago."

"We didn't know," Jessica said, "not until Jon told us."

Caitlin looked at me. "You said you'd tell me why you went away to live down south and left your family without telling them."

"I was young, and I couldn't get over being ashamed of what I'd done, of getting Sabrina pregnant and then not being able to take care of her. I tried to establish my career, gave concerts, made recordings, but after a few years I just couldn't live with myself. I decided to change my name and leave it all behind me."

"I should do that," Caitlin said. "Is everyone gonna know all about this? Am I gonna be the scandal of the month in the *National Investigator*, on all the tabloid racks in supermarkets? Or even worse, in the Bournemouth *Bugle*?"

"Your adoption, who your parents are, that's your business,"

Russell said. "We'll never tell anyone. What you and your... Jon... your birth father decide to do is up to you."

Caitlin stood up uncertainly, looked at everyone in the room in turn, then paced slowly to the front door and opened it. Without turning back she said softly, "I don't think I want to live here anymore." She walked out and shut the door behind her.

Russell looked stricken. "Should I go after her?"

"I don't think that's a good idea," Jessica said. "She has a lot to deal with, and she needs to be by herself. She's terribly angry with us right now."

"I'm just afraid she'll do something foolish, maybe even hurt herself somehow."

"I know where she's going," I said. "The boat. She sits on the deck when she wants to be alone. If you want, I'll go down to the marina and keep an eye on her. I'll stay out of sight so she won't know I'm there."

They agreed, and I left their home and walked to the shore.

One Hundred Three:
Loss

I handled this badly," Russell said.

"I disagree," Jessica said. "You did what had to be done. Our mistake was not telling her about her adoption years ago. Secrets: the pain they cause is so much worse than the truth."

"She hates us."

"Maybe, at least right now. All we can hope is that when she has time to think it over, she'll be willing to accept how much we love her and understand why we did what we did. It was wrong, but it was for all the right reasons."

"I never thought any of this would come out."

"I know."

"I wanted to shield her," Russell said. "If we had told her she was adopted, sooner or later she would have wanted to know about her birth parents. What could we have told her? It wasn't like an adoption through legal channels. There are no records, the lawyer said."

"It doesn't matter any longer."

"And she's found him. Her father. What if she wants to live with Jon? What if she hates us that much?"

"Then we let her go," Jessica said softly.

"I can't do that! She's our daughter, in all the ways that matter."

They sat in silence for long minutes, both lost in thought.

"I won't fight you about this," Jessica said at last. "But I hope…" She sighed. "Think about what she's been through, the kidnapping, her incredible escape and her courage in taking that little dinghy out into the ocean. She was only *thirteen* then. No one that age should have to look death in the face, but she survived, and it has changed her. It would change anyone. And as I told you before we left Florida last winter, she has earned the right to make decisions about her life."

"I let her sail home with Jon when she asked."

"Yes, and I know it frightened you. It also proved how much you really love her, to give her the chance to find herself in that way. I wasn't completely sure until then."

"Of *course* I love her," Russell said. "But this is different. We could lose her forever."

"Yes, we could, if she's determined to go and you try to make her stay with us. You have to trust her, now more than ever, to make the right decision. I hate to quote a cliché to you, but there's a lot of truth in the saying that came out of the 1960s. *If you love something, let it go. If it comes back to you, it's yours. If it doesn't, it never was.*"

One Hundred Four:
The Marina

I approached the boatyard cautiously so as not to be seen from the dock, and when I spotted Caitlin sitting atop the cabin, facing out to sea, I took a circuitous route to the office and stopped in. Bill Palmeter was sitting at his desk, writing in a ledger.

"How goes it, Bill?" I greeted him.

"Can't complain," the manager said. "What can I do for you?"

I walked to the window facing the water where I could see Caitlin's head and shoulders, the rest of her hidden by the top of my cabin. "I'm just keeping an eye on my buddy Caitlin. She received some bad news today, and she's a little upset."

"I saw her arrive. You told me she can go to your boat anytime, so I didn't stop her."

"That's fine. Thanks."

"Sorry to hear there's a problem."

"Family stuff. We're just giving her some space right now until she gets over it, but I want to be sure she's all right in the meantime. Mind if I stay here awhile and watch?"

"Glad to have you. Coffee?"

"Thanks."

Bill poured me a cup, and I sat down in front of the window. It was a hot and humid afternoon, although a light easterly breeze off the ocean kept it bearable. A fair number of slips were empty, more than usual for a weekday. *Northern Light*'s neighbours on either side were absent.

A big SUV pulled into the lot and disgorged a litter of kids. Their parents followed along and began unloading a cooler and sailing gear. They carried everything out onto the dock where a sharp looking CS 30 glistened in the sunlight. *Barbeque on the water*, I thought enviously. *Hard to beat that.*

"I took a good look at your electronics when we cleaned up your boat last month," Bill said. "You did a neat job putting them in."

"Thanks."

"You ever catch the guy who trashed your stuff?"

"I didn't get the chance. He blew himself up in a gas-powered trawler down in the Gulf. He was in too much of a hurry and didn't clear out the bilges."

"Stupid. People like that, I don't know, they think the rules don't apply to them."

"He paid the price."

A convertible with its top down coasted into the parking lot. I recognized the occupants, the owner of the town's Canadian Tire franchise and his wife. Their teenage son climbed out of the back seat and retrieved a couple of kit bags from the trunk as his father raised the top. Once it was secure, the woman emerged too and locked the doors. The three of them walked out onto the dock, boarded an electric-powered tender, and headed for a modest catamaran tied to a buoy close to the channel.

Caitlin hadn't moved from where she sat.

A black Mercedes drove to the dock and an elderly man got out, leaning on a cane. He had a mane of thinning hair, white on top and gray around the edges. Despite the heat he wore a long-sleeved sweatshirt, and shuffled toward the dock with a decided limp, his shoulders hunched forward. He looked around and spotted the activity on the CS 30, where two children were unsnapping the sail cover. He eased himself onto a bench close to the marina's gas pump and surveyed the inner harbour.

"You might have a customer," I said to Bill. "Older man. I don't think I've ever seen him here before."

Bill swivelled around to peer out the window. "Nor me. Looks like money, though, judging by the car. If he's in the market, maybe I can unload that Nauticat 47 that's been taking up room in the yard for the last two years. She needs a lot of work. The owner wants two hundred big ones, which is too rich for the local clientele."

He stood up, favouring an arthritic knee, and left the office. I watched him approach the newcomer, who rose stiffly to meet him. They stood talking for a few minutes, and Bill retraced his steps and re-entered the office.

"No sale?" I asked.

"Just looking, apparently. He's a funny duck. Dressed and acted like he was cold on the hottest day in July. Not as old as I thought at first, judging by his face."

"Takes all kinds. I bet the air's plenty cool inside that fancy car, though."

A compact sloop approached the pier, a twenty-eight-footer crowded with teenage sailors returning from a morning on the water. Faint sounds from the CS 30's diesel filtered into the office as it idled in its slip. The older of the children cast off the lines and hopped aboard, and the engine's tone deepened as the skipper eased away from the dock.

"Busy day," I said to Bill.

"Been like that for weeks, money in the bank; three rentals today and a lot of food, gas and diesel. If the weather holds, we're looking to make a good profit this year. Rain, rain, stay away."

I turned my attention back to Caitlin, sitting immobile close to the mainmast. The CS 30 reached the channel and turned toward the open sea. The old man Bill had talked to was making his slow and laboured way back to his car. He opened the door, hesitated and looked out in the direction of *Northern Passage*, then ducked his head and climbed awkwardly inside. He started the engine, managed an awkward K-turn between two yacht cradles, and eased slowly toward the exit.

"I think I'll check on Caitlin," I said. "She should be settled down by now."

Bill waved me away. I opened the door and stepped out into the muggy air. A few clouds scudded across the sun and the wind gusted, setting halyards to ticking against their masts. The teenage arrivals had tied up their boat and were in their cars, driving away. The CS 30 was out of sight, probably heading for an isolated beach somewhere so the kids could swim before dinner. For the first time since I arrived, there was no activity in the marina. I began walking toward the dock.

When I was halfway to my boat, Caitlin spotted my approach. She shrugged and looked away as if not wanting to deal with me right then, and I debated turning around. But then she appeared to change her mind and raised her hand in a tentative wave. I drew up close to the hull and called out, "Permission to come aboard?"

"It's your boat," she answered. She smiled weakly as I worked my way forward of the cabin and lowered myself to sit beside her.

"Hi," she said softly.

"Hi." I decided to remain quiet and let her talk, but only if she wanted to. Then I'd follow her lead.

"I don't know what to call you," she said morosely. "'Dad' doesn't feel right."

"You already have one of those," I said. "How about just plain Jon? That's worked out okay up to now."

We sat in silence, both of us lost in thought.

"I wasn't mad at you," she said after a few minutes.

"I didn't think you were."

"I'm mad at Mom and Dad. Really mad. I meant what I said, too."

"About what?"

"I feel like I'm nobody. I *am* nobody."

"I don't think that," I said gently. "In addition to having two wonderful parents who love you very much, you and I share a special heritage, handed down from my grandfather Gustav, who is also your great-grandfather. You're an amazing artist in your own right. I wouldn't call that nobody. And your mother is a talented and caring psychologist who helps a lot of people. You know darn well how much she loves you."

"But she's not really my mother. And Dad isn't my dad."

"What is a mother, Caitlin?"

"Huh?"

"You heard me."

"Someone who gets screwed and pops out a kid, that's all," she said bitterly.

"Is that all you think Sabrina did? Caitlin, she and I loved each other, more than you can ever imagine. We were just too young, which is part of why it didn't work out."

I waited in silence. She didn't speak for almost five minutes. Then she sighed. "Aren't you gonna start lecturing me some more?"

"What can I say? It sounds like you want to throw away all the wonderful things that have happened to you over the past fourteen years, just because you weren't born into your family in the usual way."

"They *bought* me!"

"They *needed* you, and if you think about it for a minute, you needed them. Babies have no say over what happens to them, and if your mom and dad hadn't found you, who knows where you would have ended up. In any case, you can't turn back the clock. We all have to accept where we are right now, and find some way to deal with it."

A vintage wooden skiff, compact at about seventeen feet and in desperate need of paint, coasted into the second slip down from my own. The pilot was a thirty-something man with a yellow oilcloth sou'wester pulled down low over his face, and we watched as he manoeuvred in close. He slung three shabby life rings over the side, and they squeaked as they rubbed against the dock. He wrapped the painter around the outermost cleat and let the incoming tide swing her around, stern in. He hauled out a toolbox and took the cover off his oversized outboard engine.

Down the line a diesel engine came to life, and I spotted an elderly couple aboard a sleek cuddy cabin cruiser preparing to move out into the channel. A beamy catamaran headed upstream against the wind with half a dozen teens aboard. A busy day at the marina: happy people, present company excepted.

Caitlin was fighting back tears. "I just feel like I've lost everything," she said.

"Okay. Want to make a list?"

"What do you mean?"

"Can you still play the piano? Do you still have somewhere nice to live? How about friends at school who don't know anything about what we told you today. They won't think you're any different. And there's the mother and father who've raised you pretty darn well for fourteen years. I agree that they made a terrible mistake by not telling you where you came from when you were small, and they're really sorry that it hurt you so badly. And I know they're hoping you'll forgive them and want to come back to them." I gave her a couple of minutes to absorb that. "And there's something else, too."

"What?" Her head was bowed, eyes looking at the deck as she toyed with the laces on her sneakers.

"Your world is larger now, not smaller, and you have something that almost no one else has. You have a second father who loves you more than you can ever imagine."

She looked up at me, startled. "You do?"

"Don't be so surprised. If it means anything, I've loved you ever since we first played duets together on *Versteck*. At the time I couldn't figure out why I felt that way, but even then, it seemed as if we were connected somehow."

Her eyes were shining. "I felt that way too." She leaned heavily against me. "Only now more than ever, I don't know where I belong. What am I gonna do?"

"What's changed today?"

"I told you, I don't know who I am."

"Who were you yesterday? Was that really someone different?"

"You're one to talk! You ran away and changed your name to Rolf and tried to be someone else. You threw away your talent, playing in a bunch of saloons, hiding from your past."

"I know, and you're right. But something wonderful came out of it—I met you—and I wouldn't change that even if I could. A year ago, I didn't know you existed. Finding out that I have a daughter has given my life a whole new meaning. Without that I'd still be drifting. Alone. Lonely. You think I saved you down there in Florida, but it's really you who saved me."

I paused to let that sink in. Then: "I'm eternally grateful to your parents for being willing to share you with me. They don't have to. I would never contest the adoption; that would cause a world of trouble for all of us. So now maybe you can return the favour by putting everything you've heard during the last two days behind you and get on with your life. Part of that should be forgiving them for not being honest with you."

"I love you so much," she said. She buried her face in my shirt and began to cry, very softly.

Breaking my heart.

We sat quietly for several minutes. "Want to take the boat out?" I asked her at last.

She rallied a bit. "Can we?"

"Why not? Maybe just a short run toward Mahone Bay and back again? You can do all the work."

She poked me in the ribs. "Yeah, okay."

"We better call home and let your folks know we may not be back in time for dinner. Is that okay with you?"

She shrugged. "I guess."

"Got your cell phone?"

"I left it home. I just wanted to get out of the house when... You

349

know."

"Bill will let me use his. Back in a minute."

The manager was still at his desk when I entered the office. "Okay if I use the phone? Local call."

"Mi casa, tu casa," he said. "Any time."

I reached Jessica and told her that all was well, but that Caitlin still needed time to get her anger under control, and that maybe a short sail would help. "We might be back in time for supper," I said, "but if you don't see us by six, go ahead without us." We said goodbye and I hung up.

"How's the girl?" Bill asked.

"A bit fragile right now," I told him, "but she'll get over it. I'm going to let her take me out to sea for a couple of hours, give her something to do."

"Have fun."

I left the office and headed toward the dock. Caitlin was no longer sitting by the mast. I approached the boat and stepped into the cockpit, but she wasn't there either. The companionway was padlocked, so she couldn't have gone below. I scanned the slips, looking for her, then remembered the little wooden skiff tied up below my bow. I stepped up on top of the cabin and saw the man in the yellow sou'wester climbing out on the dock, dragging Caitlin with him. He had his hand clamped over her mouth to keep her from calling out. He glanced up at me and I suddenly placed him. I had seen him on the cruise ship, wearing the suit and tie of a security guard. I'd heard him called Shaffer.

He waved a snub-nosed pistol in my direction and loosed a single shot that soared over my head. I ducked down and dropped back into the cockpit. I felt a slight shift in the yacht's hull and twisted around to find the elderly man from the Mercedes coming over the side. He was pointing a black Colt revolver at my chest. His posture was erect, a wicked looking stiletto clutched in his left hand. His intense black eyes bored into mine, daring me to defy him. He moved with the agility of a younger man and it was apparent that the gray hair and cane were part of an elaborate disguise.

"Keep cool, man," he growled at me. "I have no argument with you."

"What do you want?" I said, stalling for time.

"I'm sorry about this," he said, "but it seems likely that the girl you rescued in Florida can identify me. I can't let that happen."

"Identify you? What for?"

"Like I said, I'm sorry. I never wanted it to come to this. But from what I've been told, the little piano player might recognize my voice. Once I'm rid of her, I'll be free and clear."

I glanced behind me to where the security guard Shaffer had dragged Caitlin to midships. She was staring intently at the man who was holding the gun on me. And I realized that I had heard his voice before, a distinctive tone and cadence, on TV or the radio.

"Who are you?" I exclaimed. "Are you behind everything that happened to her?"

"You can call me The Spider. And if you know so much, I have to off you too."

He raised the barrel of the gun to my face just as Bill Palmeter came running toward the dock, alerted by our raised voices. The gunman heard his footsteps on the gravel and looked around, and I dove forward and slammed into him, driving him back against the port rail. Caitlin screamed. He hammered the gun into the side of my head and I stumbled back and fell against the wheel. Shaffer fired at me again.

"*Caitlin,*" I shouted, "*spring ins Wasser und schwimm schnell unter das Dock! Sofort!*"

She stomped down on Shaffer's foot, squirmed out of his grasp, and flew off the dock in a neat surface dive. Caught by surprise, Shaffer spun around and fired after her. The Spider scrambled past me to look over the rail. He turned back and levelled the gun at me once more.

"She's gone!" he yelled at me. "What the hell did you say to her?"

I climbed to my feet and faced him. "You'll never catch her," I said. Shaffer was kneeling at the edge of the dock, trying to locate Caitlin. Bill ran up behind Shaffer, spotted his gun, and booted him into the water. The gun flew out of his hand.

The Spider fired at Bill wildly, missing but driving him back. He spun toward me and fired again, and white-hot pain lanced my left shoulder. My arm went numb. I reacted without thinking and charged into him waist high, smashing him to the deck beneath me.

I managed to grab hold of his gun with my right hand and twisted it aside, but my left arm was useless and I couldn't keep him down. He squirmed out from under me and tried to scuttle away, but I caught his foot and brought him down again. He twisted around and buried his knife in my right bicep and I had to let go. He scrabbled backwards toward the hatchway and fired the gun blindly, missing my right ear by inches.

I threw myself forward and tried to pin him to the deck, but he swung the pistol at me and the gun sight ripped my scalp open. Dizzy and disoriented, I lost my grip, and he got to his feet and smashed a vicious kick into my kidney that tumbled me against the helm. He backed away and leapt to the top of the cabin. Grabbing the boom to steady himself, he fired the gun again, the shot sailing over my head as I tried to roll behind the binnacle, but before I could reach cover he fired once more, and a slug tore into my chest.

The gun's recoil knocked him off balance. His leather-soled shoes slipped on the deck and his feet went out from under him. The gun sailed into the water. He fell backwards over the starboard rail, bounced off the gunwale, and dropped into the water.

Slashed open by the knife, my right arm was no longer functioning, but I had a worse problem. My shirt blossomed red, a severed artery pulsing in my chest, and I managed to slap my left hand over the wound to stem the flow. As weak as I was, I might as well have tried to stop the incoming tide.

Bill looked into the cockpit but couldn't see me lying behind the binnacle. "What the hell's going on?"

"Man overboard!" I cried out weakly. "Watch out, he's dangerous! He'll try to get to Caitlin."

"Where is she?"

"I'm here," her small voice came from the water beside the dock.

"I don't see him," Bill said. "Wait, there he is. Holy shit, is that the old guy from the Mercedes?"

"The hair's a disguise," I yelled. "Don't let him get back on board!"

Caitlin scrambled up onto the dock, then turned and pointed. "He's gone again! He went under!"

"I'll go for help," Bill said, and ran off toward his office. I tried to call after him but choked on a mass of blood that welled up in my throat and spilled out of my mouth. I slumped against the rail, woozy and disoriented, my heart pounding uncontrollably. My arms were useless, and nausea overwhelmed me. Bloody vomit spilled onto the deck.

"Bill, I'm shot," I gasped weakly, but he was already too far away to hear. I tried to stand up but couldn't get my balance and toppled over on my side. My vision clouded, and the last thing I saw before falling down a deep, dark well into nothingness was Caitlin running toward me, clothes plastered to her body, arms flailing and mouth wide open in a scream I couldn't hear.

One Hundred Five:
Caitlin

Jacob Shaffer had vanished. Jon lay on his back on the sole of the cockpit, Caitlin hovering over him with her tee shirt wadded up and pressed tightly against his chest. His eyes were open but rolled back, only the whites showing; his breath rasped weakly in his throat. Three EMTs clambered aboard and tried to treat Caitlin first, but she fended them off, shouting that she wasn't hurt, that it was *his* blood all over her, not hers. The two men and a woman eased her away and quickly assessed the situation, and Caitlin huddled next to the binnacle as they took over for her.

She was unable to see what the paramedics were doing as they swarmed over Jon's limp form. Working quickly, they strapped him to a stretcher while keeping pressure on his chest, and the woman inserted an IV into his arm. They slid him into the EMT van, slammed the door, and sprayed gravel as they tore out of the marina, the siren blaring.

Bill Palmeter sat down next to Caitlin and put his arm around her shoulder.

"Is he dead?" she sobbed.

"They'll do everything they can for him," Bill said gently.

A police officer boarded the yacht and squatted down. "Can either of you tell me what happened here?" he asked.

"Better ask this young lady," Bill said. "She saw it all. Her name's Caitlin."

The officer turned to her. "Do you feel well enough to talk, sweetheart? The paramedics said you're not hurt. Do you know who shot that man?"

Caitlin sucked in a deep breath and straightened her shoulders. "I don't know his name, but I can help you find out."

One Hundred Six:
Jon

He's waking up."

A familiar voice filtered through dark clouds of fog that shrouded my mind. I lay adrift, flat on my back on the sole of my cockpit, helpless and unable to move my arms as huge waves poured over the gunwale and tried to wash me into the sea. I blinked and forced my eyes to focus, and found myself in a white-walled room under harsh fluorescent lights. Wires and tubes pinned me down.

Bill Palmeter, next to Jessica and Russell, swam into view on my left, and I turned my head to see Caitlin hovering over me on the right.

"Where am I?" I managed to mutter.

"In hospital," Jessica said gently. "Try not to talk."

"I guess I'm not dead," I said, my voice a raspy croak, "unless you're all angels. What happened?"

"What do you remember?" Russell said.

"I was on my boat, talking to this little runt here." I gestured toward Caitlin and discovered tubes sprouting out of the back of my hand.

"You damn well better treat her with respect," I heard Bill say. "If it hadn't been for the young miss here, you'd be worm food by now."

"I can't remember anything."

"You were shot twice, and a guy buried a huge pig sticker in your arm. One of the bullets punctured your right lung. By the time the EMTs got to you, you were white as a haddock fillet."

I turned to look at Caitlin. "Are you all right?"

"She got to you first," Bill continued. "And you owe her some new clothes too. She'll never be able to wash all your blood out of what she had on."

"I didn't do anything," she said, leaning in close to my face. "It was the other way around. You saved me from that freak who was after me."

"Liar," Bill said softly.

"How long have I been here?" I asked. "What time is it?"

"Three days, and it's two in the morning right now," Russell said. "At least one of us has been here with you around the clock. Caitlin has hardly been home at all. They pumped about a gallon of blood into you, opened you up, and plugged up all the holes. Your mother was here until just a short time ago, your grandfather too. How old is that man, anyway? They looked pretty beat, so as soon as we were sure you were going to make it, I drove them home. I'll give them a call in a few minutes and let them know you're awake."

"I still don't remember what happened. Someone shot me? Why?"

"It was The Spider," Caitlin said quietly.

"Spider? Wait a minute, old guy with white hair?" My head began to pound. "He was... He said Caitlin could..."

Dark clouds closed in. Voices droned, but I couldn't make sense of what they said. Then everything shut down: oblivion.

* * *

I woke with a start, tense and confused. Bright sunlight streamed into the hospital room, which was empty except for a nurse who was adjusting the controls of my IV. A monitor beeped quietly somewhere behind me, then accelerated as I came alert.

"What time is it?" I shouted. "What *day* is it!"

"Take it easy, Mr. MacIssac," the nurse said. "I'll get your doctor for you."

"No, I need the police! I have to tell them about The Spider. Caitlin's in danger!" I tried to sit up, and the nurse restrained me.

"You have to relax," she said. "Everything is okay. The police have been here several times, and your friends have taken care of everything."

"No, you don't understand!"

"All I know is, they have the man who shot you in custody. It's been all over the radio and TV. Now promise me you'll stay put, and I'll get your doctor and let your family know you're awake again."

I let myself sink back into the pillow. In custody? The Spider? How could they know who he is?

It was at least five minutes before Russell appeared and quickly checked my vital signs. I peppered him with questions, to which he would only say, "Caitlin will tell you. It's her story. She's on her way from home."

Ten minutes later Jessica and Caitlin came into the room, both smiling and obviously happy to see me alert once more.

"Will you two please tell me what's going on?" I insisted.

Caitlin pulled up a chair beside the bed. "They got him," she said, grinning.

"Talk about a big fish," Jessica said.

I was fully awake and becoming irritated. "Will you please stop the Laurel and Hardy routine and tell me what you're talking about?"

"I recognized his voice," Caitlin said. "The Spider. I heard him talking to Shelagh in the cabin and memorized his voice, and when I heard him talking to you on the boat, I knew it was him. I told the police, and guess what? They believed me. Mom and Dad helped, told them about my tonal memory, and they assembled a list of 'all the usual suspects'—that's what Dad calls them."

"It was quite a show," Russell said. "They set up a fake press conference with a parade of politicians and their aides from the Freedom Party, and a CBC reporter interviewed them for half an hour. Caitlin listened from the next room where she couldn't see them. Or them, her."

"I was beginning to worry," Caitlin said. "I was so sure I knew what The Spider sounded like, but none of the voices matched. Until almost the end."

"Tell me," I said. "Who was it?"

Caitlin was grinning widely. "You'll never guess. The Premier of Nova Scotia!"

"Carter Williams himself," Jessica said. "Caitlin identified him before ten words were out of his mouth."

"Did they catch Chloe's security guard? The guy in the wooden boat?"

"Jacob Shaffer," Russell said. "He ratted out everyone, including members of the Freedom Party Executive."

"He tried to shoot her."

"And he'll pay for that," Jessica said. "Listen, you'd better rest. Russell says you're out of danger, but you need time to heal. Do you need anything?"

"I'll be fine. I'll be out of here before you know it. Go home. No point in standing around gawking at me."

"Sounds like he's gonna be okay," Caitlin said, grinning. "And I am, too," she told me. "You saved me again, and like you told me last New Year's, you're responsible for me now. You better get well, real quick."

Epilogue

The Provincial government was in turmoil when the media reported the attack at the marina and the Premier's involvement in Caitlin and Chloe's kidnapping. The RCMP launched an immediate investigation into the membership of the Freedom Party, and a number of sitting members were facing charges. The question of leadership was in doubt and no party could claim a majority, so the Governor General dissolved the Legislature and ordered a new election.

With furry little Jenny tucked comfortably into one corner of the cockpit, Caitlin and I are enjoying a day at sea. *Northern Passage* is carrying us eastward, and Nova Scotia's South Shore lies brilliantly green off the port stern, bathed in late summer sun. I'm at the wheel; the autopilot is turned off. Weeks after the shooting I still sport a few bandages and my left arm rests in a sling, but I can use it if I'm careful, the right one, too.

It's the first time we've been alone together since they let me out of the hospital. We had booked an extensive Atlantic Provinces tour, scheduled to begin shortly after the big emotional blow-up in the Sheridan living room that threatened to turn Caitlin's life upside down. But then Carter Williams put me out of action.

To her credit, despite the upheaval that caused such conflict between her and her parents, Caitlin agreed to honour the commitment. She and Jessica departed for St. John's in Newfoundland a day late, but still in time for her first concert. Without me, of course.

"Does your shoulder hurt much?" she asks.

"Not as much as my pride. I should have been able to clobber that guy before he plugged me."

Caitlin laughs. "You sound like a TV gangster."

"We're even now. You saved *me* this time."

"Uh-uh. Bill did. He called nine-one-one."

"That's not how he explained it to me. He said you made a compression pad out of your tee shirt and nearly stopped the bleeding. Where did you learn to do that?"

"I saw it once on TV. One of those medical dramas. It was pretty embarrassing, though, nothing on top but my bra when the EMTs got there. One of them, a big guy, let me borrow a shirt. Extra-extra large, fit me like a tent."

"One does what one must. I'm sure no one paid any attention to you. And I'm incredibly grateful."

"I wanted to ride in the ambulance with you, sirens and all, but they wouldn't let me. I was so scared. I was sure you were already dead."

"No chance. Only the good die young." I twist the wheel and a muscle cramps my arm. "I need a rest," I tell her. "Want to take over for me here? It's time to head back."

We trade places. The sun is low in the sky. Caitlin turns into the wind and the sails cross the deck in a gentle controlled gibe. She checks the GPS, notes the compass reading, and adjusts the traveler to set a course for the harbour.

"So my mother, my *biological* mother, really was a pianist?" she asks.

"A fine one."

"Which means the music inside me came from both of you, and from *Opa* Gustav too. You're all a part of me. He's really great, ninety something and can still play. It was so amazing to find out I have such a talented great-grandfather. And I love your Mom. My grandmother. That feels so strange, calling her that, but I like it."

Once Russell and Jessica decided not to hide the fact of Caitlin's ancestry, I introduced her to the two surviving members of my family, and they quickly bonded. Caitlin especially enjoys playing duets with Gustav. Despite the inevitable arthritis that so often accompanies old age, he retains enough technique at the keyboard to impress her.

I know his presence in her life will never eclipse the memory of her granddad Orrin, but his love for her is at least partially filling the void left by that fine man's passing. Gustav takes great delight in her talent, and in getting to know her.

"I'm glad you feel that way about all of us," I tell her, "but remember, biology is only part of the equation. How are you getting along with your mom and dad?"

"You mean my adoptive mom and dad. Okay, I guess."

"I hope you'll soon stop thinking of them that way. Russell Sheridan has nurtured and protected you most of your life, and from what you've told me, he's done a darn good job of it. That's one way to define a father, after all—maybe the most important way. And your mom's pretty special, too."

"I get that, but it doesn't change the way I feel inside. Even though I can understand why Dad insisted on hiding where I came from, I just can't forgive him for lying to me all those years. It's as if he thought adoption was something to be ashamed of. I know they love me, and I love them too, really I do, but that doesn't keep me from being angry sometimes."

"'It is not in the stars to hold our destiny, but in ourselves,'" I quote.

"Uh huh, I read that once. Shakespeare, his critique of astrology and horoscopes. From *Julius Caesar*, right?"

"As usual, the old boy was right. Your future is up to you, but only if you can put all this behind you."

"It's hard, but I'll try. Will you help me?"

"We'll help each other."

We sail shoreward between paired red and green buoys. Bournemouth stretches wide along the shore, dead ahead like the uncertain future that Caitlin and I both face.

Together.

About the Author

After six years of service as Band Director at North Hunterdon Regional High School in Annandale, New Jersey, Peter Riddle aspired to a new challenge and a higher quality of life for his family. At the suggestion of his wife Gay, who grew up near the Canadian border in western New York State and knew a lot more about the Great White North than he did, he inquired about teaching opportunities in Nova Scotia, and was rewarded with an opportunity to create a new music program at West Kings District High School in Auburn.

Peter and Gay sold their home by auction, packed up eighteen-month-old son Ken and three rescue cats, and crossed from Maine to the Province of New Brunswick early in the morning of July 3rd in the Canadian Centennial year of 1967. The ferry *Princess of Acadia* took them over the Bay of Fundy to Nova Scotia's Annapolis Valley, where Peter established the WKRHS Concert Band.

Acadia University called him in 1969 and again the family moved, this time to the town of Wolfville and augmented by daughter Anne. There in the University's School of Music he initiated wind and percussion instruction, created a new music education curriculum, and formed a concert band and various other ensembles. He also established Summer Bandstand, at one time the largest music camp in the Atlantic Provinces.

Except for fifteen months absence while in residence at Southern Illinois University, where he earned a Ph.D. degree, he served the Acadia Faculty full time for thirty-six years, including a decade as Dean and Director of the School of Music. He is the author of twenty-six earlier books and over one hundred articles in various periodicals.

Gay also served the University, first in the Housing Office and later as Head of Conference Services, before retiring to work on behalf of the Eastern Kings Memorial Hospital Foundation, and also as a volunteer at Valley Regional Hospital and the Companion Animal Protection Society of Annapolis County.

Peter and Gay have three grandchildren: Alexander and Steven, sons of Anne and the late Kevin Moggy, and Sidney, daughter of Ken and his wife Betty (nee Betty Poi Lin Jang).